ARTICHOKE STARS AND CHICKEN FRIED SHARK

Craig E. Higgins

NewLink Publishing

Henderson, Nevada
2023

Artichoke Stars & Chicken Fried Shark
Craig E. Higgins
Copyright 2023
All Rights Reserved

This book is a work of fiction composed from the author's imagination. It is protected under the copyright laws of the United States of America. No part of this publication may be reproduced or transmitted in any form or by any means, electronic or mechanical, including photocopying, recording, or by an information storage or retrieval system, without written permission from the publisher. Contact the publisher at info@newlinkpublishing.com.

Line/Content Editor: Dave Hardin
Interior Design: Jo A. Wilkins
Cover & Illustrations: Stephanie Anduro

Copyright © 2023 / Craig E. Higgins
    All Rights Reserved
ISBN: 978-1-948266-84-0/Paperback
ISBN: 978-1-948266-97-0/E-Pub

1. FictionScience Fiction/Alien Contact
2. FictionScience Fiction/Apocalypic & Post-Apocalypic
3. Fiction / Small Town & Rural

www.newlinkpublishing.com

Henderson, NV 89002

Printed in the United States of America
1 2 3 4 5 6 7 8 9 0

> To my sweet wife, Kenna –
> without your love and support,
> I could never have done this.

Additionally, people think writers write books – that's true, but it's also true that to do a book worth reading you need some help. And this book wouldn't have been the same were it not for the efforts of the following:

- The membership of the Henderson Writers Group and Sin City Writers Group for their insightful critiques.
- Diana Fedorak, who did an early edit which helped to shape the tone.
- Dave Hardin, the primary editor – he did a tremendous job getting the work ready for publishing.
- Ellie Robison, my first and best Beta reader.
- And the late John Fuchs, my high school English teacher. He was the guy who encouraged me to read bent stuff; I'm forever in his debt for that reason.

ARTICHOKE STARS AND CHICKEN FRIED SHARK

1

Bay St. Louis, Mississippi, October 1980

I turn up the beach road, the cold autumn air whipping my face. With school out, my mind's on digging my toes in the sand before heading home. The sidewalk bites through my Chuck Taylor's, making the soreness in my calves worse. Coach put us through our paces yesterday, running the whole wrestling team like dogs in preparation for the December meet.

I trot past the Home Plate diner. It's the best place for shrimp in town. From the entrance, a buttery aroma smothers my nostrils. Two people, a woman and her young son, step through the front door. The little kid stumbles, nearly knocking me over. The ice cream cone in his hand plops to the concrete.

He levels a finger in my direction. "Hey, pineapple-head. You made me drop it."

"Did not." I hold up my hands in protest.

"Did, too!"

He digs his little heel into my foot, sending a jolt up my leg.

"Ow!" I grab the tiny vermin's wrist.

The woman glares at me. "Would you watch where you're going?"

"Hey, I'm sorry."

She drags the little boy away, but not before he turns and gives me the finger. "Up yours, pineapple-head!"

Why do people always make cracks about my hair? "Little boy, you need to learn some manners," I yell after them, but they ignore me.

Bumping along, they vanish around a corner. Jeez, when I was that age, my mom would've read me the riot act for telling off a stranger like that.

A quartet of girls my age in corduroy jumpers and too-tight designer jeans stand in front of a beauty parlor. Their feathered hair billows in the breeze like porcupine needles. They stare transfixed at a pyramid of cans behind the storefront window. Next to the stack an ad reads:

Aqua-Net Blow-Out! Three Cans for Five Dollars!

One girl, a freckled redhead with braces, smacks her gum and blows a huge bubble. "I'm getting me some. Going to dress up like a witch this year."

Halloween is in a week.

Her friend snickers. "Nadine, you don't need no spray to look like a witch, hon."

The other girls laugh. I brush past them, stopping at the corner before crossing at the light. A block up, I shiver beneath the twin chapel spires of St. Adolphus, a rich boys' private school. It's a spooky place. The shadows cast by those towers resemble a giant pair of shark's fins.

At the intersection, traffic blaze past in both directions, separating me from the beach. I step off the curb into the path of a white pickup blowing through a red light, swerving from side to side. I leap back onto the sidewalk, narrowly avoiding the onrushing hood.

A bumper sticker plastered on the tailgate depicts a cartoon picture of Johnny Reb. Dressed in a gray uniform, Johnny lies in state beneath a motto which reads: *Save your Confederate money, boys. The South's gonna rise again.*

Just like the little kid, the driver flips me off before zigzagging through traffic. A shiver runs down my spine. Nothing like a little brush with death to start the afternoon.

I cross the road. Below me, a concrete staircase descends to a chalky sand dotted with plastic bottles and driftwood. The briny stench floods my nose, stopping me in my tracks. I sneeze, and almost trip over a maggoty dead fish. Then, something catches my eye. Fifty yards away, a shiny cabbage-ball-sized object sits at the base of a wooden pylon beneath the pier.

It looks valuable. Okay, maybe not, but from a distance it definitely looks interesting.

The tide rolls in, scattering fingers of driftwood around the shiny object. A couple more waves like that will wash it back into the bay, and it'll be gone forever. I hesitate, my breath visible in the cool evening air.

Should I grab it?

A raspy whisper growls in my head.

Stupid, stupid, stupid. Who leaves anything nice on the beach?

Here come the voices. Again.

It's just a dumb piece of junk. Leave that thing alone.

Shut up. Maybe it fell off a rich person's boat. Might be worth a lot of money.

That's stupid.

Is not.

The surf crashes in. Cramps ripple through my stomach.

Well, if you're going to do it, stop being such a wimp and go grab the thing.

I'll grab it when I want.

Craig E. Higgins

Stupid, stupid, stupid.

Just shut up, okay?

I run to the pier. The tide rolls in, soaking my shoes. The thing sits there like it's waiting for me. It's about the size of a softball but tapered on one end, and covered with scaly, overlapping leaves that radiate an iridescent, radish-purple hue. Tiny, translucent hairs ring a puckered orifice on top.

A purple artichoke? Maybe. Except artichokes don't come in that shade. And they don't have mouths. So, what is it, really? A vegetable? Some kind of sea anemone?

Something about its irregular shape jogs my memory. The UFO magazines I collect always have articles about stuff like this. Unexplained phenomena the government doesn't want people to know about.

Which totally makes it a prize.

I try to yank it from the ground. The serrated leaves rip my hands. It hurts like crazy. Within seconds, red welts blossom on my skin, itching like a hundred ant bites.

Stupid, stupid, stupid. You'll never get it out like that.

Fine. I'll be back.

Along the main road, three blocks away, sits a squat building nestled on a blacktop parking lot. Afterschool, on Fridays, the Jitney Jungle grocery store's aisles are packed with customers. Matronly housewives pushing stuffed shopping carts fight for position with errant teenagers in search of candy and chips. The magazine rack tempts me with comics and wrestling magazines, but the image of the artichoke stuck in the sand overrides all distractions. A list of items I'll need to retrieve

4

the object circulates through my head—pair of rubber gloves, trash bags, aluminum roasting pan.

Navigating the crush of bodies and baskets, I locate the gloves and bags in the household goods aisle. But the pans are down another. A screaming boy clips my thigh on the way to retrieve the last item. This knocks me off course, right in front of a display advertising toaster pastries.

Chocolate Fudge Pop-Tarts. Only $1.99

Searching my wallet, I find a ten, just enough to cover everything, pastries included.

Customers clog the checkout lines. One is for ten items or less. A better fit but I avoid it, pushing through to the last lane. It's the busiest, but I don't care. Behind the counter, Katie Sue Carson makes the cash register sing.

Four years older than me, Katie Sue is the most beautiful girl in the world. She's thin and kind of tall. Long, chestnut-brown hair falls like rain down her back. Oversized glasses frame sparkling eyes set like sapphires in her round face. Full lips curl into an ever-present smile.

"Mickey Finley," Katie Sue says. "It's so nice to see you."

Time stops. My tongue thickens. In my head, I reach across the conveyor belt and pull her to me. As groceries pile up at the end of the belt, we make out like the couple in the Irish Spring commercial on TV.

Katie Sue drags me back to reality. "Mickey?"

"Hey kid," somebody says behind my back. "You're holding up traffic."

Whoops.

"Oh, hi." I put the items on the conveyor belt. "How's life in the grocery business?"

"Kind of sucks but it's college money." She scans each

item. "How's your cousin?"

"Tommy? He's alive, I guess."

Big-shouldered, curly-haired Tommy is Uncle John's and Aunt Margene's son. He played football in high school and all the girls adored him.

"Alive? I heard he went into the Navy." The register chimes like a pet store parakeet. "Y'all must be so proud of him."

Katie Sue blushes. She used to be one of those adoring girls, which doesn't fit my plans for us at all.

"Yeah, he's pretty cool."

"Well, tell him I said hello. That'll be nine-dollars and thirty-four-cents."

The way she tells me the price sounds sexier than Farrah Fawcett selling shampoo on TV. "You got it." The ten floats out of my wallet.

She stares at my hands. "My word, Mickey. What did you do to yourself?"

Embarrassed, I stuff them in my jacket. "Slipped on a rock at the beach."

"We've got some hydrogen peroxide in the breakroom. If you want, I could send somebody—"

"No, really, I'm okay."

"You sure?"

"Yeah."

"Okay, well take care now." She smiles like an angel. "Don't run in the traffic."

A half-hour later the artichoke still squats in the shifting silt, its lacquered leaves drying out as the tide recedes. Cold bites into my knuckles before I put on the gloves. The artichoke shivers and its ugly mouth puckers, spewing purple ooze that smells of rotten eggs.

"Yuck." I grab the thing by its base and try to yank it out

of the ground, but the artichoke's roots or whatever's holding it in place won't give.

"Jeez." I step backward, a little rattled. This is going to be harder than I thought.

I crouch down and pull, lifting with my legs. The artichoke emits a high screech, but I finally hoist its squirming form into the roasting pan. It spurts a load of plum-colored dust into my face, making me sneeze. I wipe my nose on my sleeve. The resultant snot is peppered with purple soot.

"Aw great. This thing's going to get me sick."

I take stock of the situation. The concrete stairs are fifty feet away. I can leave this thing right here and just forget all about it. But then I remember all those pictures in the UFO magazines. What if I took a snapshot of this sucker and sent it into the editor? Would somebody call the house? Maybe word would get out about my find and reporters would show up, like from the *National Enquirer* or something. They might put me and the artichoke on the cover, us occupying a space at the Jitney Jungle checkout counter right next to all the famous people in *People.*

Katie Sue would forget all about Tommy.

I turn and slip the pan with its lumpy burden inside the garbage bag. The sharp leaves shred the plastic. I slip a second bag over the first as reinforcement. My nose itches. I rub it and purple mucus runs from my nostril.

"Aw crap, this thing is getting me sick." I sneeze a technicolor nightmare, then toss the gloves and throw the bag over my shoulder. The artichoke squirms and erupts in a fury of grunts and growls, but the pan protects my back from its thrashings.

Grabbing the Pop-Tarts, I head home with my prize.

Aunt Margene and Uncle John's place sits on a quarter-acre lot, a thirty-minute walk from the beach. By the time I get there, the sun burns orange on the horizon. I enter the house through the back door which leads directly into the kitchen. Inside, a whiff of pot roast smells good in spite of my blocked sinus passages, making my mouth water. I leave the artichoke on the porch, and step inside.

Aunt Margene sits on the couch in the living room, telephone nestled between her chin and shoulder, cord wrapped around her arm. She's about forty-five, plump with graying hair. I find it really easy to talk to her, and consider her one of my few friends, even going back to before I moved in.

"Aunt Margene. I found this cool thing at the beach—"

She glares at me. "Not now, Mickey."

"Sorry."

Frowning, she speaks into the phone. "Alright, Isobel. Now, tell me what happened…really? The officer at the scene said that? What happened to the other driver?"

"Who are you talking to?" I set the bag of Pop-Tarts on the table.

Aunt Margene holds her hand over the mouthpiece. "Mickey, please. This is serious."

She listens to the person on the other end of the line. I tear into a package of the pastries and breathe in an aromatic chocolate smell. Then I grab a bite. The Pop-Tart tastes unusually bittersweet.

Tears well in Aunt Margene's eyes. "Oh, Isobel. I'm so sorry to hear about this…yes, I'll miss her, too. We loved that girl…uh huh, uh huh…she was like family to us, too."

The hairs on the back of my neck stand on end. Who was like family? What are they talking about?

"Okay…we'll be by the church later. Love you, too. Goodbye." She cradles the receiver. "Mickey, do you remember the Carson girl? Katie Sue?"

"Um, actually, I just saw her like an hour ago."

"You did?" She frowns.

"Yeah, why?"

"That was Miss Isobel, from church." Aunt Margene grabs a tissue and blows her nose. "There's been a terrible accident."

"An accident?"

"Yes. Katie Sue's been—" She clutches her chest and closes her eyes.

"Katie Sue's been what?"

"She's dead."

The pastry falls from my mouth. My fingers and toes go numb. The loss of sensation travels along my limbs and stops at my heart, deadening my pulse.

Katie Sue, gone? It can't be true.

Aunt Margene cries, "Oh Lord. What's become of this world?"

I wrap her up in my arms and we hug each other tightly.

Outside, the sun slips behind the trees like a hanged man choking on a noose.

2

On TV, a reporter barks the story of Katie Sue's death into the camera. Behind him, two police officers inspect the smashed remains of a white pick-up wrapped around a huge oak tree right out in front of the chapel at St. Adolphus. The shadows of the twin spires zigzag over the scene like dueling shark fins.

Barely visible, a bumper sticker on the tailgate confirms my worst fears.

Johnny Reb.

You took Katie Sue from me, and I'll hate you forever for that.

My stomach churns.

Stupid, stupid, stupid. This is all your fault.

Just shut up, okay.

"Do you believe it?" Aunt Margene says, blowing her nose. "Because I can't. I just…can't."

The reporter relays a meaningless set of details while an ambulance arrives. Two orderlies get out and place a body wrapped in a bloodied sheet onto a gurney.

I sit there and try not to cry. Boys aren't supposed to do

that, even when the tears come because of a girl they have a crush on. Or, when their parents die. Or, any other reason, really.

The voices don't make things any easier.

Boys don't cry. Remember mom and dad's funeral?

Shut up. I know where you want me to go with this, and it's not happening.

Only cry-babies turn on the waterworks.

"Just shut up," I mumble under my breath.

"Mickey?" Aunt Margene stares at me, a crumpled tissue in her hand. "Who are you talking to?"

"Nobody." My left ear grows hot, a sign I'm embarrassed.

"Are you sure?"

The front door closes with a shudder. Uncle John steps across the threshold. He's a big man, almost six-foot-five. He smells of sawdust and motor oil, on account of he works at a paper mill near Hattiesburg. His lanky arms hang like telephone poles at his sides. With eyes narrowed into perpetual slits, he scans the room as if expecting the bogey man to jump out and attack him at any moment.

Aunt Margene leaps from the couch and throws herself into his arms. "Oh John." They embrace and her head sinks against his shoulder. "You know Katie Sue, Pastor's oldest girl?"

"I heard on the radio." He rubs a rough palm against her wet cheek. "The Lord has surely tried that family worse than ours."

"I just can't believe it happened. She was so young."

"Death is always hard." He turns to me. "Mickey, you need to be extra good to your aunt the next few days, understand?"

"Yes, sir."

Uncle John puts his lunch pail down on the coffee table.

Aunt Margene turns to him. "John, when did you want to

go?"

"To church? Give me a chance to freshen up." He steps toward the kitchen. "And I'd like a bite to eat first."

Me and Aunt Margene follow him into the kitchen.

"There's stew on the stove," she says. "Sorry, but I didn't get the onions chopped."

"No worries. Mickey?"

"Sir?" I say, hearing a thrashing sound from out on the porch.

Crap, it's got to be the artichoke. I hope it doesn't catch Uncle John's attention.

He turns to me. "Why don't you come with us?"

"I don't know. It's...not my kind of place."

Uncle John grabs a soda out of the refrigerator. "The Lord's house is for everybody."

I roll my eyes. Here we go again. "Look, Uncle John. I'm sorry but I just don't believe in, you know, Jesus and stuff."

He scowls. "What did you say?"

"John," Aunt Margene says, touching his arm. "Let the boy be."

"Alright." He tries to smile, like he's ignoring some insult but doesn't want to show his true feelings. "Mickey, can you do one thing for me?" He pours the drink into a glass.

"What's that?" I say.

Uncle John takes a sip. "Will you at least go to the service? I know that's hard—"

"It's not. She was my friend too."

"Good." He drains the glass and puts it on the counter. "Have we tried hailing Tommy?"

Aunt Margene smacks a palm against her forehead. "Isn't his ship out in the Atlantic? I'll call tomorrow."

A rustling sound like metal scraping against concrete reverberates through the screen door. Oh, crap. What if the artichoke falls off the porch and gets away?

Aunt Margene turns in the direction of the noise. "What was that?"

"Nothing. I'll be back in a little while, okay?" Darting past them through the back door, I grab the bag and head for the backyard.

Uncle John's shed sits fifty yards behind the house. I step inside the dark space since only a single bulb illuminates the entire room. The walls are corrugated metal, and dust lines the cracked windows. Grease stains splotch the concrete floor, and everything smells like burnt motor oil. A pile of junk and tools rot under a dusty canvas tarp. Uncle John doesn't come in here much anymore, so the shed's my personal haven, a hideout from everyone but the freakshow in my head.

The voices have been coming since before my parents died in the accident. I don't know what triggers them exactly, but usually they show up when I'm stressed or frightened. They're always negative, a broken record of put-downs and belittling that can make my life a living hell.

I set down the bag containing the squirming artichoke. The cavernous shed amplifies its scratching and caterwauling. What if it escapes? I scour the room for something to put it in.

A nauseous wave hits me and upends my gut. My knees buckle and my eyes moisten with tears. I await the voices that will pile on, belittling me, filling me with self-loathing. Instead, I receive a vision, lovely but terrifying.

In my mind, Katie Sue hands me change at the grocery store.
"I need to talk to you," I say.
Her skin brushes mine, warm and tender like silk.
"Something terrible is going to happen." I grab her arm. "Stay off the main road."

Katie Sue pulls away and smiles, revealing pearly teeth.

"Why won't you say something?"

She doesn't answer. Her image collapses into dust, golden like the last rays of sunset.

The bile in my stomach curdles like spoilt milk. Here we go.

Stupid, stupid, stupid. She was never meant for you.

"Shut up."

What a worthless little nobody you are.

"Shut up." I ball my hands into fists, the skin still red and swollen. "Just leave me alone."

The voices don't.

You don't deserve good things in your life.

I punch the wall, leaving a fist-sized dent in the metal. "Shut. Up." Pain shoots through my hand. I double over until it passes.

Stupid, stupid, stupid.

"What did I tell you?" I spy a wooden stool. Hoisting it above my head, I smash it to the floor.

Stupid, stupid, stupid.

"Shut up. Shut up. Shut up." I pick up an empty soda bottle and hurl it at the wall, showering glass everywhere. "Just shut up!"

Why don't you make me?

I will.

My heart pounds and sweat pops on my brow. I try to kick an old tire but miss, hitting a steel toolbox instead. A jolt of agony shoots up from my toes, driving the voices away. My chest feels constricted, like somebody knocked the wind out of me. Am I hyperventilating? I sit still for a minute until I recover my wits and inspect the damage from my tantrum. Apart from the dent in the wall and the shattered glass, nothing else is broken. The stool lies undamaged. It's not as bad as usual, but something's missing.

The plastic bags that held the artichoke are shredded on the floor next to the crumpled aluminum pan. A trail of purple slime stains the concrete, disappearing behind Uncle John's 1973 Dodge Challenger. The ancient vehicle sits on blocks, gathering cobwebs under a heavy tarpaulin.

A smell like ozone floods the shed. Something scrapes the floor beyond the car, followed by a clicking like a rattlesnake's tail. I swallow a lump in my throat. The artichoke didn't have claws or a tail. Did it grow extra parts or something? A knot in my gut tightens.

Stupid boy. It's going to get you.

Something approaches, scraping the concrete like shrill and grating fingernails on a chalkboard.

A shiver runs up my spine, making me grit my teeth. What do I do?

The scraping grows louder and faster. It's coming for me.

Inspiration hits and I bolt for the toolbox. Flipping open the lid, I grab a cross-shaped lug wrench. The artichoke emerges from behind the car, propelled by two stalk-like legs. Bloated to the size of a football, it's grown three clacking mandibles. Attached to its bottom is a segmented tail that's dragging a bony spur.

"Stay where you are." I grip the wrench with white-knuckled fists. "I'll smack you with this, I swear."

The creature hisses, spewing noxious dust from its mouth. The tail twitches back and forth like a slithering snake.

"Stop." I bang the wrench against the toolbox. "I'm warning you."

On a high-pitched whine, the artichoke gathers its tail, and launches through the air. One mandible slices my shoulder as it rockets past. I drop the tire tool from the pain and blood.

"Jeez!" Throbbing spreads through my arm, chilling the

blood in my veins.

Whirling on its haunches, the beast faces me. It's clacking mouth-jaws are illuminated by the dim light from the window. The dragging tail scratches a divot in the concrete, releasing gray dust in its wake.

Oh, man. This thing isn't playing around. "Just stay back," I say, inching backward until I'm right in front of the Challenger. Maybe I can hop on the hood where the artichoke can't reach me.

The artichoke gains momentum, crawling along the floor faster than a sand crab. It only five feet away. No chance to escape. Either I fight, or I die.

"Alright, that's how you want it, huh?" I smack the lug wrench against the Challenger's trunk. "Well, come and get it."

With a scream, the beast vaults toward me, its jaws aimed at my throat. I raise the tire tool with both hands and bring it down in one, clean stroke. Screeching, the monster crashes to the floor, shedding lacquered scales from a wound on its side. Belching a plum-colored fluid, the creature whips its tail around my ankle.

"Leave me alone!" I impale the artichoke with the wrench. The monster spits noxious purple pulp and thrashes like a hooked fish, until it lies still.

I let go of the tool and slip to the floor. Something hot and sticky rises in my throat, tasting like blood. I retch, vomiting a chunky purple substance.

Knuckles rap on the shed door. "Mickey?" Aunt Margene says, "What on earth is going on in there?"

"I'm fine." I lie. The floor is covered in broken glass, pulped artichoke and puddles of steaming, plum-colored slime. "Just goofing off, you know?"

"Really? Because I heard shouting—"

"I'm okay, really."

A moment passes that seems to last for hours.

"Alright, we're going to the church now. Get some sleep. Don't stay up all night playing Atari."

Wow, that was close. "Okay."

I hear her footsteps trailing away from the shed. Outside, Uncle John's truck rumbles to life, engine growling like a bear. After a moment, the roar recedes into the distance, and I'm alone.

I wipe the sweat from my brow. My chest burns and my joints ache. Overcome by a coughing spasm, phlegm spills down my chin. "Ah crap." I wipe the mucus off on my shirt. Even in the dim light, my spit is a fine purple on the sleeve.

Am I sick?

The artichoke is a pulped mess at my feet. Stringy bits of flesh are splattered across the concrete. A single leaf from the monster's hide flops like a severed octopus tentacle. I scoop up the squirming appendage with a shovel, placing the specimen off to the side. I check the shelves behind the car, finding a big mason jar and a collection of lids. Returning to the artichoke, I scoop the moving leaf into the jar, then screw the lid tight.

Now, where to put this thing? A quick scan of the room reveals no obvious hiding place, so I stick it beside a block underneath the Challenger's rear axle. My sample saved, I clean the floor with shop towels, careful not to cut myself on the shattered glass. The rest of the artichoke's remains I dump into a metal drum, then seal the lid.

A half hour later, I sit on the floor with my back against the car. Mucus gathers in my throat, making me cough. I shiver and wish I brought a jacket with me. I can't stay out here long, but I'm still too amped up with adrenaline to go back inside.

What to do about the leaf in the jar? Should I send it to

a UFO magazine? The *National Enquirer*? What should I tell them? *Oh, hello, Mr. Magazine Editor? I'm a teenager and I just fought this evil creepy-crawly thing in my shed, but all I have to show for my troubles is this freaky leaf-thing that fell off when I killed it. Do you want to drop by for a tissue sample?*

More phlegm rises and I spit it into a nearby wastebasket. Who would ever believe this story? I mean, I read about this stuff all the time, but if somebody at school told me about a thing like this, I would laugh in their face.

There are still traces of the wet slime trail made by the creature. What if Aunt Margene came in while I was away and found this gunk on the floor? Or what if she looked in the drum?

A flopping sound echoes under the Challenger. I lean over and inspect the source of the disturbance.

Inside the jar, the severed leaf bats against the glass like it's trying to break free.

I jump backward. "Crap, you're still alive?" Getting to my feet, I put my ear against the drum.

Silence.

But how do I know the artichoke's really dead? If it's not, how do I get rid of it? Bury it? Burn it? Whatever I do, it can't stay in the shed.

I make a decision. Come morning, I'll bury what's left of it.

3

The morning sun's rays bend through dark clouds outside my bedroom window, illuminating a fine layer of dust on the floor.

Getting out of bed, I head for the bathroom and cough out a long rope of phlegm into the toilet, just like I'd done throughout the night.

After flushing, I listen for any activity in the house. Uncle John and Aunt Margene are predictable in their weekend habits. He's probably fishing at his favorite pier while she's at the store.

If I'm going to get rid of what's left of the artichoke, now's the time. But one thing needs doing before I destroy it.

Rummaging through my desk drawer, I find a copy of *Outer Worlds* tucked under a pile of dog-eared comic books. *Outer Worlds* is my favorite UFO rag, the inspiration for my alien obsession.

I found the magazine advertised in an old *Captain Asteroid* comic. *"Astounding Real-Life Stories of Alien Lifeforms!"* read the blurb beneath the title. Gambling a stamp, I mail-ordered a copy. After it came, I sat enraptured on my bed, gorging on stories about bug-headed visitors from other planets. Some, the writers said, are suspended in pneumatic glass tubes in a government facility in the Nevada desert. Others sat trapped under the ruins of ancient cities drowned at the bottom of the Gulf of Mexico, yearning for a chance to break their shackles and conquer our little blue sphere in a fiery bloodbath. One picture even featured an Alien Demon-Seed found off the Florida coast. A smiling girl in a bikini and flippers posed with the specimen as if displaying a prize swordfish. Though the black-and-white photo obscured the details, the thing greatly resembled an oversized artichoke. A tip line on the last page listed an eight-hundred number beneath a title that blared, *"For Those Who Know the Truth!"*

But I didn't then. Now I do.

The phone number jumps out on the yellowed page like an invitation to the grand opening of a video arcade. After copying down the digits, I run to the kitchen phone. The dial tone reverberates in my ear. After three rings, an answering machine picks up, the female voice on the recorded message sounds robotic and tinny.

You have reached the tip line for Outer Worlds. Leave a message after the beep and someone from this solar system will return your call within three business days.

Three days? Why so long?

The receiver chimes, and I speak. "This is Mickey Finley from Bay St. Louis, Mississippi. I have this real alien artichoke part? I'm pretty sure it's something from one of your magazines. So, like I killed it only not really? I think it's still alive and I need advice on how to deal with it. This is super, super important, so please call me at this number."

After leaving a message, I cradle the phone with bubbles curdling in my stomach.

Stupid, stupid, stupid. You don't think they'll really believe you.

They will, so shut up and leave me be. I'm off to destroy a monster.

Outside, I open the shed with a canvas duffel bag slung over my shoulder. Mucus rises in my throat, making me gag. The artichoke's gas must've made me sick. The lack of sleep doesn't help, either. I rub my eyes, my throat burning from hours of hacking and coughing.

The symptoms are getting worse. For all I know I could be dying. I've got to get rid of this thing while I'm still able.

An acidic cloud assaults my sinuses when I remove the lid from the oil drum where I dumped the artichoke's remains. A lump of muck and spiny limbs are congealed at the bottom of the drum. Two crab-like stalks scrape at the sides of the barrel, blindly groping for a way out.

The thing's not dead, after all. Guess I'll have to make it deader.

I grab a post-hole digger off the wall and hoist the handles above my head. I aim the blades at the middle of the purple pile of gunk. After five stabs, nothing moves inside the drum. I tip the barrel on its side. Dark fluid spills onto the floor, but most of the mess remains at the bottom. Using a flat shovel, I ladle the rest into a duffel bag lined with plastic trash bags to prevent it from being permanently stained. The bag belongs to Tommy. He'll want it in one piece when he returns home.

Hoisting the burden, I exit the shed.

The morning sky is cloudy and gray. I exhale white puffs of breath against the cool, humid air as I walk toward a pine thicket in back of our property. The duffel filled with artichoke parts is slung over my shoulder. Gripped in my hands is an entrenching tool, a keepsake from Dad's time in Vietnam. Light and portable, it doubles as both a shovel and club. A quarter mile beyond the thicket stands a meadow of tall grass, dandelions, and rock-a-chaws. I hate those little sticker-bush things—they're murder when they get in your socks or between your toes.

Past the thicket is the town cemetery. It's full of old headstones, and a lot of my family is buried there. But my destination is the meadow. That patch of ground is pretty isolated, and nobody ever goes there. If I dig down about three feet, drop the artichoke in the hole and bury it there, it should be too far away from people to do any damage.

Moving on, I plod through the dense woods. Gray clouds overhead cast a pall over the needle-covered branches, obscuring the red dirt littered with twigs and pinecones.

The bag's burden weighs heavily on my shoulder. It doesn't help that I'm getting sicker by the minute. Fluid builds in my nasal cavities and phlegm curdles in my throat. No voices, though. A small comfort considering everything that's happened in the last twenty-four hours.

A raindrop hits my forehead. Then another.

Crap, it's probably going to rain cats and dogs and I'm not even to the edge of the thicket. If I'm going to beat the coming downpour, I'll have to step on it.

Something brittle crunches under my shoe. Setting down the bag, I stop to investigate. The shattered object is a large pinecone. Its overlapping fronds resemble the artichoke's hide.

The duffle bag at my feet rustles, rocking from side to side. A spiny limb rips through the canvas and I jump backward, trying not to get stuck. I approach the sack, entrenching tool in hand, ready to bash whatever brains the thing inside possesses. As if sensing my intentions, the probing stalk retreats into its prison.

Raindrops plummet through breaks in the pine canopy.

Artichoke Stars and Chicken Fried Shark

The deluge penetrates my jacket, soaking my shirt.

Great. Now I'm really in for it. I have no choice but to hoist the writhing sack over my shoulder and make for the thicket's edge.

Coarse needles give way to soft grass when I reach a steep bank bordering the meadow. My foot slips on the wet grass and I tumble like a log shooting a water flume. "Aw crap, crap, crap!"

A murky pool breaks my descent and I sink face-first, getting a mouthful of grass and slushy mud for my troubles.

Rain pelts my face and body, the sky getting darker by the second. I search for the duffel bag and shovel, but both are gone. Then an oblong shape catches my eye. It's the bag, sticking out of the mud. Nothing moves within. Heck, maybe I got lucky, and the artichoke died in the fall.

I approach but twin stalks burst through the sack, shredding it to pieces. The artichoke emerges on newly grown legs, triple-mandibles gnashing like thresher blades. Emitting a high-pitched shriek, it dashes away from me, high stepping through the sucking mud.

"Aw man." I smack a palm against my forehead. "Come back here, you stupid thing!"

I search the mud for the entrenching tool. Beating on the monster hasn't done much good so far, but maybe I can stun the creature long enough to bury it and drop a rock on its ugly mug. The spade's sharp shovel-end pokes out of the water. Another two feet, and I would have stepped on it. "There we go."

Pulling the tool from the muck, I get to my feet and take off after the artichoke.

The rain comes in buckets now, soaking my clothes. My wet jacket and jeans weigh me down like a truck tire. Tracking the artichoke isn't hard because the parallel gouges it leaves in the mud are easy to follow.

I follow its trail through the meadow all the way to the cemetery.

"Oh brother," I mumble under my breath. Of all the places it could've gone, why would it pick the boneyard?

Clutching the weapon, I run, slogging through the slippery mud. In seconds, I find the artichoke. It's snagged on a wrought-iron fence, spindly stalk-legs waving in the rain. It must've gotten stuck there trying to hop over.

Finally, some good luck. I plod through the mud, water droplets ricocheting off the shovel's business end. On the fence, the artichoke squeals and tries to shift its weight so gravity will tip it over. Raising the weapon above my head, I shout, "You're dead meat, buddy!"

Before I lower the boom on the monster, it flicks out a leg, nearly nicking my throat. I stumble backward, losing the shovel in the mud. "Aw crap." Searching for the weapon, I'm forced to keep my back exposed to the creature. By sheer luck, my fingers close on the tool's wet handle.

Spinning around, I raise the shovel, ready to strike. "Yeah, let's go."

But the artichoke is gone. On the other side of the fence a fresh set of muddy tracks vanishes into the graveyard.

Why does it want to be in the cemetery so bad? Pelted by rain, I try to hop the fence, but my soggy clothes weigh me down. I get hung up on a sharp spike. It gouges my thigh before I tumble over the barrier and land in the muck. Picking myself up, I inspect the wound. It's bleeding, but I can still run.

Gritting my teeth, I grasp the spade in two white-knuckled fists and plunge into the cemetery. My heart pounds like a floor tom, adrenaline running like lightning through my blood.

Thirty yards ahead, I catch sight of the creature. Swaying on spindly legs, the beast wobbles on the lip of an open grave. A newly set headstone towers over the plot, flanked by a pair of shovels planted in a mound of dirt.

I bolt for the artichoke, swinging the tool like a battle ax. The creature manages to twist its bulk, avoiding the shovel but my blow cuts through the earth. Upended, the screeching creature loses its footing and topples backward into the hole.

"No!" I drop the spade and scramble to the edge.

The artichoke writhes at the bottom, sinking in a puddle of mud. I rake the dirt with my fingers and plant one foot on the plot's rim. If I can just get down there, I can cut that thing to pieces.

From out of nowhere, two pairs of hands clamp around my legs and drag me away from the grave.

"Hey," someone says, "what are you doing out here?"

"No, no, no." I attempt to kick free. "Why did you stop me?"

Above me stand two men in overalls, glaring at me like I'm crazy.

"Kid," the taller one says, "you've got no business out here."

"Yes, I do." I point into the hole. "Look down there. Do you see it? Do you see it?"

"See what?" the other says.

Jeez, what is wrong with these guys? "The artichoke. Please, you have to look down there!"

"Nothing's down there but mud," the taller man says, offering me his hand. "Maybe you need to get your eyes checked."

I turn and stare into the grave. My own reflection peers back at me from the muddy pool below.

The shorter man pats my shoulder. "C'mon, let's get you home."

Craig E. Higgins

    They lead me away. But not before I catch a glimpse of the headstone. The name chiseled into the granite sends a chill down my spine.

Katharine Susan Carson,
Beloved daughter,
1960-1980

4

"I hate the word funeral." I raise the window on the passenger side. "It's totally misleading." Frigid air blasts my face as the gap narrows and closes.

"Mickey, what are you talking about?" Aunt Margene says, dressed all in black. She sits in the middle of the front seat. Uncle John drives. Both me and him wear suits and neckties.

There are better ways to spend a Monday.

The temperature dropped this afternoon, so it's cold inside the cab. A layer of frost covers the windshield in the places where the wipers can't reach. But the truck straddles the beach road, so I have a perfect view of the bay. The sky is placid, a sea of gray and white. A long-necked egret soars overhead, wings flapping slowly.

"What do the first three letters in funeral spell?" I say.

"Mick, stop bothering your aunt." Uncle John pilots the vehicle with one hand.

"Fun. How are funerals any fun? They should call them *sad-erals*, or *grim-erals*."

Aunt Margene rubs her knuckles against her temples. "Mickey, if you're going to act like a selfish little boy, we can take you back to the house right now."

Uncle John scowls. "Mick, didn't I tell you to be nice to your aunt?"

"I don't mean...look, it's just an observation."

His knuckles whiten on the wheel. "Well, keep those observations to yourself."

Mucus rises in my nostrils. It's all I can do to stop from sneezing.

Aunt Margene runs a hand over my forehead. "Maybe you should've stayed home."

My illness got worse Sunday morning after trying to destroy the artichoke. The sniffles and coughing deteriorated into a severe headache mixed with uncontrollable chills. The shakes subsided but now congealed mucus blocks my sinuses when my nose isn't running. When I'm able to blow some of it out, the gunk is the color of overripe plums, which is weird.

Whoever heard of purple snot?

I'm grateful Aunt Margene didn't make me go to school this morning. But despite the cold and the chunks of stuff in my throat and nose, I want to say goodbye to Katie Sue. It wasn't me that got her killed, but that image of the artichoke sinking into her grave has haunted me for the last two days. I feel ashamed, and that shame coupled with her memory, hollows out bittersweet caverns in my mind.

Katie Sue wore glasses, believed in Jesus and probably had a crush on my stupid cousin. But she was also pure and sweet and real. And she had a smile like an angel's, especially that last day when she sold me the Pop-Tarts.

"Don't play in the traffic," Katie Sue said. I wonder if she thought about that, right when Johnny Reb caught her in his headlights?

God? If you're up there, and I'm not sure you are, let me

just say you should've let that truck hit me instead.

My gut rumbles and I await the voices. But they remain silent.

Uncle John pulls into a cramped parking lot beside Bay Crossroads Ministry. It's the second-biggest church in town, after the shark-castle of St. Adolphus. The building is made of yellow sandstone, windows and doors rimmed with gleaming aluminum. Three brass crosses jut high into the sky.

Bay Crossroads is non-denominational but wears its evangelical heart on its sleeve. *A place where lost people go,* Uncle John once told me.

I guess he used to be one of them. Dad used to tell me about John's wild days and lost years. I always imagined him zoned out on too many beers and little white pills, trying to blot out screaming spirits from a place Dad called Ghostland. Not long before Mom and Dad died, Uncle John changed his life and got cleaned up. Now, he and Aunt Margene call Bay Crossroads their second home, the mortgage paid by their pretend sky-friend.

Inside, the chapel smells of candles, wilting flowers, and floor polish. Blond wooden pews march lockstep to an altar situated on a stepped platform. Well-wishers line up to pay their respects, filing past an apple-green coffin.

Standing next to the casket, a short man with a dyed-black widow's peak and a small mustache comforts a parishioner with a too-long handshake. Another gets a hug. The short guy's bloodshot eyes wobble above an immobile smile.

Aunt Margene nudges me. "Do you remember Pastor Paul?"

"Maybe. Is he Katie Sue's dad?"

"That's right."

We get in line. A box of tissues sits on a nearby pew. I

reach down, grab one, and blow my nose. A plummy blot puddles darkly against the white tissue.

Wow, is that blood?

Maybe not. This stuff is too thick and not red like it should be.

Weird.

Katie Sue waits for me like she has all the time in the world. Dressed in pale green, her body lies nestled among folds of pale taffeta. Beige paste discolors her sunken cheeks. Her lips are dark and flattened, eyes glued shut.

Her hair is slightly curled and copper-colored, not her usual hue. Is it really hers, or a wig covering some nasty head wound from the accident? I almost touch the plastic-looking tresses, but figure people might be offended. So, I keep my hands to myself.

A chill radiates from the coffin, as if she were packed in ice. Brushing against her cold hand I recoil, detecting no spark. And why would there be one? She's dead, after all.

Katie Sue?

I know you're not here anymore. But I do so wish you'd wake up and smile at me one last time. Even though that would totally freak everyone out.

Aunt Margene grabs my elbow. "Mickey, your nose."

A plum-colored stream drips over my upper lip.

"Here." She hands me a tissue from her purse. "Is that blood?"

Oh, crap. Did she see what color that mucus was? "No." I shake my head. "Just, um…well, actually, yeah. I woke up with it bleeding a little."

Aunt Margene frowns. "Maybe we should run you home."

I wave her off. "No, I'm okay, really."

She drops the subject. I glance at Katie Sue one last time and turn to leave. Something acidic and small as a pea rolls around in my stomach, growing larger with every step I take. From out of nowhere, Pastor Paul grips my hand. The minister's face reminds me of Katie Sue's, same round chin and bright eyes. He smells of musk aftershave, but the smile on his face hangs precariously, like a loose shingle in a strong breeze.

"You must be Mickey." The pastor crushes my hand in his. "Thank you for coming."

I manage to extract my hand from his grasp. "I'm real sorry about this, Pastor Paul."

"That's very kind of you." Light glints off his perfect teeth. "We'll get through it. With the Lord's help, I'm sure we will."

Brushing past me, Uncle John whispers in Pastor Paul's ear. The minister claps his hands. "Well, your uncle reminded me of something that needs doing." He grabs my shoulder. "Will we see you around church?"

"Gee, I don't know. I'd have to think about that."

"That's alright. But Mickey?"

"Yeah?"

"Take it from me, no one is an island. Everybody needs a place to come home to. This could be yours."

"What if it's not?"

Uncle John frowns. "Mick."

"Let me put it to you this way, young man..." Pastor Paul smiles, muscles twitching around his eyes. "...If our master doesn't claim you, another will."

His master? Is he talking about Jesus? Because he kind of sounds like he's not. "I'll...try to remember that."

"See that you do."

Pastor Paul and Uncle John leave the chapel.

The pea swells to a fireball in my gut. "Aunt Margene? I don't feel so good."

She nods and leads me away to the front pew. "You're

burning up. I shouldn't have let you come," she says, holding a hand to my forehead.

"I'm okay." Noxious juices bathe my esophagus, making me gag.

"You're not. Soon as your uncle gets back, we're leaving."

I grab her wrist. "No."

"Yes."

The fireball blossoms into an inferno and a wave of nausea rolls over me. Sparks shimmer before my eyes. "I'll be back in a minute."

She pulls her hand back, a cross look on her face. "Make it quick."

I dash down the aisle, glad to get away from Aunt Margene's probing stare. A lump catches in my throat from my illness and the claustrophobic atmosphere of the chapel. I only wear a suit and tie to weddings and funerals. The necktie constricts my airflow, so I yank it loose, while pushing through the crowded aisle. A little boy points at me and says, "Hey, you've got purple snot coming out."

I wipe it on the back of my hand. "Thanks."

Hustling through the crowd, I reach a dimly lit corridor that seems to stretch for miles. An old woman flutters in from the shadows. "Young man, are you lost?"

Phlegm knots in my throat. "I'm looking for the toilet."

She points, nearly stabbing a finger into my swollen nose. "That way and to the right."

Another wave of pain crashes in my stomach. Sparks like comets loop past my eyes. Propping myself against a wall, I wait for the vertigo to cease.

No such luck.

Gyrations in my stomach drive the dizziness in my head. I've never been this sick before in my life. Swaying on unsteady feet, I reach the end of the corridor and turn the corner. Light flickers from an open bathroom. I step in and lock the door behind me, catching my reflection in the mirror. Nothing out of the ordinary if you're used to staring at corpses. My pale skin stretches over sunken cheeks, cavernous eyes dull as lifeless pools.

I let out a hallow laugh. If I die in here, they'll lay me out with Katie Sue.

Acid boils my stomach lining. I brace myself for another round from the peanut gallery. And it isn't long in coming.

What's the matter? Can't face what you've done?

"Shut up." I toss the tie on the counter and inhale deeply, filling my lungs to bursting.

Stupid, stupid, stupid. You shouldn't be here, you know. You dishonor her memory.

"Not listening to you." I turn on the faucet. Water flows like molasses from the spigot.

It's your fault she's dead, Girl-Killer Mickey.

What? How is this my fault?

You're bad luck. Everybody dies around you.

That doesn't make any sense.

Sure, it does. Mom died. Dad died. Girl dies. See a pattern there?

I'm not listening to this.

You make everybody go away. Even her. There's something wrong with you.

"No, there isn't."

My tongue goes numb, my gut bloating like an overfilled inner tube. The comets expand into a constellation of firecrackers.

Girl-Killer, Girl-Killer, Girl-Killer.

Doubling over, I vomit.

You liked her. She's dead. Your fault, your fault, your fault.

"Shut up." Sweat pours down my neck and pools in the hollows of my collarbones. Water from the faucet floods the sink, and the contents of my stomach spills onto the floor.

I shut off the tap, undo the top three buttons of my shirt, and swab my chest with a wad of paper towels. The crumpled wad turns purple. Even my sweat is going weird? What's happening to me?

See how messed up you are? Just like you messed up Katie Sue!

"Stop it. Just stop, okay?"

Girl-Killer. Girl-Killer. Girl-Killer.

My breath comes in shallow gasps. I glance at the steam-fogged mirror. The glass distorts and seems to bulge like a soap bubble. Darkness floods my brain and I black out.

When I come to, it's nighttime. That can't be right, though, because I'm standing on a beach by the bay.

Wait. Am I dreaming?

Chunks of blocky masonry litter the sand, black and grainy. Smoke rises in fiery orange plumes against a charcoal sky rent with gold lightning strikes. Black rain dribbles from the clouds. Burning drops singe my bare shoulders, stinking like spoiled brisket. I wince, but there's no place to shelter.

Out on the bay, something slowly approaches. Twin fins cut through the black water. Beneath the churning surface, a luminous eye glows yellow.

What is that thing, a shark? I bite my tongue, and saliva trickles down my lip.

Penetrating the waterline, the apparition's dorsal flaps make a silty foam in their wake. A great snout emerges from the surf, revealing dripping fangs sharp as meat hooks. My heart pounds in my chest, and tears stream down my cheeks. I want to run but there doesn't seem any point because this close, the shark's fins tower a good fifty feet above my head. The slit pupil of the monster's unblinking eye narrows and fixes its gaze on me.

It lets out a deafening screech.

Burning surf blasts across the beach, lashing my face. Glass from a thousand windows shatters in my ears. Screaming, I raise my arms to block steaming lava spewing from the thing's spiky jaws—

A fist pounds against the door.

"Is somebody in there?" a man's voice says.

I'm curled on the wet floor, water overflowing the sink.

"Yeah, give me a minute." I stand, tucking my shirttail into my pants.

"Hurry it up, will you?" Footsteps reverberate down the hall and everything is silent.

Sparks flash in front of my eyes, then dissipate. What was that? A dream?

Or a premonition?

After cleaning up the mess, I flush the rest of the paper towels down the toilet. My reflection stares back at me through the mirror. Still pale, the yellow tint on my flesh recedes a little. Hunger pangs replace stomach pains.

And no voices. For now.

The phosphorescent glow of the overhead lights illuminates my wristwatch. I check the time. Wow. I've been in the bathroom for fifteen minutes. Probably should get back to the chapel. I button my shirt, knot the tie, and exit the restroom.

Two voices, a boy's and a girl's, echo from up the hallway. They're arguing, the girl's voice cutting through the stale air.

"Just leave me alone, alright?" she says.

"No, I won't leave you alone," the boy says. "We're family. I got a responsibility to take care of y'all."

Stumbling along the corridor, I cover my ears, not wanting to hear about their personal problems.

The girl's voice blares through the open door of the break room. "No, Wade."

"Aw, c'mon. It'll just be a few people, right after the dance," the boy says. "You're going to be at the Fall Social, right? I could meet you there."

"But I don't know if I'm going to go. Sorry, but partying's not on my mind right now."

"I just think you'd be better off where I can keep an eye on you. You know because you'll be sad and all—"

"How do you know how I feel?" Her hollow laugh reverberates down the corridor. "Geez, Wade. Do you even hear yourself?"

I glance inside as I sneak past. The girl is short and curvy. Her fists are planted on the gentle swell of her hips. Feathered blonde hair drapes down her back almost to her waist.

The boy stands tall and muscular, sporting a barrel chest and narrow hips. His face resembles the business end of a crescent wrench. Flinty eyes and a long, thin nose above a knotty hambone of a chin.

"Suit yourself," he says. "But you'll be missing out. Going to be a lot of cool people there."

"Whatever."

"Look, Becca. I know we haven't always been good together." He grabs her wrists in his meaty paws. "But I promise that's going to change. Katie would want me to look out for you."

Who is this guy? If he's family, why does he act like a jealous boyfriend?

"Don't bring her up right now." She twists free of his grip. "And what makes you think I need your help for anything?"

Jeez, but who needs all this noise? I turn to leave but phlegm bubbles up my throat, making me cough.

The girl turns and faces me. "Can I help you?"

Now this is awkward. "I'm just passing through," I say.

"You know what? Forget it." Wade heads for the door. Stopping in front of me, he stares into my eyes. "Dude, you're in the way."

"Sorry."

"Don't make that mistake again." He rams his shoulder into my chest, nearly knocking me over.

Me and the girl are alone. For the first time, I get a good look at her face.

Her lips are full, the lower one quivering slightly. Round cheeks frame a button nose. Liquid brown eyes shimmer like pennies, whites shot through with red. Mascara streaks her face like splotchy watercolors.

"Hey," she says. "It's impolite to stare."

"Sorry." I cross the threshold. "My name's Mickey."

She meets me halfway. "Becca Mae, Katie's sister." We shake hands and she grins. "You don't remember me, do you?"

Up close, her hair smells like butterscotch, a welcome reprieve from the dead flowers in the chapel.

"Should I?"

"Yearbook club? I was in seventh grade? You were in eighth?"

Wait, I *do* remember her. "Wow. Were you like the girl with the braces who kept asking me for help with the glue gun?"

"Yes!" Becca Mae's smile is warm, a pleasant curl outlines the edge of her lips. "That was me."

"Wow." I take a seat in front of a box of glazed donuts. "Yeah, that was a pretty rough year. Stuff happened, you know, with my parents—"

"Oh, my word." She dabs a tear from her eye with her wrist. "They passed, right? How did you even bear it?"

"I mean, it was hard. It's still hard, some days."

"You always looked so sad." She grabs a spot across from me. "Sometimes, I thought about talking to you, but you were so cut off from everybody."

"That's probably true."

She brushes a sprig of cornflake-yellow hair from her forehead. "I get that though."

"You do?"

"Sure. When we lost Momma, it was like the world ended. I stayed in bed for two days. Just didn't want to get up."

"That sucks."

"It did."

"Death sucks."

"You know it." She twists a lock of hair between her thumb and forefinger.

"Say, I didn't know you were Katie Sue's sister."

"Lots of people don't." Becca Mae leans over to grab a donut and her round, firm breasts swell against the table. "Because Katie's…she was so beautiful—and thin."

"Well, I guess so," I say, completely distracted.

"Always the center of attention." She takes a bite of donut.

"Are they good?" I say, pointing to the box.

"Try one."

I do. It tastes like cardboard. "They're okay."

"Kind of stale." She takes a tissue from her purse and wipes a trace of sugar from her lips. "You know, Katie talked about your cousin a lot. Tommy, right?"

Will I ever escape that guy's shadow? "That's cool."

"She really liked him." Becca Mae's eyes moisten. "Sorry, but this is hard."

I hand her a napkin from a stack next to the donut box. "Here."

"Thanks." She wipes her eyes. "Usually, this time of day, I'd come home from school, and she'd be home from work, and we'd just talk about our day, you know? She wanted to know what I was up to. Or she'd help me with my homework."

"She was a good friend?"

"The best." Becca Mae blows her nose into the napkin. "That's one of the things I'm going to miss the most."

Without warning, she breaks down crying, cradling her head on the table.

"Are you okay?"

Becca Mae gazes up through yellowed ringlets. "I thought I could handle this, but I just can't. We lost Mom a few years ago, but Katie was there. What do I do now?"

"Speaking from experience, you have to take it one day at a time."

"You're probably right." She shakes her head. "But it's hard."

"You have to try. Although if I'm being honest, day to day doesn't always work for me. Some days I get so angry, I want to punch myself in the head."

Becca Mae frowns. "Oh, don't do that."

"No?"

"No." She places a donut on the table. "Watch." She flattens the fritter with one swift blow. "Now, would you eat this?"

"Probably not."

"Exactly." She tosses the mashed snack in the trash. "So, why punch your head? Isn't it worth more than a donut?"

"I guess."

"Don't let me catch you beating yourself up. I won't allow it." She points at my face. "There's something on your lip."

"Whoops." Grabbing a napkin, I dab the edge of my mouth. "I was sick earlier, in the bathroom."

"Oh. Is it contagious?"

"I don't know."

"You probably should get that checked out." Becca Mae rises from her seat.

"Are you leaving?"

"Yeah."

"Don't, please. At least not yet."

"Why not?"

"I enjoy talking to you."

"Fine." She sits down. "But don't give me no cooties, okay? It's been a long morning."

It takes a second before her joke sinks in. Then we both burst into laughter.

At the cemetery, the crowd gathers near a hearse parked on a dirt road. Four big men hover behind the vehicle. Katie Sue's casket sits on a rack sticking out of the rear. The open plot lies ten yards away. A machine for lowering the casket is positioned above the hole. Next to it stand Pastor Paul and Uncle John. Beside them a man dressed in dark clothes attaches a crank to the machine's frame. Nearby, a black-clad woman wearing cat's-eyeglasses checks the flash on her camera.

Me and Aunt Margene stand at the front of the mourners. Cold penetrates the thin fabric of my jacket thanks to a stiff breeze, making me shiver.

My mind wanders.

The events of the last few days play out in my brain, like film looped on a spool. The artichoke. Katie Sue at the Jitney Jungle. Losing the monstrous thing in the rain, its pulpy body slipping into Katie Sue's open grave.

Wait a minute.

What if the artichoke is still alive?

I peer over the edge of the cavity. Nothing but dried mud at the bottom, no sign of the thing that fell in a couple days before.

Wade stands across from me in the crowd, coughing into a gloved fist. Next to him another guy, tall but with dark hair and olive complexion, rubs his arms through a tweed coat.

Both wear nice clothes, not like the stuff Aunt Margene buys for me at the mall. Maybe they're St. Adolphus boys?

Pastor Paul nods to Uncle John, who takes a spot next to the quartet beside the hearse. To my surprise, Wade steps forward, as if to help, but the minister waves him off. Snapping his fingers, the pastor summons a red-haired boy with a big head lolling on slumped shoulders. I recognize him. It's Owen Duffy, senior on the debate team. He joins the others and, with a gesture from the pastor, they slide the casket from the hearse and bear it to the grave.

The woman with the camera takes a picture, the flash blinding me. Her partner turns the crank.

Slowly, the coffin descends into the ground.

Across from me, Becca Mae steps forward. Dabbing tears from her reddened cheeks, she bursts into a plaintive hymn.

"I'll fly away, o glory,

I'll fly away in the morning ..."

The ride home is bumpy. My cheeks grow hot, and mucus clogs my sinuses, so no air passes through them.

Aunt Margene puts a hand to my forehead. "Shouldn't we get him to a doctor?" she asks Uncle John.

Eyes fixed on the road he shrugs. "Let him tough it out."

I stare through the open window at the clouds above, shot through with fiery tongues of pink of dusk. They remind me of my vision in the bathroom.

Questions rattle like loose gravel in my brain. What happened to the artichoke? What was up with that vision in the bathroom?

When am I going to get well?

5

The next morning, I wake bleary-eyed and hungry but otherwise okay. Checking my face in the mirror reassures me my condition is improving. The color's back in my cheeks, and my throat doesn't hurt as badly as it did. I go to the kitchen where Aunt Margene sits, reading the newspaper. She checks my temperature and pronounces me well enough to go to school.

I attend Gulf High, the only public high school in town. On campus, kids run through the main hallway connecting the classrooms. Lockers slam amid the chatter, gossip, and the occasional distracting whistle. I tread cautiously past pockets of back-slapping boys. By a water fountain, giggling girls whisper into each other's ears.

Are they talking about me? Do they even notice me at all?

I move past colorful posters lining the cinder block walls, each advertising this Friday's Fall Social. It's the biggest school dance after Prom, and this year, like every year, the theme is Halloween. Vampires stalk the entrance of an algebra classroom. Werewolves in football helmets prowl Shop and Auto-Repair. A trio of witches hover over a boiling cauldron outside Home Economics.

Near the gym entrance stands a display put together by the

theater department. Papier-mâché ghosts and zombies haunt a cardboard cemetery. In the center, a grinning skeleton in a fisherman's outfit holds aloft the bones of a long-dead flounder. Something about the fish's hollow eye-sockets triggers a chill in my spine.

What am I afraid of? The stupid thing is just a bunch of plastic and wire.

Shaking my head, I make a beeline through a glut of bodies in the hallway.

Truth is, I hate the Fall Social. I mean, I've never gone but the predictability of everybody's behavior in the lead-up to the event bothers me. The status-climbing. The posturing for dates. It all makes me want to rip out my hair. What makes it worse is the dance happens right after the biggest football game of the season. And this year, like every year, our opponent is St. Adolphus.

I fill out a mental scorecard...

Gridiron battle with the all-preppy boys' private school? Check.

Rich kids hogging our Gulf High ladies at the combined dance afterwards? Check.

Guaranteed fistfight in the gym, or the parking lot? Check.

This will not end well.

Mr. Kraftner's English class is three-quarters full when I take my seat. He taps his wristwatch. "Mick, what time does class start?"

I gaze up at the clock. "Two minutes ago?"

"Right." The teacher returns to the chalkboard.

Scribbling down a list of names, he asks us to recall what happened in a short story about people leaving a colony on Mars. My eyelids grow heavy and a kid behind me taps me on the shoulder.

Artichoke Stars and Chicken Fried Shark

"Dude, wake up."

"Sorry."

Morning classes flash by in a blur. With each successive period, my rumbling gut grows louder. I fear the voices will raise their ugly, collective heads, but they don't.

Midday, anarchy spills over in the crowded lunchroom. In line, I receive my ration of hamburger steak, tater tots, and chocolate milk. Balancing a loaded tray, I make my way past tables brimming with the different tribes at my school—jocks, poodle-haired popular girls, kids who'll grow up to be their parents, nerds.

The winnowing process of where to sit is hard because I don't fit in anywhere. At the jock table this big kid, a lineman on the football team, rises from his seat, beating his chest like a gorilla. His friends laugh, egging him on.

No place for me there.

I avoid the Future Parental Unit contingent. Having already lost my folks, I don't see myself ending up in their shoes. The nerd table is no refuge, either. Avoiding eye contact, the bespectacled kids with their knit shirts and pocket protectors shun me. To them, I'm one of the cool kids on account of my rocker hair. Never mind the countless hours I spend playing video games or obsessing over old comics.

Drifting in no-man's land, I'm relieved when a girl's voice calls out, "Mickey Finley!"

I turn. Becca Mae Carson sits at a table a few feet away.

"Hey." I run toward her, high-tops squeaking on the linoleum.

She introduces me to a couple of girls picking over their lunch. "Mickey, this is Felicia and Ruth."

"Hi," they say in unison.

I sit next to Becca Mae on the edge of a bench. Her arm brushes against mine, and a tingle runs through me.

"Man, it's busy in here," I say.

She sips chocolate milk through a plastic straw. "And how."

Stabbing my fork into the burger, I take a bite. It's tough but tastes less like jerky than usual. Becca Mae wears a blouse that's a little too tight against her ample chest. I try to keep my gaze fixed on her face, but it's a losing battle. Up close, her butterscotch scent is another distraction.

She smiles as if sensing my discomfort. "So, Mickey. Are you going to the game?"

"What?" I say, shaking my head.

Felicia and Ruth giggle.

"I asked if you're going to go," Becca Mae says. "To the game."

"Oh." My face goes flush. "Wasn't planning on it."

"What about the dance?" Felicia says.

"Yeah, we're all going in costume," Becca Mae says. "That'll be fun, right?"

The other two nod.

"Totally," Felicia agrees.

"Maybe." I chew my food and wish the other girls weren't there, so me and Becca Mae could talk like we did at the funeral.

Somebody bumps my shoulder. "Oh, sorry, Pop-Tart," a girl's voice says. "Didn't see you down there."

Glancing behind me, I behold Alice Walsh.

"That's not my name," I say.

Alice laughs. "No, your name is Pop-Tart." She turns to a trio of girls behind her dressed in matching red-and-gold cheerleader outfits. "Ain't that so?"

They cackle in sterio like crows in a cornfield.

Tall and long-limbed, Alice's curly, liquid-black locks reek of hairspray, and her mouth is wrenched into a perpetual sneer. I don't know why she hates me. My best guess is she's held a grudge ever since that time in seventh grade when I wouldn't let her copy off my test paper.

I frown. "What do you want?"

"I got a message for you." Staring into my eyes, Alice leans close, pert nose inches from mine. "Somebody's fitted you out for a stomping."

"And who might somebody be?"

Becca Mae rises from her seat. "Why don't you leave him alone?"

The tall girl snickers. "Who's this, your bodyguard?"

Stepping into the aisle, my new friend's nose only comes up to Alice's chin. "And what if I was?"

Everybody at the table stops talking.

Alice smiles. "Then you might be in for a stomping yourself, little girl."

Becca Mae's eyelids narrow like a viper's. "Just you try it."

Whoa. She's not backing down. That's impressive because not many people stand up to this nasty girl.

Alice shoves Becca Mae, who scowls and balls her fists. One of the cheerleaders steps between them, stopping the fight before punches are thrown.

"Wade Ruthven's going to get you, Pop-Tart," Alice yells, her heels dragging as her friends lead her away. "Remember that name. And don't come to the dance if you know what's good for you."

Me and Becca Mae turn to each other. Biting her lip, she shivers, cheeks flushed. "If that witch comes at me again, I swear I'm going to—"

"Wait," I say. "Was she talking about the guy from the funeral?"

Becca Mae frowns, the red waning in her complexion. "Yeah. Wade's my cousin."

Felicia and Ruth grab their trays. "Y'all need a minute?" Ruth says.

Becca Mae nods and they leave. "Wade goes to St. Adolphus, and he's a total jerk. I really hate him sometimes."

"That sucks."

"Yeah." Becca Mae rubs her arms. "He gets a little weird around me, you know? Like he's my dad or…you know, I don't even want to think about it right now."

"He seems really creepy."

"Totally." She taps her fingers on the table. "Why'd she call you Pop-Tart?"

Geez, I hate it when people ask me about that. "It's a stupid nickname her and her friends gave me in junior high." I wipe my mouth and wad the napkin into a tight ball. "Because I used to eat Pop-Tarts a lot."

"Do you still?"

"Do I still, what?"

"Eat Pop-Tarts."

"Yeah. Chocolate Fudge especially."

Becca Mae smiles. "You know what I think?"

"What's that?"

"You have to come to Social just to spite Aqua-Net Girl."

"Wow…" I laugh. "…you smelled it too?"

"Phew." Becca Mae makes a face, fanning the air with her hand. "Anybody who uses that much product needs to reorder her priorities in life."

"What about Wade? He serious about that threat?"

"Don't worry about him." She punches my arm. "Your bodyguard will be there."

At wrestling practice, Win Cobb slams me onto the mat. On my back I strain against his grip, but there's no getting free. Shifting my weight, I try to bridge out of his hold. He tightens his grip. Sweat beads on my brow.

Coach kneels next to us and slaps the mat. "That's a pin."

Win offers me his hand. "C'mon, Mickey."

"One day, I'll beat you," I say.

"Okay, man."

We sit on the bench, rehydrating while a couple of other boys grapple. Win takes a cup of Gatorade from the trainer and drains it. He's my height and weight, but his arms and shoulders are corded with muscle. As the only Black kid on the team, Win's not tight with too many people at school, and I never have been able to figure out why. He's always been nice to me. Maybe the other kids need to get to know him better. It doesn't help that Win's from Cincinnati, which to some people's way of thinking pretty much makes him a Yankee.

He tosses the cup into a wastebasket. "You going to be ready for them prep-school boys next month?"

"St. Adolphus? I'll be ready." I lie.

Coach approaches. "Cobb? Tell your folks to order you a pizza tonight. I need you to move up to one-forty-five for the next meet."

Win frowns. "Coach, I won't be as fast."

"True. And when we go to state, we'll have you back at your regular weight. But Sanderson's out sick, and we got nobody else."

"Timmy Sanderson's sick?" I say.

The big man nods. "That's right."

I frown. "I wrestled him last week and he walloped me."

"Not likely he'd do that today."

Win raises his hand. "But Coach, the meet's not for another two weeks."

"Doesn't matter. Tim's in bad shape. Some kind of respiratory thing. They have him on oxygen right now."

"Oh, man," I say.

Sanderson out? Does he have purple stuff leaking from his eyes, too?

Craig E. Higgins

Coach wipes his glasses with a handkerchief. "You fellas didn't hear this from me."

On the walk home after practice, a cold wind cuts through my sweatshirt, making me shiver. Plum-colored mucus seeps down my upper lip, and I wipe it on my sleeve. Then a knot twists in my gut.

Stupid, stupid, stupid. You suck at wrestling.

Shut up. You're no expert.

Being on the team is just to impress your uncle, isn't it?

No, it's not.

Sure, it is. Think you're a big tough guy now, don't you?

You don't know anything about me.

I know everything about you, sissy-baby. Stop kidding yourself and do something that fits your place in life.

Like what?

Why not try out for mascot?

Why don't you go stuff it with a bag full of turds?

A pulpy wad disengages itself from my sinuses and slides down my throat. I spit it out, but another takes its place.

Swallow. Spit. Repeat. Dull purple patches stain the sidewalk like stepped-on blueberries. If this stuff is contagious, I've exposed pretty much everybody on the team.

Aunt Margene frowns when I walk in the house. "Mickey, are you okay?"

I let the bookbag slip from my hand. It crashes to the floor. "What? I'm fine."

A haze descends over me, and I stumble, my ankles wobbling in my high-tops.

"Doesn't look that way, kiddo. Let me make you onion soup."

"Aw, man. That's totally not necessary."

She guides me to the couch. "It totally is."

After the soup, Aunt Margene takes my temperature. "You're

burning up."

Phlegm balls in my throat. "I'm fine."

"And what is this purple stuff on your mouth?" She sets the thermometer on the coffee table.

I shake my head. "It's nothing."

"Mickey," she takes a tissue from the box and dabs my lower lip. "You are not well. I'm calling the doctor in the morning."

"Aw man, don't do that." Why do my words sound so slurred? My tongue feels like it's wearing a gym sock.

"Don't argue with me." Aunt Margene tosses the used tissue on the table. Then another.

"Um, I don't feel well."

She helps me to the bathroom, where I puke. After that, I'm ordered to bed. Tossing and turning between crisp sheets, I slip into darkness to the sound of distant drumming.

I'm dressed in a sleeveless tunic and stretched out atop a stone altar. Above me the sun burns red against an orange sky. Shaking my head to clear the cobwebs, I try to sit up. A frigid bolt of agony shoots through my bare feet all the way to my eyes. In spite of the bright fireball overhead, my arms break out in goosebumps. Worse, I'm covered by a blanket of murky fog, obscuring my view. Two fin-shaped shadows cross overhead, sharp as razor blades.

A dull silence descends.

Climbing down from the altar, I make my way to the edge of a platform. Terraced steps descend beneath me in all directions. Am I on top of a pyramid? That's certainly what it looks like.

Mist curls around my feet. Stone stairs fall away on all sides, descending into the fog. I catch a whiff of burning oil mixed with sulfur.

Someone behind me coughs.

I turn to face a tall man in a long black robe. Inky black

hair hangs in bangs on his forehead. Between the hair and the encroaching shadows, I can't make out his face.

He hisses, his voice hoarse and raspy. "Do you know me?"

"No," I say, inching backward. "Should I?"

"A sacrificial lamb should know its master," he whispers, drawing a glassy black dagger, "or its killer." Light glints off the blade like a tongue of flame.

The edge of the platform crumbles under my weight. Tumbling down the slime slick steps, I fall forever, my screams echoing up to the heavens.

I wake up in a cold sweat. The sheets are soaked and stained purple. Gears turn in my brain. Then, something worse replaces the terrible dream, a literal punch to the gut.

What's the matter? Afraid of a little old nightmare?

Stop talking. Please, stop talking.

When you beg, it only makes it worse.

I crumple the bedsheets in my fists. "I said, stop talking."

Who's a fraidy little boy now!

"Shut up." I punch the headboard, cracking the veneer. Standing before the open window, I notice a flicker of light from the shed out back.

Who's down there? Something rattles like marbles in my stomach.

You better not go. We already know you can't take care of things.

Oh yeah? You think I'm scared? Because I'm not.

Obviously, you are. Or we wouldn't be having this conversation.

You shut up.

I put on a robe and slippers, grab a flashlight, and head downstairs. The shed looms in the darkness. The voices go silent. Even they seem reluctant to join me as I make my way to the shed.

6

Inside, the shed is still a mess from the fight with the artichoke. The concrete floor is scarred from the beast's spur. Purple leaves and pulp are scattered everywhere. A smell like bait wafts from the drum where I hid the artichoke's remains.

But something's different. A fine layer of red dirt stands out in my flashlight beam.

Where did that come from?

There's a new scent, too, so powerful it cuts through my blocked sinuses. Something sweet, like faded lilies, mixes with the noxious stench of bait.

When my eyes adjust, I catch sight of footprints in the dirt. Too small to be a man's or even a kid my size, they lead to a spot behind the Challenger. Something or somebody wheezes, the sound of its labored breathing echoing in the metal-sided shed.

"Hey," I say, "somebody over there?"

No response except for a dull whimper.

Well, great. I'm sick as a dog and now I've apparently got one in my shed trying to kill me.

Stepping toward the car, I check under the rear axle. The glass jar is right where I left it. I lift up the container. Inside, the artichoke leaf squirms, slumps for a moment, then dashes itself against the lid. "Whoa." I nearly drop the jar.

Something scrapes against the concrete floor, followed by another round of weak gasping. This close, I'm pretty sure it's not a what but a who wheezing like a broken vacuum cleaner, because by this point any dog or rabid animal would've either bolted or come after me.

I set the flashlight on the ground, so it illuminates the far wall. Just past the Challenger's hood, an irregular shadow interrupts the pale glare. I make out the silhouette of what appears to be a wooly lion's mane hunched over a bent human leg.

"Seriously, who's there?" I say.

The stranger's breathing grows raspy and rough like a growling car engine.

A tingle goes up my spine. What if it's a hippy on a bad acid trip? Or an escaped killer from the Big House?

"You know what?" I say, getting to my feet. "Just wait right there, okay? I'll be right back." I step toward the toolbox, grab the tire iron and creep slowly around the car.

A cold wind whispers in the eaves of the shed. My shadow spills across the car's dusty canvas cover.

"I can hear you. Why don't you come out, and nobody gets hurt?"

I sniffle and my stomach muscles tighten. Vomit rises in my throat, but I hold it down through sheer force of will. You better be ready for a battle, murder-hippy.

Something stirs beyond the hood. Footsteps patter in the darkness. The tire iron sits heavy in my shaking hands, sweat beading on my upper lip. Am I really doing this? Because I can waste an artichoke, but another person?

But before I strike a woman in a pale green sleeveless dress floats into view. Her pale, stringy hair fans out like electrified spaghetti, framing a bleached-white face illuminated by blazing magenta eyes. Seeing me, she recoils and raises a pale forearm to protect herself.

Though she's changed considerably, I recognize her. My weapon clatters to the concrete and I place a hand on the Challenger to steady myself.

"My Lord, Mickey," Katie Sue Carson says. "You done scared me half to death!"

Neither of us move. We eye each other across the hood of the car. I bite my lip but I'm unable to stop a nervous yawn.

Katie Sue's alive? I can't believe it. Or is she alive? Maybe she's somewhere in between life and death. Her walking-and-talking existence blows my mind. I mean, I went to her funeral, and saw them put her in the ground. So, she's got to be dead. And if that's true, how do you talk to a ghost?

Katie Sue grabs my wrist. "Stop that, now." Her cold fingers sear my skin like I've been lashed with dry ice.

"Ow." I pull my hand away. "Stop what?"

"You know." She gestures toward me. "The whole yawning thing." A cough escapes her lips, followed by a low rattle. "You're freaking me out."

"Freaking you out?" I rub the flesh on my hand where she touched me. It's as cold as deli-counter salmon. "How about you just showing up in my shed?"

Katie Sue ignores the question. "Well, what about that thing?" She points to the artichoke leaf bumping around in the jar.

I lie. "Um, it's for a school science project?"

Katie Sue walks around the car and examines the jar. "No, it's not." Her magenta eyes burn like road flares. "Where'd you find it?"

"On the beach." I step toward her, keeping an eye on the leaf still bumping against the glass like it's trying to break free. "You remember when I came by the store the other day?"

She shakes her head. "No." Her pale eyebrows flutter like insect wings. "Well…yes, actually, I do remember." The leaf wobbles and stiffens against the lid. "I want to check this out."

Katie Sue starts to unscrew the lid. I try to stop her. "That's a bad idea."

"What are you doing?" She whirls around, pulling the container out of my grasp.

I stumble back, hands in the air. "Nothing."

Scowling, Katie Sue sets the jar on the toolbox. "Mickey, you're acting funny."

"Funny? Why would you say that? It's really good to see you." Actually, it's weird because at this point I'm pretty sure Katie Sue is dead. Her face and arms are pale, almost translucent in the dim shed light. Plum-colored lips and eyelids accentuate her bleached skin. Great sheaves of milk-white hair coil like Spanish moss around her face and shoulders, and her bare feet and hands are caked red with dust.

She frowns. "It's like you don't want me here."

"That's not true." I grab the flashlight from the floor. "Look, you may not remember this, but you were in an…accident."

Katie Sue turns, stringy hair whipping around like cattails. "I was?"

"Yeah. And we need to get you cleaned up."

I aim the light toward her, but she recoils as if slapped. "No." She swats the flashlight from my hands, and it rolls under the Challenger.

"What'd you do that for?" I scurry to the ground and reach under the car, but the light is just out of reach. "I just wanted to see you, is all."

Katie Sue sighs. "What if I don't want to be seen just now?"

"Well, it would make things easier." With a second effort, I grasp the flashlight and get to my feet.

"Easier for who?" She rubs her arms as if warming herself by a fire. In the light's glare I glimpse a purplish lump the size of a golf ball just below her collarbone. The bulb rises and falls as if it were breathing.

Katie Sue crosses her arms over her chest. "Would you stop please?"

"Stop what?"

"Didn't your momma teach you not to stare?"

A burning sensation crawls up my neck and engulfs my ears. "Ah Jeez, I'm not staring at your—"

"It's very rude."

My gut turns over like a flooded engine. Phlegm rises in my throat. Acid bites at my tongue. Needing to puke, I lunge for the oil drum. Katie Sue is kind enough to turn her head, but when I'm finished, she takes my wrist with her cold fingers. I try to pull away, but her touch doesn't burn me this time.

"You're sick." She places an icy palm on my forehead. "Do you have a fever?"

"Everything's fine," I manage to say. Except it's not. I'm sick and getting sicker. I'm also confused over the girl I've crushed on for years standing before me looking like some late-show zombie queen.

"I'm totally okay."

Hit by a wave of nausea, I droop against the car.

"Everything's *not* fine. She put an ear to my chest. "You've been infected. The spores have already entered your bloodstream. If they reach your heart—"

"Spores?" Sweat breaks out under my arms, drenching my scalp and face.

Katie Sue furrows her brow. "We have to burn them out of you."

"What?" I push against her shoulders but I'm too weak to make her budge. "I don't want you burning anything."

She grabs my head in her hands.

"Katie Sue, no. What are you doing?"

"Trust me."

Constellations explode before my eyes, the room goes black, and I go under. Colors explode along the walls, slithering in snake-like patterns. The ground rumbles beneath my feet, and thousands of bees scream in my ears. Slack-jawed, I fall, my body flopping on the floor like a hooked fish, but Katie Sue doesn't let go. Instead, she kneels beside me, sparks shooting from her fingers.

Smoke rises from my temples where her hands sizzle the flesh. A stench like a car battery about to explode invades my nostrils. I hear my own voice, disembodied and screaming a thousand miles away. "I can't do this anymore. Make it stop!"

Shaking her head, she says, "Hang on. I've got you." Her voice is low and deep like a humpback whale's song.

I gaze up at her face and colors blossom under her cheeks, reds and purples drowning into polished black glass. Am I dying? My skin numbs to her burning touch, and a screech like a feedbacked guitar wails in my ears.

Somewhere in the distance dinosaurs cry, and spirals of dark drown me into oblivion.

"Mickey? Please wake up."

I stir, my eyes adjusting to the dim light in the shed. Kneeling next to mee, Katie Sue bites her lower lip.

"What happened?" I rise to one elbow, my gut quivering.

"You went under, but I brought you back." She blots my forehead with a shop towel. I glance at the cloth and there's no discoloration.

I shiver. "I guess so. But how did you know to do that?"

Katie Sue stares at her hands. "I just…something was ailing you, so I fixed it. That's all." She wipes a drop of something purple from her cheek. "Don't ask me to explain, because I really don't know."

"Okay. Let's start from the beginning." I hobble over to a stool. "What do you remember about the accident?"

"Accident?" Her eyes grow wide.

"You got hit by a truck, remember?"

"Sorry, but I don't," she says, frowning.

"Well—"

"Wait, it's coming back to me," she says, bringing a hand to her forehead. "There *was* a truck."

"Go on."

"I was crossing at this red light, and it blew right into the lane. Just, boom, then..." She claps her hands. "...then things went dark, and it got really cold."

The stool creaks under my weight. "What about after that?"

Plum-colored mucus oozes from her eyelids, down her cheeks. "Next thing, I was walking in that thicket. You know, the one right by the..." Her lips curl into a frown, and I'm certain she's about to cry.

"Katie Sue?"

She grasps my hands in hers. "Mickey?"

"Yeah?"

"Am I dead?"

How can I even answer that question? "You're...you..., possibly. As far as I can tell."

For a long time, we avoid eye contact, neither of us saying anything. Then she turns to me.

"How do I look? Be honest."

"What do you mean? You look the same as always."

She holds up her translucent hands. "No, I don't."

"You want to see yourself?"

"I do."

Craig E. Higgins

Together we search the shed. She finds an old hand mirror in a cardboard box on a shelf.

"Shine a light so I can see."

"You may not want to do that."

"Yes, I do."

Luckily, the flashlight still works. I hold my breath and illuminate her face.

Katie Sue's scream reverberates against the walls like the wail of an ambulance.

7

The next morning, Aunt Margene pulls a thermometer from my mouth and shakes her head. "Guess we don't need to call the doctor after all."

The walk to school is uneventful. My gut churns but the voices stay silent. At least, that's something to be thankful for.

I skid through the door to Mr. Kraftner's class just before the bell. He wheels on one foot to face me. "Mr. Finley, good to see you here on time."

The kid in the next seat drops a folded piece of paper on my desk, and I sneak a peek.

> *Dear Pop-Tart,*
>
> *This is a helpful reminder to MIND YOUR OWN BUSINESS and stay away from Becca Mae Carson. You're in for a WORLD OF HURT if you don't.*
>
> *Signed,*
> *Your Betters*

A girl's laughter interrupts the silence. I turn in the direction of the disruption and there sits Alice Walsh. She and a friend of hers stare at me, then cackle again.

Mr. Kraftner puts down his chalk. "What's going on over there?"

The giggling stops but the furtive glances don't.

Becca Mae's nowhere to be found at lunch. Felicia and Ruth sit at the same table. I approach but they glare at me, and in a not-friendly way.

Okay, what did I do wrong?

My nerve endings feel as though they're being clipped by tiny scissors.

See? It's not just Alice and her friends.

Oh, shut up.

Everybody thinks you're a weirdo—even Becca Mae.

No, she doesn't.

Then why isn't she here?

I don't know, but—

What would she say if she knew you were hanging out with her dead sister?

I kneed my temples with my knuckles. This is all too much to process. And here I thought Katie Sue and I had it all figured out this morning, around sunrise.

Sunlight crept through the windows while me and Katie Sue sat on the shed floor, struggling with the implications of her resurrection.

"What if I'm condemned?" she said.

"That's silly."

"Silly?" She spread her arms wide. "*This* is silly?"

"That's not what I meant."

Katie Sue fingered a small silver cross on a chain around

her neck. "What if he doesn't want me?"

"Who doesn't want you?"

She sniffled. "You know who."

"You mean Jesus?"

A plummy droplet leaked from her eye. "Yep."

"Maybe Jesus has, I don't know, like this magic bus to pick people up? What if the bus is just late? Or there are a lot of passengers today?"

She scowls. "That's stupid."

Okay, that wasn't a very good job on consoling Katie Sue about her relationship with her imaginary sky-friend.

Katie Sue hugged her knees to her chest. "No, I know what's happening here."

"You do?"

"The Rapture." Her eyes met mine. "Mickey, that's the time where, if you're good, you go to be with God before...bad stuff happens."

"Is that what you think this is?"

"Maybe. I'm not sure." Katie Sue sighed. "Rapture or not, if there's no place for me in heaven, where do I go?"

The solution to that problem eluded us, but we did decide on a hiding spot for her, on account of the fact she couldn't go home. Katie Sue's very existence would confront her minister dad with an inconvenient fact about his view of the afterlife.

"I just can't do that to him," she said. "He'd totally freak out."

We tossed around a few possibilities. Even though the shed was my domain, both of us agreed it was only a matter of time before Uncle John stumbled in, looking for tree-trimming shears or a shovel. Finally, Katie Sue suggested an old barn on an abandoned lot near St. Adolphus.

"Won't it be cold in there?" I said.

"Mickey, cold doesn't matter to me anymore. You

understand?"

"I don't." Peeking out the window, I spied my uncle getting into his truck. The engine growled, and he sped off, the pickup's wheels grinding into the seashell driveway.

She took a blanket from off a shelf and wrapped it around her shoulders. "I'm going there right now."

"You want me to check on you when I get out of school?"

"Yes." She bit her lip. "Mickey?"

"Yeah?"

"Not a word to anyone about this, okay? Not even Becca."

"Who would believe me if I told them?"

I followed her to the door. She paused, then wrapped her arms around me. The purplish lump on her chest pressed into me but the warmth of her smile cut through the strangeness of the moment.

"Thank you." She turned the knob and disappeared into the early morning mist.

At wrestling practice, Win Cobb sneezes and his stance slips. Taking advantage of this unexpected gift, I try to trip him. Unfortunately, he grips my arms to right himself, and topples me to the mat.

Coach slaps the mat. "Pin. C'mon, Finley. You got more fight in you than that."

The phone on the wall rings. Coach runs to grab it. Win helps me to my feet.

"The leg whip was good," he says. "You almost had me there." Coughing, he doubles over. I reach out a hand, but he waves me off. "I'm okay."

Coach stares at the phone, his face ashen. He cradles the receiver, then walks to the center of the mat. "Gather 'round, guys."

We circle him.

"I got some bad news. Sanderson's taken a turn for the worse."

A collective chatter, hushed and frantic, fills the room.

Coach wipes his forehead with a hand towel. "They've put him in the ICU. We're collecting donations for a get-well card. If y'all want to chip in, it would be greatly appreciated."

A tall kid next to me raises his hand. "Coach, what's the matter with him?"

"Nobody knows. Some kind of respiratory thing, very serious."

My gut juices boil.

And where do you think he got it from?

Don't talk to me right now. I only grappled with Sanderson, like, once the other day.

But once was enough, right?

Just shut up, okay?

Stupid, stupid, stupid. Always trying to weasel your way out of it. But there's no escape this time. Everybody's going to know it was you.

But it's not even my fault—

Everything is always your fault!

Win Cobb sneezes into the crook of his elbow. His eyes look watery in the harsh overhead lights. "Can we get sick from it, too?"

A bunch of kids grumble.

"I don't know," Coach says, glancing at the clock on the gym wall, "but if any of you fellas comes down with a high fever or a bad runny nose that won't stop, see a doctor soon as you can." He points to a laundry bin beside the benches. "Make sure you drop all towels where they're supposed to go. The custodial staff will be sanitizing the locker room this afternoon."

After practice, I dress in jeans and a gray hooded sweatshirt that used to belong to Tommy, same one he wore when he wrestled for Gulf High.

I sling my backpack over my shoulder. Inside, I've stowed a ratty t-shirt from Petra's '79 tour, a pair of Aunt Margene's gardening slacks, and my old tennis shoes. I had to air them out because they'd been sitting in the shed for the last three months.

Katie Sue waits for me at the barn a quarter mile away. It's time to make tracks if I'm going to spend time with her and still make it home in time for supper.

Exiting the gym, I stride through the parking lot but stop when I get a whiff of an aerosol scent. Turning, I catch sight of the source of the smell.

Somebody spraypainted yellow graffiti on the gym wall. It's a picture of a shark with a single cat's eye just to the rear of the snout. Two stubby fins stick out of its back, and four gnarled tentacles dangle from the body. Underneath the monster is a single word—RISING.

Rising? What is that supposed to mean?

Two blocks north of the vacant lot, I slip beneath the towering spires of St. Adolphus chapel. Those twin shadows blanket me anytime I pass the place, no matter where the sun hangs in the sky. The campus stands behind a black, six-foot, wrought-iron fence, green lawns and sandstone buildings accentuated by well-manicured rows of shrubbery.

I gaze at those spires, their bulbous domes curled like tulips. Something odd about them strikes me, a detail I'd missed up until now. The gray cobblestone façade of the towers clashes with the red sandstone walls of the chapel. It's as if somebody added the spires as an afterthought, oblivious to the rest of the architecture.

I head south, skirting the back of the school property. I

spot the ramshackle barn in the middle of a field. The doors stand open, like the maw of a hungry animal. I'm about to cross the street when the growl of an engine catches my ear. A dark green sports car, hood like a crocodile's snout, screeches to the curb.

Wade Ruthven and another boy emerge, the same kid I remember from Katie Sue's funeral. They approach at a rapid clip. I try to run but they're on me in seconds.

Wade wrenches my arm behind my back. "What do have we here?"

I struggle against his grip. "Let me go, man."

"You want to go places?" He slams me into the wrought iron fence. "There you go."

My cheek bangs against the metal and it hurts like crazy. "Ow!"

The other boy laughs while smacking his fist into his meaty palm. "What does Alice call him? Pop-Tart?"

Wait, this dude knows Alice? "Hey, cut it out."

"Pop-Tart," Wade sneers, cranking on my arm until the pain in my elbow is nearly unbearable. "That's your name, right?"

I bite my lip to blot out the hurt. "Just let me go, huh?"

"Uh-uh. You don't listen well." The bully punches me in the ribs. "Can't take a hint, can you?"

My side burns like hellfire, but I don't scream. "What are you talking about?"

"You got a note today, right?" Wade's breath is hot against my ear. "Told you to mind our own business." He twists my arm like a pretzel. "But you come around here to *my* school? You get hurt for that."

White-hot spikes of pain shoot all the way up to my neck from my wrenched arm. I clench my teeth and try not to cry.

"Yeah, a world of hurt." the dark-haired kid says, punching

me in the ribs again.

My whole side goes numb. "Man, how was I supposed to know you went to school here?"

"Let me tell you something, Pop-Tart." Wade relaxes his grip and whips me around. "You stay away from Becca. Blood begets blood. Blood protects blood."

What does that even mean? "Hey, she's my friend. You've got no right—"

Wade hammers my solar plexus. The air goes out of my lungs, and I'm left gasping on the sidewalk.

"Pop-Tart," the bully says with a sneer, "she don't need you. And just so you remember that, we're going to get you some education."

Curling into a ball, I try to protect my ribs but it does me no good. Wade slaps me and blood trickles down my lip.

The other boy smiles. "You gonna get it now, boy."

A sharp whistle pierces the air. Wade and his buddy stop in their tracks like trained Rottweilers.

Inside the fence stands a man in a long black shirt and ankle-length black skirt. His hair is as dark as a crow's wing, his face obscured by the shadow of the towers. Even from this distance the stranger gives off a negative vibe that swallows light and warmth, like he's a human black hole.

Who is this guy?

Wade glowers. "We gotta go." He points at me. "Stay away from Becca."

"And our school." The other boy kicks me one last time. "Next time we take the trash out on you, hear?"

Wade and his buddy dash to their car. The engine roars and they roll past the corner, nearly clipping a sedan before careening through the gates of St. Adolphus.

I kneel on the sidewalk, humiliated and in agony from the beating they gave me. My lungs burn with every breath, straining for the faintest hint of oxygen.

Once the pain subsides, I slowly get to my feet. A quick glance across the compound reveals the man in the black robe hasn't moved.

We stare at each other for a moment. Then he turns and disappears into the school grounds.

8

"**My word, Mickey, what** did they do to you?"

Katie Sue runs a cool hand across my forehead. I lay on my back, looking at the sky through a hole in the barn roof. Her gentle touch eases the sting of my busted lip and bruised face.

"It's nothing." I scratch at the caked blood my chin. "They just roughed me up a little."

"Looks a little worse than that." Katie Sue tears a strip from the hem of her dress and dabs my mouth. "Who did you say these boys were again?"

"One of them was a guy named Wade. I think he's your cousin."

"Wade." She doesn't say his name like he's family or an old acquaintance, or even somebody she cares for. There's just this flat tone of recognition in her voice, and no more.

The hay irritates my skin, and I sit up, scratching like mad. "Is he bad news?"

"He is." The afternoon sun sends streaks of gold through Katie Sue's stringy white hair. "Wade has always been the worst." She frowns. "Uncle Walter, that's his dad, used to own a shrimping business. But really, he was involved in some shady stuff. It got so bad his wife left him, and after that it was like he didn't want Wade around, or any of his other kids."

A cool breeze drifts through the barn, cooling my flushed cheeks. Despite my injuries, I feel better than I have in days. "Is that how your cousin ended up at rich-boy academy?"

"That's right." Katie Sue's eyes crackle like firecrackers. "We used to have them over for Christmas sometimes. Wade's tolerable in little doses, but the last two years he's been around a lot." Her pale shoulders quake. "Too much." Steam rises from her clenched hands. "And now he's beating on my friends."

Jeez, what's happening with her? "Katie Sue? I'm okay, alright? I mean, I'm not okay but you don't have to…do whatever that was you were doing."

"Sorry, but I get angry with Wade sometimes." She stares at the dissipating fumes curling around her fists. "Did you just see what I did?"

"Yeah, and it was weird."

"My Lord." She opens her hands, and they give off a hint of ozone. "Not sure what this means."

Neither do I but it makes me uncomfortable. "Here." I pull the t-shirt and pants from the bag. "Try these on. There are shoes too, only I'm not sure if they'll fit."

"I'm sure they're fine." She takes the clothes from me. "This is sweet. You're very thoughtful, you know."

"I try."

"You do. Thank you." Katie Sue plants a cold kiss on my cheek. The smooch leaves a syrupy scent, like a cherry-flavored snow cone.

My cheeks go flush. Did she just kiss me? "No problem."

"Give me a sec." She grabs the shirt and pants and steps into the shadows. With her back to me she starts to lift her dress over her head. My eyes trace the gentle curve of her hips beneath the silken fabric.

Katie Sue stops pulling the dress up, her fingers at the

straps over her shoulders. Without turning around, she says, "Um, could you not look?"

Oh wow. Was I staring? "Sorry." My burning ears catch the rustling of clothing.

"Okay, I'm done," she says. "They actually fit pretty well."

I turn and catch sight of Katie Sue. The t-shirt hangs loose and baggy, which is good because I had no idea how to find a bra on such short notice. The pants sit low on her waist, but not so low they'll fall off.

Milky tresses spill down Katie Sue's shoulders, and her magenta eyes cast pink highlights on her pale cheeks.

Dead or undead, I've never beheld a girl more alive–again.

A lump gets caught in my throat, pulse quickening in my veins. Questions tumble inside my head, each one more fevered than the last. Should I tell her the real reason I visited her at the grocery store all those times? It wasn't because there were no more Pop-Tarts in the pantry. What if I just wanted to gaze upon her lovely face? Or should I mention all the nights I laid awake, imagining myself a big success so I could afford a fine set of wheels? Me asking her out, and us going to the pier? Sitting side by side in a convertible, my arm wrapped around her shoulder while she lays her head against my chest? The kisses she plants on my lips? Warm embraces forever out of reach in the real world, where I'm too young and she's too old and everything sucks?

In this lonely barn, I have Katie Sue all to myself. If ever there was a time to tell her I love her, this is it, but the words get jammed up in my brain, stalling before they reach my mouth.

This is my moment.

Our moment.

And I'm not sure how to seize it.

"Mickey, are you alright?" Katie Sue nudges my arm.

I shake the cobwebs out of my head. "What?"

"You kind of went off into space there for a second."

"Sorry. I was just…can I talk to you about something?"

"You can talk to me about anything." She sits on a wooden bench next to a gnarled tangle of purple roots sticking out of the dirt. The cluster of vines and runners stands about a foot high and pulses like blood vessels, making a dull throbbing sound.

I hadn't noticed those when I walked in. "Jeez, what's that thing?" I take a step back.

Katie Sue grins. "Oh this?" She gives an affectionate pat to a pulsating tuber. "Something I've been working on."

"Working on?" That doesn't sound right at all.

"Yeah. I got bored." She tweaks a root-end, and it splits open, blossoming into a huge white-petaled flower with a purple bulb poking from the center.

What just happened? I stand there, open-mouthed like an idiot. "Is that a—"

"I think it's a magnolia." Katie Sue plucks the bloom and sticks it into her hair. "Pretty neat, huh? I've grown a few of those, actually." She gestures to a pile of flowers lying atop a patch of hay.

My mind is blown, but I still try to process what I'm seeing. Not only has Katie Sue risen from the grave, but now fire erupts in her hands, and she can grow freaky plant life at the drop of a hat.

What am I dealing with here? "Katie Sue? How are you…I mean, how did you do that?"

"Don't know." She glances upward through a big hole in the roof. "It's like the Lord himself wants me to learn about this new way I am, you know? And so, He's given me these little talents to learn about." She rubs the root-clump like she's petting a dog. "Like creating Tammy here."

I stifle a chuckle. "Tammy?"

"Yeah," she says, smiling, "that's her name."

This is so weird. "That thing's a she?"

"Yep."

Oh great. She thinks this is her imaginary sky-friend's doing. "Well, um…" I swallow hard. "That's really cool, I guess."

"Yeah, she's neat." Katie Sue pats the bare bench next to her, tilts her head, and smiles. "But you said you had something on your mind."

Sure, but that was before I knew you had magic alien powers. "Yeah."

"Come here." Her glowing eyes meet mine. "Is everything okay?" She laughs.

"Oh sure, sure it is." The chill from her body makes my arm-hairs stand on end. Here's my big chance only now I'm not sure if it's even what I still want.

Then again, maybe I do.

Katie Sue pats my hand. "So, what's your story, morning glory?"

"Wow, where to begin?" I take a deep breath, then exhale. "Um, Katie Sue? This is going to sound so weird—"

"Trust me, I know weird, now."

Okay, here goes nothing. "What would you say if I said I liked you?"

"I would say that's very sweet." Up close, her hair gives off a fragrance like faded lilies. "And I like you, too."

"That's not really the way I meant it."

"Well, what do you…oh." She gazes into my eyes, and there's a note of recognition in her voice. "You mean you have feelings for me?"

"Yeah." I shrug. "Sorry."

"What is there to be sorry about?"

"Well, I mean, you're *you*, you know? You're smart and beautiful, and…" I gesture toward the purple root-ball. "…you're into, I don't know, making plants and stuff now. It's actually kind of weird."

"But Mickey, I'm still me." Katie Sue's eyes flash in the dim light. "You know that, right?"

I don't. "And the other thing is, I'm a dork, and anyway, I know you totally like my cousin." I sigh and it feels like a huge weight's been lifted from my shoulders. "That's what I wanted to say."

A laugh escapes her lips. "You want a true confession?"

"I guess."

Night falls outside and moonlight filters through the barn door, illuminating her pale skin. "When I met Tommy, I thought he was the most handsome boy ever. Whether we were at church or school or wherever, I just wanted to be right by him. He's a really special guy, you know?"

Oh brother. "That's what they tell me."

"But we never connected." Her hand rests on the bench, agonizingly close to mine.

"No?" In spite of everything, there's a part of me that wants to lace my fingers with hers.

"No. And I don't know why. I gave him plenty of hints."

"Girls give hints?"

"Oh yeah," she says. "You're old enough where you'll start to see them. At least, smart boys do."

"What about dummies like me?"

It's dark inside the barn. Tammy's base glows faintly. "Is that thing going to eat me?" I say.

"No, silly." She gently tugs my fingers. "And you, sir, are not a dummy. You're a sensitive, sweet boy who's going to find the right girl when it's time."

My throat tightens. "Why can't that be you?"

"Mickey, look at me." Katie Sue stands, palms resting on her cocked hips. "I don't know that I could be anybody's girl anymore."

She's wrong. "We'd work it out. I'm sure we would."

"So sweet." Her lips curl into a thin smile. "But you know what I need right now, more than anything?"

"What?"

"A friend." Her voice cracks. "Because honestly? I don't even know what I am."

Blood rises in my cheeks, and my heart pounds like a jackhammer on concrete. This isn't what I wanted at all. I thought I could tell her I love her and then we'd live happily ever after. But I don't know how I feel now. And Katie Sue's voice is filled with so much pain, I can't tell her no. "Okay."

"Okay what?"

"Friends." I offer her my hand.

"Friends." She grazes my fingertips with hers and walks me to the barn door. Up in the sky, the full moon sits like a cockeyed king amid a congregation of stars.

A half-hour later, I'm trudging home through high grass. The ground ahead is dead and barren. I spy a lumpen, furry mass, swarming with flies. When I get closer a stench like fish-guts assaults me. The moonlight casts the thing in stark relief. It's a nutria, one of those oversized swamp rodents twice the size of a regular rat. The skull is crushed, its yellow buck teeth snapped clean off.

The bloated belly makes a sudden quiver, and a green tentacled thing the size of a cricket squirms from underneath the carcass. A single lizard eye blinks at me before it disappears into the deep grass.

At home, a man's wretched coughing greets me when I

push open the kitchen door. A pot of stew boils on the stove, sending up a column of steam. I turn down the burner, so it won't boil over.

The hacking echoes down the hall. Aunt Margene sits in the living room, hair tied back, a worried look on her face, wringing a damp cloth into a bowl. Uncle John is on the couch. Stinky, plum-colored sweat drenches his ashen face. His right eye is swollen shut, as though he'd taken a punch. He raises his head to whisper something to Aunt Margene. She nods, and he slumps back into the cushions, unconscious.

"What's going on?" I kneel beside them, pushing the coffee table aside.

She wipes away a wisp of hair with the back of her hand. "Your uncle took sick at the mill today. Pastor had to drive him home."

"What?" A drop of plum-colored saliva dribbles from the corner of his mouth.

"He's not well." She sighs. "I'm about to call an ambulance."

"You know how he'll feel about that," I say. "He hates doctors because of Vietnam."

"And the Vietnam War is over." Aunt Margene dabs his forehead. "If he doesn't pull out of it by morning, he's going to the hospital."

I grasp Uncle John's meaty hand. His skin is cold and clammy to the touch. "Think he got sick because of me."

"What, this?" She sneezes, blowing her nose into a tissue. "Maybe."

"The symptoms are like mine."

"He's got it worse, though." She rests her palms on her knees. "Mickey, when people get older, sometimes it takes them longer to recover."

"Is it the same thing, though? Same sickness, I mean."

"Lord, how should I know?"

Uncle John wakes with a start. "What's going on?"

Aunt Margene grips his arm. "It's okay John. You just dozed off."

He opens his good eye. The yellow orb is shot through with purple veins. "Mick? That you?"

"Yeah, it's me."

"Where have you been?"

"Um, out?"

He struggles to smile. "You're going to get your aunt worried sick about you." Phlegm slides over his chin, stinking like battery acid.

"Sorry about that." I ball a wad of tissue and wipe him clean.

He reaches into his pants pocket and retrieves two crumpled tens. "After school tomorrow, take this to Pastor Paul. You know where he lives?"

I nod. "Tommy drove us there one time. I can find it."

Uncle John's smiles. "Here." He hands me the bills. "Make sure he gets this."

Aunt Margene frowns. "John, Pastor said he didn't need the money."

He shivers under the blanket. "Mick, tell him to put it in the building fund if he won't take it for himself."

"Yes, sir." I place the cash in my wallet. "Are you going to be okay?"

"I survived 'Nam." He coughs. "I can make it through this."

I swear something wiggles underneath his swollen eyelid. Must've been a trick of the light.

Uncle John slips back into unconsciousness and I stumble off to bed. My gut churns when my head hits the pillow.

Stupid, stupid, stupid.

Let me sleep.

The ground's giving way under your feet. And when it falls

Craig E. Higgins

apart, you'll never find the bottom.
    I don't have to listen to you.
    My eyelids grow heavier than a ship's anchor.
    The voices recede and I drift off into oblivion.

9

Wednesday comes and there are more empty chairs in Mr. Kraftner's class. Those kids who do show up, sit with blank expressions on their faces while the substitute, Mrs. Cranberry, writes the day's assignment on the board. She's older than dirt and wears a perpetual scowl, like somebody spiked her prune juice while her back was turned.

Alice Walsh fluffs her perma-dyed poodle hair, her mouth a complaint-churning misery machine. "Mrs. Cee, you give us too much work." The inky-haired girl gazes at the others in the room, fishing for support. Slack-jawed, no one responds to her protest.

Mrs. Cranberry turns from the board. "Miss Walsh? You take what's coming to you."

Alice frowns, struggling to come up with a witty retort. I chuckle under my breath, enjoying her misfortune.

No wrestling practice today after school because a bunch of kids turn up sick. Coach meets me at the locker room door, his forehead wrinkled as a prune.

"I think Win Cobb's got it," he says.

Static builds in my ears and a knot twists in my gut.

Of course, he does. And where do you think he got it from?

I try to stop myself from speaking so my words don't match my worries, but it's too late. "No, that's not possible."

"What's not possible?"

"Sorry, I was just thinking I forgot my book in English class."

He stares as though he doesn't believe me. Embarrassed, I make my way down the hallway and out into the street.

The two ten-dollar bills Uncle John gave me to pay Pastor Paul are folded in my wallet. I need to pay the minister, but the exchange with Coach boils inside.

Stupid, stupid, stupid. Now he knows it's your fault everybody's getting sick.

No, he doesn't.

Or course he does. You just blurted it out, dummy.

If I'm the dummy, then what are you?

I stride past parked cars, windshields reflecting light from the afternoon sun. It's warmer out than it's been in almost a month, and my path to the Carsons takes me past well-kept lawns and wood-framed houses. I spot a Jack-O-Lantern on a porch behind a white picket fence. Oblong and big as a medicine ball, it's nothing special. But the carving along its side creeps me out.

Etched into the rind is a one-eyed, tentacled shark.

The Carson place is yellow, almost the same shade as the brick at Bay Crossroads. Crossing the yard, I step on a rusty rake and the handle flies upward. I manage to dodge a skull fracture but lose my footing and tumble to the ground. Hopefully nobody saw how stupid I looked just now.

Brushing myself off, I head for the front door, and rap my

knuckles on the brass plate. Loud music blares inside, jarring the windows. Despite the din, I make out the patter of footsteps.

Becca Mae answers. "Mickey. So good to see you!"

She's dressed in a black sleeveless top over a white t-shirt, gray leggings under rainbow-striped leg warmers. One of her knees is wrapped in an ace bandage. Her cornflake-colored hair is plastered to her forehead, held in place by a damp headband. Sweat darkens her shirt. When she hugs me, I'm overcome with an aroma of butterscotch.

Instinctively, I enfold her in my arms. We stay locked together for a moment that slips by slower than it should, like a raindrop sliding down a window pane. I've never been close like this with a girl before. Becca Mae's flesh is soft and yielding, and her heartbeat thumps against my chest. The experience is weird and kind of scary, but absolutely fabulous. A spark cascades along my loins and I disengage quickly, afraid of involuntarily expressing my appreciation.

"Nice to see you, too," I say.

She smiles. "To what do I owe this pleasure?"

"Got some gas money for your dad?"

"Oh, right." She dials down the loud rock beat blaring from the TV. "Daddy said he gave your uncle a ride. Come on in."

"Yeah." I cross into the room, heart racing and throat dry. Still recovering from the hug, I struggle to focus on what she's saying.

Becca Mae makes things worse when she bends over backward, thrusting her ample chest skyward. "I was just doing my Jazzercises."

It's hard not to stare, but somehow, I manage. "Is that like yoga?"

"No, silly. It's floor routines. You know, like in dance?"

"Guys don't do stuff like that."

"That's true." She blots under her arms with a towel. "Oh,

I'm sorry. That's gross, isn't it?"

"What's gross? Girls sweat. Don't they?"

The business end of the towel pops an inch from my ear.

"Hey, what was that for?"

"Making me feel self-conscious." Becca Mae turns and walks through a doorway, heading down a hall. "Follow me."

My eyes track the hypnotic sway of her hips, jiggling in tight spandex.

I take a step but the growling in my stomach stops me in my tracks.

What's this? The dead girl blows you off, and now you want her sister?

It's not like that.

Of course, it is. No wonder you're a lonely little boy. Always grabbing at things you'll never have.

I'm not.

Don't make me laugh! Maybe you need a reminder of how pathetic you truly are.

The room spins and I'm standing in a darkened chamber with stone walls. The air smells like candle wax. My mother lies on a stone slab, thin frame shrouded in midnight blue, her favorite color. Her eyes are closed, and she holds fresh lilies in her gnarled hands. Mom's auburn hair is the consistency of dead weeds, her ruddy cheeks lifeless and tough as rawhide. Light filters in from somewhere above, casting shadows over the floor.

This must be a dream. And since you're not real, Dream-Mom, why don't you sleep until I come back for you?

She opens her eyes. They're jaundice-yellow, veins the color of plums.

"He's coming," Mom says. "Run."

"Mickey?" Becca Mae shakes me by the shoulders.

My eyes snap open. I'm not sure where I am except that I'm on my back and staring up at the ceiling.

"Sorry." I slowly get to my feet. "It's been a long week."

"You totally passed out." She stares at me, wide-eyed. "Is this like a medical condition? Should I call your aunt?"

"It's okay. Maybe I should sit down for a sec."

"Of course." She grasps my hand, leading me to the sofa. "And you're right about the week. I've been struggling myself."

Struggling? Did I get her sick, too? Have I infected the whole town? "Any coughing or sneezing? You know, there's something going around."

"Oh, I don't get sick from stuff like that." Her eyes trail toward an open window. "But I've been thinking about Katie, you know? That makes everything hard." She points to the brace on her knee. "And I used to do gymnastics and sometimes my knee pops out. Like, it dislocates?"

"Ouch."

"Yeah. So, Daddy made me stay off it for a few days. That's why I haven't been at school."

Whew.

After a short rest, she guides me down a hall, stopping at a door with a brass knocker. "He's in here."

She taps the knocker. A man's voice says, "Who is it?"

"Daddy? Mickey Finley's here to see you."

"Oh? Well, let him in."

The door opens, creaking on its hinges. Becca Mae turns to me, teeth gleaming in the half-light. "Get in there."

Inside, Pastor Paul sits at a roll top wooden desk covered with stacks of paper. He's dressed in a faded blue shirt and dark pants, a tie loose around his neck. Resting on the table is a vinyl-bound book, probably a Bible.

"How are you, Mick?" Only Uncle John calls me that. It's

like the minister wants me to warm up to him. I hate when people do that.

"Okay, I guess."

He motions for me to grab a nearby seat. "Let's have a chat."

"Sure." The cushion is worn and threadbare. "Thanks for taking care of Uncle John." I reach for my wallet and pass him the money.

"Oh, no." He pushes the bills away.

"But he said to give it to you."

"Your uncle's a dear man, but noble to a fault." The minister lays the book on the desk. "I'd help him anytime, free of charge."

"Y'all must be pretty tight."

"Tight? Want to see something really cool?" He takes a framed, black-and-white photograph off the wall and presents it to me.

In the photo, men in fatigues and helmets camouflaged with leaves huddle around a dead crocodile. A grinning woman stands nearby. Dressed like the men, she's tall and thin, a Red Cross armband on her arm. There's something unsettling about her dark eyes and the tilt of her smirk. It's like she knows something others don't. A boy in black pajamas sits cross-legged beside the carcass, grinning and pointing at the fearsome teeth.

One guy sticks out from the rest. Taller than the others, he towers in the background, hefting a big machine gun trailing a belt of cruel-looking bullets.

Pastor Paul points to the giant. "See that fella?"

I inspect the picture. "What about him?"

"That's your Uncle John."

It takes me a moment, but then I recognize him. "Wow, you're right."

"Let me show you something else." His finger skates across the glass, stopping at a dark-haired grunt with a buzzcut and thin mustache.

I stare at him, then back at the picture. "Wait, you guys served together?"

"For about three months." He takes the picture from my hands, then hangs it back on the wall.

"Then you must've known Dad, too."

"What?" He sits in his chair just as the frame slips on its nail, coming to rest at an off-kilter angle.

"Dad and Uncle John were in the same unit." I give the picture a second glance, eager to spot my father among the ghosts in uniform.

"But not at the same time." Stepping in front of me, Pastor Paul adjusts the frame. "Your dad got into our outfit about two months after this was taken. John and I were already gone."

I bite my lip. The picture is still crooked, worse than before. "Oh yeah. Dad mentioned that once."

"I'm sure he did." The minister takes a tissue and polishes the glass. "By that time, I was done with my second tour."

"So, you just missed him?"

"That's right."

My eyes scan the picture, inspecting every face. "But Dad got drafted before Uncle John."

"How interesting." Pastor Paul sits, then props his feet on the desk. "He must've been somewhere else at the time. Big jungle, you know."

"Sure," I stare at the croc's milky eyes. "Why'd y'all shoot him?"

"We were waiting on a patrol boat to get us out of a jam. Dang thing crawled out of the water and almost got this little lady here." He points to the woman in the picture.

I take a second look and swear I've seen her face before. "Who is she?"

"Thought you'd have picked up on that one."

And then it clicks. "Pastor, I don't mean to be weird, but she's a dead ringer for Katie Sue."

"Of course." Even the minister's smile is oily. "That's my Enid, Katie and Becca's mother."

Way to put your foot in it this time. "Oh, I'm so stupid."

"Don't be silly." He pats me on the shoulder. "You know, crazy as that day was, it was also one of the best for me. Right there in the jungle, the Lord brought me my greatest joy, even though I didn't know it at the time."

Sunlight creeps through a window, casting shadows that snake across his desk. "My, but it's getting late," I say.

Pastor Paul holds up a hand like a traffic cop. "Wait. I have something for you."

His hand slips into the drawer.

"Check this out." He hands me a piece of paper. "You like seafood?"

I scan the flier. A cartoon shark and a buck-toothed fisherman with a spin rod fight it out.

Beneath the sketch, a caption screams, *It's Shark Fest at Bay Crossroads, this Thursday, November Sixth! Grilled, baked, or fried. Come fill your belly and make new friends!*

I place the advertisement on the desk. "Sounds cool, but no thanks."

"Are you sure?" Pastor Paul licks his lips, displaying big white teeth. "Bunch of kids your age will be there, Mick."

"And I hope they have a good time."

He chuckles. "Becca's going. She says you've been a real friend to her of late."

Jeez, why won't this dude leave well enough alone? "Let me think about it."

"Please do." The minister fiddles with a locket attached to a gold chain around his neck. It's a triangle shaped pendant. In the center is a little brass shark with jeweled tentacles.

Crap, but what is it with this guy's obsession with sharks? Or is it me? It can't be a coincidence that the same image crops up everywhere I go. Maybe I'm still sick and just *imagining* all this?

Pastor Paul snaps his fingers in front of my face. "You okay, Mick?"

"Oh, sorry," I say. Sweat beads on my upper lip. "Be seeing you."

It's dusk by the time I make the main road along the beach, heading for home. Cars hiss past, like crickets in a thunderstorm. The sky is black and shot through with orange wisps, perfect for Halloween.

Something groans from a muddy pond nearby. I turn, expecting a clutch of toads hopping through the muck, but there's only a handful of trees. I make out an oak, a row of pines, and a lush magnolia.

"Mickey," a voice whispers from the shadows.

"Who's there?"

A cool breeze whips off the bay. The magnolia's shiny leaves flutter and fall, one landing at my feet. A noxious smell, like bait, permeates my nostrils. Placing its origin is difficult. Is it coming from the dumpster behind the convenience store across the street? Or maybe an animal carcass?

My stomach turns.

Stupid, stupid, stupid. They got you now!

A shadow slips behind the oak. I catch sight of a man darting between two pines. In mid-step the runner stops and doubles over, stifling a raspy cough.

"Hey," I say, "you okay over there?"

Saying nothing in reply, the figure stands there silently, breathing heavily. Is he staring at me?

"Say, what's the deal, man?" I shout. "Can I help you with

something?"

The stranger takes off in a clumsy gallop, hacking all the way.

I should probably ignore the guy and just head home. But something about his herky-jerky movements and smoker's rattle unsettles me. Is he sick with the same stuff I had?

High-tops sinking in the muck, I give chase. He rounds the pond then stops in a small clearing, his cough overcoming him.

I stop a few yards away. "Dude," I say, "I'm not trying to hurt you. But why were you stalking me?"

All I get in response is a series of raspy gasps.

Cautiously, I step forward. "Look, man. You sound like you need a doctor—"

Suddenly, the dude yells, and rushes at me, full clip. I try to push him off but he throws a punch, nailing me in the jaw. Stars flare in front of my eyes.

I raise my arm, trying to block his next shot, but the stranger drills a fist into my solar plexus. Breath explodes from my lungs. I double over, chest tightening from lack of oxygen. He's got a free shot, but all my attacker can do is cough out his lungs.

Getting my breath back, I rise to my feet and barrel into him, locking my arms around his waist. We tumble into the mud. He flails wildly at my head, but the dude has no fight left in him. Rolling off me, he lies on his back, wheezing and hacking.

"Hey, Mickey," he says between gasps. "Ease up, huh?"

My face is flushed, lungs burning. It's dark outside, so the dude's features are hard to make out. But up close, his voice, scratchy and strained, is suddenly familiar.

"Dang." Win Cobb struggles to his feet. "How come you don't fight like that on the mat?"

10

"Man, I never had anything knock me out like this," Win Cobb says. "Feel like death warmed over."

Me and him sit across from each other at a booth inside the Home Plate Diner. The cramped room smells of old coffee and burnt cooking oil. Pies tower in a glass cylinder on the counter, next to the ancient cash register. I keep a close eye on Win. Infected by the same stuff that got me, he wilts more precariously by the moment. But he insists he's hungry in spite of his condition, so here we are.

"Why were you following me?" I say.

He unloads a wad of mucus into a paper napkin. "I wanted to know how you did it."

I hand him another from a dispenser on the table. "Did what?"

"Get better from this." After blowing his nose, he wheezes, then coughs. "You gave it to me, you know."

A wave of embarrassment knots my gut. "Did not."

The waitress stops by with menus. She glowers at Win. "You okay, kid?"

He gives her a weak smile. "Never been better. How's the

grilled cheese in this place?"

"Best in town." She pulls a pad and pen from her apron. "Y'all need a minute?"

I nod. "Sure."

The server pivots on one heel, then drifts toward the next table. Above her head, a TV bolted to the wall replays the presidential debate from earlier in the week. On screen, an old guy with dyed-black hair berates his opponent, all slumped shoulders and premature wrinkles. At the counter, a couple of good old boys cheer the proceedings.

"Aw, yeah," says one. "You go, Mr. Reagan, sir."

"He asked Carter if we were better off four years ago," the other says. "Ain't that funny?"

Win Cobb stifles a cough. "My old man hates Reagan."

"Really? My uncle loves him—thinks he's a hero."

"Huh." He takes another napkin from the dispenser. "Well, he's no hero to anybody I know." Win doubles over, shaking with a loud coughing spasm. A couple in the next booth eye him cautiously.

Twisting his head around, he scowls at them. "What are you looking at? I got a cold, okay?"

The man rises from his seat. "What'd you say, boy?"

"Excuse me?" Win's on his feet in a flash, fists balled.

In the nick of time, the waitress arrives with their check. "Here y'all go."

The woman stares at her date and tugs at his sleeve. The man's expression softens, and they get up and leave.

"Boy, huh? He's lucky I'm out of it." Win wads up the soiled tissue. "Is there a trash can around here?"

"I got it." Spying a small trash can near the hostess station, I grab the receptacle and place it by his feet. "Sorry about that."

"About what? It's not your fault what that dude said."

He hacks up a chunk of phlegm and spits into the can. "But where I'm from? Nobody talks like that."

"No?"

His eyes flash. "Not if they don't want to get jacked up, they don't."

"I'm sorry you think I got you sick. But it's fall. There's probably a flu bug going around."

Win frowns. "My Ma makes me get a flu shot every year. We just go right over to the pharmacy. So, I know it's not that."

"Look, I wouldn't lie to you. I don't think it was me."

"You kidding?" He pulls down a reddened eyelid, exposing a fine purple half-moon. "Man, it was definitely you. I even recollect the exact moment. Remember at practice when Coach told me to move up weight?"

I shrug. "Well, I was coughing that day."

"Dang straight," he says. "Just be honest about it."

"Yeah, you're right. I'm sorry."

"I ain't mad. Stuff happens sometimes."

The server places two glasses of water on the table. "What's it going to be?"

"The chili, please." My mouth waters at the very thought of the greasy delight. "And can you put that on fries?"

She points to an item on the menu. "You mean like chili fries?"

"Oh, yeah. Didn't see that one."

"Coming right up." She grins and turns to Win. "Still want that grilled cheese?"

He places the menu in her hand. "You know it."

Win takes a sip of water and begins to gag. "So, here's my thing. You got sick, but you're over it in, like in a couple days. How'd that happen?"

Because I possess a miracle cure to artichoke infection in

the form of an undead girl with magic powers. But sharing it with him means exposing Katie Sue.

"Just got a strong constitution I suppose," I lie. "You'll shake it pretty soon."

"The heck I will. This keeps getting worse. My folks got it, too."

Maybe with enough stalling, he'll let it go. "But y'all been sick only a couple days."

"Mickey, stop playing." He takes my wrists, fingers digging into my flesh. "You've got to help me out."

My gut churns like grinding gears in a busted transmission.

Aw, isn't that cute? He wants your help. But we know a sissy-baby can't do nothing, can he?

Just shut up. I don't have time for your crap right now.

Stupid, stupid, stupid.

"Mickey?" Win's fingernails cut into my skin. "Please."

"Alright, alright." I twist my wrists out of his hands. "There's...a place we can go where there's help. But you have to promise me a couple things."

"Anything." He reaches into his pocket, producing a handful of grubby bills. "You need money? I got some."

"Put that away. I'll help you, but you can't tell anybody where you got your cure, understand?"

"Where we going? A clinic?"

"Not exactly. But here's the other thing." I lean across the table to whisper into his ear. "You got to promise you won't freak out when you meet her, okay? She's in a weird place right now."

"Her? You got a *girl* doctor?" He grins. "She fine?"

The waitress sets our plates in front of us. "There we are."

I take the money Uncle John gave me from my wallet. "Sorry, we got to get going. Can you bring us the check?"

The walk to the barn is torture for Win. He leans against me, hacking and spitting, breath coming in fits and gasps. I worry he'll drop any second. When the sun slips below the horizon, the weather changes, and a cold wind whips down the street, making us both shiver.

We pass a hardware store. Behind the display window, a bank of TVs are tuned to the same channel. Like synchronized ghosts, they advertise an upcoming Halloween special on Friday night. It's a double bill featuring a slasher movie, followed by one with an aquatic man-monster terrorizing a Florida town.

Win grimaces. "Who watches this stuff?"

Block by block, we stumble along, arriving at the barn beneath a darkening sky. The lot is strewn with fast-food wrappers and empty soda can tabs. Threadbare weeds like burnt matchsticks grow in patches all the way to the barn's lonely silhouette, a hundred yards away.

Win turns to me. "This is it?"

I nod. "Yep. Let's get going."

The grass crackles like kindling beneath our feet. An odor lingers like spoiled bait. Tall cattails to our right rustle violently. Must be the wind or a raccoon hunting through trash piles. Then the tall reeds begin to flatten in places, accompanied by a chorus of atonal chirping.

"What is that?" Win points in the direction of the disturbance.

I shrug. "Probably crickets."

He frowns. "That's some loud crickets, there."

The rustling stops. Cattails sway in the wind. An unnerving silence descends on the empty lot.

"See? It was nothing," I say, but I wish I'd brought the tire iron. At least we'd have something to defend ourselves with.

Fifty yards between us and the barn, the ramshackle

structure squats in darkness, wind howling through the empty sockets of its windows.

"Place looks empty," Win says. "You're sure your doctor friend's coming?"

"She's here, I think." Who am I kidding? The place is deserted.

"You *think*?" He spits on the ground. "Man, don't tell me we walked all this way for nothing."

A high, piercing screech breaks the silence. My nostrils fill with a stench like a burning electrical socket. Amber lights flicker amid the piles of fallen reeds, and slithering sounds fill the air. Dozens of small tentacled monsters emerge from the reeds, hopping and hurtling toward us like bullfrogs.

"Mickey?" Win grabs my arm. "What the hell *are* those?"

Lightning crackles across the sky, striking a nearby tree. Its trunk bursts open and more of the nasty things emerge.

"There," I yell, pointing to the barn. "That's our best bet."

We run at a full clip—the pursuing horde close behind. Clumps of weeds fly past my face, and the ground slips and slides beneath my feet. One creature vaults ahead of us and turns, its yellow eye glowing like a bug zapper. Hissing, its open mouth reveals double-rowed fangs.

"Out of my way." I kick it right above the jawline. Screeching, the beast flies into the air and splats against a rusted barrel.

Another latches onto Win's calf.

"Aw, come on now!" He rips the creature free with both hands and tosses it into the mob behind us. The racket escalates to a fever pitch, louder than a jetliner's scream.

My heart pounds in my chest like it's about to explode. I gauge the distance to the barn and it's maybe twenty yards to safety. But the creatures have outflanked us, massing around the barn.

"They're trying to cut us off," I shout over the din.

"Tell me something I don't know," Win says. "We're running out of time."

Another monster leaps at him. Catching it by a tentacle, he swings the thrashing beast above his head like a bola and smashes it to the ground. The creature splats into a pile of green goo and razor teeth.

Dozens or hundreds more slither through the grass, yellow eyes burning like the headlights of a thousand oncoming trains.

"C'mon." I grab his arm and together we run toward the barn. Ten feet from pay dirt, the barn doors open. A lone figure emerges from the shadows.

I laugh out loud. "We got it now."

Katie Sue steps into the moonlight, white hair waving in the breeze like a tattered flag. Magenta flames blaze from her eyes, matching the intensity of the purple fire around her fists. Me and Win run past her.

"Inside," she says.

Win nudges me. "She don't look like a doctor."

"Get in the barn, man." I push him behind a wooden crate, then turn to face the chaos outside.

Waving her arms, Katie Sue spins a circle of fire in the air. The legion of creatures hiss and scream. "This is *my* house," she shouts. "Y'all git!"

A crew of little monsters swarm from her left. She sweeps her arms and thorny vines burst from the ground, impaling dozens of the creatures. Then a second wave gets within a few feet of the entrance before Katie Sue clutches her fists. The monsters scream when sharp roots lash their squishy hides, crushing them. A third group never reaches the barn. Katie Sue throws her hands outwards, unleashing a clutch of blackened reeds from the fiery circle.

Win gets to his feet, coughing and hacking. The adrenaline must be wearing off now that we're out of danger.

"How you feeling?" I say.

A wad of phlegm slips from his mouth. "I been better." He points to the battle outside the door. "Anything we can do to help?"

I shake my head. "I doubt it. We're in her hands, now."

Wave after wave of creatures fall at Katie Sue's feet. A chill wind blows in a stench like smoking brisket mixed with rotted fish guts. Random purple fires dot the weeds outside. Thirty minutes in and the chattering din reduces to muted screeches, then slithering whispers, and finally silence.

Katie Sue lowers her arms and the landscape settles back into silence. She turns to us smiling, eyes casting a pink glow over her pale flesh. Her white hair covers her shoulders like a lion's mane.

I'm not sure if I'm dealing with Katie Sue anymore, and I don't know how I feel about that. "Hey," I say, "thanks for bailing us out."

Win steps toward her. "Yeah, that was cool, man."

She laughs. "Wow, that was really crazy." She stiffens, a tremor running across her body.

"Katie Sue, you okay?" I say.

"Sure," she says, her speech slurred.

Her eyes roll up in her head, her knees buckle, and she reels backward.

I catch her before she hits the ground.

11

Two hours pass. Me and Win keep watch in the barn. We shut the doors but, every once in a while, I peek through a crack in the wall, wary of any more monster swarms. Win leans against a hay bale and tries to sleep, only to be jarred awake by the occasional coughing jag.

Katie Sue lies on a pallet of purple grass. The purple bruise between her collarbones pulsates with a regular rhythm, and her cold flesh feels even colder.

I gaze upon Katie Sue's face, white and shiny as alabaster, and then at the bulge in her chest. What is that thing, anyway? Is it a part of her anatomy? The only thing I'm certain of is that her bruise and the artichoke are somehow connected. She wouldn't be alive or undead or whatever she is if I hadn't let that thing get into her grave.

A towering magnolia tree brushes the barn's ceiling, its upper canopy sprouting through the hole in the roof. Since the tree occupies the same spot where Tammy, Katie Sue's little creation, once stuck out of the ground, I'm guessing this is the same organism all grown up. Tammy's thick trunk glows with a faint luminescence, oval leaves and white petals sparkling with an oily sheen.

Win stumbles over to the tree. "This thing here last time?"

I crane my neck to glimpse the highest branches. "Wasn't this big, but yeah."

His forehead wrinkles. "And that was…what, a day ago?"

"Two days." I run my fingers across the striated bark and sparks flicker.

"Man," Win stifles a cough, "how is that even possible?"

The barn doors slam open. Me and Win rush to the entrance, ready for a fight. But nothing's out there save weeds and a stink of fish guts, the remains of our attackers dissolved into noxious-smelling puddles.

"Let's shut this thing," I say. "Can you help me?"

He joins me and together we swing the doors closed.

"Mickey," he says, "I hope this doesn't come off the wrong way, but the tree ain't even the weirdest thing about this whole deal."

"What do you mean?"

"I'll come right out and say it." Win points at Katie Sue's still form. "How come that chick is all bleached? She an albino?"

"No, I…I don't think that's what you would call it."

"So, what would you call it?" he says, eyes wide as manhole covers. "I mean, if I didn't see her walking around and going off on those things like she did, I would swear she was—"

"Dead? Yeah."

He stiffens. "For reals?"

"Oh yeah. Dead and come back. Don't ask me how. She just…came back."

"Well, okay then." Win gestures toward the door. "But how come she can do all that stuff, huh?" He waves his hands around like he's a spaceman blasting death rays. "She tore them monsters up like they were nothing."

"I have no idea. Look, you're as much in the dark as I am right now." That's a lie, but would telling him the truth do either of us any good?

Katie Sue stirs, stretching her arms and yawning. "What happened?"

"You saved our butts is what happened," I say.

"Wow." She takes my hand and pulls herself up. "You know, for a second there I thought I dreamed all that."

Hands in his pockets, Win squirms on the balls of his feet. "No, it was the real deal. How'd you, you know, get that going?"

"Get what going?"

"You know," he says, twirling his arms and imitating her motions during the battle. "The big fire-wheel and all that."

Katie Sue glances at me. "Mickey, who's this?"

I shrug. "Win Cobb, this is Katie Sue Carson. Katie Sue, meet Win."

She reaches for his hand, but he recoils.

"Don't worry," she says. "I can turn it off when I want to."

Reluctantly, Win takes her hand, and they shake.

A sigh escapes his lips. "Guess that wasn't so bad." But the effort has him wobbling on his feet.

Katie Sue shakes her head. "Mickey, I think your friend here has—"

"Whoa." Eyes fluttering, Win slumps to the ground.

Katie Sue sinks beside him. "He's sick."

"I know. That's why we came to see you."

She grabs his ankles, and I take him under the arms. "Let's get him beneath the tree."

Together, we lay him beneath Tammy.

Purple shoots sprout from the dirt, coiling around his arms and legs. Body shaking, Win's breath comes in short, erratic blasts.

"Aren't you going to do something?" I say.

Katie Sue clutches the boy's wrist. "He's further along than you were." She places a hand on his chest and then his ribcage. "Don't know if I can help him."

I dab sweat from his brow. "He's got no chance if you don't."

A dewdrop, smelling of honeysuckle, falls on my cheek.

Overhead, a gentle tide rocks against the ceiling.

Gazing into Tammy's canopy, I make out a translucent, mushroom-shaped mass floating amid its upper branches. The organism is big as a VW bug. Long, opaque tendrils mesh with the magnolia's branches. Every few seconds the invertebrate quivers like Jello, its watery reverberations spraying colored lights along the ceiling like reflections from a disco ball.

"Aw no," I say. "Is that a jellyfish?"

Katie Sue shakes her head. "I wouldn't call Tammy that."

I turn to her. "Wait, is Tammy a tree or," I point to the jellyfish, "that thing?"

Katie Sue traces a circle on Win's forehead. "Can we talk about that after I save your friend?"

He opens his eyes. "What's happening?"

She takes his head between her hands. "Win, you've been infected by something that'll eat you alive if we don't burn it out. This will hurt, okay?"

Win squares his jaw. "Go."

Light bursts from her hands. A rush of superheated air fans outward. He screams, hair smoking under her burning touch.

Win sleeps off his ordeal up in the loft. Me and Katie Sue sit beneath the magnolia.

The jellyfish has stopped pulsating, but rainbow lights swim within the creature's body, casting a kaleidoscope on the ground. I gaze into the creature's translucent innards. "So, this is Tammy, right?"

"Yep." Katie Sue brushes a strand of hair out of her face. "She got huge while I slept."

"I'm totally confused about something, though," I say, mesmerized by the quivering mass. "Jellyfish don't usually grow inside magnolias."

"Well, that's just it," she says, running a hand along Tammy's luminescent bark. "She's not a tree." Vines descend to brush her fingers. "Not a jellyfish, neither."

"Then what is it? Or her, I mean."

"A friend?" Katie Sue tickles a tendril, and it blossoms small tubular bulbs. "She speaks to me."

"Wait, really?"

"Well, she doesn't speak like we do. It's more like...a feeling."

"Not like voices in your head?"

She frowns. "No."

"That's a relief. Only crazy people hear voices."

"Well, I may be dead, but I'm not crazy." Smiling, Katie Sue draws her knees to her chest. "I sense Tammy—if that makes any sense. Know her spirit. Her heart beats same as mine. It's almost like when Momma was alive. Sometimes, it was like Mom and me shared the same brain."

What? That's weirder than a jellyfish tree talking in your head. "You know, I actually wish I could do that."

"Do what?"

"Talk to my mom. Course, she's not around anymore."

Katie Sue turns to me. "Are you sure?" She opens her arms wide and throws back her head. "Mickey, there's more out there than this world. You know?"

"I don't." Sap from above lands on my knee. "So, is Tammy like your power source? Because that would explain how you did all that hocus pocus."

"You keep trivializing things." Katie Sue shakes her head. "Tammy speaks through me, but not for me."

"Then who am I talking to right now?"

"Who do you think?" Katie Sue's magenta eyes blaze, sending a chill up my spine.

"I mean, I don't know." I throw my hands in the air. "Every time I see you, something changes. You have all these powers and stuff. You talk to trees or jellyfish or whatever. It…it's like I don't know you anymore."

Her eyes grow moist. "Mickey, we've been through this. I'm still me, remember?" A purple tear stains her cheek. "Please believe that."

Crap, she's about to cry. "Look, I'm sorry. We've all been through a crazy week. I didn't mean to say those things."

Katie Sue rubs her eyes and smiles. "It's okay. Want to know something else?" She lays a finger to her temple. "Sometimes, Tammy gives me visions."

"Visions?"

"Yeah. Almost like stuff that's going to happen in the future. They're not fully formed, but…" Steam rises from her pale hands. "…there's a great battle coming." Katie Sue's eyes flash in the semi-darkness. "You and Win both have a part in it. There'll be somebody else to help, too."

She must be talking about Tommy. "Yeah? Anyone I know?"

Her brow furrows. "I don't think so. Face is unclear but…

somebody who's familiar with things."

"*Familiar* with things? You're not making any sense."

Katie Sue shrugs. "Sorry, that's all I've got."

We stare off into the darkness for a moment. Then her nostrils prick up, like a dog catching a scent. "What's this?" She takes a whiff of my shirt.

"What are you doing?" I say.

Katie Sue grins. "Been hanging 'round my sister?"

My cheeks flush with embarrassment. "I went over to your house on an errand, and we talked. You're not angry?"

She chuckles. "Why would I be?"

I trace a circle in the dirt with my foot. "It's just that... after the other day, I was worried you would get mad, is all."

Katie Sue plants her hands on her hips. "What you mean to say is, you were worried I'd get mad at seeing you with another girl, right?"

"Kind of." My eyes moisten, and something wet trickles down my cheek.

"Oh, Mickey." Her cold hands grasp mine, translucent flesh gleaming beneath the jellyfish lightshow. "We've been through this. What you want, can't be. Even before everything that's happened..." She shakes her head. "...I just never saw you that way."

"But it's just not fair."

"What's not fair?"

"I came to see you all those times, and you never cared, did you?"

"You mean at the store? Mickey, it wasn't that I didn't care. I always thought you were the sweetest kid."

I pull free. "That's just it, isn't it?" Hot tears stream down my face. "I'm just a kid to you, right? Just this little crybaby, always needing pity."

Katie Sue frowns. "Now you're the one who's not being

fair. I've never acted like that towards you."

I cross my arms over my chest. "You have, too."

"And to think this is coming from someone I thought was my friend."

"So, that's all I'm good enough for, right? I'm like your little pal."

Katie Sue shakes her head. "No. I love you as my friend. Why are you so afraid of that?"

She's got a point. My arms fall limp at my sides. "I don't know."

We hug, shoulder to shoulder, for a long moment. And it's hard, but somehow, I manage to stop crying.

She wipes my face with a leaf from the tree. "Anyway, how's Becca?"

"Hard to say. She looks happy, but I think she's a little sad—like on the inside."

"You didn't tell her about me, did you?"

"What? No. That would freak her out."

"Agreed."

"I mean, unless you wanted me to."

"Not now." Katie Sue shakes her head. "She's not ready for this." She caresses a clutch of Tammy's vines. They sprout white flowers with fat triple-petals. "And what about Daddy? How's he doing?"

"He's okay, I guess. I don't know him all that well."

"Very few people do." One of the flowers billows to the size of a softball. "He's kind of guarded, really. Lots of layers to pull back, and he never makes it easy." She plucks a petal, then places it in my hand.

"What's this for?"

"For Win's parents. They're sick too, right?"

How did she know that? "Sure. But what good's the flower for?"

Katie Sue points to the tree. "How to say it? She makes me feel it will help them." She smiles, fingertips lightly brushing the white petals.

They wiggle and expand, giving off a honeysuckle scent.

"Here, smell." She holds a flower to my nose.

I gag from the scent. "Whew, that'll wake the dead, just about."

Katie Sue smiles. "Tell Win to put it by their bed. Let them soak that stuff in for a few days, and it'll heal them."

"You sure that's how it works?"

"Mickey, I'm not a doctor." She runs a hand along the magnolia's bark. "We have to trust Tammy."

"Guess so."

"Anybody else that needs fixing?"

"Well, Uncle John's sick. He's got it really bad."

"He's older." She plucks a second bloom from the vine. "Maybe his immune system's not so strong."

"True." I take the stem, and absently twirl it in my fingers. "I guess we've only got my case to compare it to. And my symptoms didn't show until a couple days after I found the—"

The word freezes in my mouth. I never told Katie Sue about the artichoke.

"Found what?" she says.

My eyes drop to the purple lump beating below her collarbone, its rhythm slow and deliberate.

"Mickey? Is there something you're not telling me?"

"There, on your chest."

"You mean this thing?" She lowers her collar, revealing a glossy lump of plum-colored flesh, like a bruised muscle. "It keeps growing, but it doesn't hurt."

I'm sweating now. "Um, Katie Sue? Remember your last day? Like when you were alive?"

"Unfortunately, yes. The details get clearer all the time."

"Well…" The words stick in my mouth like peanut butter. "…I found something on the beach that day. That's actually why I came to the store, to get stuff to retrieve it."

"Okay. So, what does this have to do with me?"

I squirm in my seat. "Um, this part's going to be hard to explain. It's kind of weird."

"Mickey, trust me. Nothing's too weird to talk about anymore."

"Promise you won't be mad?"

Her eyelids narrow. "Tell me."

I explain everything, in graphic detail—finding the artichoke, yanking it from the ground, getting attacked in the shed, the thing escaping when I tried to bury it during a thunderstorm.

She nods with each new detail. "So, it ran? Where did it go?"

"Whoa." I throw a hand up. "Katie Sue, I swear to you I didn't want any of this to happen."

"Mickey, where did it go?"

"Um, it kind of ran into the cemetery," I say, dipping a hand like a plane in a nosedive. "And it, well…it fell into your grave. Plop—" I snap my fingers. "—into the muck."

"Mickey."

"And, like, I tried to get it out? But I couldn't reach it." I rub my arms. "And these dudes who worked there grabbed me, and I told them to let me finish what I started but they pulled me away."

Katie Sue glares at me. Magenta fire churns in her eyes. The purple lump under her collar throbs violently.

White-hot fear runs up my spine. I turn my head to avoid her gaze. "Please don't be mad." Ashamed, I bury my face in my hands.

She grabs my wrists and pries them free, her touch cold as the grave. "Mickey, look at me."

I raise my head. Katie Sue's face is inches from mine. Her lips curl into a frown. "Are you saying you allowed this to happen?" She points to her chest. "You let that *thing* into my grave?"

"Katie Sue, you got to understand. I couldn't stop this from happening. I tried—"

"I could be at peace now," she says, fingering the purplish lump. "At rest."

"I didn't mean for any of this to happen, I swear. You have to believe me!"

"Mickey, I don't know what to believe," Katie Sue says, face shrouded in darkness. "But you need to go when your friend wakes up."

A knife turns in my stomach.

Stupid, stupid, stupid. Now, you've done it.

I rise to my feet. "Katie Sue, please. I got in touch with an expert. We can fix this."

Katie Sue scowls, face streaked purple. "Little boy, you can't fix anything." Above her head, the jellyfish expands, filling with a dark plum-colored liquid. A low rumble shakes the rafters. Dust falls from the ceiling.

Climbing down from the loft, Win calls out. "What's going on down here?"

She gestures toward him. "Collect your friend and go."

"But you're going to need my help," I plead.

Steam billows from her clenched fists. "I don't need anything from anybody. Least of all you." Tears in her eyes, she points to the barn entrance. "Now, git."

Ten minutes later, me and Win walk back up the main road, streetlights dim amid sparse traffic and glittery storefront displays. We cut down a side street to the railroad tracks, headed for the east side where he lives.

Win pats me on the back. "Mickey, it's going to be alright. She's going to get over it. I know she will."

"You didn't see the look in her eyes. I'm worried, to be honest with you."

"Worried about what?"

"You kidding me? You saw what she can do. What if she turns on us? On the world?"

12

It's almost ten o'clock by the time I get home. Aunt Margene waits for me in the kitchen. She looks terrible. Her nose is red, big bags under her eyes.

"Mickey, where have you been?"

I place my bookbag on a chair. "Just out, you know."

"Out? It's a school night."

"Well, I was at Win Cobb's house."

"That the boy from the wrestling team?" Aunt Margene sneezes. "Why didn't his parents call?" She blows her nose into a tissue.

A lie escapes my mouth that nobody would believe. "I think the telephone lines are down in their neighborhood. You know, from the storm last weekend?"

She doesn't press the point. "Next time, you call me to pick you up, okay? It's dangerous for a boy your age to be out this late."

Suddenly, Aunt Margene stiffens. She coughs and coughs, leaning on a chair to support herself.

She doesn't look so good, come to think of it. "Did Uncle John go to work today?"

"No." She shuffles to the table and takes a seat. "And he

refuses to go to the hospital. But if he doesn't get better soon, we're taking him."

"What about you?"

"I'll be fine. This is just a head cold." Aunt Margene tears a note from a pad next to the wall phone. "Somebody called while you were out. A woman, actually." She sets it on the table.

The pantry door stands open. Spying a box of Chocolate Fudge Pop-Tarts on the top shelf, I pull out a pack. "Did she leave a name?"

"Look at the note."

I scan the note while tearing open the wrapper. "Who's Callie Whistler?"

Aunt Margene shrugs. "She called you, so you tell me. Said it was something about UFOs?"

"UFOs? Did she say she worked for *Outer Worlds?*"

"That's right. I think she mentioned that name."

I bite into the Pop-Tart and almost choke on the first nibble. Wow. *Outer Worlds.* They really called me back.

I try to make out the scribbled name. "Did she mention any other details?"

"Details? Mickey, it's your phone call. You deal with it."

Her vague answers frustrate me, especially after everything I've been through the last few days. "Aunt Margene, this is actually kind of important."

"What's important to me is my nephew staying out of trouble with strange women."

Aunt Margene sneezes, almost doubling over in a coughing fit. She's getting sicker, just like me and Win and Uncle John.

I step over to my bag and retrieve the magnolia blossom Katie Sue plucked from her tree. "You like flowers?"

She wipes her reddened nose and gives me a funny look. "We haven't finished this conversation."

I place the bloom on the table. "I know. But I wanted you to have this. It's really, um, pretty."

"Pretty?" She inspects its wide petals. "Hmmm. I would say it is. Such a nice magnolia. Thank you."

"No problem."

"Absolutely lovely." Getting up, Aunt Margene heads for the cabinet by the sink. She grabs a bowl, then fills it with water. "We used to have a magnolia tree you know. Your uncle cut it down, just after he got back from the service."

"That sucks."

She puts the flower in the bowl. Petals quivering like pennants in a gentle breeze, the bloom emits an overpowering scent that floods the room.

Aunt Margene twitches her nose. "What an odd fragrance. Kind of nice, though." She covers her mouth, stifling a sneeze. "Mickey, are you sure this is a magnolia?"

"Yeah. They grow right next to the boys' school."

Aunt Margene frowns. "St. Adolphus? What a dreadful place." She gestures toward the living room. "Your uncle wanted to send you there, but I told him no."

"Really?"

"Really." Her chest heaves then falls, the rhythm labored. Color returns to her face. "The brethren who run that place have a bad reputation."

"They do?"

"There are a lot of stories," Aunt Margene says, frowning. "It costs as much to go there as paying college tuition, but a lot of boys never finish. That school is just a revolving door."

She wipes her nose. Good thing the tissue is clean.

I'm impressed. From a coughing, sneezing wreck, she's better within minutes of being exposed to the flower.

"You saved me from a fate worse than death." I crumple the Pop-Tart wrapper. "Which is why you're my favorite aunt."

"Well, thank you." She places the flower bowl on the table.

"This has got me to thinking, though. Maybe I need another big tree in the yard."

"Aw, Uncle John would just rip it out." I toss the wrapper into the wastebasket. "Where is he?"

"Still on the couch."

I grab the bowl. "Can I put this in the living room?"

"You know, that's a good idea." She places a few dishes in the sink, then turns on the water. "They'll look nice on my knickknack shelf."

That's too far away from the patient. "Actually, I thought it'd look good by the couch."

"Whatever."

Uncle John lies unconscious on the sofa. The odor of his sweat fouls the room. His face is pale yellow, streaked with purple veins, nose and cheeks pitted with black spots. And his eyes are puffy like somebody stuffed cotton balls beneath the lids.

I place a hand on Uncle John's shoulder. His skin is icy to the touch. Is he dying?

"I know you can't hear me." I set the bowl on the coffee table near his head. "But this'll fix you up right quick. It's going to be all over soon."

The petals slowly undulate. A pungent aroma fills the room.

Instantly, Uncle John's face shrivels like a dried apricot. A gasp escapes his lips. The flower, so vibrant and alive only minutes before, wilts, reeking of rotten bananas.

"You know what?" Aunt Margene enters the living room. "I just thought of a better place to put your—"

We stare at the withering bloom. Blackening to the stem, it dies before our eyes.

"Mickey?" she says. "What's going on here?

13

Friday morning arrives. Tired from last night's craziness, I robotically rise from my bed. A quick check around the house reveals Aunt Margene's off on an errand. Uncle John moans in his sleep on the couch. His breathing is labored, and that swollen eye is as puffy as ever.

You rest, Uncle John. I mean, it's not like *my* help has done you any good.

I go back to my room and stare into the mirror, flinching at the dark circles under my eyes. My stomach growls and I need to eat, but I'm so tired and fresh out of ideas, and hope. I've got to regroup, just get away some place where I can figure things out.

Last night, Katie Sue threw me out of her life, or un-life in her case. Rejection hurts, but I get why she did it. I feel so stupid that I didn't tell her about the artichoke before. Guess I was so excited at her return from the grave, the magical strangeness of that reality blurred my judgment. Now I have this all-powerful zombie-witch hating my guts. What worries me isn't the zombie-witch part. It's the fact I hurt her that disgusts me the most.

Donning a jacket, I grab my bookbag and head toward

school. Along the way, I pass a pale-green van parked outside a drug store. A couple of guys in green beekeeper's outfits are setting up a table and chairs. Another one hoists a plastic box with a hazardous-materials sign stenciled on the side. He sets the box onto the table and opens it.

From a distance, I make out the kit's contents—a set of syringes and a plastic tube nestling in foam rubber. Questions roll through my head like bowling balls down an oiled lane.

Who are these dudes? Health officials? Doctors? And why are they giving out shots on the street?

One of the beekeepers stops and turns toward me.

I wave. "Hey, how's it going today?"

The faceless figure says nothing. His buddies step in behind him like they're squaring off to bulrush me.

Nervous, I kick the curb with the toe of my sneaker. "Um, what's in the shots?"

The hiss of passing cars fills my ears. These guys, whoever they are, just stand there staring at me from inside their stupid helmets. I won't get any answers from them, and it doesn't seem healthy to keep asking.

I shrug. "Okay, well, have a nice day." I cross the street as fast as my legs will carry me.

At school, a group of maybe two dozen kids stand, lined up against the fence. A second green van is parked near the main gate. More beekeepers are busy setting up tables on the sidewalk. A bunch of football players hog the front of the line, punching each other's arms and cracking jokes about how bad they're going to beat St. Adolphus. I catch sight of a dude from English class. He's wearing a Walkman.

I tap his shoulder to get his attention. "What's going on here?"

"What?" The boy shrugs away from my touch. "Oh,

Finley," he says to me. "How's it going, man?"

"I asked you first."

"Oh yeah." The dude shakes his head. "Principal said to come out here and get a shot. Something about a bug in the water."

That sounds weird. "The water?"

"Yeah, like the water in the bay. Look," he points to a sign that reads, *Retrovirus Vaccine–brought to you by the Bureau of Disease Management.*

I turn to him. "What's the Bureau of Disease Management?"

He grins and I catch of whiff of something that stinks like sage on his breath. "They're like government health dudes or something?" The boy rubs his bare arm. "All I know is we need to get this shot because a kid died last night."

Holy crap. "Died? From Gulf High?"

"Yeah. Whatshisname?" The boy scratches his chin. "Sanderson."

My heart lurches in my chest. "Tim Sanderson?"

"You know him?" The kid smacks his own forehead. "That's right. Wasn't he a wrestler?"

"Yep." I nod. "He was."

The kid pats my shoulder. "Sorry for y'all's loss." The boy gestures toward the back of the line. "Better find your spot, dude. This could take a while."

"Thanks." I stumble away, feet heavier than forty-pound dumbbells.

Tim Sanderson dead? I can't believe it. Did *I* get him sick?

At the end of the line, I catch sight of a poster stapled to the fence. It spells out in big bold letters the symptoms of this new disease.

If you have:

Excessive coughing/vomiting
Jaundiced skin
Colored discharge from the mouth and/or eyes

You may have contracted Fleischer's Syndrome. Left untreated, this disease can cause extensive lung and kidney damage. Even death!

Get your shot today!

Bureau of Disease Management

A chill runs up my spine. Colored discharge? I gaze at my fellow students. A few cough, and one or two dab purple gunk from their eyes. Acid boils in the pit of my stomach.
Stupid, stupid, stupid. Got them all sick, didn't you?
I shake my head. "No way," I whisper, "No way I did all this."
Yes, you did. Got them all sick. Sick boy, sick boy, sick boy.
Man, just shut up.
The voices fade and I count in my head all the people I came into contact with after battling the artichoke. Win Cobb? Yeah, me and Win wrestled after I got exposed. But he's okay now, thanks to Katie Sue. Uncle John? Makes sense.
But Tim Sanderson? He turned up sick *before* I found the nasty thing. Even accounting for some super-high infection rate, there's no way he gets the artichoke-crud before I do. So, if he didn't get it from me, then when was he exposed? Something doesn't add up. Is there more than one artichoke?
A big hand falls on my shoulder. I spin around and stare into the crabapple face of a middle-aged man with tousled

dark hair, a broken nose, and piercing brown eyes. "Hello, my friend," he says, "ready to take your shot?"

I take his full measure. He wears a white lab coat over a green shirt, black slacks, and black flat-bottom necktie. Must be a doctor or something.

I brush his paw aside. "Guess I will. Who are you?"

"Doctor Blightman. I'm head of the special response team for the BDM."

Dude's got a weird accent. "The what?"

"Oh, sorry." He points to the sign. "Bureau of Disease Management. We handle...unusual tropical diseases like the one infecting your school."

"You do?" Something about this guy is *too* familiar, but I can't place where I've seen him before. "So, like, are we all going to get sick and die?"

His hollow chuckle rattles like an old muffler. "Oh, hardly. Fleischer's Syndrome in its early stages is entirely treatable."

Yeah right. "Must be, because I never heard of it before."

"Most people haven't," Blightman says, gesturing to the line. "But you'll be alright just as soon as you get inoculated." At the shot table, a football player winces as a beekeeper buries a syringe into his arm.

I frown. "Say, doc? Is this vaccine, I don't know, safe for people?"

He smiles, revealing sharp incisors. "Of course, it is." His laugh could cut glass. "We'd hardly make sacrificial lambs out of you lot."

What a weird thing to say. "Don't you mean guinea pigs?"

"Oh, so I did." He holds out his hand. "Well, do take care now."

"You too, buddy." I fold my arms in front of me and take a step back.

Clicking his heels, the doctor goes off to join the

beekeepers. Weird. There's maybe a couple dozen people in line, and he starts bugging me? Why would he do that?

And why does that guy look so familiar?

I ditch the line and head to class. No way that stuff can protect me better than Katie Sue's medicine. A clutch of kids crowd the building's front steps, where an assistant principal checks for proof they've been vaccinated.

"Everybody got your shot records?" he says.

A ton of kids hold up their hands, each clutching a white index card. The AP can't keep track of them all. In the chaos, I slip past him into the main hallway. The walls are still decorated with black and orange streamers, and the theater department's cardboard cemetery still stands. But there's no crush of bodies like last year. A few individuals shuffle between classes, some burying their faces in their elbows, trying not to sneeze. Teachers stand on monitor duty in the hallway, pulling aside those who are obviously ill.

It figures. Word must've gotten out how the beekeepers would inject them at school. And since tonight is Fall Social, there's bound to be a few who don't want to catch something before the game. Maybe they think staying home will protect them.

Entering Mr. Kraftner's English class is like falling into a well. Half the seats are empty, and there's a big assignment on the board. The substitute Mrs. Cranberry sits behind the teacher's desk, sipping tea while reading a newspaper. Grabbing my seat, I stare at a list of readings scribbled on the board.

Something pointy hits me in the ear. I turn toward an eruption of girlish giggles. In the corner Alice Walsh, her poodle-mane puffier and oiler than usual, grins at me while batting her eyelashes. Seated next to her are a couple of girls from the Cheerleading Mafia, the whole lot done up in game-time red sweaters and striped skirts.

A knot forms in my stomach.

Stupid, stupid, stupid. They're making fun of you.

Would you just shut up? Why should I even care what they think?

No. They're all laughing at you. They'll always control you.

"They don't control anybody," I say aloud.

The girls gape, then burst into hysterics.

"Do you *believe* this guy?" one of the Mafia whispers.

"What a weirdo," says another.

Alice points at the airplane, upside down on the floor. "Aren't you going to read it, Pop-Tart?"

I reach for the note, but Mrs. Cranberry snatches it up first. She unfolds it, and there's an audible gasp from my tormentors.

"What have we here?" the old woman says.

The girl rises from her seat. "That's private property, Mrs. Cee."

"Then why is it on the floor?" The substitute glares at her through thick bifocals. Alice slinks back to her seat behind her desk, shoulders slumped.

Mrs. Cranberry adjusts her spectacles. "Let's see." Her finger traces back and forth across the paper. "Something about Mr. Finley minding his own business...don't go to Fall Social...a vague threat of bodily harm, and..." The old woman chuckles.

Alice raps white knuckles on her own desk. "Don't read it. Don't. Please don't."

"My, my," the sub says, crumpling the plane. "Why, Ms. Walsh. It takes a special young lady to be willing to show a fella, as you put it, *a night you'll never forget.*"

The rest of the class laughs. Alice's cheeks turn the color

of canned beets.

Nobody's home when I return. Stuck to the refrigerator door is a crudely scrawled note from Aunt Margene, saying she drove Uncle John to the hospital in Biloxi.

I stumble into the living room. The stained couch reeks of his foul body odor. That dying flower weighs heavily on my mind. Now that Tim Sanderson is gone, I'm convinced Uncle John needs more than a trip to the ER.

A wild notion flutters in my brain. What if I ran back to the barn? Begged Katie Sue to grow another flower?

That won't work. She hates me now. Me and the artichoke beating in her chest, keeping her stuck between life and death. No help from that quarter. And anyway, would a second flower do any better than the first?

The phone rings down the hall. Thinking it's Aunt Margene, I run toward the source of the sound.

My heart races when I lift the receiver. Were there complications at the hospital? Is Uncle John dead?

"Who's this?" I say.

The voice is that of a middle-aged woman. "Can I speak to Mickey Finley, please?"

Who is this person? "Depends on who's asking."

She talks in a clipped Midwestern accent. "Young man, I don't have time for games. Someone named Mickey Finley left a message on the tip line of my magazine, and it's vital, absolutely vital we speak. So, are you him or not?"

"Okay, I'm Mickey. Who are you?"

"This is Colleen Wentwhistle."

"Did you say Whistler?"

"*Went-whistle.*"

"From *Outer Worlds*?"

"That's right."

"You the secretary?"

She clips each syllable, crisply. "I own the magazine."

I laugh. "Oh, give me a break."

"Excuse me?"

"You heard what I said." I coil the phone cord around my arm and stifle a chuckle.

"Young man, what's so funny?"

"Whoever heard of a girl running a UFO magazine?"

The venom in her voice could poison a cobra. "*Girl?*"

An uncomfortable silence fills the space. For a moment, I think the connection is lost, but suddenly, she clears her throat. "You don't think I'm qualified to investigate extraterrestrial activity," she says. "Fine. Here are my credentials, Mr. Finley. I hold doctorates in anthropology and aeronautical engineering, both from prestigious universities. In a previous life I worked Mission Control at Cape Canaveral. Nowadays I'm the chief writer, researcher, and publisher of *Outer Worlds*. That enough of a resume for you?"

Another giggle bubbles to the tip of my tongue. "Really? I mean, you sound all expertly and what not, but I just don't believe you."

"You think only *men* do science?" A loud sigh floods my ear. "It never ends. It really doesn't."

Jeez, talk about being sensitive. "Look, I didn't mean it as a cheap shot."

"Nothing changes. They start you little chauvinist pigs early, don't they? Maybe I should post a mugshot of me in my cap and gown."

Please don't. You're probably hideous. "Sorry. I didn't mean to laugh at you. It's just I never met any girls who were even into science, much less the cool stuff."

"Cool stuff? I can assure you, Mr. Finley, some extraterrestrials are *not* cool."

But some are? "Look, lady. We got off on the wrong foot. I really have a situation down here."

"I'll bet you do." A staccato burst of tapping clatters in the background. "Let's get some information. So, you found an artichoke? Was it alone or in a pod with others?"

So, there *can* be more than one. "A pod? No, it was alone when I found it."

More tapping. "Was there any other suspicious-looking plant life nearby? Mutated animal carcasses?"

"Um, no on both. But there's been other stuff since then." I nearly drop the phone, recalling last night's battle at the barn. "Weird stuff that chased me and tried to eat me."

"What kind of stuff? Insect-mammal amalgams?"

"No. More like these little green tentacle monsters."

"Tentacles? Hmm." A bell rings, followed by a scraping sound. "What about weird fish? Like with flappy wing-things instead of fins?"

"Would you settle for giant sharks?"

The tapping stops.

"Miss Wentwhistle?"

"Doctor." She coughs like someone with smokers' hack. "I'm sorry. Did you say you saw a shark? Like a messed-up-looking one?"

The tapping resumes.

"Well, no." The telephone cord is wound around my arm to the shoulder. "I haven't *seen* a shark. But all over town, someone's putting up, like, shark images? They're everywhere. Carved into jack-o-lanterns, spray-painted on walls." Becca Mae's dad is a shark groupie, too. But does this weirdo need to know that?

"Oh, no. Oh, no." The tapping resumes.

"And there are these weird scientist dudes who showed up at my school today."

"Were they dressed in green hazmat suits? Did they administer shots?"

How could she possibly know about them? "Yeah. Oh, yeah."

Another flurry of keystrokes rattles my eardrum. "Tell me more about these shark pictures. Do any of them feature a big eye, dead center in the stomach?"

"Some do."

"And you mentioned tentacles. Do the shark pictures have them? Tentacles, I mean?"

"Pretty much all of them."

She mumbles something under her breath, tapping all the while. "Mickey, you and everyone in that town are in mortal danger. It's absolutely vital I get down there as soon as possible."

Guess her help can't hurt, even if she's a crackpot. "Cool."

"Excellent. Give me until this afternoon to get there. Once I've set up my equipment, we can establish a perimeter. You'll be helping me, of course."

What? Wait. No. "I'm not a scientist. I don't even know you."

"You can learn on the job. Where do you live?"

"Bay St. Louis."

"I know that part. What about your home address? I'll pick you up soon as I get to town."

"Hold on a sec." I put my hand over the receiver. Crazy thoughts stampede through my head like wild horses. How do I know this is all on the up and up? What if this woman is connected to the beekeepers, or that creepy doctor? What if she's using me to get to Katie Sue?

"Mr. Finley?" she says impatiently.

I put the phone to my ear. "Sorry, but you're crazy. I made a mistake contacting you."

Craig E. Higgins

"No, you haven't. I just need a hot minute to—"
I hang up on her.
A moment later, the phone rings. I ignore it.
Time to go to the game.

14

Night falls and a crescent moon hovers over the stadium. One of those creepy BDM vans sits in the parking lot. Beekeepers stick the arms of a trickle of kids, come to get their medicine. This confuses me until I spy a sign stapled to a fence.

> *It's recommended that all students attending tonight's game be vaccinated.*
> *Bureau of Disease Management.*

Oh well. At least at the game they're not *making* people take their stupid shots.

Ducking the van, I trot over to the entrance, buy a ticket, and enter the arena. The Gulf High Tide, my team, warm up on the sidelines. The stadium itself is a drab affair—two opposing tiers of aluminum bleachers, a press box, locker rooms, and concession stand. Chunks of broken earth pockmark the thinning grass. Students, parents, and alumni fill the stands, tipsy with school spirit or in some cases, booze and weed. A few kids wear surgical masks on account of the sickness going around. But most sport jackets and beanies to ward off the cold.

Some wear costumes in preparation for Fall Social. Afterward, there will be lots of parties in backyards or the houses of older kids whose folks are either tolerant of alcohol and loud music or are simply out of town. But I'm done after the dance. Mostly, I'm going because I told Becca Mae I would come, and I need a break from my real-life Halloween movie.

On our sideline, Alice Walsh and her Cheerleader Mafia raise pom-poms above their heads, kicking their legs like a bunch of showgirls. With toothy smiles radiating mindless fun, they raise their voices in unison, shouting empty slogans.

I don't hate Alice, even when she does stupid stuff like today. But it's times like this I'm reminded of how different we are. People like her crave applause and attention. I'm happy with my comic books and Atari. She's oil to my water, or in this case, Aqua-Net to my Pop-Tarts.

On the field, our quarterback throws a spiral to one of his receivers on the fifty-yard line, hitting him in stride. It's a nice pass, clean and on-target. But our guy's skills pale in comparison to St. Adolphus's passer. Six-five and built like a tank, this kid's consensus All-State, a future college star.

Their scat-back explodes across the scrimmage line. The quarterback nails him in the numbers, then follows that pass with a bullet to a tight end. I'm impressed. This dude's like Godzilla with the guitar-hands of Eddie Van Halen, lighting up one target after the next. Their coach lumbers onto the field, blows a whistle, and the quarterback and the rest retreat to their bench.

The St. Adolphus cheering section takes up the entire visitors' bleachers, a collection of rich boys with longish hair, sporting nice coats and expensive shoes. A selection of very hot girls mingle among their ranks, so well dressed they must be from out of town. Perky and decked out in the latest fashions, their teased, feathered locks and heavy make-up distinguish them from the common stock on our side of the field. But since St. Adolphus is all-boys, the quotient of females is noticeably thin.

Win or lose, the St. Adolphus boys will invade Fall Social. They'll hog two parking spots with their fancy European sports cars, and lord it over anybody who gets in their way.

Alice and her Mafia, status seekers and social climbers all, will coo and flaunt themselves like peacocks, each hoping to snare their own rich boyfriend.

A familiar voice calls my name. "Hey, Mickey."

I spy Win Cobb. "Hey, man. You feeling better?"

"Oh yeah." He smiles. "And that flower your friend gave me? It fixed my folks right up."

From where we sit, the parking lot is visible. I point to the BDM vehicle, still servicing last-minute customers. "Win, did you take that shot?"

He smiles. "Nah, man. Because I heard about the symptoms. Same as ours, right?"

"They are. You heard about Tim?"

"I did." Frowning, Win plays with the zipper on his jacket. "I feel pretty lucky, you know? That could've been us."

"Yeah, it could've," I say. "Let's get a seat. It's getting pretty crowded."

We grab spots a few rows up from the field. A fat kid from my algebra class sells popcorn and drinks from a hawker tray balanced on his gut.

Win flags him over. "Give me a popcorn." The boy exchanges one greasy container for a dollar, then weaves away through the crowd.

"You want some?" Win offers me the box.

"Don't mind if I do." The kernels taste buttery-smooth in my mouth. While crunching the popcorn, I track a familiar blonde making her way high in the bleachers.

It's Becca Mae. She takes a seat with her friends, Felicia and Ruth. A song comes over the loudspeakers and she tosses her cornflake-yellow hair, waving her arms in synch with the music.

Win's claps me on the shoulder. "Why don't you go talk to her?"

The very thought cranks like a corkscrew into my stomach. "What?"

"You heard me. That girl you're looking at. Go talk to her."

"I mean, what would we talk about?"

"Dude, you like her. Just go talk."

"You think it's that easy?"

"If you don't…" He points to the row behind her. "…that fella will."

Wade Ruthven and the dark-haired boy from Katie Sue's funeral make their way to Becca Mae's aisle, pushing people out of their way. Wade knocks one kid against a guardrail. The boy glares at the bully, but Wade's friend grabs the guy by the collar and tosses him over the side.

Win scowls. "Man, talk about rude."

"He is." Enough is enough. "I'm going to straighten him out." I rise from my seat, determined to intervene. But before I can plant a foot in the aisle, a pain like a knife in the gut doubles me over.

Are you crazy? That kid's going to splatter you just for being here.

Maybe he will, but I've got to stop him.

Stop him from doing what? Talking to his cousin?

Wade and his friend reach Becca Mae. He says something, and the girls laugh.

See? Nothing to worry about. Be a good little sissy-baby and sit back down.

Out of the corner of my eye, I catch sight of a familiar

Artichoke Stars and Chicken Fried Shark

figure in red, standing on the sideline.

Alice Walsh stares into the crowd, arms limp and poms-poms drooping in her hands. She's scowling. Even from way over here, her pupils seem no bigger than pinpricks.

Man, Alice is mad at somebody. Turning, I catch sight of the target of her ire.

Wade.

Win nudges me, pointing at Alice. "Man, what's up with Miss Jerry-Curl?" He gestures toward the bully. "She don't like that dude, huh?"

In a flash, the reality of the situation hits me. "Alice must be seeing him."

"Who's him?"

"Wade. Becca Mae's cousin."

Win turns around and searches the bleachers. "The blond, right?" Win laughs. "Man, for people you claim not to like, you seem to know a lot about them."

Alice flings her pom-poms to the turf and stamps her feet. A couple players on the sidelines laugh. Elbows out and fingers curled into talons, she bounds for the bleacher steps, only to be stopped by a couple of her Mafia.

Above us, Wade places a hand on Becca Mae's back, and her smile instantly evaporates. She brushes the paw away, and he barks something that doesn't reach my ears. Becca Mae tosses her head and crosses her arms like a bouncer. Wade throws up his hands, then storms away, the dark-haired boy in tow.

Win gestures toward the sidelines. "Uh-oh. Here comes drama."

Down below, Alice frees herself from her friends. Bounding up the steps, she meets Wade halfway up the aisle, within earshot of me and Win.

The poodle-haired girl lays into him, her face coming up to

his chest. "Excuse me, Mr. Ruthven, but *exactly* who was that you were talking to?"

"She's kin," says Wade.

"Kin?" Alice drives a long fingernail into his chest. "That girl ain't no kin. She's not even…" The cheerleader screws up her face, as if searching for a lost tune. "…a sophomore!"

He shrugs. "What does that have to do with anything?"

Mascara seeps down Alice's cheek. "You know how embarrassing this is for me? How humiliating?"

He drops a beefy hand on her shoulder. "C'mon, honey-baby. You don't have to worry, none. That's just my cousin."

She slaps the hand away. "They're *all* your little cousins, aren't they? Every girl you run around with. You think I don't hear the rumors? People gossiping about what you do at your secret boys' club?"

Secret boys' club? I lean closer to get a better listen.

"Honey-baby, just relax. You know you're my number-one girl." For a moment, she leans her head against his hand, her frown settling into something like a grin.

Suddenly, Alice shoves him away. "You don't fool me. Come up with some better lies than that, Wade."

He protests, but she pushes him away.

The National Anthem blares from the PA. Me and Win rise with the rest of the crowd, trumpets blaring in our ears.

The anthem finishes and Alice rejoins her fellow cheerleaders. They retrieve their pom-poms and hustle to the sideline.

Before I can take my seat, someone clamps my arm in a vice. I try to yank it away, but the grip tightens.

"Hello, Pop-Tart," Wade says, breath stinking like a distillery. "Thought somebody told you not to show your face tonight."

Win steps between us, fists balled, nostrils flaring. "Hey,

buddy. You want a piece of him, I got something for you."

The blond kid laughs, releasing my arm. "Well, what do you know, Freddie?" He nudges the dark-haired boy behind him. "Pop-Tart's got himself all kinds of back-up."

"Yeah, he do." Freddie snickers. "But it won't matter none, if he shows up at the dance."

Wade jabs a finger into space, inches from my nose. "That's right. Then you'll get to meet *my* people."

My Adam's apple bobs, and a tremor runs up my spine, immobilizing me.

Win shoves Wade in the chest. "Just try and stop us. We're going to be there no matter what kind of help you got."

Wade sneers. "Famous last words. You receive my note, Pop-Tart?"

The words tumble out of my mouth as if spoken by somebody else. "What note?"

"Alice gave it to you, yeah?" He smiles. "Stay out of my way. Or I promise you, this *will* be a night you'll never forget."

We lock eyes. Something in his dark orbs flickers, like a brush fire consuming everything in his path. I'm the first to blink. Acid percolates in my belly.

Stupid, stupid, stupid. Now he knows you won't stand up to him.

Wade laughs. "There we go."

He and Freddie hustle down the aisle.

I sit on the bench, angry and afraid. Every nerve in my body misfires like a faulty engine.

"Don't worry, man." Win hands me the box of popcorn. "That dude's all talk. We go to the dance, and your honey's going to be there."

"She's not my honey." My hands shake, pulse pounding in my temples like kettle drums.

Win frowns. "Mickey, you alright?"

"No." Why am I so scared of Wade?

Win smiles. "You listening to me? That girl's going to be at the dance. And you two will get together and it's going to be so cool."

I reach into the box of popcorn and toss what I grab into my mouth, wincing when I bite down on a hard kernel. "Yeah. Pretty cool."

Something across the field grabs my attention. Standing in the shadows behind players pouring onto the field, a man wearing a long black robe, and an oily pageboy haircut gazes across the field. His features are hard to make out amid the pom-poms and cheering spectators. But I know him. He's the dude who called off Wade and Freddie when they tried to beat me up.

The apparition waves at me, then fades into the gloom beneath the stands.

15

The moon hangs three-quarters full behind a gray cloud bank above the gym. When me and Win get there, a line of kids stretches all the way from the parking lot to the entrance.

No creepy green vehicles or beekeepers or weird doctors this time. Maybe they took the night off. But predictably, several shiny European sports cars clog the parking lot, some taking two spaces.

Since the St. Adolphus Spires beat our Tide in the bragging-rights game, the horde of arrogant rich boys have come to gloat.

An Econoline van is parked nearby, beige with raised rear mag wheels. The windows are blacked out. Airbrushed on the side is a matador rescuing a flamenco dancer from a charging bull.

Win points to the strange picture. "You know that painting?"

I give it a once-over. "Nah. Kind of familiar, though."

"Remember that Cuban grocery closed down? The one by the Quik-Rite past the railroad tracks?"

"What about it?"

"You know how they sold those black velvet paintings?" he says, sounding a little awe-struck. "I think this was copied

139

off one."

"Wow." I give the picture a second look. "You're right. And I thought I was a nerd."

Win chuckles. "Man, ain't nothing nerdy about 'em. Those prints are way cool."

"Whatever you say, my friend."

Some kids are in costume, most of them girls. A few wear surgical masks but otherwise it's a perfectly normal crowd. I catch sight of a stocky blonde standing a few feet away, her feathered hair spilling out from beneath a witch's hat. Next to her slinks a tall brunette in a shiny black catsuit and ears. A long tail waves languidly behind her. Completing the trio is a big, rawboned girl. She's pretty, done up in a blue-and-white gingham frock and red pig tailed wig.

The witch laughs a familiar laugh that reverberates in the dark.

"Wait," I say. "That's her."

"Blondie?" Win scans the trio. "Hey, you're right." He nudges me. "No excuses now, my man. Go talk to her."

Go talk to her. As if it were that simple.

The other night, me and Becca Mae's undead, all-powerful sister had the fight to end all fights. How would Katie Sue react if she knew I was talking to her sis? What would happen if Becca Mae found out I didn't tell her about her sister's return from the grave? And don't I still love Katie Sue, no matter how terrifying she's become?

My stomach turns.

You're going to screw this up. And anyway, you don't care about this girl. You're just doing this to take your mind off the dead one.

No, I am not. Me and Becca Mae are just friends, that's all. How could it be anything else?

"Earth to Mickey." Win snaps his fingers in front of my face.

The blonde doubles over laughing, sharing some joke with her friends. I stand there, tugging on a finger, then another. There's a tightening in my chest that travels down my legs, rooting me in place. "Man, I don't know."

Win throws up his hands. "You know what? I give up. Do whatever you want to do."

He's right. It's time to decide.

Heart pounding, I push past a necking couple, and tap Becca Mae on the arm.

Her eyes flare like Christmas lights. "Mickey. What a surprise!" She wraps her arms around me, the creamy aroma of her skin and hair flooding my nostrils. I sink into the hug, embracing her soft flesh. Time slows just like it did that day at her house, and the rest of the world fades into stardust.

The cat-girl taps Becca Mae on the shoulder. "Hey, Becca, you forget about us?"

Raggedy-Ann nods. "Yeah. This is our night, remember?"

She disengages herself from me. "Aw, come on. My dad never lets me out of the house. I got to have some fun here. Y'all remember Mickey, right?"

"Yes," they say in unison.

"Mickey, you remember Felicia and Ruth?"

They both stare at me, just like in the lunchroom.

"Sure do." A chill runs up my spine. "How're things?"

"Fine," Ruth says flatly.

"Super-peachy," adds Felicia the cat-girl.

"We just changed into our outfits," Becca Mae says. "You come with somebody?"

Does she think I came with a date? "No, just a friend. We went to the game and thought it would be fun to come to the party."

Felicia snickers. "Parties are *after* the dance, dude."

Becca Mae frowns. "Now, don't you listen to them. You

come in and have a good time. And if my cousin shows up, don't worry. I'm your bodyguard, remember?"

I shrug. "Yeah, that's true."

"Sure is. Are we going to dance later?" she says.

Dance? Does that mean this girl likes me? Like, *like* me? If so, what do I do with that? "I suppose," I say.

Ruth laughs. "You *suppose*?"

"He's just shy." Becca Mae punches my arm. "But extra-sweet."

Her friends whistle. My cheeks flush.

Win gestures at me from back in the line.

"Uh, I think I should be going," I say. "But I'll see you later, okay?"

Becca Mae readjusts her hat. "Yes, you will. And don't forget about that dance, ya hear?"

The girls break into hysterical giggles while I return to my place in line next to Win.

"How'd that turn out?" he says.

"I think she wants me to dance with her?"

He cocks an eyebrow. "Slow-dance or regular?"

There's a difference? "She didn't say. But girls never want to dance with me either way."

"Well, this one does." He holds out a hand. "Give me five, brother."

We slap hands. My chest fills with warmth, and something else besides.

Pride?

Confusion?

Fear of Katie Sue?

A shadow crosses the parking lot, almost too quick for my eyes to register. It's followed by a buzzing sound, like a hive of angry bees. My heart flips, pulse pounding in my ears.

Win grips my arm. "You alright, man?"

"I'm fine."

At the entrance, a girl from chemistry class sits behind a table. In front of her is a cash box. "Two dollars each."

Win plunks down a five. "That's like highway robbery."

The girl adjusts her horn-rimmed glasses. "Give me a break. It's cheaper than last year."

She hands him his change, and we step across the threshold.

Inside the gym, wooden bleachers are accordioned against the walls, freeing up space on the basketball court for mingling and dancing. Gauzy streamers hang from the ceiling, terminating at a spinning mirror ball, its glittering facets cast rainbow-hued shards over the animated throng gyrating on the hardwood floor.

A pulsating dance beat pounds from the PA. Manning a pair of turntables, a balding, middle-aged DJ in a shiny purple track suit rummages through a box of vinyl records. Selecting a platter, he drops it on one turntable while adjusting a slider on the other. Cranked up, the PA buffets the crowd with a wall of sound.

Me and Win squeeze through the sweaty clutch of dancing bodies. My heart pounds in my chest, nerves firing like pistons. I hate crowds and loud noises that don't involve metal music. The collective musk of the perspiring crowd sets my teeth on edge.

Win bumps my arm. "Mickey, you got to relax. It's just people."

"Sure. Let's find some empty wall, okay?"

He shrugs. "Whatever you want, man."

In front of the bleachers a punch bowl and cups sit on a table. Win points to the server, a girl dressed as a pirate wench, her billowy sleeves slipping over her hands.

"You know her?" he says.

"No." The music fills my ears with syrupy static, blotting out my thoughts.

"She's fine." His white teeth shine like marbles in the glitter ball's glow. "Be back in a bit." He saunters off in the direction of the punch bowl table.

Standing alone beside the bleachers, my mind drifts, ears ringing like gongs. Usually, I wilt under these conditions. Too much noise and the smell of so many sweaty people overwhelm me. But somewhere in this glut of kids, Becca Mae waits for me to take her hand and lead her out on the floor. Then it'll just be me and her, awash in the mirror ball's flickering glare.

That image sinks into my brain. Despite the madness that's descended into my world the last several days, I can't deny the thought of her near is a rush. All the puppy love stuff I imagined about her sister blurs like raindrops peppering the surface of a lake. With Becca Mae, it's something more.

Something real.

But the crowd is huge, and the enveloping darkness shot through with colored lights looms larger than the bay itself. How will I find her?

Then, a knife jabs me in the gut.

Stupid, stupid, stupid. Where did she go?

Shut up. She's got to be around here somewhere.

What does it matter? You don't have the guts to dance with her.

We can play this game if you want, but you won't stop me.

Yes, we will. You're easy. Just a gutless little sissy baby who can't get a date.

"Stop talking," I say.

Can't get a date. Can't get a date.

A two-inch-long stiletto heel nearly impales my foot.

"This is all your fault," a girl shouts in my ear.

I recoil, gazing up into the mascara-ringed eyes of Alice Walsh.

Dressed in a silky red robe held together by a slinky silver sash, she glares at me. Alice's hair is a mass of dark ringlets held back by a shiny tiara. Her breath reeks of alcohol.

"I'm sorry?"

She purses her lips like she just sucked a whole lemon. "Don't you sorry me, Pop-Tart. You're ruining *my* life."

"What are you talking about?"

She levels a long red fingernail in the direction of three girls giggling among themselves across the dance floor. One's dressed as a witch, the other two as a cat and a ragdoll.

"Blondie over there," Alice says. "She's your girlfriend, right?"

The blaring music makes it hard to reply. "What?"

"But you're not enough for her, right?" She tosses her poodle hair and gives me a look that could burn firecrackers.

I shake my head. "Me and Becca Mae are just friends."

Alice snarls. "Give me a break! Look at her laughing at me, her and her little crew."

"But they're all the way over there. How can you even tell what they're—"

"I can." Alice's eyes well up. A teardrop trails down her cheek. "She's making a fool out of me, getting with Wade right in the open."

"You know they're cousins, right?"

"I'll show her." She sweeps across the hardwood in a flurry of red silk, pushing people aside on her way to confront Becca Mae.

Oh crap, she wants to fight. I dash after her. Kids curse when I push past them, but Alice has to be stopped.

I reach the girls, but I'm already too late. Alice stands there, hands curled into claws, her hair a snaky mess slipping over her bare shoulders.

Scowling, Becca Mae balls her fists. "What can I do for you,

Miss Thing?"

Felicia and Ruth giggle.

Alice frowns. "You stay away from my boyfriend, little girl."

"Is that what this is about? You can have him—the creep."

"What did you say?"

"You heard me. Wade's a creep, and how'd you get me mixed up in this anyway? Me and him are—"

"Just shut it." Alice grabs Becca Mae's blouse, ripping a sleeve. "You're going to get yours, little girl."

I try to get between them, but I trip on the hardwood and fall on my knees. Snarling, Becca Mae punches Alice in the face. The taller girl slashes her cheek with her long red nails. Becca Mae locks her hands around Alice's throat. Like angry cats the two descend into a mess of flying fists and sharp nails, grappling on the floor. A circle forms around the fight. Kids push against each other to get a better view.

Alice claws Becca Mae's shoulder, drawing blood. Becca Mae returns the favor, kneeing Alice in the stomach. The dark-haired girl howls in pain. Things degenerate into a blur. Alice and Becca Mae rip into each other's hair. Inky curls and cornflake locks scatter across the floor. Jumping on top of Becca Mae, Alice bites her forearm. The blonde girl screams and the music lurches to a stop. A piercing whistle cuts through the roar of the crowd.

"Stop this right now." Coach drops to the floor and separates the two girls. He pulls Alice to her feet while Miss Singleton, the librarian, wrestles Becca Mae from the floor.

A big, balding man approaches, shoving kids out of the way. In the semi-darkness, it takes a moment to recognize him.

Mr. Barton, the school principal, wags a finger at Alice. "Miss Walsh, you're in a lot of trouble."

Alice points at Becca Mae. "She started it!"

"Did not." Becca Mae lunges at the other girl, but Miss

Artichoke Stars and Chicken Fried Shark

Singleton grabs her arm.

Coach frowns, holding the squirming Alice fast. "What should we do with these two?"

"I'll talk to them separately on Monday," Mr. Barton turns to Alice. "Now, you owe Miss Carson here an apology."

"Apology? Seriously?" Alice sneers. "Y'all always blaming me for everything."

"Stop it, Alice. You're only making this worse for yourself," Miss Singleton says.

The principal sighs, then turns to the crowd of kids gathered round. "What are you all staring at? Show's over."

Slowly, they retreat, Mr. Barton herding them back onto the dance floor.

Coach nods to the DJ, who stands gawking, as if seeking permission to restart the music. "Go on ahead. Play."

The flamboyant middle-aged man fires up the speakers.

Felicia approaches Becca Mae. "We'll have to catch up later."

Ruth adjusts her pigtail wig. "Yeah. Stay safe, okay?"

Becca Mae shrugs, wiping blood from a cut above her eyebrow. "Sure. Call me?"

Felicia shrugs. "For sure."

The pair rejoin the crowd.

Shaking her head, Alice strains against Coach's grip. "I'm going to get you, blondie," she screams. Blood streams from a cut on her lip. "You're going to regret messing with me!"

Becca Mae dabs her swollen eye. "Oh, dream on, Aqua-Net."

"What did you call me?" Alice stomps Coach's foot.

He winces but doesn't let go. "Now Alice. You done taken it too far this time. Mr. Barton already said there'll be consequences—"

"Don't tell me about no consequences." Her stringy biceps tense against his grasp. "This little girl's trying to take my place. And she's never going to do that. I'm Queen Bee around here. Queen Bee!"

Pushing through the crowd, the Cheerleader Mafia appears behind Coach, dressed in matching white tunics, their short skirts trimmed with purple.

"What's this?" Coach says.

Like chorus girls, the Mafia parts, making way for a tall blond guy in a toga, plastic laurel leaves bracketing his temples.

Becca Mae frowns. "Well, well, Wade. Come to collect your trash?"

Ignoring her, he approaches Coach. "Sir? I'm Alice's date. Let me take her home."

Turning to examine the smirking young man, Coach scowls. "Sorry son, but I don't know you—"

A sliver bolt of light cuts through the darkness. Coach swats the back of his neck, dropping Alice's wrist in the process.

He drops to one knee, eyes rolling up into his head and goes stiff as a board.

Seizing the opportunity, Alice charges Becca Mae. But the dark-haired girl's heel catches on her own dress, and she goes sprawling.

Wade steps in, breaking her fall. "That's enough out of you."

Alice beats her fists against his chest. "No, Wade. Let me go. Let me—"

He slaps a hand over her mouth to muffle her complaints.

Coach writhes on the floor, his complexion the color of over-ripe plums, his breath coming in shallow gasps.

Win squats next to the man. "You okay, Coach?"

Coach struggles to bring a hand to his neck. "Can one of y'all get this thing out?"

Freddie steps from the shadows, a two-pronged purple tongue flickering over his lips.

Sweat beads at my temples. Nobody has a tongue like that.

Well, except maybe Gene Simmons from Kiss, but he's weird. And so are these guys.

Freddie leers.

I glare back. "What did you do?"

The dark-haired boy laughs. "What you talking about, Pop-Tart?"

With one arm tight around Alice's waist, Wade nods to Freddie. "We can't wait any longer."

Alice bites Wade's hand and he winces. "Ow."

She struggles from his grasp and whirls on him. "How can you treat me like this?" Alice stamps her feet. "You said they was preparing me—"

"Alice!" Wade hisses at her. "I told you not to talk about that."

Talk about what? "Wade, I don't know what's going on here," I say, "but you leave her be."

He snorts. "Pop-Tart, don't involve yourself in things that don't concern you."

Wade nods to Freddie. Smiling, the dark-haired boy's tongue lolls out of his mouth.

"Ewww," Becca Mae says. "Put that thing away."

Miss Singleton thrusts the blonde girl against the bleachers. "Stay out of this."

Freddie spits. Something whistles through the air, nearly clipping my ear. Becca Mae ducks, and the tiny barb sinks between Ms. Singleton's shoulder blades.

Shaking like a leaf, she falls forward and takes Becca Mae with her.

Kids begin to gather around, encircling the renewed fight.

Becca Mae lies pinned under Miss Singleton's writhing body. "Mickey, help me."

Together, we roll the unconscious woman onto her back.

Win glances up. "Coach needs a doctor."

Wade and the rest of his gang are gone. The cascading lights and pulsating beat of the music fill me with anxiety. Every kid in the gym is gathered around, staring at us.

"We thought the fight was over," one girl says.

"It is." I help Becca Mae to her feet. "Any of y'all seen a dude dressed like a Roman? Got a girl with him?"

A boy points to the lockers on the other side of the gym. "They went that way."

My gut twists into a pretzel.

No, no, no. A sissy-baby like you can't stop him.

I take stock of the situation. Becca Mae is cut and bruised from her fight with Alice. Win flags over another adult, who yells for a first aid kit. Coach lies pale and shivering against a bleacher, dark foam dripping from his lips.

Stupid, stupid, stupid. Better stay out of trouble, or—

Oh, shut up.

Don't tell us to shut up. You're not going to—

You heard me. If I don't do something, who will?

Becca Mae grabs my wrist. "Whatever you're thinking of doing, I'm coming with you."

I brush her hand aside. "Wasn't planning on doing anything."

"Don't lie." Her brown eyes meet mine. "You find Wade and then what? Those boys will hurt you."

"Maybe. Look, I know Alice is horrible."

Becca Mae sighs. "Trailer trash is what she is."

"Whatever. We both hate her, but the way Wade dragged her out, I don't think his intentions are pure."

She frowns. "Trust me, they're not."

The music stops and the house lights flicker on. At the DJ table, Principal Barton barks into a microphone. "Okay everybody, go home. I need you all to vacate the premises."

Amid a chorus of boos and shouts, kids make their way to

the exits.

"I still think I should come with you." Becca Mae trails a fingertip across my cheek.

Pushing through the dwindling throng, Felicia returns. "Hey, Becca? Your dad's outside. He told me to come collect you."

She turns to me. "Promise you won't do anything stupid."

Atonal buzzing fills my head, blaring from the girls' locker room's double-doors.

"You hear that?" I say.

Becca Mae cocks her head like a confused spaniel. "No, I don't." She grasps the front of my shirt with both hands. "Promise?"

"I promise."

"Okay." She kisses me on the cheek, then leaves with the other girls.

I head straight for the locker room, feet pounding the polished floor.

16

The locker room hallway reeks of must and mildew. Grime fills the spaces between the tiles, most of them cracked or warped. Fluorescent lights flicker, casting spidery shadows on the walls. I pass a trophy case decked out with gold cups, multi-colored ribbons, and mottled, discolored medals.

Silence fills the passageway.

Did Wade drag Alice through here? I see no stray bits from her costume or skid marks on the tile from a broken stiletto. Angry as she was, Alice would've put up a fight, especially considering Wade pulled her off the dance floor against her will. Did he knock her out before he dragged her away?

Treading cautiously, I press forward. Something shiny and yellow flickers in the darkness at the far end of the hall. Jeez, is that an eye?

From the shadows a creature stirs. Big as a cat, it crawls along on a mess of squirming tentacles, making a sound like a wet mop. A second creature emerges, slime dripping from a double-fanged mouth. They are joined by a third and a fourth. Screeching floods the corridor, accompanied by a foul whiff of bait.

I bite my lip. These are the same things that attacked us at the barn. Only this time, there's no Katie Sue to hide behind.

Crap.

Whirling around, I scan the corridor for a weapon, but nothing stands out, save a bag filled with volleyballs sitting in a laundry basket.

Like that's going to do anything.

The quartet of monsters lurch toward me. One breaks off and scales the wall. Next thing I know, the thing is coming at me on the ceiling.

Man, they can climb stuff, too? "Uh, hey, y'all." I reach for the volleyball bag. "Let's not have any trouble."

They're on me before I can formulate a plan. One beast leaps into the air. I swat it with the bag, and the creature careens against the wall.

A second scurries into view, pointed fangs flashing. I sidestep and bring the bag down on its head. The creature slams into a display case, shattering the glass. A heavy bronze trophy slips from its shelf and brains the thing, splattering it on the floor.

Slime drips on my shoulder from directly overhead. With a screech, a monster drops onto my chest, its teeth snagging on my shirt.

"Man, get off me!" I throw a punch, but the creature holds on. A tentacle wraps around my ankle. I kick it free, then grab the chest-hugger with both hands.

"I told you, get off!" I turn and smash the beast against the wall, turning its body to pulp on the brick. Hot slime splatters me.

Two down. The creature I kicked free reattaches itself to my leg, its big yellow eye bright as the headlight of an oncoming train. Slipping on something wet, I fall backward. The beast climbs on my chest. A thick tentacle wraps itself around my neck.

It's happening. I'm really going to die this time.

Something shiny catches my eye, a glass shard from the trophy case. I grab the fragment and stab the beast through the eye. The monster slips from my chest, its screech reverberating against the walls. Pain shoots through my hand. I let the shard go. Blood drips from a red line on my palm.

I hop to my feet and come face-to-face with the last monster. Its tentacles slap the floor and the beast hisses, exposing razor-sharp teeth.

"You're going to have to do better than that, you—"

A sound like a swarm of bees fills the corridor. Dozens of tiny yellow orbs with mouths full of white fangs swarm my way. This bunch is smaller physically, but then *piranha* are small too. Chirping and chattering, these beasts squirm toward me along the floor, so fast and many I can't count them all.

Yeah, there's no way I win this fight.

Getting to my feet, I dropkick the blinded creature, and run for the gym doors. Slime from above drips on my shoulders and cheeks. Are there more on the ceiling? I reach the exit but it's blocked by a horde of the little creatures. One about the size of a rat manages to sink its teeth into my arm.

"Crap!" I shake it free and whirl around to dash down the hallway. Maybe they haven't gotten into the girls' locker room yet. If I can get in there and lock the doors, maybe I'll have time to find a window to escape through.

The floor is slippery from the things I've already killed. The door is propped open by a wooden wedge. I kick the wedge loose and slam the door shut. On the other side the little monsters squeal like stuck pigs. It's so loud, I can't even think straight.

I survey my surroundings. Nothing but rows of metal lockers and hardwood benches beneath flickering lights. My arm stings from where the creature bit me. Inspecting it, the bite marks look superficial but hurt like hell. Crap, but that's a relief.

The wooden door begins to splinter. Well, that's great. How long before those things get in here? I stumble past lockers, the burning stench growing more intense with each passing step. Three rows down, I discover the showers.

A round hole about three-foot-wide has been cut through the titled floor. Its golden edges crackle with electricity. A column of orange smoke billows from the breach, stinking like a chemical fire. Obviously, this wasn't part of the blueprints for the ladies' lockers. But what is it, really?

A snap echoes from the other side of the room, followed by a chorus of screeches.

They're in, and I'm out of time. With no means of escape. Or is there?

Peering into the hole, I spy a black oval filled with tiny pinpricks of light. In the center, an orange sphere glows like an amber jewel.

Is that supposed to be outer space in there? What happens if I jump in?

The sound of tentacles squeaking on the floor grows closer. Out of the corner of my eye, I catch sight of a handful of the nasty buggers crawling past the lockers.

This is it, then. Swallowing hard, I dive in.

Immediately, I'm enveloped in sticky gelatin that fills my mouth and nose. Sparks dance in front of my eyes, and it gets hard to breathe. I try not to swallow the gunk but some slips down my throat. Suddenly, my lungs fill with air. What is this stuff? Jellied oxygen?

I fall for what seems like a thousand, thousand years.

Then my ears pop and the jelly covering my body dissolves into soapy bubbles. Hot air whips against my face, like somebody is blasting me with a giant blow dryer.

The girls' showers are long gone, replaced by murky clouds drifting through an orange sky.

Crap, I'm airborne, and dropping like a rock. Which is bad because I've got no plane or parachute. I accelerate, the wind buffeting me as if I'm tumbling in a clothes dryer. I catch sight of the blackened earth below. The wind howls in my ears, the ground rushing to meet me. I make out clumps of red treetops and churning, smoking bogs.

Is that a jungle down there?

As I reach terminal velocity, I catch sight of a blue-green marble set against the amber sky. Is that Earth? Where am I? I'm so confused.

Just before hitting the ground, I spot a stepped pyramid towering above a verdant jungle, stretching as far as the eye can see. A sound like an air-raid siren echoes in my ears, followed by a burst of light.

Did I just die?

Darkness engulfs me.

17

A small, many-legged thing crawls across my chest, rousing me from delirium. I frantically brush the thing away.

Jumping to my feet, I size up my surroundings. Thick-rooted trees topped by canopies of red leaves tower above me. A stink of sulfur mixed with swamp grass spoils the air. The sky above is bright orange. Dark clouds drift overhead, shot through with amber bolts of lightning. What happened to the gym? Come to think of it, this doesn't look like Earth.

Something loud hums to my left. A two-headed fly the size of a sparrow lands on my forearm. It scampers on dozens of hairy legs, heading toward my shoulder.

"Jeez!" I swat at the thing, sending it buzzing off into humid air.

Even after everything I've seen lately, that was *too* weird. I take stock of the strange plant life and oppressive-looking orange sky.

It's official—I've got to be on an actual alien planet.

The opening to a seashell-covered path cuts through the jungle just ahead. Beside the trail, broken tree stumps jut from the ashen soil. The pyramid I spotted from the air looms above the tree line, casting a shadow over the trail. Nagging questions tug at my brain. How did I get here? How do I get home? And if this *is* an alien world, shouldn't there be some aliens around? What do I do if they're hostile?

The skyline, clouds, and terraced temple are just like the ones in my dreams since touching the artichoke. The only thing missing is my tormentor in the black robe.

I can't figure that guy out. A few days ago, he saved me from Wade and Freddie. Last night, or at least my last night on Earth, he stalked me at the football game. Is the dude an alien? Is this his home turf? If so, he must've brought me here. But why?

Something awful screeches overhead. I don't know what it is, but I'd rather have a weapon to deal with it. Searching the ground, I find a sturdy branch and hoist it in both hands.

A clatter of boots crunch on gravel nearby. I duck behind a thick tree stump, clutching my improvised club. A tonal clicking echoes in the air, and a column of gangly creatures appear. Each is about six feet tall and armored in brass chest plates, helmets, and armguards. Their faces are covered by metal masks decorated with insect-like bulbous eyes and angular snouts.

Wait. Are those people dressed in bug outfits, or bugs dressed as people? Either way, I'm pretty sure I'm about to meet actual spacemen. If I wasn't so scared, this would be really cool. But I'm seriously scared right now.

The column draws closer. They carry spears tipped with a greenish metal. The last two drag along a skinny girl in a tattered red robe. Her head is shaved and bruises cover her face and arms. Whoever gave her the buzzcut did a terrible job. Stray locks of dark hair stick out in patches behind her ears and scalp.

Oh, crap. They got Alice Walsh.

As the column draws even with my hiding place, Alice cries, "Where are y'all taking me?"

None of them respond. Instead, they plod forward in silence, the sound of their trudging feet muffling her cries.

I hate Alice, but she doesn't deserve whatever they're about to do to her. I grip the club tightly. No way I'll take them all down, but what if I ambush them and knock a few off the trail? Maybe Alice can break free, and we can both run for it.

Something cold clamps onto my arm. I whirl around and stand face to face with a bug-faced soldier. Covered in brass armor, the creature hisses behind its facemask, spear at the ready.

Stepping back, I ram the club into the thing's face, dislodging the mask. The exposed creature glares at me through glitter-ball eyes set above two long nose-slits and razor-sharp mandibles clicking madly.

"Wow, you're super-ugly," I say, jamming the weapon into the soldier's knee.

Hissing, the creature brings the spear up. I clip the thing's elbow, making it drop its weapon. The soldier falls, frantically clutching at its mask.

Do they need those visors to breathe?

I swing the club and bring it down hard on the creature's head. With a hiss, the beast nearly slashes my thigh with a three-taloned hand.

"Aw, no you don't." I sidestep and smack the creature in the face. The alien staggers, then recovers, knocking my club away. The bug-faced creature wraps his long arms around my midsection and drives me backward to the lip of a ravine. We grapple on the edge before we lose our footing and plunge over the side.

Me and the alien trade punches the whole way down. Brambles tear my cheeks, shirt, and pants. I block most of the shots, but the creature connects with a sharp jab, breaking my nose. We land hard, rolling within inches of a bubbling tar pit. Thrusting with both legs against the soldier's chest, I spring free.

Slowly, the alien staggers to its feet, shaking its head. Is it stunned? If so, this might be my only shot to take it down. With both hands, I seize a big stone and hoist it above my head. Before I can launch the rock, the soldier draws a knife and rushes me.

Bubbles burst in the pool next to us. Oil splashes and a giant tentacle rears out of the muck. Mandibles clicking, the soldier turns and tries to run. But the tentacle lashes itself around the creature's ankle and drags it into the boiling tar. A glut of steam bursts from the pool's surface, then both are gone.

I drop the rock and slump to the ground. My nose throbs with pain, and tears cloud my vision. Things could be worse. I could've been eaten by whatever's on the other end of that tentacle.

Another bubble breaks the surface. What if the bog-monster's still hungry? Loud noises echo from somewhere at the top of the ravine. I make out the sounds of snapping branches and rattling metal, followed by a series of guttural clicks.

This isn't good. They're probably searching for their buddy.

It's time to leave. I pick up the knife and begin climbing the ravine. Back on the trail, I make out a smoke plume rising from the top of the pyramid. Is that a signal? If so, then what are the aliens signaling for? The start of a ritual? A sacrifice? What if the aliens are into *human* sacrifice? I shudder and try not to think about Alice's shaved head and torn robe. Wade and his buddy with the freaky tongue-launcher must have kidnapped the girl to bring her to Planet X and offer her up to their shark-god. And maybe the dude in the black robe is the high priest who does the sacrificing.

I hear the sound of heavy boots on gravel. They're coming back this way. I dart into a grove of black trees with quaking red leaves. My feet itch and burn, like a bad case of poison ivy. Something must have oozed into my shoes during the fight, but there's no time to stop.

Branches snap in the dank underbrush. The soldiers must be searching off the trail, too. I duck behind a tree. Two creatures trot into view. Treading cautiously, the aliens follow my trampled path.

Blood pounds in my temples. I grip the knife and ready to defend myself. If they come for me, I'm going down swinging.

A sound like a whale's cry bellows in the distance. The soldiers pause, turn in the direction of the call, then dash up the trail.

I slump to one knee, letting out one deep sigh. Sweat covers my body, sticking to my clothes. Jeez, but that was close.

The horn blasts again.

Alice is running out of time.

Something glints in the underbrush. It's the spear dropped by the bug-soldier I fought. In my hands, the weapon feels heavier than a lead pipe. Its tip reflects the blood-orange sky. There's a thumb-sized depression above its rawhide grip. Wonder what that's for?

So, I have two weapons, and the will to fight. Guess that'll have to do if I'm going to rescue Alice.

18

The last year she was alive, Mom did charity work for the Catholic Archdiocese, dropping off food parcels of powdered milk and mac and cheese for needy families. On one such trip, I joined her. I had just turned thirteen and thought the world should serve me chocolate fudge sundaes every day for the rest of my life.

We drove into this trailer village east of town and parked behind a single-wide. Mom just sat there frowning, hands gripped tightly on the steering wheel.

"What's the matter?" I asked.

A sigh escaped her lips. "This is Gertie Walsh's place."

"Who?"

"A girl I knew from high school." Mom got out of the wagon, then pulled some groceries from the back seat. "Here, you can help."

The outside of the trailer was speckled with dust and grime. A metal trash can stood nearby, filled to the brim with crumpled take-out boxes and empty two liter bottles. We stumbled up the stairs to the small porch. She rang the bell.

Alice Walsh answered, which freaked me out a little because I had no idea she lived there. Her hair was in curlers, no make-up on her face.

"Hey, we're here with your groceries," Mom said with a big smile, holding the bag in front of her.

Alice stared directly into my eyes, hers wide as quarters, blank and waxy. I swallowed a lump in my throat. We were already on the outs by that point, and the whole situation was totally awkward.

She pointed at me. "What do you want?"

"Oh, don't mind him," Mom said. "Where's your mother?"

Alice's face contorted into a mask of fury. "I don't want him knowing where I live."

"I'm sorry, but what does my son have to do with—"

"We don't need nothing from y'all." She slammed the door in Mom's face.

Mom shrugged. "Maybe I should call ahead next time."

The memory of that day curdles in my brain the whole walk to the pyramid. I flip it over and over like a quarter in my head, and finally clicks in my brain.

Alice didn't hate me because I ate Pop-Tarts or wouldn't let her copy off my paper. She hated me because she and her mom were dirt poor and lived on the wrong side of the tracks. And no matter how much she primped up her hair or threw paper airplanes at my head, she could never be bigger or better than me, because I would always know who she really was and what she really came from. But none of that will stop me from saving her life, if I can.

Up ahead, I hear boots crunching on shells. Ducking behind bushes, I keep an eye out for Alice and the armored creatures. As if on cue, they emerge around the next bend. She stumbles along with her captors, her stubbled head shining under the orange glow of the sky. Alice moans, her wailing reverberating beneath the murky canopy.

Threading my way through the underbrush, I follow them as close as I dare.

Drummers pound their skins at the top of the pyramid, steady rhythm echoing over the jungle. The massive structure towers at least fifty feet, four terraced sides climbing into the orange sky, the great stone steps wedged together at odd angles. Strange glyphs are cut into the rock, eroded with time and hard to see. Not that I would know what they meant if I could read them.

From my hiding place at the jungle's edge, I make out brass-clad soldiers standing at attention on the stairs. Beside them tower statues with grotesque faces carved like insects, rodents, or long-fanged fish. One of the tallest and most imposing is a tentacled, one-eyed shark.

Alice's captors deposit her on a thick mat at the base of the pyramid. Standing on the bottom step is a blond dude dressed in a red robe splotched with black circles like leopard's spots.

Wade Ruthven. I figured he'd be here.

Wade pulls Alice to her feet. Without warning, she snarls and lashes out with her nails, raking his face bloody. Laughing, he shoves her into the arms of one of the bug-soldiers. I watch as the wound closes over, the skin weaving itself whole.

Oh, crap. The dude's not human. At least, not anymore.

"What are y'all going to do to me, Wade?" Alice strains against the creature's grip. "This ain't what you promised!"

His chuckle sounds like rattling bones. "But it is, though. This is what you wanted, right? To be Queen Bee. To have power." He sweeps a hand toward the top of the pyramid. "Right up there, he's going to make you one of us, give you all the power you ever wanted."

"Wade, you tell your bug-zapper friends to let me go. I mean it!"

"Aw, honey-baby." He takes her chin between his thumb and index finger. "You'll thank me for this later."

He nods, and soldiers appear. They drag her screaming up the steps. Halfway up, Alice goes limp, dragging her feet in a vain attempt to slow the progress.

My stomach boils over.

Quick, go back, go back. No way you can save her now.

Shut up. I fell out of the sky. No way home but straight through these guys.

Stupid, stupid, stupid. Going to get us all killed for that no-account piece of garbage who hates us anyway.

I don't have time for this.

Lifting the spear, I leave the tree cover and dash across the clearing. A couple of bug-soldiers stand guard at the base of the pyramid.

I rush them, waving the spear. "Hey! Hey, you!"

They crouch, weapons at the ready. Both stand taller than the one I fought in the ravine. And there, I had help from a giant tentacle. This doesn't look good. Maybe I'm going to die this time.

By accident, I press the notch on the spear's shank. A blinding flash of energy bursts from the tip. One of the bug-soldiers falls backward, smoke pouring from a gaping black hole in its chest plate. The alien wobbles in its tracks, then crumples to the ground.

Well, what do you know? This thing's a blaster.

The second creature raises its weapon, but I fire first. In a flash, the soldier joins its pal in the dirt.

There's no time to lose. I mount the terraced steps two at a time, adrenaline propelling me upward.

A loud thunderclap explodes nearby. The stair just below me erupts in a ball of fire and collapses into rubble. Glancing back, I make out dozens of bug soldiers below taking aim with their blasters. A stone riser explodes to my left. I peel off one random shot in their direction, then mount the stairs. Legs pumping, I cover the remaining distance to the platform. The edge extends outward like the eaves of a roof. I toss the blaster over the lip, grab the rough stone with both hands, and hoist myself over.

The platform is maybe fifty yards square. Two tents squat in its center, one green, the other purple. Wade stands with his arms crossed, an idiot grin on his face. Hooded figures in dark green robes surround him. The whole crew rings Alice, who's writhing atop an altar, her wrists and ankles manacled to the rough-hewn stone.

Over her looms the man from my nightmares, his gaunt frame draped in a loose, black cloak accented by a green sash that glints like snakeskin.

Gazing up, he smiles at me. "Mr. Finley. How good of you to join us."

Alice turns her head. "Pop-Tart? You got to get me out of here!"

I pick up the spear and level it at the guy in black. "How do you know my name?"

He chuckles. "A master knows his sacrificial lamb."

Sacrificial lamb? Where have I heard that before? "You don't know a thing about me."

"Oh, but I do." The man in the black robe extends his arms like a priest giving a benediction. "Your body bears the stink of transformation. Not enough to *change* you fully, as some have," he gestures toward Wade, "but enough to mark you as one who serves that which would oppose me."

"Dude, I have no idea what you're talking about."

"You don't, and it doesn't matter." He chuckles. "Because you won't live long enough to see an end of things." The priest pulls his robe aside, revealing a black, serrated knife in his sash. "My enemy would use you as an errand boy. But me?" He snaps his fingers. "You're a lamb I slaughter."

The green-robed wraiths close in, whispering a guttural chant. I thumb the button on the blaster. "Just you try it." Wow, that didn't sound too threatening.

Wade laughs at my obvious discomfort. "Oh, you're in for it now, Pop-Tart."

Alice strains against her bonds. "Mickey, do something!" She wails, a tear running down her cheek. "Please."

"Don't worry Alice." I struggle to swallow the lump in my throat. "I'll get us out of this."

The priest smiles. "You're brave, I'll grant you that. But bravery won't save you."

I hear the sound of talons on stone from somewhere below me. It won't be long before the soldiers clear the lip of the platform.

My heart leaps. Do I rush these guys? Blast my way to Alice? If I do free her, where will we go?

The man reaches underneath his cloak. "There's nothing you can do, Mr. Finley." From its folds, he draws a squirming green beast the size of a cat. Tentacles lashing, the creature glares at me through a one slit-pupiled eye, its saw-teeth snapping within its long-nosed snout.

"No light to protect you from darkness." He holds the flailing monster over Alice's chest. "I will show you."

"No!" I fire the blaster. The squirming beast melts into slime on the priest's hands. With a howl, he drops the molten carcass and gestures toward the wraiths. "Kill him."

The hooded guys rush forward. I blast one and dart between two others.

Wade appears, blocking my path. "Forget it." He raises a hand. "There's nowhere to go." Bones snap in his forearm, and something slithers beneath the skin. He clenches his fingers, and they fuse into knobby spikes.

"Jeez." I level the blaster. "What are you, Wade? A monster like them?"

"Worse." Steam rises where the flesh shreds along his expanding arm. "I'm the *king* of monsters."

Laughing, Wade reveals a chitinous limb, the thickness of a man's thigh. In place of a hand, the new limb terminates into lethal-looking crab's pincers.

Fear arcs like electricity up my spine. "That...that's not real."

"I'm going to gut you, boy." Wade snarls, snaps his claws like pruning shears. "Gut you, and then I'm going to—"

Thunder breaks across the sky. Bolts of purple lightning rip through the clouds, the last touching down about a mile away, setting fire to the jungle.

Tremors roll across the landscape, shaking the platform beneath our feet. A fiery brazier tips over and collapses near the tents, setting them ablaze. One of the priest's robes catch fire, and like kindling the poor beast is consumed under a curtain of flame.

Pandemonium breaks out, the air filling with shrieks and hisses. Smoke from the tent fires blankets the platform. Stumbling through the haze, Wade makes a lunge for me but trips over the remains of the incinerated priest. Seeing an opening, I deliver a blow to the bully's head with the butt end of the blaster.

"No!" Wade swipes at me with his claw and nearly severs my foot.

Another lightning bolt strikes the platform, shaking it violently. Bug-soldiers and priests scatter like bowling pins. One alien tries to run me through with its spear. Dodging, I blast the monster. It falls on Wade, pinning him.

"Where you going?" He bucks under the dead creature's

weight but can't budge the heavily-armored carcass. "I'm not done with you."

I shrug. "Yeah, you are."

"This isn't over, Pop-Tart. You hear me?"

"Whatever, dude." I leave him thrashing and cursing. Smoke billows everywhere, concealing the altar where Alice remains shackled. I catch a glimpse of a bare leg through the fumes. Reaching the slab, I smash her manacles with the blunt end of the blaster and extend a hand.

Alice rises from the barren rock and wraps her arms round my neck. "Mickey?"

"Yeah?"

"Watch out."

Her eyes go wide, and a spear tip bursts through her chest. Behind her stands a priest, holding the weapon's shaft in both hands.

"Alice!" I blast the alien, then drag her from the altar. Alice's flesh is growing cold, her eyes clouding over.

Oh no. No, no, no.

Please don't die on me.

Alice lifts her head. "Mickey?"

I grab her arm. "Come on, we can still make it."

From out of nowhere, a dark purple cloud descends upon the pyramid. Milky white vines burst from the cloud and rake the pyramid, sweeping aliens aside like dead leaves.

In my head, a voice whispers. Only, it's not one of the ones who usually torments me. Instead, it's the soft, reassuring tones of a woman.

"Let's get you home, now," Katie Sue says.

A large purple tendril descends from the cloud, it looks like the business end of a tulip, and about the size of a station wagon. The huge bulb unfolds like a flower, revealing a leafy pallet a good ten feet wide.

Alice pulls away from me and falls, slumping against the altar, a trickle of blood running down her chin. "Better get going. Don't worry about me."

I grab her elbow. "No, I can get you out of here."

From out of the smoke, the guy in the black robe emerges. Pulling the sash from around his waist, he snaps it like a whip. Instantly, it goes rigid and turns into a blaster with a shark's head tip.

"Oh, no you don't." He levels the weapon at us. "Leave the girl. She's already mine."

"It's okay." Alice smiles at me. "You go on now."

I can't let this happen. "Alice—"

"I...I'm going to be alright." Crying, she shakes her head.

The man fires. Alice is shrouded in a corona of green light. Something crawls out of the wound in her chest, sprouting snaky tentacles.

"No!" I lunge, but a wide crack opens in the stone between us.

Lightning flashes above my head. Alice writhes as squirming limbs coil around her.

The dude in black smiles and raises his hands. "Blessed be the Rising."

With a final awful thrash, the tentacles envelop her.

Blood pumps slow as molasses in my veins. Alice, dead? I can't believe it.

Smirking, the man in the black robe aims his weapon at me. An iridescent halo swirls at its tip.

"Mickey," Katie Sue's voice echoes in my ear. "It's time to go."

I fire a shot at Alice's killer, shattering the stone at his feet. Then I turn and run toward the pallet. Stepping onto the spongy expanse, I close my eyes, tears streaming. I'm lifted up before the dude in the robe gets off another shot. Leafy

Craig E. Higgins

petals big as billboards enfold and protect me. Another crack of thunder erupts, echoing somewhere beyond the horizon. Numbness creeps into my limbs, the blaster heavy in my hands.

    I drift into blackness, deeper and darker than the bottom of the Gulf.

19

I awake in a hospital bed with an IV drip in my arm and a heavy brain fog, like somebody stuffed a wad of cotton balls between my ears. My muscles ache, and my throat is scratchy. A dull pain throbs in my splinted nose.

Everything hurts, so I know this is not a dream. But how'd I get back to Earth?

Aunt Margene sits next to me, her smile blissful and bright as the morning sun. "Mickey, thank the Lord."

Uncle John stands over her, beaming. "We thought we lost you, boy."

I gaze into his block-jawed face. There's not a mark to indicate his recent illness. No blemishes or swelling, or even the puffed-out eyelid. The last I remember, he was on death's door, barely able to breathe. But now? He's fine.

What's going on here?

A woman wearing a white coat ambles in and checks my chart. "Well, well," she says. "Welcome back to the land of the living, Mickey. I'm Doctor Carmelo."

I try to raise my arm, but the IV line impedes my movement. "Where am I?"

"Waveland General." She puts a cool hand on my forehead.

"You're still burning up. We'll keep you in observation for at least another day. After that, you can go home."

I shake my head to clear the cobwebs. "How did I get here?"

Doctor Carmelo taps a pen to her chin. "Someone dropped you off at the ER early this morning."

"Who?"

The woman shrugs. "No idea. I wasn't here. But the nurse on duty said the person she spoke with claimed you were found on the beach."

My mysterious benefactor didn't leave a name? "What day is it?"

"Sunday," the doctor says.

Uncle John frowns. "You were gone two days."

"Where were you, Mick?" Aunt Margene says, grasping my wrist. "Who did this to you?"

Trust me, you don't even want to know. "Um, well…I'm not sure," I say. "I remember being at the dance. There was this fight between two girls, and then things kind of…escalated."

"That's what your principal told us." Uncle John smiles. Jeez, when did his eye teeth get so sharp? "I see somebody broke your nose" he says. "You get a few good licks in?"

Is that all he cares about—that I put up a fight? "Yeah, Uncle John," I lie. "I stood up for myself, just like you always tell me to."

He claps his hands together like he's killing a fly. "You see?" Uncle John growls, punching my arm and almost knocking the needle out of my vein. "I told you wrestling would do you some good."

"But how did you end up on the beach?" Aunt Margene rummages through her purse and produces a handkerchief. "And how did you get knocked out?" She uses the rag to dab sweat from my brow.

"I don't know. I think what happened was…I mean…gee, I

guess I tripped over something in the gym. And, like, I hit my head? Or, maybe somebody hit me, I'm not sure. But I really don't know how I ended up outside. I'm sorry, but I just don't remember."

"That's okay." She pockets the handkerchief. "You got in some trouble, but now you're okay. This is a time to be grateful." Aunt Margene turns to Uncle John. "Don't you think so, John?"

"Yep." He nods. "He made it through Ghostland."

I gaze up at him, confused. "Ghostland?"

"Yeah." Uncle John stares out the window. "Ghostland was the jungle in 'Nam."

A couple seconds pass until what he's talking about clicks in my brain. "Oh yeah. Dad told me about that place. He said you could get lost in there and become one of the ghosts."

"And he was right." Uncle John grunts. "Some guys did go in there and never came back. But you?" He turns, a smile spreading across his face. "You beat 'em, right? You beat the ghosts." The big guy socks me on the shoulder, jostling my bones. "You're tougher than you look, Mick. But Ghostland's tougher. You know who helped you?"

Gee, I don't know, Uncle John. Your imaginary sky-friend? "You mean Jesus, right?"

Uncle John snaps his fingers. "That's right."

The door opens and Becca Mae enters the room.

"Mickey?" she says.

Oh, wow. She's here. All the pain, exhaustion, and bad things wash away like mud in a rainstorm.

"Yeah, it's me," I open my arms wide, the IV needle forgotten.

Becca Mae throws herself onto my chest, the butterscotch scent of her hair fills my nostrils. Man, but she smells so good. Her body heat and the softness of her touch send shivers down my spine.

"I was so worried about you." Tears stream down her cheeks, salty where they fall on my lips.

I take her hand in mine, and it feels so good. "I'm okay. Really, I am."

"Did Wade and them do this?" She points to my nose splint.

Behind her, a man clears his throat. "Ahem. Becca?"

I gaze up, and there's Pastor Paul. He looks tired, and there's a day's growth of stubble on his chin.

Becca Mae straightens. "Sorry, Daddy."

He pulls up a chair. "It's alright." The pastor sits down. "Mickey, Becca kept watch on you all yesterday."

She nods. "I would've stayed all night too, if he'd let me."

"Your uncle and me did the graveyard shift." Aunt Margene pulls a Bible from her purse. "You know what, Pastor Paul? Do you think we should take this time to, you know, show our thanks to the Lord?"

Oh, brother. "I mean, I appreciate y'all staying up with me," I say, "but that's really not necessary."

There's a knock on the door. Uncle John opens it, says something to the person on the other side, then turns to me. "Mick, there's a policeman wants to talk to you."

"About what?"

Becca Mae casts her gaze toward the floor. "Alice Walsh is missing."

How can I explain to anybody here what happened to Alice? "Wow. I'm sorry to hear that."

Pastor Paul pours a cup of water from a nearby jug. "They're getting statements from everybody who saw Alice that night." He hands me the cup.

I take a sip. "Okay, I'll talk to him. But like I said, I don't remember much."

Becca Mae leans over and whispers in my ear. "I didn't tell

them you went looking for her."

"So, you didn't see Alice at all?" the minister says, frowning.

"Oh, I saw her," I say. "She was at the game, and then there was that fight she had with Becca Mae. But I'm not sure what happened after Wade took her."

Pastor Paul cocks an eyebrow. "Wade was with this girl?"

Becca Mae nudges the minister's elbow. "I told you that, Daddy. She thought *I* was seeing Wade. That's what got her upset."

"Well, I'll have a talk with him," he says, straightening his collar, "soon as he turns up again."

"Wait." I set the cup down on a tray. "Wade's missing, too?"

He nods. "S*eems* to be. The police went looking for him to get his statement. But he wasn't in his room at school. Nobody's seen him since the dance."

Of course, they haven't. Wade's been busy trying to kill me. "Wow, that's weird. I hope he's okay."

"I worry about the choices he's making." The minister scratches his head. "He has a great future in front of him, and I don't want him ruining his life over some girl."

Uncle John steps toward the smaller man. "Pastor? Mick still needs to give his statement."

Aunt Margene glares at him. "John, not before a prayer."

Everyone bows their heads in supplication to their imaginary friend in the clouds.

Pastor Paul nods, then closes his eyes. "Dear Lord, we thank you for lifting this young man from the darkness and bringing him back to us."

Five minutes later they leave me to the tender mercies of a sleepy-eyed cop who takes my statement. I try to give him the truth without spilling the beans about the whole alien-adventure thing.

He jots everything down with a ballpoint pen. "So, was this…what was his name…Wade involved?"

"Kind of," I say. "He showed up afterwards."

"So, it was you who broke it up?" The cop smirks. "Between the two girls, I mean."

He doesn't know who stopped the fight? "Well actually it was Coach who did that. Him and the librarian. Principal Barton was there, too."

The officer flips a page on his memo pad. "We got their statements."

"You did? All three of them?" That's totally confusing because Coach was on death's door after Freddie nailed him with a tongue-dart. "Some of them got hurt."

"That's true." He jots something on the pad. "Fortunately, those government guys…you know the ones in the hazmat suits? Come into town a couple days ago?"

"Yeah, I've seen them."

"Well, their van happened to be nearby the hospital and that doctor who was with them helped out." The officer taps his pen against the bed's handrail, "Now, what was his name again?"

The word slips out of my mouth. "Blightman?"

"That's it. Blightman." He smiles. "Guy had a shot of something all ready to go. Fixed your coach right up. The librarian, too."

I mull over what this man is telling me. Coach and Miss Singleton both got darted, and Coach didn't look like he was going to make it. Blightman's vaccine, or whatever's actually in those syringes, healed them in no time. But the doctor and his beekeeper crew just happened to be there to deliver a miracle cure to the people Wade and his buddy hurt? That's just too convenient to be a coincidence.

The cop snaps his fingers in front of my face. "Son, you

okay?"

I shake my head. "Sorry." An idea occurs to me. "Officer? Can I ask you something?"

"Sure."

"Are you *sure* Coach is okay? Was he acting a little weird, either before or after his shot?"

He shrugs. "How should I know? I wasn't there when they let him out of the ER."

"But—"

"Don't worry, kid," the officer chuckles. "Everybody's okay except the two who are missing."

"But he was really bad off. You can ask my friend—"

"Like I said," the officer cuts me off, "everyone else is fine." He pockets the notepad. "Now, what exactly is your relationship to Miss Walsh?"

The officer leaves and hours pass. Just before midnight I sit on the bed, arms wrapped around my knees. Darkness shrouds the room, and silence echoes in my ears.

Dazed and weary, I work out a timeline of everything that's happened in the last two days. Friday night I fell through a hole in space and ended up on an alien planet. Fought some bug-soldiers, the priest, and Wade. Watched Alice die, and then got rescued by a giant magnolia flower with Katie Sue's voice. And this morning, I was found on the beach by some good Samaritan.

In my mind, the questions are a jumble of random jigsaw puzzle pieces. Where *did* I go? Did Katie Sue really help me, or was that just a hallucination? And who brought me to the hospital?

There's a rap at my door. "Mr. Finley?" a woman's voice says. "Are you decent?"

I pull the sheet around my shoulders. "Sure."

A nurse enters and turns on the light. "There's a phone call for you."

"At this hour? Who is it?"

"A Doctor Whistling?"

"Is that the person who checks my chart?"

"No, it's nobody who works at the hospital. She claims to be a friend of yours."

I roll over on my side. "Can you take a message? I want to get some sleep."

"No problem. I'll leave her number on your breakfast tray. You need anything right now?"

I point to my broken nose. "For this to go back to normal."

"Get some rest." She exits, closing the door behind her.

Whistling? It doesn't ring a bell. Could she have meant *Wentwhistle*? I don't want to talk to that nut. I pull the covers over my head, and my eyelids grow heavy.

Before sleep overtakes me, I hope for pleasant dreams or at least oblivion to wash away the pain in my nose and all the other parts of my body.

Instead, my mind fills with images of stepped pyramids, dying girls, giant magnolia leaves, and purple lightning. I recall what the priest said to me.

My enemy would use you as an errand boy.

Errand boy? What did he mean by that?

20

Monday morning, Uncle John picks me up from the hospital. Rain pelts the truck's windshield, wipers slapping a tight rhythm on the glass. "Your aunt will be at the house," he says. "She wasn't up for traveling."

Gazing at him, I still can't get over how quickly Uncle John recovered from being infected. His once-jaundiced complexion is tanned and rugged, eyes steely and fixed on the road. But there are signs something's not right. Uncle John's jaw is clenched, constantly working like he's chewing on a cockroach. A vein pulsing in his bull neck seems to shift from side to side beneath the skin.

Or is this just in my imagination? I'm exhausted, and my nose hurts, and the pain meds the nurse gave me are wearing off. So, maybe I'm in no position to judge. But the man behind the wheel was practically a corpse a few days ago. How did he recover so quickly?

"Can I ask you a question Uncle John?" I say, trying to sound as casual as I can.

He flicks the turn signal on. "Sure thing, sport."

"Last I saw you, you were sick. I mean, like really sick."

"I was." Uncle John guides the truck into the next lane.

"But I'm fine now."

"Yeah, yeah you are. But Friday, Aunt Margene left me a note that y'all were going to the hospital. Same place we just left, I'm guessing."

"Your aunt overreacted." He chuckles and a stench like rotten meat fills the cab. "I was getting better on the way to Waveland General."

That doesn't sound right at all. "Really? You recovered before you got to the hospital?"

"No, that's not right." Uncle John shakes his head. "Actually, I got me a shot from one of those government fellas."

His shirt sleeve is rolled up, and for the first time I note a small circle of raised flesh on his bicep, like a burn mark. "You mean the beekeepers?"

"Beekeepers? That's funny." Uncle John's laugh could frighten a bear. "This is what happened. They was giving out free vaccines, right by that drug store. You know the one I'm talking about?"

How could I forget? "I think so, yeah."

"And we're driving past and your aunt, she's worried I'm not going to make it to the hospital."

"Okay."

"So, and I think the Lord guided her on this, we see these beekeeper fellas and she says, 'John, maybe you need that vaccine.'" Uncle John abruptly cuts off a Ford Pinto and the other driver hammers on his horn. "And we pulled over and I took the jab. She got one too, just to be on the safe side. By the time we got to Waveland General, I was getting better."

He smiles, the vein in his neck squirming like a snake in the grass.

I don't believe any part of his story. "So, she just *guessed* you needed that shot, and y'all stopped and got one?"

"That's right." Uncle John's knuckles whiten as he makes a

hard right at an intersection, nearly clipping a cyclist. "Fixed me right up."

"But—"

"Mick—" Uncle John grabs my wrist. "—you're always asking questions you got no need in asking." His grip is like iron, and I wince. The truck plows through a puddle and water cascades against the passenger side window. "Always looking for the what-ifs. Sometimes, there are no what-ifs."

"No?"

"No," he says, giving his head a violent shake. "Sometimes, Mick, the Lord looks out for His own. There's a plan, and He ain't going to lead us like no lambs to the slaughter."

Lambs to the slaughter? "Okay." I nod. "I guess that makes sense." I pull my arm free. The outline of Uncle John's fingers are imprinted on my skin.

"Sure it does." Uncle John chuckles, swerving to avoid something the size of a cat skittering across the street. "He'll look out for you too, you know. You just have to believe."

There's no getting answers from this man. And I don't want him grabbing me again. "Well." I lean back in my seat. "I'm glad."

"Glad about what?"

"Glad you licked it."

"Sure did." He runs a red light, nearly flattening a pedestrian scrambling onto the sidewalk.

The guy stands, soaked through, shaking his fist at us. "You know you almost hit that dude?" I say.

He ignores my question. "Say, Mick. You want to come with me to the VFW hall tomorrow?"

The windshield wipers whoosh through the rain like a grain thresher. I can't answer him because he's driving like a crazy person, and I'm shutting down so as not to think about why he's doing this. What he said earlier keeps rolling around in my brain... *Lambs to the slaughter.* What do you get when you lead lambs to the slaughter?

Slaughtered lambs.

"Mick? Did you hear me?"

"Sorry." I sit up. "Still getting over these meds."

Uncle John grunts and gives me a cross stare. "I asked if you wanted to come to the VFW hall."

"Maybe." I shrug. "What's happening there?"

"Tomorrow's the election. Reagan's going all the way."

"That's nice."

"Want to be there to help me cheer him on?"

About as much as I'd willingly submit to a root canal. "Um, I don't know. If I'm feeling better, I guess."

"Oh, right. Then, if you're up to it." He hums the tune to a hot-dog jingle and drives us the rest of the way home.

Rain falls in buckets now, obscuring the road ahead.

After dropping me off, Uncle John kisses Aunt Margene on the cheek, then dashes back to the truck. I hear a door slam, and the sound of the growling engine fades into the distance.

Aunt Margene sighs. "Oh well." Dressed in pajamas and a bathrobe, she plops on the couch. Her eyes are glassy and purple veins bulge under her cheeks.

I point to Uncle John's sweat stains on the cushions. "Don't you want to put a sheet over that?"

"That's alright, Mickey. We'll get it later." She smiles.

A plum-colored droplet falls from her nostril. I thought Uncle John said she took the shot. How come she's showing symptoms?

"Aunt Margene? You got something on your nose."

"Oh." She takes a tissue and dabs the weird blood from her upper lip. "You're right."

Grabbing a chair across from her, I try to ignore the

blaring TV. On the screen, the Skipper, Gilligan, and the Professor are drooling over the red-head Ginger, gyrating in a grass skirt.

"There's a bunch of good programs on." She presses one of the remote's three buttons with a stubby finger. "What do you want to watch?"

"Not Gilligan."

"Oh, I *love* Gilligan." She stares at the TV, then breaks into a cackle on cue from the laugh track. "Isn't this funny?"

"Sure," I lie. "Think I'll head to bed for a bit."

"What am I thinking?" Aunt Margene sits up, the light returning to her eyes. "Oh, how awful of me. You must be exhausted."

I touch the splint on my nose. "This hurts, too."

"You need something to eat?" She rises from the sofa. "Maybe some aspirin?"

"I've got my meds. And maybe I'll eat later, thanks."

Aunt Margene's eyes frost over again. She sits and turns to the TV, changing the channel to some western set in a small town. Beside a covered wagon, a woman in a hoop skirt and oversized bonnet gazes longingly at the chiseled face of a man in a cowboy hat.

"You know what I love about old movies?" she says. "The really old-timey ones?"

I stop just short of the hallway. "What?"

"They're so romantic."

"Sure."

"But a boy your age wouldn't understand such things."

"Maybe not." I stumble to my room, then close the door. Falling into bed, I unfold the note that's been in my pocket. The nurse did get the name wrong.

Mister Finley,

Craig E. Higgins

> *I was the one who found you on the beach and brought you to the hospital. Vitally important we meet.*
>
> *Will be calling on you soon,*
>
> *Wentwhistle*

The woman is persistent, I'll give her that. But how did she know where to find me? How did I even end up *on* the beach?

Down the hall, the phone rings, and rings.

Aunt Margene's voice echoes through the walls. "Mickey? It's for you."

I meet her halfway. She hands me the receiver, then shuffles back to the living room.

"This is Mickey," I say.

"Mr. Finley," Wentwhistle says, "how goes your recovery?"

"Well, I just got home like a half-hour ago, so that's hard to say."

"Is this a bad time?"

Like you really care about that. "I guess not. What do you want?"

"You got my note? It's vitally important—"

"That we meet. I get it." My stomach growls and I wish I had a cheeseburger. "Look, doc. I really appreciate you getting me to the hospital."

"Think nothing of it."

"But, like I just went through a really bad time, you know? The stuff I've seen, you wouldn't believe—"

"Believe what? About the energy spear I found next to you?"

"How did you know about that?"

"Tested it." She chuckles. "Thing packs quite a wallop, more than the relics I've found. Is it new?"

She's found relics like my blaster? "You could say that."

"Where'd you get it?"

"I don't think I can tell you over the phone."

"Understandable. You going to school in the morning?"

"I doubt it."

"So, I'll come pick you up. Say, around noon?"

"No, I'm all beat up, remember?"

"Well, when can you get un-beat up?"

This woman is really cheesing me out. "Look, can you just call me back tomorrow? I'm on meds and can barely think right now."

"But we don't have much time. By this point, surely, you're aware of the gravity of the situation."

More than you, I'll bet. "Jeez, lady. I don't know. After this weekend, I'm not sure I even want to be involved in… whatever this is."

"Mr. Finley, I don't mean to scare you. But with everything that's happening now, you can't walk away."

She's got a point. "Alright. So, what do we do?"

"I'm at a motel in town. So, I'll need you to copy down the number here."

"Okay." Grabbing a pen and notepad, I listen while she recites her digits.

"Got it," I say.

"Good."

While I scribble, I hear Aunt Margene's slippers scuffling at the end of the hallway.

"Mickey?" she says. "Who's that on the phone?"

"Just a kid from English class," I say. "I'm just getting today's homework assignment."

"Oh, that's nice." Aunt Margene drifts back to the living room.

"That your aunt?" Wentwhistle says. "She doesn't sound so good."

"She's not."

"Okay. So, call me tomorrow before eleven. We'll meet and work out a game plan. The BDM being in town complicates things, so we'll have to avoid them."

I scratch my head. "BDM?" Oh yeah, I remember them. The beekeepers.

"Bureau of Disease Management." She whistles into the receiver. "You've seen the hazmat-suit guys, right?"

"I have."

"Call me—" The line goes dead with a click.

Exhausted and bleary-eyed, I head back to my room, but something metal crashes to the floor in the kitchen. I stop in my tracks. Maybe one of those big aluminum cans of potato chip Aunt Margene keeps fell off a shelf.

Silence permeates the house. Then a gentle cooing, like a baby's prattle, vibrates through the drywall.

"Oh, I'm sorry," Aunt Margene says. "Mommy has the clumsy fingers today. Clumsy."

Who's she talking to?

The clicking sounds of a small animal with lots of claws reverberates down the hall. "Yes, that's right. Why don't you come out where mommy can see you?"

Whatever she's talking to yelps, then gasps for air.

Every fiber in my being demands I investigate. But my knees wobble from pain killers, the drugs knotting my tongue like I ingested rat poison. On cue, a wave of nausea grips my gut.

Are you out of your mind? Who knows what's going on in there?

A loud slurping noise echoes from the kitchen, followed

by another round of cooing.

"Oh, that's nice," Aunt Margene says, her voice hoarse. "This will make you grow big and strong."

The hairs on my neck stand on end. What's that thing doing to her? Or, what's she *letting* it do to her? Woozy or not, I need to check it out.

"Aunt Margene?" I say. "We have any Pop-Tarts left?"

A metallic sound like a lid slamming shut makes me wince.

"What? No. Don't come in."

"Why not?"

The sound of claws scratching against metal echoes in the hall. "Just don't, okay?" she says. "I'll get you some Pop-Tarts in the morning."

"But—"

"Mickey, you're sick. Go to bed."

I don't want to leave her in there with that thing. Pressing myself against the wall, I stand listening with a hand on the doorknob. The cooing resumes, and then another round of awful slurping.

Aunt Margene joins in, her sing-song voice rising and falling like the tide. On unsteady feet, I make my way down the hallway, slip back into my room, and close the door behind me. As I lay under the covers, I press my knuckles against my forehead, wishing I was anyplace else on Earth.

They got Aunt Margene too, didn't they? Turned her into a monster like the rest of them.

What do I do now?

21

In the morning, I bolt out of bed, awakened by a roar of sludgy guitars vibrating through my window. Drums pound like an elephant stampede. It takes me a second, but I recollect what's assaulting my ears. Somewhere outside, somebody's playing Black Sabbath.

Before I moved in with my aunt and uncle, an older guy from my old neighborhood invited me to his house. He was kind of a weird dude, but I was in a bad headspace at the time, so I went. We sat on the floor of his room. The guy put some Sabbath on the turn table, and I dug it. Then he smiled and pulled out a baggie full of weed, which seemed a little weird because I don't do drugs. But what really freaked me out was when he walked over and started rubbing my shoulders, like, really slow. Making an excuse about getting some homework done, I pushed him aside and headed out of there quick as I could.

This morning's atonal dirge is definitely Sabbath, and the memory it dredges up makes my stomach turn. But we're several blocks from the next house, and Aunt Margene and

Uncle John only listen to Christian rock.

So, who's playing the devil's music?

I stumble out of bed, the sun's rays blinding me. My body aches and my nose is still a throbbing mess. Rubbing my eyes, I orient myself, and head to the bathroom to brush my teeth. Then I realize that I haven't bathed since I left the hospital. Jumping in the shower, I let the water blast my bare skin like a thousand acupuncture needles. Turning my head, I'm careful to avoid getting my nose splint wet. After toweling off, I pop a painkiller the doctor gave me, then dress in a pair of jeans, a ratty Petra t-shirt, and high-tops.

Refreshed, I step out of the bathroom. The windows still vibrate, Black Sabbath given way to "Highway Star" by Deep Purple, another un-Christian band. That song's mumblety-peg keyboard solo works my nerves. Who would play this stuff early on a weekday morning?

Annoyed, I scan the shell-covered driveway and uncover the source of the disturbance.

The windows of Uncle John's shed vibrate. Someone has covered them on the inside with old rugs. But this development is totally weird because it's Tuesday. Shouldn't he be at work? I'm going to have a talk with him. Only problem is, how do I get to the shed without running into Aunt Margene?

Treading lightly down the hallway, I keep my ears peeled for her or her monstrous new friend. Okay, maybe it's not her friend. More like a pet? Or, maybe it's less a pet and more her kid. The way she talked to it last night, and worse, the cooing and suckling sounds it made. It reminds me of a mother and child, only in a totally creepy way.

And if that's true? I don't even want to think about what that means for a woman Aunt Margene's age—assuming she still *is* a woman.

In the living room, a tune from an old Elvis movie blares

from the TV's tinny speakers.

"Honey, I'm just about to go for you," The King says.

Aunt Margene's cackle reverberates down the hallway.

Oh, great. She's definitely in there. To get to the front door, I have to walk right past her, which totally weirds me out. What if the monster baby's sitting on her lap, ready to eat me? Backtracking, I lose my footing and bump into the wall, nose-first. Pain shoots through my nasal cavities. I steady myself to keep from passing out.

"Mickey, is that you?" Aunt Margene barks from the other room.

I take a deep breath and rest my weight on my knees. "I'm okay. Just going outside."

"Oh, okay. Don't be out too long. You need your rest."

"Sure."

An unsettling thought crosses my mind. I didn't hear my aunt's little bundle of joy cry when she shouted at me. What if the critter's not in her lap? What if it's in the kitchen instead?

Acid percolates in my gut, and the voices shout in my ear.

That thing's going to get you, get you, get you.

I shake my head. No, it's not.

Stupid, stupid, stupid. Yes, it will.

Well then, it'll get you, too. And then I won't have you to deal with anymore.

I got no response from the peanut gallery on that one.

Creeping down the hall, I enter the kitchen, my high-tops squeaking on the linoleum.

A gold-colored chip can the size of a hat box sits on the refrigerator. Emblazoned on the side is a cartoon turtle digging one flipper into a colorful snack bag, the little critter's head haloed with a slogan that reads, *El Tortuga, for a great snack anytime!* Plum-colored slime drips down the sides, leaving a trail dribbling down the front of the refrigerator and coagulating on the floor. I tiptoe past the sink, holding my breath, one eye on the can.

Inside the container, something lurches, nearly toppling it to the floor. A plaintive mewling bellows beneath the lid. The sound of rending metal stops me in my tracks. Three parallel ridges mar the side of the can. I guess the can was too strong for it to bust out the first time, but I'm betting a second attack will shred the metal.

I make a dash for the screen door, yank the handle, and leap from the porch. Running down the driveway, I stare at those rugs against the shed's dirty windows. Questions rattle around in my brain. Uncle John got *better* after getting Blightman's shot. But what if he's gone bad, too? I stand at the door, hand on the knob. Inside, Bob Seger supplants Deep Purple without so much as a record skip.

A knot forms in my stomach and sweat beads on my forehead. My heart flutters in my chest like butterfly wings trying to start a hurricane an ocean away. I want to run back to my room and hide under the covers. Maybe I'll pass out and, when I awake, the last week will be just memories of a bad dream. But there's no going back now. Steeling myself, I turn the door handle and step inside.

And there, next to the Dodge Challenger, Uncle John takes a swig from a Bud longneck.

"Mick." He smiles like an alligator. "Come on in."

"Hey," I cross the threshold and step into the shed. Uncle John is dressed in a yellowed sleeveless t-shirt and stained jeans. There's a pungent stench of motor oil, stale alcohol, and sour sweat hanging in the air. Bob Seger's voice wafts from the Challenger's maxed-out stereo, weaving a tangled tale of night moves Bob made on some dark-haired girl down on Main Street.

I cup my hand to my ear on account of the racket. "Sorry,

I can't hear you."

"You can't?" He sets down the beer, then leans into the driver's side. "Give me a second." The wailing vocals fade to a low murmur. "That better?"

"Yeah."

"So, what brings you out here?" He wipes oil off his hands with a filthy rag.

"Just heard the music, and...you know, I just was wondering why you were out here?"

"Well, it is my shed." He chuckles. "That good enough for you?"

"Shouldn't you be at work?"

"Ah, I took a day off." Uncle John tosses the rag on the floor. "Me and the boys'll be at the hall tonight, and I might just bring this baby." He pats the car's hood. "You know, to show her off."

Sounds thrilling. "Oh."

The toolbox sits on the floor next to the car, I spot the tire iron I used to take down the artichoke. On top sits a glass jar dripping with a dark slime.

Hold on a second. Isn't that the jar I put the alien leaf in? If so, then where did it go?

My thoughts flash to the creature in the chip can. Did Aunt Margene find the leaf and bring it into the house where it grew into something else? Or had it already mutated into a monster when she found it?

Man, why did I keep that nasty thing?

"You know, Mick," Uncle John says, selecting a huge lug wrench from the toolbox, "maybe it's time you learned something about cars." He holds the wrench in front of him like a sword. "I can teach you."

He's expecting an 'attaboy' for that suggestion, so I try to give him one. "Well, you know what? Maybe we could do that this summer."

"Great idea." Uncle John smacks the wrench against the toolbox, making a sound like a temple gong. "Because soon, Mick, you'll be a man." He taps his own chest. "You know, before he died, I swore to your dad that I'd raise you right. And I will."

"Thanks, Uncle John."

"Don't mention it." He steps toward the car and a strange realization hits me.

Usually when Uncle John engages me in one of these one-sided talks, he can't help but toss Jesus into the mix. But he didn't just now. It's like his sky-friend got drowned in the swill pickling his brain.

I struggle with what's happening here. Before he found religion, Uncle John lived for rock-n-roll. He owned crates full of LPs, forty-fives, and eight-track cassettes. Hendrix, Janis, and Black Oak Arkansas used to scream from the speakers in my dad's garage while they fixed up hot rods.

But the vinyl and tapes vanished after he and Aunt Margene started going to Bay Crossroads. Now, they're back, and so is the beer. And something else besides.

Near the trash can sits a stack of glossy magazines, dog-eared pages curled with age. A beautiful blonde with smokey eyes and pursed red lips gazes at me from the cover of the one on top. She wears nothing but a strategically arranged boa constrictor.

Girly magazines? Aunt Margene would freak if she got a look at that pile.

Humming to himself, Uncle John kneels beside the Challenger and struggles with a rusted wheel nut. The car is a mess. Engine parts are strewn across the concrete, but the body work looks good. The fenders and hood gleam with a fresh coat of dripping lacquer.

"Um, Uncle John?" I step toward the car. "You fixing her up to show around town?"

"No." He sets the wrench on the floor and gets to his feet, a good head taller than me. "Something's coming up."

"Oh yeah? Like a race?"

Uncle John nods, white teeth shiny against his lips. "Yeah, like that." He punches my arm, nearly flooring me. "How's the old nose?"

Instinctively, my fingers touch the edge of the splint. "It's been better. Say, Uncle John?"

"Yeah?" He grabs another beer.

"Since when did you start drinking again?"

Uncle John's cheeks blush. "Oh, you mean this?" He drains the longneck, then swings it between his thumb and forefinger. "I was just throwing it out." With a flick of his wrist, he sends the bottle tumbling end over end into a nearby trash can, shattering on impact.

I guess that display was for my benefit. "Hey, that was a pretty good shot."

"Durn straight." He tosses a rag over the magazines. "Shouldn't you be in bed, Mick?"

"Aw, but I feel so much better, though."

"Good enough to go to school?"

I laugh. "Okay, maybe not *that* good."

Uncle John scratches his chin. "Well, look. I got some work to do." He pops the hood, then looks over his shoulder. "Unless you got a mind to help me?"

"Maybe some other time."

"Sure. Say, since you're feeling better, will you be up for the hall this evening?"

An image of middle-aged men devouring brisket sandwiches like medieval barons inhaling wild boar invades my mind. "I'm good. I might stay home and play Atari."

"Suit yourself." He dives under the hood, muscles in his bare arms flexing while he struggles with a bolt.

The sudden exertion splits the back of his shirt and the skin underneath wide open. Purple pus oozes from the ruptured fissure. A stench like bait hits my nostrils. My heart's beating faster than a snare roll.

"Mick?" He reaches behind his back, groping blindly at the dripping wound. "Is something the matter?"

I've got to get out of here now. "No, nothing's wrong." I inch toward the door. "Everything's cool."

"You're lying." He turns toward me, eyes yellow and blazing like wildfires.

"Uncle John?"

"Now, Mick." His mouth opens, revealing twin rows of razor-sharp fangs. "Ain't nothing to be afraid of. You brought this gift to us, me and your aunt." He opens his arms wide, hands transformed into hooked claws. "Now it's your turn."

I hit the shed door at a run and tear off down the seashell driveway, the devil close behind.

"Mick, don't run," he shouts. "Come and join the family!"

I veer into the pine thicket, needles tearing at my face and arms. Branches snap behind me, Uncle John's heavy footfalls keeping pace.

"Don't run off, boy," he calls after me. "You can't get away."

After what I've been through the last few days? Yes, I can, Uncle John.

A bramble patch looms ahead. Ducking under briars, I put distance between us. A heavy limb sails past my head like a javelin and buries itself in a tree, showering me with splinters. Jeez, that thing is huge. How did he throw it?

"Mick!" Uncle John's muffled footsteps reverberate in the dense undergrowth. "There's nowhere you can go from here."

Ignoring his warning, I break through the far side of the

bramble patch and stumble into the meadow. A smell like lilac mixed with saltwater floods my nostrils. In the center of the meadow towers the blackened trunk of a tree. White flowers beckon like safe harbor against the dark green of its waxy leaves.

It's a magnolia.

A pink-hued jellyfish the size of a man-o-war floats high in the canopy. It unfurls a curtain of translucent tentacles that cascade to the ground.

"Come here," Katie Sue's voice echoes in my head. "I got you."

I duck beneath the behemoth's leafy branches, energy crackling around my body. The sound of Uncle John crashing through the brambles recedes behind me.

"Grab on," she says.

I reach for one of the tentacles and it bears me aloft. Uncle John lurches into the clearing. His face is waxen, a festering polyp over one eye. The tree is enveloped in a shimmering aura that extends from the ground to the uppermost branches. Uncle John throws himself against the luminous veil, slashing with his claws. His bony appendages burst into flame. Ignoring his own injuries, Uncle John strikes again and again. "I'll kill you, boy! Kill you!"

"You will not," Katie Sue thunders. "Git."

Uncle John raises his ruined claws high over his head, the double rows of fangs grinding like lawnmower blades.

From somewhere nearby, a loud whistle sounds. Uncle John stops abruptly and his shoulders slump like oxbows. The ruined man gives me one last sullen glance, and vanishes into the thicket.

I stand, trying to catch my breath beneath the shelter of the tree. A frond gently caresses my face.

I place a hand on the leaf. "Hey, cut that out."

"This is going to help," Katie Sue whispers.

"Okay." I drop my hands and close my eyes.

The tip probes the bridge of my nose. A warm sensation floods my nostrils. Something pops in the cartilage and my nose straightens itself. The process hurts like crazy, making my eyes water. "Hey, you said this wouldn't hurt."

"I said this would help. Let me finish."

Lilac floods my sinuses, overpowering me. My legs wobble, and my head feels like it's filled with sand.

I drop to one knee. "Whoa, what is that? It's pretty powerful—"

"It sure is," she says. With a flick, the vine tears off the splint. "You won't be needing this anymore."

White blossoms engulf the bandage and burn it to ash.

I slump against the tree's rough bark, too exhausted to stand. "Katie Sue? Is this really you?"

"It's an aspect of me and Tammy, like, mixed together?" A waxy leaf floats down and lands in my hands. "Her real body's in the barn. This construct can only exist for a short time."

"What does that mean? Are y'all dying?"

"No. I just can't maintain this form for long. Something's been trying to block us and keep us in the barn."

"Oh." A shimmering pool of water rises in the cup of the leaf. "What's this?"

"I want to be able to see you." Kate Sue's face emerges on the surface, and she smiles. "That's better."

A chuckle escapes my lips. "Wow. It's like having a little TV in the palm of your hand."

"I reckon."

An unpleasant memory creeps into my brain. "Last time we talked, I thought you hated me."

Her expression softens. "Oh, Mickey, I was too hard on you. I'm sorry."

"You aren't mad?"

"Well, maybe a little. But after y'all left I got to thinking about what you said. You tried to stop that thing, right? When it jumped in my grave, you tried to get it out."

"I honestly did."

"And remember the other day when I really needed a friend? And you said you'd be my friend?"

My eyes moisten. "Yeah."

She gazes up at me. "So, what kind of friend would I be if I abandoned you when you needed me most?"

"It's nothing. Thanks for saving me when I was on the pyramid."

She frowns. "I wish we could've saved that girl, too."

"Say, where *did* I end up, exactly? That place was weird."

She purses her lips, as if considering how to proceed. "You were taken off-world, Mickey. Where that is, I'm not rightly sure."

"Like an alien planet?"

"Something like that."

"And who were those bug people?"

"Folks with bad intentions."

Wow, that's all kinds of helpful. "How did you know where to find me?"

Her eyes sparkle. "You have a very expansive mind."

"I do?"

"Yep. Makes your thoughts really easy to track."

I brush the leaf's veiny folds with my fingers. "The girl I tried to save, Alice. She died, right?"

"Yes." Katie Sue says, averting her gaze. "Or, at least, she's dead to what she was."

What does *that* mean? "You know who brought her there?"

"Wade," she says flatly. "He's been corrupted by his... master."

"That dude in the black robe? What's his deal?"

She ignores my question. "Mickey, something terrible is about to happen. We need to get everyone we love to safety. I'm counting on you to be my hands and feet on this."

The dark priest's words about me being an errand boy echo in my head. "You're not using me, are you?"

"Using you?" Her laugh makes the leaf shake in my hands. "No. I'm just telling you what I need you to do. You want to save Becca?"

I nod. "Yeah."

"And your friend?"

"Of course."

"Then you need guidance."

"Wait a minute." I sit cross-legged in the shadow of the tree. "By something terrible, you mean that battle we talked about?"

"Yes." A gentle breeze rustles the canopy, brushing against my cheeks. "It's coming soon. We don't have much time to get ready."

Dark clouds appear and begin circling ominously. Thunder peals and I instinctively cup the leaf. The magnolia shudders and begins to sway in the wind. Branches and bark are torn away, showering the ground with debris. Splinters pop from the tree's bark like spent nails onto the earth.

"Katie Sue?" I ask. "What's going on?"

"Not sure." Blossoms swirl around me, tossed around in the stale air. "I think he's blocking me again."

"Who? Who's trying to block you?"

A lightning bolt slams into the ground, just past the clearing.

I jump, spilling the water from the frond. "Jeez, I'm sorry."

"It's alright." Katie Sue's voice whispers in my head. "You have to get everybody to the barn. Becca, Dad, Win and his folks. Then we'll—"

The ground quivers and shakes. A massive branch crashes near my feet. Glowing lavender pulp spews from cracks in the tree's bark.

"He's found me." The luminous vine beside me fades and grows dark. "I can't stay much longer." Other branches darken and fall, flopping in the dirt like bleached fish.

"Katie Sue?" I say. "Are you okay?"

"No." Her voice wavers in my ears. "Mickey, I'm sorry."

Leaves, branches, tentacles, and blossoms shower down around me, dissolving to ash when they touch the ground. A stench like burning rubber floods the air. I scramble to my feet. "What do I do?"

"Find Win. Get Becca and Dad. Anyone else you can find who isn't infected."

A great fissure opens in the earth, swallowing everything in its path.

"Katie Sue?"

"Get them to the barn. It's the only place I can protect y'all."

An unearthly screech pierces the air. Greenish globules rain from the clouds, popping like bullets on the soft ground.

Hissing fills my ears, and I make out smoke rising from the edge of the clearing. A curtain of flame consumes the woods behind me. No way out in that direction. Getting to my feet, I run from the fire.

A loud crash grabs my attention before I get twenty yards. Turning, I catch sight of what's left of Katie Sue's tree. Enveloped in a funeral pyre, the blackened trunk disintegrates and its twisted remains corkscrew into the ground. Flames dart from the tree's corpse onto the grass, sending plumes of smoke into the air. Inhaling the acrid-smelling stuff makes me cough. My eyes water, and the heat is unbearable.

Craig E. Higgins

If I stay, I'll die.

I dash for the far side of the meadow. Here, the ground ascends in a sharp gradient. Legs pumping, I run across a hill and through another line of trees.

A lightning bolt slices into the clearing behind me. The ground shakes and I tumble to the ground, rock-a-chaws biting into my bare hands. In front of me stands a familiar iron fence surrounding a sea of gray headstones and crosses.

Holy crap.

I'm at the cemetery.

22

Dark clouds loom over the graveyard. Sketchy shadows lengthen, cast by rows of leaning headstones. I dash through the underbrush and vault the fence. On the far side of the cemetery, five figures in green beekeeper outfits huddle around a fresh grave.

BDM guys. But what are they doing here? Even at this distance, I make out the name chiseled on the headstone's polished granite.

Katharine Susan Carson.

Aw, crap. Somehow, they know about Katie Sue.

Two beekeepers thrust flathead shovels into the earth and start digging. A third waves something that looks like a metal detector over the soil. The last two face outwards, blaster spears like those of the bug-soldiers on the alien planet.

Wait a minute. Are BDM from outer space, too? The synapses in my brain pop like fireworks.

Stupid, stupid, stupid. They followed you to Earth.

No, they didn't.

Did, too. And look whose grave they're defiling.

Shut up. It's no big deal. Katie Sue's not even there.

They seem to think it's a big deal. Maybe they know something you don't.

Just shut up. You don't know anything, either.

Like an idiot, I trip on an exposed root, and fall sprawling to the ground. The beekeeper with the gadget turns and points, hissing something at the others. The two gravediggers drop their shovels and draw crude-looking hooks from their belts. Leveling their weapons, they open fire.

One blast takes out a headstone to my left. A second hits a tree, reducing it to burning matchsticks. I duck behind a row of headstones, the air crackling with ozone. Blast after blast rips the earth to ribbons.

Can't fight these dudes with my fists, so what can I use as a weapon?

A few feet away, I spot a crumbling gravestone surrounded by a pile of rocks. Dashing toward the pile, I grab a handful of granite projectiles and turn to face my attackers. One leapfrogs a mud puddle, a perfect target. I bean him in the facemask with a barrage of rocks, but to no effect. Shaking his head, the beekeeper closes the distance between us. With a shriek, he swings his hook at my head. I duck and the curved blade gets stuck in a headstone. Hissing, the attacker tries to free the blade.

Bad move, sucker. You left yourself wide open.

I trip his ankle with my instep. Arms flailing, the beekeeper slips in the dirt. He tries to rise but I slam him repeatedly in the head with a chunk of granite. After a couple shots, the beekeeper goes down.

An energy blast reduces a nearby headstone to rubble. They'll pick me off at this rate if I can't find an equalizer.

Fortunately, the hook is still embedded in the gravestone. Grabbing the weapon by its handle, I yank it free. Footsteps reverberate to my right. I turn and there's a second beekeeper, a hook in his hand. Raising the weapon, he fires. A piercing whine assaults my ears and the grave marker behind me explodes into shrapnel. Peppered and bleeding, I hit the ground.

Something hisses next to me. Without its helmet, I get a good look at the first beekeeper's face. Mirrored eyes glitter above hooked beetle-jaws.

I knew it. These guys are aliens.

Scrambling to my feet, I smash the bug-soldier with the flat of the hook, knocking it out. The second beekeeper approaches at a full clip. Raising my weapon, I discover a button along its grip.

Wait, does this thing have a trigger? Maybe it's a blaster, too?

I turn, aim the weapon, and fire. The hook vibrates and a loud whine pierces my eardrums. Hit by some invisible force, the bug-soldier lurches backward and gets tossed against a big stone angel. It wobbles on unsteady feet, then falls.

That's two down. But I'm not out of the woods yet.

The remaining trio close in. I get off a blast, but the shot goes wide. They return fire, filling the air with white hot arcs of light.

Aiming its hook, the leader fires and reduces a nearby gravestone to dust. I get a glimpse of the weapon. Its blade is bigger than the others, the metal a dull red. Must be a deluxe model.

More energy blasts sear the ground around me. Headstones explode. An ozone stench fills my nose. I try to scramble for cover, but a beekeeper is already on me, hissing and shrieking like a banshee. It swings its spear, nearly taking my head off.

Then a flash of bright light fills the air, blinding me. Rubbing my eyes, I catch sight of the bug-soldier collapsing to the ground, smoke belching from its back.

There, at the top of the hill overlooking the cemetery, stands a figure in a brown leather bomber jacket and cargo pants, holding a blaster spear. Face hidden behind oversized goggles and a brown scarf, my rescuer fires another blast, neatly decapitating a stone cherub. A second shot vaporizes one of the two remaining beekeepers.

That leaves a sole survivor. Returning fire, the bug-soldier retreats in the direction of Katie Sue's grave. The stranger advances, getting off a couple more blasts for good measure. Up at the gravesite, the beekeeper abandons its weapon and stops in front of a headstone. Then it raises its hands, holding aloft a triangular-shaped object.

My rescuer brushes past me, running toward the last alien.

"You got something of mine?" I say.

The stranger offers no reply.

Lightning flashes, illuminating an opening in the clouds. Thunder roars and a glowing column of green light streaks from the sky, sweeping the ground around the bug-soldier. I shield my eyes, but my rescuer merely gazes on unfazed.

With a thundercrack, the energy stream retreats into the clouds, taking the beekeeper with it.

Gradually, the roaring subsides. Getting to my feet, I knock the dirt off my knees. A sudden screeching sound cuts through the air. I catch sight of a bug-soldier trying to scramble for safety.

Jeez, but what's it going to take to finish these guys?

Wheeling around, my new friend in the bomber jacket fires, reducing the creature to smoking ash.

"Should've played dead, chummy," the stranger says in a muffled voice.

I step toward the masked figure. "Who are you?"

"This bunch packs a wallop." My rescuer walks past me and gestures toward the alien's dusty remains. "But they're not too bright."

Up close, I size up my mysterious benefactor. This person is at least two inches shorter than me. And beneath the jacket, baggy pants, and goggles, I detect a rounded softness of the hip.

"I'll ask again," I say. "Who are you?"

"I thought that part was obvious." My rescuer removes the goggles and scarf to reveal a woman's drawn face, her clear hazel eyes offset by thin brows and a perky nose. She wears her brunette hair in a bun streaked with gray. Not sure how old she is. Thirty-five? Sixty? Her face is not exactly pretty, but not bad to look at. *Handsome features* is the way my mom would've described her.

"Colleen Wentwhistle," she says, offering her hand.

I extend mine warily. "Mickey."

"I know." She grins. "Mr. Finley, you are one hard man to get hold of."

23

"**Do you *believe* all** the toys they left us? My, oh my."

Colleen Wentwhistle scurries from one fallen alien to the next, like a terrier on a scent. She picks up the leader's hook by the handle. "A cleric's sickle, compact but with more shear-wave firepower than the standard-issue." She smacks the flat of the bladed weapon against her gloved hand. "Most impressive."

I scan the hilltop, anticipating the red-and-blue lights of a police car. "Um, shouldn't we be making our getaway?"

"Not without collecting the spoils of war, my friend." She pulls a large Ziplock bag from her jacket, then places the weapon, blade-first, inside. "Good thing I got that bugger before he got me." She regards me with a wolfish grin. "You see the *size* of the hole I put in that one? Yow!"

"Sorry, but no. I was too busy trying not to die."

Wentwhistle drops the bag in a big canvas satchel, then she turns and heads for Katie Sue's plot. The soil around it is covered with a greenish ash that stinks like burnt rubber. Scattered bits of beekeepers' outfits litter the ground.

Wentwhistle pulls on surgical gloves and runs her fingers lightly over the spoiled earth. "See this dust? It's a mineral by-product from extra-planetary thermo-photonic transmigration."

"Thermo-what?"

"Teleportation, basically." She draws a small baggie from her satchel and collects a sample. "You know, like in *Star Trek*?"

"Well, duh," I say. "I've watched that show."

"I call this tele-poop." Wentwhistle deposits the sample in her bag. "You don't see this often in the field. They must be getting desperate if they're evacing their guys in broad daylight."

This woman seems to know what she's talking about. Maybe she's not that crazy, after all. Maybe.

"Cool. But what were they doing at Katie Sue's grave?"

Wentwhistle cocks an eyebrow. "Who's Katie Sue?"

Shouldn't have let that slip out. "She's nothing…I mean, nobody."

"Oh really?" The woman turns and inspects the inscription. "So, your Katie Sue has no relation to poor…what's the name?" She runs a finger over the letters cut into the marble. "Katharine Susan, who just happened to have passed so recently?"

I have to think of something fast. "Um, well…I guess so…maybe."

"Well, which one is it?"

"I mean…this girl got killed like a week ago. So, like there was a big story on the news? That's how I know her name."

"Um-hmm." Wentwhistle smirks. "And aliens desecrating Ms. Carson's final resting place is a coincidence in your view?"

I bite the inside of my cheek. "Yeah, I guess."

The metal triangle the alien used to summon rescue sticks out of the dirt. It's about six inches long with jewels embedded at two of the three points.

She points to the object. "What's that?"

"What's, what?" I say.

"That pendant."

"How should I know? You're the expert."

"Pick it up."

"Me?"

"Yes, you."

I kneel beside the grave. The tattered remains of the beekeepers' uniforms stink like soiled diapers. "Phew. These guys are nasty."

"Here." Wentwhistle tosses me another Ziplock. "Bag it and let's go."

I pick up the pendant and give it a closer inspection. The triangle is made of some brass-colored metal, its striated surface is rough like pumice. A purple amethyst is set in one corner, a green emerald in another. The remaining end is scratched and empty.

Ornate symbols are carved into the metal. The outline of a shark, its pointy snout framed with tentacles, surrounds the emerald.

No big surprise on that one.

A tree crowned with a jellyfish is inscribed next to the amethyst. Katie Sue's lady-tree friend Tammy? The similarity can't be a coincidence. The symbol on the third end is scratched out, as though somebody intended to obscure its identity.

Light flickers from the emerald. Suddenly, my limbs go cold, and a wave of nausea rushes over me.

Why do I feel so ill?

"Would you get on with it, Mr. Finley?" Wentwhistle says.

I try to move, but I'm frozen in place. The memory of everything that's happened since Fall Social–the trip to the alien world, Alice's death, Aunt Margene and Uncle John's corruption–fills my brain with static. Confusion mixes with guilt for stuff I never did, and things I didn't do when I should have. Which makes everything else all the worse. But I don't think those things are the reasons why I feel sick.

Wentwhistle says my name again, her voice too low and slow to be coming from a human mouth. "Mr. Finley?"

I gaze up at the sky. Dark clouds bleed and churn, mixing together like oils on canvas. A steady buzzing floods my ears, penetrating my mind. My face and neck break out in a cold sweat.

"Hey, wake up." Wentwhistle whacks my shoulder with the blunt end of her spear. "Get it together."

"What?" I collapse to my knees. Shadows pass before my eyes. Am I blacking out?

"Here," she says, "let me help you."

Standing behind me, Wentwhistle presses a knee into my back, grabs my arms, and draws my shoulders up and back. My lungs fill with oxygen. After a moment, I struggle to my feet, greedily gulping the stale, acrid air.

Wentwhistle glares at me. "You're not a pothead, are you, Mr. Finley?"

A pothead? "What?" I chuckle. "No, I never do any of that stuff."

"Good." The woman sighs. "Because I can't work with potheads." She pinches my nose.

"Hey!" I brush her hand aside. "What did you do that for?"

Wentwhistle approaches me. "What about glue?" She lets out a snort next to my ear. "You one of them glue-sniffers, huh? Sniff, sniff, sniff?"

I back away. "Lady, are you out of your mind?"

The woman frowns. "Just answer the question." She snorts twice more, loudly for emphasis. "That's how some of them do it, you know. It's disgusting."

"I swear on my mother's grave, I don't sniff glue, or do poppers or whippets, or none of that."

The woman cocks her head like a parakeet. "Alright. Given

that it's vital, absolutely vital, we get started, I'm also going to rule out you being a dope fiend."

I shrug. "That's a relief, I guess."

Wentwhistle punches me in the arm.

"Man!" I say, rubbing the spot where she hit me. "What was that for?"

"Your combat reflexes are terrible."

"Sorry." Tears well in my eyes. One droplet falls down my cheek.

She smirks. "Oh, no. Did that hurt?"

Is she making fun of me? "No. It's just been a weird week."

"Sorry to hear that." The woman shakes her head. "But trust me when I tell you, these things we're fighting? They don't care about your weird week."

That's when it hits me. Every death, injury, mutation, and other crazy thing that's happened in the last ten days plays on a tape loop in my brain. I can't shut out the images or pain that comes with them. They just won't go away. I plop to the ground and begin to cry.

Wentwhistle's expression softens. "Hey, I'm sorry." She pats me on the shoulder. "Let it out. We've all been there."

"Oh yeah?" I press the heels of my hands to my eyes. "Lady, you have no idea what I've been through."

She raises her hands as if warding off a curse. "I wasn't implying that I did."

"It's like everything happened at once," I say, the pulse pounding in my temples like a backbeat for all the anger and frustration pouring out of me. "First, I got sick as a dog with some freaky virus. Then everybody else got sick. Then I got transported to some alien planet where they perform human sacrifices—"

"Alien planet? That would freak anybody out."

"You think?" I yell, slapping dust from my jeans. "Now,

on top of everything else, I find out my uncle's a monster who's trying to kill me, and my aunt is keeping a baby alien or something in a potato chip can. And it probably wants to kill me, too."

Wentwhistle pulls a handkerchief from her jacket and wipes my face. She's surprisingly gentle.

"Kid," she says, "do you need to hug it out?"

"I'm sorry?"

"You know, I read a study the other day which showed that hugs can be very beneficial for relieving stress."

Normally, I'd be long gone by now, but something about her says I can trust her. "What does that even mean?"

"Well, what it means is, there's a physiological response to—"

"Okay." I don't know this person, but I need a hug, and don't care where it comes from.

"Okay, what?"

I bury my head in her shoulder and weep like a lost child.

She strokes my hair, whispering to me like my mom used to. "Sweet boy, you're not made for this work, are you? But we'll set it right."

We hug for what seems like forever.

Then she pulls away and straightens the fur collar of her jacket. "You know, I'm really not the touchy-feely sort."

"Me neither."

"So, this won't become a regular thing. This…clingy stuff. Kind of embarrassing, really."

"That's fine." What was I thinking? "That's *totally* fine."

"Guess we made a mess here." She surveys the graveyard, then helps me to my feet. "Somebody might come checking around. Let's grab what gear we can and get going."

The woman retrieves another canvas bag from her jacket and hands it to me. A wave of fear washes over me when I place the pendant inside the satchel.

What did that thing do to me?

Wentwhistle bags the hook, and the salvage hunt begins. Scouring the cemetery, we collect two spears and the remaining hook. I search for the leader's metal detector and find only an ashen outline in the grass.

"Here." Wentwhistle hands me the long weapons and I sling them over my shoulder. Grasping her blaster spear, she leads me to a gate, and we exit the graveyard.

While we walk, a thought occurs to me. "Why were those dudes dressed as beekeepers?"

"Hazmat suits." She corrects me.

"Oh."

"Bureau of Disease Management is a corrupted branch of the CDC," she explains as we climb the hill. "It's like a SWAT team for uncategorized disease outbreaks. But our alien friends have secretly been running the BDM for years, using it as a cover for their activities."

She walks fast, and I try to keep up with her. "You mean they just sort of took it over?"

"Right under everyone's noses."

"But what about Doctor Blightman? He's human, right?"

Wentwhistle smirks. "He's a puppet, I think. The T'Kalul often use human pawns to do their dirty work."

I frown. "Wait a minute. What's a...how do you even pronounce that?"

Footsteps echo on the wind, followed by a creaking sound. We both freeze. Twenty yards ahead, a potbellied man in overalls carrying a bouquet of spring flowers opens the gate and enters the cemetery. He stops when he sees us, standing there like a dime store mannikins.

Wentwhistle waves to him. "Hi there." She gestures toward the graveyard. "We're just passing through."

The man furrows his brow but doesn't reply, which is totally understandable. What do you say to two people who resemble *Star Wars* extras hanging around a cemetery, especially when said boneyard's all blown to hell?

"Yeah, we won't be long," I say. "Not a lot of action around here."

His eyes narrow like coin slots in an arcade game. Snorting, he retreats from view.

Wentwhistle turns to me. "He's probably going to call the law. Let's get out of here."

We run and reach the top of the hill. There sits a van parked along a seashell road. It's brown with rusted red patches. Airbrushed on the side are a matador, flamenco dancer, and charging bull.

"Been stalking me all weekend?" I say, tossing the spears in the back of the vehicle.

She ignores me. "You hungry? I could murder a tomato."

24

Me and Wentwhistle stop at a Sonic just outside the city limits. She parks the van beside an intercom and presses a button for service.

A girl's voice buzzes through the speaker. "How can we help y'all?"

"Give me two slices of tomato and a piece of bacon. Oh, and bring extra salt packets—like ten if you got them." She turns to me. "What do you want?"

I quickly scan the menu. "I don't have any money."

"My treat."

"Okay. Get me a Sonic burger with fries and a soft drink."

Wentwhistle frowns. "What kind of soda?"

"Lime."

She barks into the microphone. "Also, a Sonic burger, fries, and a lime drink."

The girl on the other end says, "Ma'am, about that first part? We don't have *just* tomato on the menu."

"What? Almost every sandwich you make comes with tomatoes."

"I know, ma'am. But we can't just have that special ordered, is all."

"Then get me a Sonic burger with bacon and hold everything except the tomato and bacon."

"Bacon costs extra. That's a special order too."

"Then add special bacon. And don't forget the salt." Wentwhistle removes her thumb from the intercom button and sighs. "Oh, my word. Mr. Finley, do you have designs to spend the rest of your life in this town?"

"Not really."

"Good. You deserve better."

Soon, a thin-legged girl with curly hair and bad acne rolls toward us on roller skates, bringing our food on a plastic tray. My drink nearly spills when she bumps the tray against the driver side. Apologizing profusely, the girl holds out a hand for money and Wentwhistle pays her. Then the carhop glides away, skate-wheels creaking.

"Let's regroup." Wentwhistle stares at the rearview mirror while backing us out of the lot. "I need to know more about this little off-world excursion of yours."

We park beside an abandoned paper mill two miles up the road. Rust scours the metal sides of the dilapidated structure. The decaying innards are shadowed by a single mechanical crane jutting over the gravel lot and surrounding thicket. Wentwhistle sets out a couple of folding chairs with attached aluminum trays. Sitting in the cool shadow of the crane, we eat our lunch. The woman unwraps her sandwich, discards the burger, and places the tomato and two scraggly bacon slices on the wrapper. I unwrap my burger and bite down. The meat tastes like cardboard, but I'm so hungry even a shoebox would satisfy me.

My lunch companion still hasn't started eating. Her efforts make for a distracting show. With deliberate slowness, Wentwhistle sprinkles one salt packet after the other over the fried pig fat and pulpy vegetable. Gobbling fries, I silently count each packet. Ten in all, just like she ordered.

She smiles. "Are you watching me?"

"Yeah." I shrug. "Why don't you just eat?"

"What's the rush?" Wentwhistle spreads the white granules over the tomato, creating a fine silty layer.

Jeez, this woman is obsessive. "Aren't we supposed to be fighting aliens?"

"Be patient." Cradling the concoction in both hands, she slides the mess into her mouth and finishes it off in one swallow. "Attention to detail is vital—absolutely vital—in all things."

"Even with tomatoes?"

She wipes her lips with a napkin. "Especially with tomatoes."

While I gobble the rest of my meal, Wentwhistle unlocks the van's rear doors and hops inside. She returns with a large, bulky bundle and lays it on the ground. "There's a flat board on the floor. Could you get it for me?"

Rising from my seat, I enter the vehicle's cargo hold. The interior reeks of something pungent, like the stink of the dead skunk I accidentally ran over once with my bike. A shiny metal plank glows on the plush shag carpet. Tucking it under my arm, I turn and exit the vehicle.

"Just lay it there," Wentwhistle says, pointing to the ground. She arranges the bundle on the board and undoes the twine. The cloth rolls away, and I get a good look at what's inside.

On the board lies a treasure trove of rusted, snaggletooth-tipped spears, and a hook like the ones I found—only this one's covered in barnacles. There's also a necklace of bones and small animal skulls that don't resemble anything on Earth, and several crinkly, two-foot-long rolls of yellowed paper.

Wentwhistle pulls two pairs of surgical gloves from her

pocket and gives one to me.

"Put these on," she says.

After gloving up, the woman selects a spear from the pile. "I found this off the coast of the Yucatan peninsula, in Mexico. You know where that is?"

"Not really."

"It's along the Gulf. The boot off the Mexican coastline?"

Geography is not my strong suit. "If you say so."

She runs her fingers over the crusty tip. "Lance, my second ex, nabbed it when we were deep-sea diving fifteen years ago. In the last decade I've collected about two dozen of these things from fourteen different dig sites throughout the Gulf. But I never knew what they could really do until I had a spin with the one I found on you."

Wentwhistle aims the thing at an old metal drum and presses a small button. A dull hiss emits from its tip. "See?" She returns the spear to the collection. "Yours is new and mine are museum pieces." Reaching into the van, she retrieves one of the spears from the cemetery. "Now, we have three in working order."

I inspect the ancient hook, its blade pockmarked with rust. "How old are these things?"

"Metallurgist I knew at Mississippi State tested them for me. She said they were made somewhere around two-thousand years ago. But the metal's not from Earth, you understand, so they may be older."

"Wow." I return the hook to the pile. "What'll we do with the ones we got off the beekeepers?"

"Well, we need them for the moment. After that, I may sell what doesn't get busted up."

"People buy this stuff?"

"For *insane* amounts of money." Wentwhistle snags a rag from her satchel. "How do you think I stay in business? Selling fanzines?"

The whole notion of some secret, super-rich crowd of alien-weapon enthusiasts blows my mind. "What do they do with them?"

"Keep them in vaults or safes I suppose, locked away from prying eyes." She unfurls a scroll, spreading it on the ground. "The circle's pretty small, and the initiated like to keep it that way."

Wentwhistle extracts a three-inch-length-of-pipe from her satchel. "If word got out about their little hobby, the Feds would bring the hammer down on their collective heads in short order, I assure you."

"That actually kind of sucks when you think about it. Buy some cool alien weapons, and you can't show nobody."

"That's not my concern." Using the pipe, she pins down one edge of the roll. "What matters is that they pay. You wouldn't believe what they cough up for the antiques. Imagine what a working blaster will fetch."

"No way." I plant my high-top on the other end of the scroll. "I'm the one who called *you* in, remember? You make any money off those, I get a cut, too."

"Would you please *not* wipe your feet on my star chart?" She grabs my ankle and yanks.

"Star chart?"

Wentwhistle frowns. "Yes, star chart. One of a unique set, and all in my possession."

I inspect the scroll, but it makes no sense to me. Frayed and tattered, the edges are naturally scalloped, as though made of leaves rather than pulp. Scrawled along the border are characters like the ones on the temple where Alice died. In the center there's a drawing of a stepped pyramid inside a circle. Lines radiating out from the structure divide the map into three sections. Reddish brown splotches float among the swirls, some of them marked by smaller symbols that look like numbers. Two sections feature sketches of the shark and the tree. A set of squiggly lines in the third section obscures the images.

"Where'd you get this?" I ask.

Wentwhistle spreads her arms wide and yawns. "After he found the rod, Lance and I uncovered a cave entrance hidden in a coral reef. Our tanks were almost out of oxygen, but we wanted to check it out. So, we went inside and swam until we found this pocket of fresh air and plant life. You know what else we found?"

"More spears?"

"Yep. And all the rest in front of you." She holds her thumbs and fingers together in an oval shape. "We emerged in a *cenote*, you see, an oasis formed in an eroded limestone chamber."

Wow, too much science talk and my brain will fog over. "You don't say."

"Oh, but I do. They were created when an asteroid hit earth sixty-five million years ago. Some scientists think that space rock killed the dinosaurs."

"Freaky." I run my finger from the temple drawing to a red dot just beneath the tree. Bigger than the others, the mark is situated next to a blue-green sphere. "That supposed to be near Earth?"

"That, Mr. Finley, is where I think you traveled to. Look." Wentwhistle gathers some small stones. "Imagine this is an asteroid or maybe a moon. Bigger actually than the asteroid that hit the Yucatan." She places a larger rock next to it. "My knowledge of *T'Kalul* is pretty sketchy, but from what I've learned of their history—or at least the legends of it—some kind of apocalyptic event happened on their home planet."

"Hold the phone." I shake my head. "What was that word

you just said?"

"What word? T'Kalul?"

"Yeah, that. Taka-whatever are the aliens' name?"

Wentwhistle nods. "That's correct."

Suddenly, I feel as though I've wandered into a history class I didn't sign up for. "Okay. Go on."

"Anyways, the apocalypse happens and…boom!" She flicks the larger stone away. "Home planet goes bye-bye, and all they have left is this little piece, which they somehow terraformed, powered up and made into a traveling world."

Planets can travel by themselves? That's crazy. "So, they hopped on this asteroid and…what? They searched the universe for a new place to live?"

"Precisely, Mr. Finley." Her eyes light up like New Year's sparklers. "You're getting the flavor of it, my friend."

"Not really. I can't even pronounce what you're saying. Taka–"

"*Tuh-kah-lool.* Means, *space-faring race.* At least, that's what I *think* it means, given I've been able to translate from these suckers here." She pats the other scrolls, as if soothing a crying baby. "They contain the closest thing on Earth to a record of their language."

"Such a weird name." I trail my fingers along the parchment. "They've been here for two thousand years, and stayed out of sight all that time?"

"The T'Kalul hide their tracks well. And they eliminate those who get in their way." A chuckle escapes Wentwhistle. "No muss, no fuss. It's not like they hang a shingle when a Rising is near."

"Okay, okay." I hold out my hand to stop her. "What's a Rising?"

"I'll get back to that." Wentwhistle taps her finger on the red dot. "Your instincts were right, Mr. Finley. This spot marks the interstellar location of T'kahuatl, the traveling world. T'kahuatl drifted for thousands of years through two different galaxies until it reached our solar system. And for at least the last two thousand years it's been in an orbit near Earth. But where exactly, I've never been able to determine."

"And that's where I went, right?"

She nods. "Pretty sure. What I can't figure out is how they got you there, or how you got back." Wentwhistle arches an eyebrow. "And why you, anyway? No offense, but why take some random kid to space?"

"There was a fight at the gym last Friday." I take a stick and draw a rectangle in the dirt. "This girl, Alice, was involved. Afterwards, this other dude Wade—who I really hate a lot, by the way—grabs her and drags her into the lockers. I follow them, get attacked by these other crazy things, and fall through like a hole in the girls' bathroom."

"Seriously?" Wentwhistle chuckles and shakes her head. "They left a dimensional aperture behind in the toilet?"

"Well, in the showers, actually. Maybe they didn't have time to abduct her on a UFO. Anyway, I get sucked into this thing, wake up falling from the sky and I land here," Drawing a series of curving lines, I sketch a path from the rectangle to the pyramid.

She frowns. "And how did you not die on impact?"

Sweat beads my forehead. "I don't know. Falling made me black out, and when I came to, I was safe on the ground."

"That doesn't sound right."

"Whatever." Suddenly, tears well in my eyes and I struggle to speak. "Anyway, I was there and, and…one of those bugs tried to kill me but a worm monster sucked it into a swamp and, and, then I was fighting up on the temple where Alice got…got killed by this dude in a black robe." I'm shaking like I got a fever and chills.

I double over, tears running down my cheeks.

"You've had a traumatic experience." Wentwhistle takes my hand. "It's vital—absolutely vital—you understand that recognition of trauma is a first step toward healing—"

"It's not okay!" I pound the dusty ground with my fists, tears streaming down my face "None of it is. Alice is dead and everything's going to crap, and I'm so sick of all of this. I just want things to be normal again!"

She draws me close, and I cry like a baby. My breath comes in shallow gasps and something cold settles into the pit of my stomach.

Stupid, stupid, stupid. All your fault, all your fault, all your fault.

Wentwhistle's gentle pat on my back dispels the voices. "Mr. Finley, I know this is hard. And I can't promise things will get better right away. But you've got to be strong now, hear? I need your help if we're going to beat this Rising."

I pull free. "Okay. You've got to tell me what that means."

She frowns. "Rising is when the T'Kalul resurrect *Azokuitli*, their god of destruction."

"I can't pronounce that one either." I sniffle, fighting back a runny nose. "But that's the shark with tentacles, right?"

"The very same. The legends say when Azokuitli comes, he carves a path of blood and pain that blackens the sky and sunders the land. And woe to all those who try to stop him. Get up." She helps me to my feet. "Now, tell me about what happened to the artichoke."

25

Wentwhistle drives us back to town. I sit in the passenger seat and give her everything I know. Finding the artichoke and fighting it. Katie Sue's accident. Getting sick. Learning that Katie Sue was back from the dead. Getting healed by her.

She taps her fingernails on the steering wheel. "So that's what the artichokes do. They're resurrection vessels."

"What?"

"I'll explain later. Go on."

The rest of it pours out of me—Becca Mae, Win Cobb, Wade and Freddie, Aunt Margene and Uncle John getting sick and turning bad, Alice and Becca Mae's fight.

The dude in the black robe.

"A black robe? Like a priest's robe?"

"Yeah, something like that."

Her knuckles whiten on the steering wheel. "Tell me what his face looked like again."

"Kind-of beat up, like he had a broken nose once and didn't get it fixed. And his hair flops over his eyes, you know like a girl's bangs?"

Wentwhistle purses her lips, inhales deeply through her nose, then empties her lungs in one great exhalation. "Blight."

"Who?"

"Midian Blight." She smacks her palm against her forehead. "Egad, but we're in Mississippi. This used to be *his* neck of the woods. Why didn't I make that connection before?"

I'm totally confused. "What connection?"

She pulls the van into the parking lot of the Home Plate Diner. "Go call your friend." Her hand trails to a blaster spear next to her seat. "We need to get off the street as soon as possible."

A pay phone hangs forlornly on the wall next to the front door. Phone numbers and crude graffiti are scrawled everywhere. Next to the phone a White Pages dangles on a chain. Leafing through it, I find Win Cobb's number. I pull a dime from my pocket, drop it in the slot, and dial my friend.

"Who's this?" an older woman says on the other end of the line.

"Ma'am? I'm Mickey Finley. Friend of Win's?"

"Oh, Mickey." Her tone softens. "Win told me some good things about you. Something about you being the stud of the wrestling team?"

I would laugh, but nothing's funny right now. "He didn't say that, did he?"

She chuckles. "Let me go get him."

Footsteps echo through the receiver. There's a hush in the air, and then Win says, "Mickey, when did they let you out of the hospital?"

"Couple days ago."

"Man, am I glad you called. I was worried Wade and them guys got you."

"I'm fine. I mean, I'm actually *not* fine, but I'm alive, anyways."

"That's good. You home right now?"

A burly guy with a thick beard brushes against my shoulder

on the way into the restaurant. "No, I'm at the Home Plate," I say. "Can you come down here? It's important."

"Hold on a second. What happened to Alice?"

I don't want to break the bad news. "I...can't talk about that right now."

"Oh."

"What about Coach?"

A silence swallows the air between us.

"He didn't make it," Win says.

"Oh crap."

"It was tough. People were standing around crying. But you know what was really weird?"

"No."

"You remember those dudes giving out shots at the game? Kind of dressed up like they were tending bees?"

"Yeah."

"When the ambulance pulled up, their van came, like, right afterward. And this guy gets out, and he's dressed like a doctor, right?"

He's talking about Blightman. "Go on."

"Yeah, well the doc takes something out of Coach's neck and pulls a sheet over his face. He didn't try to resuscitate him or anything."

"But are you *sure* Coach is dead? The officer who grilled me at the hospital said—"

"Mickey? He's gone. End of story. They just grabbed him and took off. Police left, too."

So, the cop lied to me. Are the aliens controlling them as well? "That's insane. What about Ms. Singleton?"

"Not sure about that one."

"Well, that's just great." I punch the wall hard enough to scrape my knuckles. "Anything else I missed?"

"Everybody thinks Alice is dead," Win says. "You know the

whole school's having a vigil for her? They're lighting candles in the gym and everything."

Why didn't Becca Mae tell me about that? "That's cool."

"Isn't it, though?"

I grip the phone's handset tightly in my hand. "Look, Win. The situation's bad, and we need your help."

"Who's we? I thought you and dead lady were on the outs."

A cold, blustery draft whips down the street, making me stuff my free hand in my pants pocket. "We got that worked out."

"You do?"

"Yeah. And somebody I called in showed up, too."

"Who's that?"

"An expert."

He chuckles. "Who's an expert at this stuff?"

"It's a long story, but I found a person who knows what she's talking about. All we need is for you to—"

"No way." His tone sharpens as if honed on flint. "Mickey, I don't need to do anything. Honestly, I don't want to be mixed up in this anymore. Got it?"

"I understand."

"No, you don't." He lets slip a long sigh. "I got to thinking about things over the weekend. Stuff we been doing? It could get my Ma and Pop hurt, or worse."

"Look, I hate to ask you, but things are worse than we figured."

"How could they get any worse?"

"I'll explain everything to you when you get here."

"Sorry, but I don't like it. I just don't."

It takes some haggling, but he reluctantly agrees. Shivering, I put down the receiver.

Wentwhistle hops out of the van and joins me. "How's your friend?"

"Freaking out." I shrug. "But Win's the best fighter I know. He'll come."

She chuckles. "You act as though you're both in the Super Friends or something."

"Well, really, it's just me and Win. And Becca Mae too, I guess. And Katie Sue."

She smacks her gum, faint odor of peppermint hanging in the breeze. "You know, I do this stuff for a living, and I still don't believe your story about this dead girl with the resurrection vessel in her chest."

I frown. "Why do you call it that?"

"Some T'Kalul legends tell of an organism—a biological machine, really—that keeps a body alive and walking around." Wentwhistle plucks the gum from her mouth and tosses it in a trash can. "That's got to be what your so-called artichoke does." She stares past my shoulder into the diner. "Now, what about the other sister, the one you obviously have the hots for?"

My cheeks flush. "It's not like that."

Wentwhistle smiles and nudges me with an elbow. "The way you describe her, it totally sounds like it is."

"Well, I mean, that's getting kind of personal."

"Fair enough." The woman pats her jacket. I detect the outline of a hook beneath the cracked leather. "You know, we could pick your friend up instead of waiting here. It would save time."

"In *your* van? You've got to be kidding me. Plus, I don't want his folks to meet you. They might think I'm hanging out with an old hippy."

She rolls her eyes. "I beg your pardon."

I laugh. "You heard what I said. Old. Hippy."

"Look, just because a person enjoys a little Mamas and Papas doesn't make them a hippy." Wentwhistle sniffs under her own armpit. "Do I smell? Because hippies don't bathe."

"Whatever, man."

"Have it your way."

"I will."

"Fine, then." She zips her jacket. "What say we get out of the cold?"

We walk into the Home Plate. A crowd sits at the counter, their collective gaze fixed on a TV bolted to the wall. Two talking heads in dull suits and oddly bright neckties discuss the merits of the respective presidential candidates.

"Preliminary results are in. Ohio is projected for Reagan," one head says.

The big guy who almost knocked me over earlier high-fives a burr-haired man wearing a polyester hunting vest.

"Hot dog," Beard Man says, hoisting a mug of amber liquid. "America, let's kiss ol' Carter goodbye."

He puckers his lips. Burr-Head slaps him on the back. Beard Man spills his brew, and they descend into bickering.

Wentwhistle shakes her head. "Republicans."

Me and Wentwhistle grab seats at a back booth.

"What are the specials like in this place?" She leans over to grab a menu.

There's a muffled clank against the table.

"What you got there?" I ask.

Wentwhistle looks around. "A hook," she whispers, neatly arranging napkins on her lap. "Just in case."

"Makes sense." I inspect the menu options and none of them stand out—burgers, crawfish jambalaya, onion rings, and salads.

Wentwhistle points to the crowd at the counter. "Egad, but they really think that old vampire is the bee's knees, don't they?"

My mind drifts to Uncle John right before he monstered

out, pushing me to join him at the VFW Hall. "You don't like Reagan?" I say.

"Hmph," Wentwhistle scowls. "I was at Berkeley when he was governor of California. Man is a barbarian, I tell you, a fascist. We're in for a world of hurt if he takes charge."

"Well, my uncle likes—" I stop myself. "—liked him. Lots of people do."

"Lots of people think soap operas are high art."

I tune her out, taking in the festive crowd of good old boys cheering the election results. They remind me of Uncle John—not the thing that tried to kill me but the real man. Guy who taught me how to fish or sight a rifle so I could pop driftwood floating in a pond. I remember him and Tommy taking me out on the marsh one time. Uncle John sat me in back of his old motorboat and taught me how to adjust the engine choke and run the tiller.

When Mom and Dad passed, he became my father. Why is he a monster, too?

On cue, a knot twists in my gut.

Stupid, stupid, stupid. It's your fault he's gone bad.

I'm not sure I believe you.

Believe your own eyes. He would've eaten you like a shrimp po-boy if we hadn't gotten away. And you know what's another problem?

What's that?

Win's not going to come.

Why not? Win's in as deep as me at this point.

Didn't sound that way over the phone. And why are we trusting this woman anyway? She's old and crazy. Probably owns a lot of cats—

"Look," I say aloud, "how do you know how many cats she has?"

Wentwhistle's eyes go wide, and she grips my wrist. "Mr.

Finley. What are you doing?"

I pull away and fight the urge to run. "Doing? What do you mean?"

"Talking to yourself in public." A cheer rises from the counter while the TV talking heads count another state for Reagan. "Stop that. People will think you're crazy."

I groan. "Man, just leave me alone."

The front door bursts open. A big kid with gray flabby cheeks, and orange hair piled haphazardly on his bulbous head looms in the open doorway.

"Shark," he says.

Everyone in the place stops talking and turns to stare at him.

The muscles in the kid's jaw clench. "Shark."

A little boy crosses the intruder's path, chasing a rubber ball. Orange Hair hisses at him. The child runs screaming for his mommy.

Beard Man slides off his stool and steps toward the intruder. "Hey, boy. What's wrong with you?"

Ignoring the warning, Orange Hair knocks over a specials chalkboard propped on an easel.

The waitress approaches warily with outstretched hands. "Sir, you'll have to leave right now—"

He slaps her, knocking her to the ground. She doesn't get up.

People whisper among themselves. A woman cries, "Somebody stop him."

I gaze at the chalkboard. Scrawled on the surface is an image of a smiling, toothy cartoon shark.

"Shark," Orange Hair lifts the chalkboard over his head, and points to the cook behind the counter. "Shark."

Beard Man drops a big mitt on the kid's shoulder. "Son? You need to cool it."

Orange Hair spins and smacks the board on Beard Man's head. He grabs the big man and throws him across the room. Dishes fly, silverware and broken china scatter across the floor.

Two more guys rush the attacker. One throws a punch that clips Orange Hair in the jaw. Plum-colored spittle flies from his lips. Smiling through a double row of fangs, Orange Hair bites the dude's neck and the man slumps to the ground, bleeding heavily.

Wentwhistle rises from her seat, fumbling in her pocket for the hook. "Mr. Finley, get a blaster from the van—*now!*"

People lurch from their seats and run panicking for the exits, trampling an older dude. A musty bait smell permeates the air. I want to blast Orange Hair to kingdom come, but my legs won't move. It's like somebody glued my feet to the floor. Sweat pours down my face, heart beating faster than a snare roll.

Coward, coward, coward! Do something!

Orange Hair snaps the second dude's neck, dropping him like a ragdoll.

Everyone else living is gone but me, Wentwhistle, and Beard Man.

Silence fills the room except for a talking head on the TV. "Well, the time has come, you've seen the map, we've looked at the figures and NBC News now makes its projection for the presidency…"

Beard Man gets to his feet. Dazed, he wipes blood from his mouth, and charges again. The two crash into each other. Using his long arms for leverage, the bigger dude avoids Orange Hair's grip and grabs him by the neck.

Wentwhistle draws the hook, and it hums in her hand. "The blaster, Finley. Move it. What are you waiting for?"

She's right. If we don't stop this guy now, we never will.

I make a run for it. Just as I near the door, something big

sails past and crashes through the front window, showering the floor with glass. Beard Man lies half in, half out of the diner, gore oozing from a serrated bite on his neck.

Wentwhistle fumbles with her hook, which has stopped vibrating. "Why won't this stupid thing work?"

Orange Hair glares at me through yellow eyes, his double fangs dripping blood. Why does that guy look so familiar?

And then, I recognize him. Owen Duffy, the kid from Katie Sue's funeral. I call out to him. "Owen?"

"Finley," he says. "The Master wants you."

Out of the corner of my eye, I spy Wentwhistle beating the hook against an overturned table.

"Mickey, try to stall him." She slaps the back of the weapon's handle. "Get him talking."

I turn to the monster. "What's he want me for, Owen?"

"Dead." Drool and blood drip from his pulpy chin. "Dead and gone."

"Oh yeah?" I shake my head. "Well, I can't help you with that."

Owen makes a grab for my neck. "Yes, you can."

"Got it." The hook vibrates to life in Wentwhistle's hand. She points the sickle at Owen, and it emits a high screech. Across the room, a booth explodes, sending wooden splinters everywhere. The boy-monster sails over the counter, ducking out of the line of fire.

I inspect the damage. The blast obliterated the wall, leaving a smoldering hole big enough to walk through.

Wentwhistle blows on the hook like it's a six-shooter. "You know, the kick on this thing isn't half as bad as I figured."

The sound of rending metal and wood drowns out the TV. Owen rises, meaty paws holding aloft a smoking section of the counter.

"No rest for the weary." Wentwhistle takes aim, but with a

shudder, the hook stops humming and goes dead.

"Huh?" She shakes the sickle. "Oh, come on!"

Owen flings the countertop across the dining room. Wentwhistle avoids a direct hit but takes a glancing blow to the head.

"Finley? I think I'm going to be ill." Eyes rolling back in her head, she slumps to the floor.

Oh, crap. "Hey, doc? You okay?"

But there's no time to get her out of the line of fire. Owen steps toward me, kicking aside a stool. Bending my knees, I drop into a wrestling crouch and put up my fists. With no weapons and no backup, I'm going to get killed by this thing. But at least I'll go down swinging.

A high-pitched shriek pierces the air. I scan the room but can't detect the source.

Owen cocks his head like a well-trained Doberman. The whine echoes again. With a grunt, the boy-monster turns and escapes through the hole in the wall.

Oh, great. Now Owen wants me to chase him. But I have bigger problems at the moment.

Kneeling on the ground, I try to rouse Wentwhistle. "Wake up," I say, gently shaking her by the shoulders. "We're in a lot of trouble here."

Her eyelids flutter open. "Mickey?" She grasps my hand, her touch cold as ice. "What just happened?"

I tear a piece of cloth from the hem of my shirt. "You got hurt." I dab the blood from her forehead. "I'm going to get you out of here."

"No." She shakes her head. "I don't think there's time."

Something shatters in the room next door, making a sound like glass breaking. A loud series of animal grunts follows, punctuated by the slamming of a heavy door.

"You have to stop him, Finley." Coughing, she puts a hand

Craig E. Higgins

to my cheek. "Alone."

"Let me at least get you off the floor," I say.

Grabbing her under the arms, I drag Wentwhistle behind the smoking remains of a booth. She's actually kind of tiny so it's not hard to move her. I prop her against the barrier, and she swoons.

Silence resonates in the diner. Getting to my feet, I retrieve the hook, blade gleaming under the fluorescent lights.

Doing my best to ignore the bodies, I duck through the opening and go after Owen.

26

An odor like bait mixed with aerosol hangs in the kitchen. The floor is a mess of broken glass, canned goods, and spilled flour. Atop a stove, a big pot of chili has been upended, beans and sauce spilling along the oven door.

Treading cautiously, I almost trip over a middle-aged woman sprawled on a pile of spilled macaroni. It's our waitress. She's shaking like a leaf, purple ooze dripping from a bite wound on her shoulder. Her eyes are glassy and she's clutching her purse and a can of hairspray. The woman keeps repeating the same word, over and over.

"Shark…shark…shark…"

Kneeling beside her, I wave my hand in front of her face. "Lady, you okay?" I whisper.

"Shark…shark…shark," she mumbles.

Gently, I take the can from her hand. The label reads, *Aqua-Net*.

Weird. Owen must've come this way. Did she try to hairspray him to death?

A trail of plum-colored slime disappears around a stainless steel table. A purple handprint drips from the door of a walk-in cold box in the back.

Fighting back the urge to flee, I inch forward through the kitchen. If I'm going to take Owen down, I need some firepower. Grasping the hook, I work the weapon's trigger. The sickle is dead as a doornail.

Wonderful.

A knot twists in my gut.

Stupid, stupid, stupid. No way you can take this guy. We are dead, dead, dead.

"Are we?" I say out loud. "If he's so scary, why'd he run?"

You're going to get us killed, killed, killed.

"Look, just let me do this, okay?"

Somebody grabs my shoulder. I break free and raise the sickle above my head, ready to strike.

Win throws up his hands. "Whoa," he whispers. "Don't take me out, man."

"Sorry." I lower the hook. "You snuck up on me."

"You're easy to sneak up on."

"I guess that's true."

He points to the waitress, shaking on the floor. "What do we do about her?"

"Don't know."

A muffled moan escapes the cold box, followed by a sound like a ravenous dog chewing on a bone.

I point to the freezer. "That way."

Treading carefully, me and Win reach the door.

Win turns to me. "Who's in there?"

"Actually, it's more of a what," I say. "Used to be a dude from school, but now he's all…well, you know."

"I wish I didn't." He points to the hook. "Where'd you get that?"

I shrug. "Would you believe it's from an alien asteroid full of pyramids and bug people?"

"No." He chuckles. "Except coming from you, it's probably

true."

"We got more in the van, like blasters and stuff."

"Blasters?" His eyes go wide.

"Yeah. But they're all locked up and Wentwhistle's got the keys."

"That the old hippy chick I saw when I walked in?"

"Yep."

"Couldn't we just get the keys off her? Go get those weapons and, you know, lock and load?" He makes a clicking sound while racking an imaginary pump shotgun.

A bumping sound reverberates through the cold box's insulated door.

I grip the hook tightly in both hands, heart pounding. "I don't think there's time."

"Okay." Win frowns. "Um, Mickey? We busting through, right?"

"We are. You ready?"

"Yeah. But can I give you some advice?"

"Right now?" I glare at him. "We're going in."

"I know, I know." He stares at me the way your dad does when you get caught taking the last soda out of the fridge. "But Mickey? Seriously, you got to stop talking to yourself."

Aw jeez, he must've heard me earlier. "What? I don't do that."

"Yeah, you do. And I don't know who you *think* you're talking to, but they're not real, man."

Win's got me, and there's no point in pretending otherwise. "Look, I got a confession to make."

A ragged belch rattles behind the door, followed by a sound like cracking eggs.

"Yeah?" Win stares past my shoulder at the door. "Make it quick. I think our friend in there has the munchies."

"Um, this is going to sound weird. But I hear these voices?

They're not actually in the room but like inside my brain or something."

"Seriously?" He frowns. "That's messed up."

"Yeah, and they never go away. It's like there's this evil spirit inside me, telling me my life's always going to be horrible or I'm going to screw something up."

A rattle like cracking eggs reverberates from the freezer, accompanied by a sound like somebody smacking gum.

"I don't like the sound of that," Win says, grabbing a cast iron skillet off a nearby stove. Gripping the handle, he tests the heft of the pan. "Oh yeah. This'll work." Then he turns to me. "You ever talk to your folks about your problem?"

"They'd just think I'm crazy. Anyway, they're monsters now so I guess it doesn't matter."

"Mickey?" He shakes his head. "It matters to me, man."

"Thanks." I reach for the handle to the freezer and the hook vibrates to life, humming like a hairdryer. "Well, alright," I say. "Now we're cooking."

A muffled voice calls to me from inside the freezer. "Finley? That you?" He sounds like a lost little kid looking for his mom.

"How are you, Owen?" The sickle glows, throwing off heat.

"That witch sprayed me with something," he says between slurping noises. "Hurt me really bad."

"Sorry about that man," I say.

Win nods at me and takes up a position beside the door.

"But I'm going to be...it's going to be okay," Owen says. "Just had to get me something to eat." An awful racket like somebody hocking up a loogie echoes through the door.

"Owen?" I say, "why don't you just come out, now? Tell me about the Master. He anybody I know?"

"Oh, you know him, and he knows you. Sees you wherever you go." Owen pauses and a muffled crunching noise fills the air. "Even in your dreams. That's what he did to me. Kept coming to me in my dreams and changing me. But you? You *can't* be changed, and that's why you've got to die."

"Mickey," Win whispers, "let's go."

I nod. "Say, Owen? Whatever happens next? It's nothing personal, okay?"

"You come through this door and I'll get you," he shouts at me. "Get you and kill you and eat and eat and eat!"

Win grips the skillet like it's a baseball bat. "That's it."

I yank open the door, and we plunge into the freezer, frigid air filling my lungs with biting cold. A stench of maggoty fish guts permeates the cramped space. There's water on the floor and Win almost slips in it. I wield the sickle like a sword, trying to keep my balance.

Owen sits in the muck, legs splayed in front of him. The dim freezer light casts spidery shadows over smoking blisters on his puffy face, a greenish fluid dripping from his fangs. An ice cream carton lies in the creature's lap, propped up against his distended belly.

A cartoon turtle smiles on the side of the carton, dancing above a logo that reads, *El Tortuga.*

Well, crap. They even put monsters in the ice cream. "Owen," I whisper, leveling the hook at him. "You know what this thing can do. Give it up."

He smiles, his eyes dripping plum-colored sludge. "What, these?" Owen digs a paw into the carton and pulls out a squirming green creature about the size of a mouse. "No way." It wiggles in his plump fingers, screeching like a tiny cat.

Win clutches the skillet in his hands. "Dude, what is that thing?"

The light flickers above my head and I get a glimpse of tentacles lashing around the critter's pointed snout, a single reptilian eye blinking on its belly.

"Owen," I say, "don't eat that."

He laughs. "You know they're putting these in the grocery store tomorrow?" The boy-monster pops the squealing thing into his mouth and swallows. "That way, everybody gets a taste."

"What are you talking about?" My knuckles now burn from the humming hook. "Dude, you've got to stop this right now."

"Too late to stop anything." He belches. "The Rising's already happening."

A tentacle pokes above the carton rim. Win's eyes go wide as silver dollars. "What do we do?"

Owen laughs. "They come in all sizes. This one's bigger."

From inside the container, a second tentacle tests the air. A tiny creature emerges, its single yellow eye and razor-sharp teeth gleaming under the flickering lights.

With a roar, the boy-monster tosses the thing like a hand grenade. It lands on Win, tentacles encircling his thigh.

He tumbles into the muck, bashing at the creature with the skillet. "Man, get it off me!"

That does it. I'm going to fry this dude.

The hook explodes with a deafening whine. White light fills the small room. Knocked backwards by the blast, Owen slams into the wall. Green flames erupt from his chest, casting noxious smoke into the room. The fire consumes the boy-monster and he screams, his high-pitched yammer loud as a jet taking off.

Win smashes the skillet over the thing on his leg. The creature lets go and makes for the exit, tentacles slogging through the muck.

"Win, get out of the way." I aim the sickle at the beast.

"You don't have to tell me twice." He presses himself against the wall and I blast the monster.

Artichoke Stars and Chicken Fried Shark

It splatters like a June bug smashed on a windshield. A stench like rotten eggs fouls the air. I turn to Owen, but he's just a skeleton dissolving into a gelatinous mess. Mist hovers over the bones until they disintegrate, reduced to an oily puddle.

Something moves on a shelf above our heads. Win points to an ice cream carton shuddering on the rack. "Is that what I think it is?"

"There's more of them." I grab his arm. "Let's get out of here. Burn the whole place down."

"Oh, no. I don't think you'll be doing that," a voice says.

I grab the sickle and drop into a crouch. "Who's there?"

Three figures enter. The first two are Freddie, the tongue-dart spitter from the dance, and a fat kid with baggy eyes. The third, is blond and barrel-chested. He strides in like a lion.

"Hello, Wade." I train the hook on him. "How's your throwing arm?"

Wade cracks his neck. "Never been better." He gestures to the hook. "Why don't you drop that thing and come with us?"

"Nah, we're not doing that." Win grips the skillet. "Why don't you just back on out of here?"

Wade's laughter is so icy it could cut glass. "Ah, Pop-Tart," he says. "Lately, when I got an itch needs scratching, you seem to be that itch. Too bad for you."

"Shut up, Wade," I say. "Why'd you do it, huh?"

He raises his hands in protest. "Do what?"

"Let them hurt Alice." The hook hums in the still air.

He inches closer. "Hey, she wanted to be Queen Bee. I just made all her dreams come true. Why do you care, anyway? You two hated each other."

"That's far enough." I wave the weapon like a road flare. "What are you doing here, anyway?"

"Master wants you as a specimen, errand boy. So. y'all 're

coming with us."

"Owen said your boss wanted me dead."

Wade smirks. "Owen was an idiot." He points toward the open door. "Let's get going."

"Don't think so." Win lunges at Wade, bringing the skillet down on his arm. The bully smirks and backhands him, sending him sprawling into the muck.

I fire and a wild scream reverberates in the freezer. Wade dodges the blast and gets inside, unloading a jab that makes me see stars. "You made a bad enemy, Pop-Tart." He punches me again. "But lucky for you…" He slams me into a shelf. "…I got other plans."

I slip to my knees, my pants legs soaking from the water on the floor. My eyelids grow heavy, and my ears fill with static. Win lies on his back, Freddie's tongue dart gleaming from his neck.

We're screwed now.

Before I black out, Wade grabs the sickle. "Somebody put this away. Let's get them to the boat house."

27

Stripes of sunlight hit my face through a broken window blind. Ropes constrain my arms behind my back, the cord cutting into my wrists. Judging from the glare baking my skin, I guess it's around five in the afternoon.

I'm sitting on the floor of a small, plywood-paneled room, the air stinking of gasoline and brine. Wind buffets the building's exterior, making the walls sway gently. Am I on a boat? That would explain the bait smell.

There's a leaden feeling in my arms and I figure they've been tied for most of the time I've been unconscious. My ankles are bound, too. Most of the room lies in shadow, and nothing moves except a dim figure against the opposite wall.

I make out Win struggling against his bonds. "Mickey? You awake?" he says.

"Yeah," I whisper. "You okay?"

"I guess." Win flips onto his back trying to squirm free, to no avail. "You know what? I think we lost the last round."

"Looks that way. Any idea where we are?"

"No. I didn't wake up until a couple minutes ago."

"Well, that sucks."

"It is what it is. See that over there?" He nods to an old oar standing in the corner. "Must be a boat to go with it."

"You're right. Smells like shrimp a little, too. So, we're out on the Gulf?"

"Maybe *near* the Gulf." He shrugs. "Floor's concrete, so we're not on a boat."

"Right. So, how do we get out?"

Win nods to a table. "See that? Look at what's on top."

"Okay." I catch sight of a pair of scissors sticking out of a coffee mug. "What's your plan?"

He rolls to his knees, pitches forward, and lands on his shoulder. "I'm going to try to knock the table over. We get those scissors we can cut each other loose."

"How?"

"I slide them over, we sit back-to-back, I'll get them open, and you push your ropes against the blade. Got it?"

"You think that's going to work?"

"You got a better idea?" Squirming across the concrete, he reaches the table.

"No," I drop to the floor, kicking myself toward him.

Bringing both feet together, Win hammers a table leg. It shudders but holds.

"Man, they going to make me do it." Win attacks the leg again and again. On his fifth attempt, splinters fly.

Sweat beads on my forehead and runs down my nose. "That's it. It's about to—"

He kicks again and the table topples over. The cup shatters on impact, spilling the scissors on the floor.

"There we go," Win says, pushing himself through the debris. He rolls over broken shards of pottery, fingers grasping at the scissor-handles. "Aw, I can't see."

I direct him toward the scissors. "You've got, like, three more inches."

Win inches backward, then twists his body until his fingers

clutch the handles. "Got 'em."

"Cool." I nudge forward. "Let me just get to you."

Something rustles the blinds. I hear a rush of flapping wings from outside.

"Man, what was that?" Win whispers.

"I think it was just birds." With a final push, I reach Win. We're back-to-back. I can feel his fingers working to open the shears.

"Think they got guys watching us?" Win opens the blades. I can feel their sharp edges on the rope, nudging my wrists.

"If they are, all that noise we just made would've sent them running." I start to work the rope against the blade, working slow so as not to cut myself. "So, I've never done this before."

Win chuckles. "Just keep sawing."

"What if the scissors won't cut through?"

"Dude!"

"Okay, okay." I drag the cord back and forth, the taut fibers cutting into my skin. At first, the binds hold. "Man, I don't think this is working."

"Keep trying," he says.

It seems to take forever. I'm drenched in sweat and my arms are beginning to cramp. Finally, the rope frays enough for me to wiggle free.

"I got it," Sitting up, I stretch my arms.

"Okay, now do mine," Win says.

Using the scissors, I hack away at his ropes until they break.

"Cool." He grabs the shears. "Give me those."

Win slices through his ankle ropes with a few strokes, then he frees me.

I get to my feet. "Man, it feels good to stand."

"Let's check out where we're at." Win goes to the window, and peeks through the blinds. I join him.

Outside, the sun is a dull orange fireball sinking into a

marsh field. Tall cordgrass waves amid still patches of brackish water.

"Say, Win? I think I know where we are."

"You do? All I see is a bunch of swamp."

"There's marshland just north of town, and like a lot of rich people live out there?"

"Huh." He frowns. "Why would somebody rich want to live by a swamp?"

"Well, it's mostly fishing camps and stuff. See that house?" I point to a large white two-story dwelling squatting on a bank maybe a quarter mile away. "You got to have money to own a place like that."

"So?"

"So," I smile, "if that's where we are, there has to be a way to reach the main road. We can hitchhike back to town from there."

"Cool." Win walks toward a grime-covered contraption against the far wall. "What's this thing?"

"Not sure." I follow him.

The metallic relic is about five feet tall, and there's a hose with a spigot sticking from a holster on the side. Bolted to the front is a sign that reads…

FUEL ONLY. CONTAINS LEAD.

Win raps his knuckles against the metal, making it ring. "This is an old boat pump. So, they've got to have a boat, hopefully a fast one."

"And I can run it." I grab the oar. "My uncle taught me how to use an outboard."

"Then, why are you bringing that?"

"We need weapons."

Win snaps his fingers. "Yeah, right." He pockets the scissors, and we make for the door. I reach for the knob but stop at the sound of boots slogging through mud. Win nods, and we take up positions on opposite sides of the entrance.

He waves the scissors. "Whoever comes in, you hit 'em high, and I'll stick 'em in the gut."

"Um, no. Can't you just punch them?"

"You're right," Win says, sliding the shears into his back pocket. Outside, a boy swears. A key slides home, and the doorknob slowly turns, then stops. Sparks run the length of my spine. Win balls his fists, sweat pouring from his brow.

The knob turns back slowly, then stops. Then the person on the other side of the door leaves, footsteps receding into silence.

"Whew." Win rests his hands on his knees. "But we still got to take him on, whoever that was."

"Yeah, but maybe on better terms."

Me and Win wait until nightfall. When the guard doesn't return, I smash the doorknob with the oar, and we slip outside. Our makeshift jail is nothing but a small shed with a tin roof. A wind cuts across the marsh, chilling me through my sweaty t-shirt. Goosebumps prickle my arms.

Win disappears around the corner of the shed. After a second, he yells, "Look, here's our boat."

Next to the weather-beaten structure, a small dock floats above the cordgrass. Tied to a wooden piling is a two-person skiff, red paint peeling from the hull. The outboard looks like it hasn't been started in years.

Gingerly, Win places one foot in the stern, the other firmly on the dock. "Looks sturdy. Guess we better get out of here."

I hand him the oar, step in and yank the cord on the outboard. It grumbles but doesn't start.

Win leans over the dock. "You sure you know how to start

that thing?"

"Yes."

Something the size of a medicine ball plops into the water.

"What was that?" Win whispers, wielding the oar with both hands.

"Probably a nutria."

He frowns. "A what?"

"It's like this giant water rat with big orange teeth." I dangle two fingers in front of my mouth, like vampire fangs.

"*Orange* teeth? Sounds nasty."

The roar of a car's engine breaks the silence. Birds scatter.

Win gestures to the boat house. "Better take cover."

Staying low, we dart behind the structure. Voices echo across the marsh.

Win glimpses around the corner. "Mickey, take a look."

Wade Ruthven's fat accomplice stands beside a long-nosed sports car. Wade gets out of the passenger side, grabs the chunky kid by the shirt and shakes him. The boy struggles to free himself, but the bully slaps him across the face, then gestures to a ramshackle two-story house built on ten-foot stilts.

I stare at the dilapidated building, remembering what Alice Walsh told Wade at the football game. *You think I don't hear the rumors? People gossiping about what you do at your secret boys' club?*

You were right, Alice. The club is real, and I'm staring right at it.

Wade shoves the boy again, knocking him backward a few feet. Then the bully gets in the vehicle. It takes off, hurtling down a gravel path and out of sight.

The kid watches the car disappear, then retreats into the house.

Win bounces on the balls of his feet. "You know, maybe we could just wait for those dudes to come back with that car. We could get the drop on them and use that as our getaway."

"Maybe." I scratch my chin. "But remember, Wade and his buddy are no longer human. I fought Wade, and he can like… change parts of his body into…other things."

Win furrows his brow. "What do you mean, *other things*?"

"Dude can turn his arm into a crab claw," I spread my arms wide, "this big around."

"Seriously?" Win's eyes grow big as half-dollars. "That's weird. And Whatshisname spits those freaky darts and all."

"Exactly." I nod in the direction of the house. "But what if…I don't know. What if we took out the dude in the house?"

"You mean…?" Win draws a finger across his throat.

I shake my head. "No, no. I mean we overpower him. He's just one guy, and he might not be amped up like the other two."

Win grins. "And he looks like a total wimp."

"Righto. Him, we can take."

Win snaps his fingers. "Then we tie him up and call the cops from the house to bust Wade and them." He grins at me, nodding in a self-satisfied way. "Say, Mickey? Right now, you feel like we're in an episode of *Magnum P.I.*?"

I shrug. "I never watch that show."

"What? Me and Pop watch it all the time. Thomas Magnum is the greatest!"

"If we survive this? I'll come to your house every week just for Thomas Magnum."

"And Zeus and Apollo."

"Who are they?"

"The butler's dogs."

"Magnum has a butler?"

"Mickey, where have you been? We got to catch you up."

He aims a finger at the stilt-house. "You ready?"

28

Me and Win trudge through the muck toward the house. Mud cakes my pants, falling off in clumps with the rise and fall of my feet. Exhaustion and humidity weigh heavy on my legs and arms. I wish there was time to rest but if I stop now, I drop.

The house is a shipwreck on stilts, with a weather-beaten roof and walls riddled with termite holes. Its upper deck appears to be held together with chicken wire. A rickety staircase leads to a second-story screen door dangling on one hinge.

Win mounts the stairs two at a time, and I follow. A rotten tread snaps under my weight.

Upstairs, a light goes on.

Win puts a finger to his lips. "Shh."

Huddled on the decomposing second-floor deck, Win tries the doorknob. The door swings open without any fuss.

Inside there's a short hallway. Wallpaper peels away in great bunches. Rotting insulation spills from holes punched through the plaster. Cockroaches scatter from rusted cans and crumpled fast food bags.

Win pinches his nose. "Man, these guys are disgusting. I

Craig E. Higgins

thought Wade was rich?"

"I think he is," I whisper. "Maybe they're just squatting here." I lift my foot to avoid a puddle of something pulpy and brown that stinks like roadkill. "Wow, this just gets better and better."

We make our way to the back of the house, floorboards creaking like an old sailing ship. The hall ends at a short passageway. To the right, weak light flickers on the walls and ceiling. To the left, complete darkness.

Win nods to the right. "Let's try this way first."

A few feet down, we stop at an open door. An unmade bed stands against the wall, the headboard decorated with animal bones, the mattress covered with dark stains. Ropes dangle from the four corners of the metal frame. A smell like rotten apples mixed with shrimp-bait lingers in the air.

I spot a curly blonde wig on the floor. The remains of a torn dress lay crumpled on the bed. On the other side of the room, moonlight reflects off the cracked mirror of an old vanity. Aerosol cans litter the floor, dresser, and windowsill.

I pick one up and shake it. It's half-way full.

Win glances over at me. "What you got there?"

I turn over the can and read the label. "*Aqua-Net.* What is it with these guys and hairspray?"

"What do you mean?"

"Remember when we found Owen, and his face was all messed up?"

Win chuckles. "His *everything* was all messed up."

"Yeah, but he said the waitress hurt him before he got in the freezer." I shake the can. "Only thing she had on her was this."

Win shrugs. "You think *Aqua-Net* took Owen down?"

"Well, maybe it didn't kill him. But maybe it weakened him enough so that when I blasted him, he flamed out."

"Don't remind me," Win says with a shudder. "I'll never be able to unsee that."

Without another word, he slips out of the room and down the hall. I fill an empty sack with Aqua-Net and run to catch up.

We retrace our steps, and make our way down the dark, unlit corridor. A television in a room at the other end of the hall casts a blue glow, and static chatters from its speakers. Through the open door, we survey mounds of trash, moldy furniture, and strange brass objects scattered around on every flat surface.

The top of someone's head is visible above the back of a filthy sofa.

"That's him," I whisper.

Win nods. "Yeah."

"What's the plan?"

Win grabs the paddle from me. "I hit him high with this, and you hit him low."

"That's a plan?"

"Follow my lead." Win charges the couch, swinging the oar like a club.

The boy rolls to the side, springs to his feet, and deflects the blow. Win raises the weapon again but gets decked before he can use it. Stumbling backward, he slams into me, and we both collapse in a heap. The oar clatters uselessly to the floor.

Towering over us, the fat kid hisses. His cheeks split into three mouths that open and shut like nutcrackers.

"Y'all thought you could jump me?" The big boy's hands melt, contorting into sharp, spiny barbs. "Thought you could take me down, huh?" He swipes the back of the sofa, spilling stuffing onto the floor. "Come get some!"

Win hops to his feet. "Mickey? This dude ain't a wimp."

I rise on unsteady legs. "No, duh."

A desperate thought crosses my mind. I pull an aerosol can from the sack. But before I can spray him, he's on top of me. The fat kid stabs his sticker-hand into the floor, narrowly missing my face.

"Going to carve you up, you little—"

The paddle careens off the back of the kid's head and he drops like a sack of potatoes.

Win grins. "Guess you weren't so tough after all."

Suddenly the kid rises, triple-mouths snapping like turtles. Win whacks him again and again, but nothing seems to stop him.

I get to my feet, grab a can of Aqua-Net and point it at the kid's face.

He throws his hands up in surrender. "No, don't do it to me! Please, don't!"

Win hits him with the oar again, and the boy topples over.

We stand there, breathing hard. I'm suddenly aware of the television static and the stench of bait in the air.

"What do we do with this dude?" Win cradles the paddle like a spear.

I stare at our fallen kidnapper. "Tie him up, I guess?"

He nudges the boy with his shoe. "Think we should, I don't know, interrogate him?"

"Don't think there'll be time. We better get out of here."

Headlights play across the wall, and the sound of tires on gravel filter through the windows.

Win turns to me. "Is that their car?"

"Probably. They'll be here soon. We got to make for that boat."

"But which way do we go once we get out in the swamp?"

"Toward that house up the marsh."

"You mean the plantation?" Win sounds less than thrilled.

"Yeah." I position myself next to the exit. "Maybe

somebody there will let us use their phone." I lean through the doorway. Only silence echoes in the hall. Still, it's only a matter of time before Wade and Freddie get here.

The fat kid groans and tries to take a knee. "Man, y'all play rough."

I spray a burst close to his head. "We haven't even gotten started. Your friends are coming. Can you get us out of here?"

He regards me through plum-shot eyeballs. "I ain't helping you. M-Master Blight would kill me."

So, Blight *is* the master. "Don't worry about him." I hold the *Aqua-Net* under his chin. "You help us out or you'll be tuna melt."

The fat kid growls from all three of his mouths, then stumbles to his feet. "Okay."

Win high-fives me. "Now, that's some stone-cold Mickey Finley right there."

I look at Win and smile. "Thanks, man."

Stone-cold? Sounds better than Pop-Tart.

Our prisoner lurches toward a screen door. "There's a back staircase. We can go that way."

Win grabs the oar. "Then lead on, buddy."

29

We get outside and I search the marsh for a sign of Wade and his buddies. Overhead, a yellow moon illuminates a path through the cordgrass. An engine's roar catches my attention. Headlights bright as snake eyes cut the darkness. The twin ovals grow bigger and bigger, the motor's growl rough and steady. They'll be here soon.

I glance at Win. "You ready?"

He nods. "Let's go," he says, pushing the fat kid ahead of him. The monster's wrists are tied behind his back, and plum-colored blood drips from his six swollen lips.

About fifty feet on, I whirl around at the sound of an engine backfiring. At the house, Wade and Freddie climb the stairs at a quick clip. They enter the building, and seconds later a light springs to life on the second floor. Garbled screams and curses echo from above. Then an upstairs window shatters, glass showering the ground below.

The fat kid smiles. "Wade's going to get y'all. And when he does—"

"Shut it." Win yanks the boy-monster's wrists, making him cry out in pain.

I glance upward, waiting to see them rush down the stairs.

Craig E. Higgins

Nothing moves on the second floor. Silence permeates the night air, save for chattering noises of frogs and crickets.

"It's too quiet," I say.

Win shakes his head. "Doesn't matter. We got to go."

We stumble through the marsh. Twenty yards from the shed, my shoe gets stuck in the muck. From the direction of the house, a familiar voice shouts, "Where you going, Pop-Tart?"

Wade stands at the bottom of the stairs, flanked by Freddie and two other boys, their shark-grins gleaming in the moonlight.

"Alright!" The fat boy wrenches away from Win's grasp and bolts toward his buddies. Something whizzes through the air and hits the kid in the neck.

"Dang," Win says, "that must be Freddie."

The chubby boy tries to pull the stinger from his flesh. His eyes go wide. Dark fluid spills from all three of his mouths. He moans, staggers, and collapses face-first into the muck.

"Jeez," I say. "They kill their own guys."

Win nudges me. "Go."

He sprints for the boat, his leggy stride sailing over the high grass. I struggle to keep up, mud sucking at my high-tops. Something zips past my ear. Another of Freddie's tongue darts? I put my head down legs keeping time with the tripwire cadence of my heart. Sweat pours down my face, and blood pulses in my temples.

Behind me, Wade's mocking voice fills me with dread. "You can't get away, Pop-Tart!"

The dock is only a few mud-choked yards ahead. When I'm a few feet from safety, a submerged stump sends me sprawling. I choke on a mouthful of grime. Have to get up and keep going. If I don't, we'll both die. Boots slog through the marsh a few yards away. I rise, mud dripping from my soaked pants legs.

Win stands with one foot on the boat's gunnel, a big-barreled flare gun in his hand.

Where did he get that?

Another projectile splashes just ahead of me. Wade and the rest are closing in. Win levels the flare gun.

"Mickey, toss the rest of them cans at those dudes." He closes one eye and takes aim. "On my signal. Ready?"

"Go for it," I say.

"One."

I swing the bag like a sack of groceries. The timing has to be just right.

"Two."

Out in front, Freddie hurdles a grassy mound, tongue lolling like a monitor lizard.

"Three."

I hurl the bag with as much strength as I can muster. It lands right in the dark-haired boy's path.

Laughing, Freddie picks it up. "This ain't going to do nothing to me."

Win fires.

The cans in the bag explode in a great blue fireball. Screaming, Freddie sinks into the muck, enveloped in a fiery curtain. Wade rolls his pal, trying to douse the flames. The others hesitate, waiting for orders.

Win sticks the weapon in his waistband. "Don't think that'll give us all that much time."

I leap into the boat and give the cord a yank. The outboard coughs and goes silent.

Wade rises, arm distorting into a crab claw. "You think this changes anything?" He waves the bony appendage at us. "Where are y'all going to go, anyway?"

I take another shot at the outboard. More coughing, then a wet sputter. The little motor catches and I give Win a nod.

The blond bully strides through the muck. "I'm going to gut you like a fish, little boy. And what we don't eat? That'll make for a nice rug!"

Win shoves the boat with his foot, and dives in. "Go, go, go!"

I swing the bow around, and the boat lurches into the cordgrass.

"You sure you can drive this thing?" He yells over the wind.

"Yeah." I grit my teeth, trying to ignore the possibility I don't actually know what I'm doing.

We speed from the dock just before Wade and his crew arrive.

Win kneels in front of the boat. "So long, suckers!" He flashes them a double, one-fingered salute.

Wade whistles, and a torrent of bubbles churns in our wake. Two bony fins the size of battleship anchors break the surface, cutting through the cascading water.

"Oh crap," I say. "What is that thing?"

"Just drive." Win checks the flare gun, frowns, and starts picking through piles of junk in the bottom of the skiff.

"What are you doing?"

"Got to reload." Win finds two more shells in a white plastic box. He snags one and slips it into the flare gun's breech. "This is all we got, so it'll have to do."

The prow slices through the black water. Foam sprays my face and I steady the tiller, so we don't run aground.

A dull roar like a freighter's horn cuts through the air. Something big splashes behind us, sending the tide back in our direction. I barely avoid a half-submerged tree, but backwash from the giant wave behind us nearly upends the boat.

The plantation house is dead ahead. I make out Grecian columns supporting a wide veranda littered with trash. Even in the darkness, it's easy to see the old place has been long abandoned.

Win smirks. "So much for the plantation. Now what do we do?"

"We can still hide there." With both hands clutching the tiller, I guide the boat toward the house.

"We can't hide from that." Win points to the thing chasing us. The yellow moon is high. For the first time, I get a good look at the creature.

The beast's torpedo-like body stretches twice as long as Uncle John's Challenger. Its head is shark-like, bristling with needle-sharp teeth. One unblinking yellow eye sticks out of its side, and its fins twitch like stabilizers on a jet plane. The monster hops more than swims, loping along on giant tentacles. Even at a distance, I choke on its briny stench.

"Can we outrun it?" Win yells.

"No way." I give the motor full throttle. Black marsh water sprays in my face from off the bow, and everything stinks of sulfur mixed with gasoline.

The monster screeches again, and something the size of a

nutria leaps into the boat.

"Aw man!" Win drops the flare gun. A squirming one-eyed thing slithers across the floor, biting at his foot. "Stupid thing!" He grabs the beast and flings it into the prop, splattering both of us in green slime.

The outboard's whine ratchets to fever pitch. Up ahead, I catch sight of a muddy embankment partway hidden behind a clutch of cordgrass.

"Win, look out." I grip the tiller with both hands. "We're about to hit the dirt."

In another heartbeat, we slam into the embankment. I am catapulted out of the boat. Time slows down before I slam into a rusted gas pump.

Everything hurts, and sparks dance across my eyes. Working to clear my head, I test my ability to stand. There's another screech. I catch sight of the monster wallowing in the shallows. It rears on its haunches a good twenty feet in the air, jaws snapping like a giant bear trap.

We're running out of options now. I scan my surroundings for a way out, a weapon, anything. The flare gun sticks out of the mud above the water line, right beside its ammo box. Scrambling through the muck, I find a single shell and slam it into the chamber.

Win stumbles toward me. "Forget it, Mickey. We can't stop that thing."

I catch a whiff of gas from the old pump. "No, but we can kill it."

"How?"

A tentacle, the thickness of a telephone pole, snakes through the cordgrass, finds the skiff, and crushes the hull.

"I'm going to copy your idea. Run to the house. Now."

The beast screams again and rolls onto shore. Hundreds of little one-eyed monsters wash in with its wake. Teeth chattering, they swarm toward me.

"Hey, stupid," I yell, waving my arms. "Over here!"

The giant beast turns, limbs splashing muck in all directions. I take off toward the house, the horde of little sharks dogging my heels. Twenty yards from the structure, I stop, take a knee, and draw a bead on the pump.

When the beast pulls even with the tank, I fire. The explosion splatters the embankment, sending a huge plume of muck into the air. A column of flames, smoke, and roasted flesh surges into the darkness.

Win slumps against a column while I fall to the porch, gasping for breath. The raging fire casts a sickly glow over the marsh and a stench of cooked meat and slimy fish guts hangs in the night air.

Win gets to his feet. "Great shot, man." He offers me a hand up. "But now we got no boat."

"Don't know if that's a problem." I shake myself off, flinging mud from my clothes. "There has to be a trail connecting this house to a road or…" I scratch my scalp. "…I don't know."

"We'll figure it out." Frowning, he sniffs at the air. "Wait. What is that smell?"

"What do you mean?"

"Mickey," he says, burying his face in his sleeve, "you stink like a fish market."

I catch a whiff from his direction. "Well, so do you, pal."

He chuckles. "This sure is some funky business."

We both laugh while the flames die on the wet cordgrass. Win points to a cracked cement driveway leading off into the woods.

"Guess we got some walking to do."

30

The sun hangs like a blood orange in the early morning sky by the time we flag a ride back to town. I thumb down a pickup. From the driver's side, a middle-aged man with teeth like piano keys squints at us from behind owl-eye's eyeglasses. "Where y'all going?"

"Back to town," I say. "Bay St. Louis."

"Well, I don't know what to tell you." He frowns. "Road's closed into Bay St. Louis."

"What?" I say.

"Something about a disease outbreak," the man says. "I can get you as far as the exit right before there, but that's about it."

"That's cool, man." Win trots in front of the truck and grabs the door handle on the passenger side. "I'm calling shotgun."

"Nope." Piano Teeth jabs a thumb at the truck bed. "Y'all get in back."

The pick-up barrels down the gravel road, kicking up a cloud of dust. Pine and cypress blur into a green smear. The wind scours my cheeks. My body is chilled as a cadaver in my wet clothes. I'm exhausted, every muscle sore, my ears ringing from all the explosions and screaming monsters.

Win plucks a splinter big as a rat's tooth out of his arm. "Wow. That's a nasty one."

"Yeah."

He flicks it away and leans close. "How long you figure we been gone?"

"I don't know. A day, I think?"

"A day? My folks will kill me for being out like this."

"I'm sorry."

"That all you got? He thumps the wheel well with the flat of his hand. "Man, we're screwed. You know that, right?"

I nod. "Yeah."

Win pounds his fist against the side of the truck. The driver glances back and shakes his head.

"So, what are we going to do now?" he says.

"Reckon we need to go see the cops. Shoulda' done that in the first place."

"But what do we tell them?" Win gestures toward the marsh. "About, you know, everything?"

"Tell them the truth, and hope they believe us."

"Yeah, right." He folds his arms. "Pop is going to be so mad at me."

"They'll probably ground you forever."

"Seriously." Win nudges me with his shoe. "What about your aunt and uncle?"

I wish he hadn't brought them up. "They've gone bad, too."

"Aw, no." He whistles under his breath. "Can things get any worse?"

The truck halts at a stop sign, sending us sliding toward the cab. "You know what?" Win rights himself and picks a chunk of mud off his shirt. "This is definitely not like *Magnum P.I.*"

Empty cars choke the intersection at the last exit into town, some overturned in a nearby ditch. Others lay crumpled on their sides or squat on their axles, burned out, smoke rising from the twisted remains. The blackened remains of a pick-up hangs on a ruined guardrail. Glass peppers the asphalt, sparkling in dark patches of motor oil. Green fluid streaks the sides of vehicles like old blood, pooling under flattened tires. All around there's a stench of bait mingling with gas, and maybe something from a dumpster.

Not a single person stirs.

Win nudges my arm. "What happened here?"

There's a squawk and a bird on a powerline teeters, then drops to the ground.

Piano Teeth comes to a stop in front of a police cruiser, roof lights flickering red. He steps out onto the gravel and walks to the rear of the truck.

"Hey." Piano Teeth bangs the tailgate with his hand. "Y'all get on out." He points to an overpass just past the exit. Burned-out vehicles stretch as far as the eye can see. "I'm not going down there."

Win hops out of the cab. "Aw man, what's happening?"

Piano Teeth glares at me. "You too, buddy."

"Give me a second," I say but do as I'm told.

"See what I mean?" the driver says. "There's been an outbreak."

"Looks like war to me," Win says.

"Outbreak," Piano Teeth says, nodding to the fallen bird. The poor creature stirs, shudders, and disgorges a steaming green mass. Tentacles sprout from the heap, and a yellow eye pops open. With a shriek, the little monster scurries under a car.

Win turns to me. "Mickey, was that what I think it was?"

"Yep." I walk toward the police cruiser. The driver's side

window is smashed, and the keys are still in the ignition.

A truck door slams behind me. I turn, just in time to see Piano Teeth get behind the wheel.

"Sure you want to go that way?" he says.

I shrug. "Where you headed?"

"North, up to Hattiesburg." He fires up the engine. "Y'all want a ride there, be my guest."

Win hesitates for a moment, then steps away from the pick-up. "Nah, we good, man. Thanks for the lift."

Without saying another word, the driver backs up, and vanishes the way we came.

I look at Win. "We could take this cop car."

He surveys the long line of vehicles in our way. "How we going to drive around that?"

"Reckon we can't. I don't know how to drive anyway."

Win opens the cruiser's passenger side. "Well, maybe they left a shotgun or something."

We search the vehicle and find a box of twelve-gauge shells, but no weapons.

"Weird," I say. "What happened to all the people?"

"I don't know." Win peers into a VW bug. "Man, there's slime on the steering wheel."

I lean in to take a peek. "Yeah. Smells bad, too."

He sighs. "Maybe we search a bunch of cars? Somebody must've left a gun, a knife, something."

Oh yeah, like a gun's going to help us against twenty-foot-tall monsters. "Dude, we got a lot of walking to do. Let's get to town."

"And then what, huh?" Win throws his hands in the air. "What do we do against all of this?" He slams the car door. "Mickey, we are out of options, man. For all we know, there's nobody left but us. No magic zombie plant ladies, no UFO experts." He stops to take a breath. "Just us," he whispers, thumping his chest.

A car horn, blaring a mariachi tune, shatters the silence. I push past Win and reach the guardrail.

Below the overpass sits Colleen Wentwhistle and her ugly van. She hops out of the vehicle, waving her hands. "You boys look like you could use a ride."

31

"**So, while you were** out, the apocalypse happened." Wentwhistle informs us while maneuvering the van around burning cars smashed together at an intersection. We're off the main road into Bay St. Louis, and all we've seen for the last quarter mile are abandoned vehicles, smashed storefronts, and pools of green muck on the ground.

She pulls over and offers me and Win fresh t-shirts. Mine says, *Keep on Truckin'*.

"What does this mean?" I ask.

"It means to persevere, you know." Wentwhistle shrugs. "Go with it. Something like that."

"Hippy stuff." I slip the shirt over my shoulders while she pulls back onto the street.

Win sits behind us, inspecting a blaster spear in the rear of the van. "What's this thing do?"

I glance back at him. "Makes stuff go boom."

He smiles. "Really?"

Wentwhistle hits the brakes so hard we skid to a halt, and I slam into the dash.

"Jeez, will you watch the road, man?" I say.

Wentwhistle sits behind the wheel, eyes wide, finger

pointing at a spot past the windshield. "Egad, but this Rising is definitely happening."

"What do you mean?" I lean out of the passenger side window. In front of us, a half-burned car sits on the road, its rear passenger door yawning open. The hood is crumpled under the weight of a bull-sized, one-eyed monster. Tentacles impale the vehicle's sides. Dark blood smears the interior of the car's windshield, obscuring whatever's left of the driver.

"This is all my fault." Wentwhistle slams the gear shift into park, leaving the engine still humming. "Finley, as soon as you contacted me, I should've immediately gotten on the horn with the cavalry."

"There's a calvary?" Win says. "What cavalry?"

"Other…collectors. We could've swooped in, guns a-blazing. But no sir." She flips her sun visor down and checks her teeth in the vanity mirror. "I just wrote you off as a cranky little boy with an artichoke story." She smacks her forehead. "Stupid me."

"Can't your friends come help now?" Win says.

"No." Wentwhistle shakes her head. "It's already too late. At this point, we're cut off from outside assistance."

"So, it's up to us, then." I grab her wrist. "But let me ask you something. One of the dudes who kidnapped us said something about Blight."

"Do tell?" She brushes my hand aside.

"Who is he?" Win says. "Or maybe what is he?"

Wentwhistle folds her hands in her lap. "Midian Blight is an alien sorcerer who's been on Earth for thousands of years. That thing right there?" She nods to Win's spear. "It was built by Blight's people, the T'Kalul."

I frown. "But the T'Kalul are bug-heads. They don't look human at all."

"Blight's one of them. He appears human because he wears

a human face." She frames her face with her hands. "Somehow, and I've never determined the exact process, Blight can assume a human identity. And since he looks like us, he can go places the other T'Kalul can't. His usual modus operandi is to dress like an authority figure. A priest, maybe, or sometimes a government flunky."

Government flunky? Wait a minute. "Like a doctor?" Snapping my fingers, I turn to Wentwhistle. "Doctor Blightman, the dude with the BDM. He's Blight, right?"

"I've never met Blightman, although I've heard about him. But when you put it that way, it makes so much sense. Blightman *is* Blight."

"Dude couldn't even come up with a different name." I laugh. "It's like he *wants* people to know who he is."

Win points to something through the windshield. "There's something in that car."

"What? The one with the shark on top?" I say.

"No. The one next to it."

I catch sight of a dull-orange Mazda hatchback. Aside from one blown tire, nothing's amiss. "I don't get what you—"

Like a jack-in-the-box, a head pops up over the back seat. I make out double rows of fangs and plum-shrouded eyes rolled up in its pale face.

Win recoils and grips the blaster. "Man, is that thing dead?"

"Let's go take a look." Wentwhistle draws the hook from her jacket.

We inch toward the vehicle, Win covering our rear.

Weapon at the ready, Wentwhistle stands a few feet in front of the door. "Mr. Finley, if you'll do the honors?"

I pull the handle. The graying husk falls out of the car and collapses on the ground.

She nudges the carcass's head with her foot. "Yep. This

sucker's not getting back up again."

Win jabs the cadaver's fleshy arm with his blaster. "That thing ain't human, is it?"

"No." Wentwhistle sticks the hook in her belt, reaches into her satchel and pulls on a pair of surgical gloves. "It's what the T'Kalul call a *kzeloc*, or a ruined man." Kneeling over the body, she inserts her fingers into the mouth and extracts a tooth. "Exposure to T'Kalul pathogens kills most humans. But some change into monsters, like this one."

"The kid at the restaurant," I say, scanning the line of cars for any other nasty surprises. "Was he a kzeloc?"

"Oh, most definitely." Wentwhistle snags a plastic bag from her satchel and deposits the tooth in it. "Not sure why this one got left behind." She discards the gloves and gets to her feet.

Win steps back, gripping his weapon tighter than the safety bar on a roller coaster. "Lady, last time we saw you, you were out like a light. What happened after we got taken? How do we know they didn't get to you?"

Oh Jeez, he thinks she's in league with the aliens. I step between them. "Win, what are you doing?"

Wentwhistle brushes dust off her pants. "If they had, I'd be slobbering over myself, trying to have the both of you for breakfast." She turns to me. "Finley, tell your friend I'm on his side."

"Hey, be cool, man," I say.

Shaking his head, Win raises his weapon. "And how did you know where to find us? I mean, that's pretty random you showing up where we were at."

"There's only one road north leading out of town," she says, taking a step toward him. Win stumbles back. "I woke up alone at the diner, okay? Once I got my act together, I got in the van and headed where the action was." She nods toward me. "This one usually tends to be at the center of it."

Win squints and gestures with the blaster. "That's it?"

She shrugs. "That's it. Take it or leave it."

"Okay, I guess I trust you." He lowers the weapon. "For now."

Wentwhistle smiles, and it occurs to me she might've been pretty, once. "Well, where did all the people go?" I say.

"Back to town." She gestures up the road. "When a Rising occurs, there's usually a big ceremony ushering in the end of all things."

From her jacket, she produces the three-cornered pendant we found earlier. "This thing keeps buzzing. I think it's a signal device of some kind."

The object's green jewel flashes as if powered by some internal force. A wave of nausea washes over me, and I stagger.

"Mickey." Win drops the spear and grabs my arm. "You okay, man?"

"Yeah, yeah." I shake my head to clear the cobwebs. "Just really tired, is all."

Wentwhistle stares at the pendant and then back at me, before tucking the glittering object in her shirt. "Do we need to get you something to eat? Sorry, but the Sonic's closed right now."

"Too bad." My laugh sounds more like a hoarse wheeze. "We could get you more of those tomato non-sandwiches."

Win stares out at the line of cars in front of us. "Ma and Pop have got to be worried sick about me."

"Kid, I hate to break it to you," Wentwhistle says to him, "but they may no longer be among the living."

Win glares at her. "Who are you to talk about them like that? They *got* to be alive." He makes for the van. "We need to go find them now."

"And we will." I say, blocking his escape. "But we can't do this alone."

Wentwhistle nods. "You're talking about the resurrected girl?"

"Yeah," I say. "Katie Sue. She told me to round up everybody close to us, and head to where she's at." I turn to Win. "Look, man, we'll go get your folks first, okay? But then we need to find Becca Mae and her dad, too. They're all in danger."

Tears slide down his cheeks. Shoulders slumping, Win buries his face in his arm. "You think I don't know that? Man, I don't mean to sound selfish, but—"

"You don't," Wentwhistle says. "All I hear is, you love your folks. That's an entirely rational expression of your state of mind."

"Well, yeah." He grins. "I'm just so worried about them."

"We'll save them," I say. "We'll save everybody."

Win looks at me and we hug, both of us in tears. Ordinarily, I'd feel weird about something like this because, you know, boys don't usually turn on the waterworks. But it's been a long day, and for all we know his folks really are dead. Besides, he's my friend and the world's about to end, so who am I to judge what's weird right now?

"Win, dear?" Wentwhistle places a foot on the running board of her van and taps the roof with her hook. "Where's the old homestead?"

A shadow passes over the van when we reach Win's neighborhood. Wentwhistle navigates the vehicle around wrecked vehicles and past rail cars derailed on rusty tracks. Used fast-food wrappers, plastic bags, old tires, and broken glass litter the broken, uneven sidewalks. We pass a windowless corner store. A surf-blasted sign advertising Skoal dangles precariously above the front door.

"Pop wanted to move us out of this area." Win says. "He thinks we'd be better off in base housing in Biloxi."

"Might not be a good time to sell," Wentwhistle says under her breath as she swerves around the charred remains of a motorcycle half-buried in a burned-out school bus. "This whole town will be slated for demolition when this mess is over. If there's a world left over to do the demolishing."

I open the window and let the chill wind numb my face. "Is there a cold snap coming on?"

"Not exactly," Wentwhistle says. "Look at the sky."

Coal black clouds shot through with gold flashes churn and percolate overhead. Now and then, lightning bolts arc from the darkness. Behind the cloud banks, a smoldering orange sphere partially eclipses the sun.

I don't see black rain, but the rest of it is right out of my dreams.

"I don't understand," I say. "Is this an eclipse?"

She cranes her neck to look through the windshield. "Of a sort, yes."

From the back seat, Win says, "Would you just tell it to us straight for once?"

Wentwhistle accelerates past a pair of green, tentacled creatures feasting on roadkill. I don't want to know what it is they're eating. "What's blocking the sun is *T'kahuatl*," she says. "That's the asteroid you went to, Mr. Finley."

I turn to Win. "It's where the bug people are from."

Win's brows furrow. "Man, all this alien stuff is making my head spin."

Wentwhistle neatly swerves around an overturned beer truck. "T'kahuatl is an asteroid turned into a spaceship, a traveling world if you will. It's blocking the sun because they brought it closer for the Rising."

Just then, something hard bounces off the side of the van.

"What was that?" I poke my head out the passenger side.

A trio of sprinting kzelocs run alongside the vehicle. One

rifles a rock at me, nearly taking my head off.

I roll up the window, as if that will do any good. "Jeez."

"Must be the welcoming committee." She guns the engine. "How far is your house, Win?"

He points up ahead. "Two blocks up that way. Can't miss it."

At the next intersection, we pass a darkened neon sign above a beauty shop window. Inside, a display advertises *Aqua-Net! Three Cans for $5!*

I grab Wentwhistle's arm. "Stop the van."

She stomps on the brake, throwing Win into the back of my seat. "Mr. Finley, what on earth?"

Win picks himself up and grins. "See that? Aqua-Net is like death for these things."

"That's for sure. Cover me." I hop out the passenger side and Win follows.

"Wait, we can't stop here," Wentwhistle protests. "We're exposed on the street."

I gesture toward the satchel at her feet. "Borrow your bag?"

She glares at me, then passes the leather pouch. "I swear, you'll be the death of us yet."

"Just keep the van running, okay?" I dart toward the beauty shop. Win is close on my heels, spear at the ready.

Three kzelocs round the corner and stop dead when they spot us. Barring their fangs, the trio attack.

Win blasts the sidewalk at their feet. Concrete sandblasts their faces but they keep coming. One spits a silver dart that narrowly misses my neck.

Win lays down fire while I dash into the shop. Aqua-Net cans lay scattered on the floor. I scoop up all I can carry and dash outside.

"Let's boogie," I say.

"You got it." Win takes out a brick wall, burying our

pursuers under falling rubble.

Hopping into the van, I drop the bag full of cans on the floor at my feet. More kzelocs arrive. They pelt the van with stones and bricks. One projectile hits the windshield, and it splinters into a mess of cracks.

Wentwhistle draws her hook, opens her door, and fires. Two creatures sail backward into a junked car. A tongue-dart flies through the driver's side window, impaling the head rest.

She turns to me. "We've got to get out of here."

The sliding door behind me slams shut. "I'm in," Win says, gasping for breath.

"Go, go," I yell. Wentwhistle floors the gas pedal and the van roars forward, clipping one kzeloc. Fishtailing down the street, the van takes out a couple more. With the road clear, we speed off toward Win's place.

The sky is pitch-black by the time we reach Win's house. It's identical to all the other homes on the block, except it's painted bright yellow.

Win leaps out of the van before we come to a complete stop and dashes for the front door. "Please, please please, let them be okay." Shaking, he grasps the doorknob.

"Just open it." Wentwhistle trains her hook on the entrance.

We step into a gallery of silent shadows.

Win cups his mouth. "Ma? Pop?"

Signs of a hasty exit are everywhere. In the living room, magazines lay scattered like autumn leaves. A half-filled suitcase is open on the bed, and clothes are spilled onto the floor. We reach the laundry room at the end of the hall. It's empty. On the opposite wall, an open door leads outside.

Win bangs his fist on the dryer. "Come on. They got to be around here somewhere!"

I grab his wrist. "Maybe they got out in time?"

"But—"

"Dude, they're not here."

Something crashes to the ground outside, and we freeze. Win levels his blaster at the door while Wentwhistle rushes to a nearby window.

"What was that?" I say.

She scowls. "Looks like a meteorite."

"A meteorite?" Win says.

"We need to get out of here." She retreats through the house at a run. "Where are the girls?"

32

Nobody's home at the Carson house. We try the door and when it doesn't budge, Wentwhistle draws her hook and blasts the lock.

I step across the threshold. "Becca Mae? Pastor Paul?"

Wentwhistle inspects an open leather-bound Bible on a coffee table. "Somebody was reading the New Testament." She turns to me. "You know the story about the loaves and fishes?"

"No," I say.

"Jesus feeds the masses in this big seafood giveaway."

I scratch my head. "Seafood?"

"Yeah." She closes the book. "Like a big cookout?"

A big cookout. Why does that sound so familiar?

Win darts from room to room, calling, "Yo, Becca? You here?"

We search the whole place. Not a soul in sight. But one detail stands out.

"Say, Wentwhistle?"

"Yes?" She turns her attention away from the Bible.

"When we went into Win's house, it looked like his parents split in a hurry. But here, there's no overturned furniture, no trash, no half-packed luggage. Nothing."

"You're right." She frowns. "How odd."

"Mickey?" Win walks in, a piece of paper in his hand. "Found this in the preacher's office."

I take the flyer from him. Inked on one side is a buck-toothed fisherman reeling in a comically grinning shark.

"Oh, crap." I crumple the advert in my hand. "Pastor Paul told me about this. They're having a shark fry at their church today."

"Any bets on what the main course is?" Wentwhistle says.

From another part of the house comes a sound like a wet mop being dragged across the floor.

Win grips his blaster and peers down the hall. "What the heck was that?"

"Don't know." Wentwhistle draws her hook. "But we better check it out."

The three of us enter the dining room. An Igloo cooler sits in the center of the table. The lid is ajar, and the air reeks like bait.

"Win? Be a dear and open it," Wentwhistle says, training her weapon on the cooler, "then step back."

Carefully, he nudges the lid with the blaster. A green tentacle slips over the top. Then another.

"There it is." Wentwhistle levels the hook and fires.

The cooler vaporizes, splattering pulped shark and tentacle everywhere.

"Yuck," I say, shaking gunk from my shirt.

"Eww," Win says. "Never going get this stuff off."

I glare at Wentwhistle. "Doesn't that thing have a lower setting?"

"Finley, sometimes it pays to be thorough." She wipes the mess from her face, then crosses the room. "What's this?"

I walk to where she stands, gawking at a picture partially covered in slime. It's a portrait of the whole Carson family from maybe five years before. Pastor Paul, mustache neatly trimmed, stands beside his wife, Enid. Long necked and bespectacled, she reclines in a rattan chair, thin lips transfigured into a self-satisfied grin. Flanking the pair are a smiling Katie Sue, long brown hair draped over her shoulders, and Becca Mae, blonde and bubbly like a cocker spaniel puppy.

Win wipes his face on his t-shirt and waves his weapon at the picture. "Dude got himself some creepy whiskers."

Wentwhistle dons surgical gloves and examines our find. With one latex-covered finger, she swipes a chunk of pulped tentacle from Pastor Paul's head. "Mr. Finley, how well did you say you knew these people?"

I turn to her. "What do you mean?"

Win speaks up. "What she means is, do the Carsons have something to do with all this?"

"No way," I shake my head. "Katie Sue got turned because the artichoke ended up in her grave. But she's on our side, her and Becca Mae."

"Really?" Wentwhistle grimaces. "What about dear old daddy?"

What about daddy? A knot forms in the pit of my stomach, and the events of the past two weeks run like a movie reel in my brain...

Uncle John and Pastor Paul whispering to each other at Katie Sue's funeral.

The minister picking John up in Hattiesburg.

The evasive answers Paul gave about the war photo in his office and his insistence I show up at the shark fry.

What if he's been involved the whole way?

Would he hurt Becca Mae?

"Aw, no," I say, "no, no, no." My gut-knot grows from acorn to basketball-size. Bile rises in my throat and my goosebumps get goosebumps. My legs go rubbery, and I prop myself against the wall to avoid falling.

Wentwhistle rushes over to catch me. "Are you alright?"

"It can't be." I slump to the floor. "This is going to suck, but I'm pretty sure they got Becca Mae. Maybe everyone else, too."

"Where, Mickey?" She shakes me gently. "Where's the shark fry?"

"Isn't it obvious?" I gaze into her hazel eyes. "Bay Crossroads. That's the church they go to."

A quarter mile from the church, something hurdles over the van, trailing flame and giving off a stench of sulfur.

The projectile plows into a nearby storefront and explodes. Wentwhistle swerves to avoid a blazing chunk of meteorite in the middle of the road.

Thrown off-balance, Win careens from side to side in the rear. "More meteors?"

"That's what happens when you drop an asteroid a few thousand miles from Earth's orbit." Wentwhistle threads the van past the smoking debris.

"So, this is only going to get worse?" Win says.

"Yep." She points to the sky. "Blight and his friends are going to rain down literal fire and brimstone on us from T'kahuatl. This way, they prep the field before dropping Azokuitli in our laps."

"Well, that's just great." I reach behind my seat and grab a blaster. "That's just completely awesome." I stare out the window at the burning storefront, then at my friends, and then back at the storefront. I'm tired and I want this whole mess of craziness to end. But it just keeps going like TV static after all the stations have signed off for the night.

What if we can't save Becca Mae?

Wentwhistle veers right at an intersection, taking the turn

on two wheels. "Blight hasn't tried something like this in over a thousand years. So, he's pulling out all the stops with this one."

I scratch my chin. "Wait. Did you say a *thousand?*"

"If this dude's so old, how come he's walking around?" Win says.

She weighs her words carefully. "*Husking* is what the T'Kalul call it. I don't know how it works but Blight started out as a bug when he came to Earth. At some point he became people—sort of."

"So, he's had the same human body all this time?" I ask.

"Probably different bodies." She passes kzelocs munching on something pinned underneath a car. "My guess is, he trades them out when they get damaged or too old. That's just a guess, though."

"How come he's been in my dreams?"

"Well, that I don't rightly know." We zip past a park filled with burning trees and smoldering grass. "But Blight's mind is reputed to be very powerful. He can perform all kinds of hocus-pocus. Mesmerism, astral projection, ESP—"

"ESP?" Win says. "I thought they just made that up for the movies."

"That's cute." She chuckles. "Look, all that really matters now is he wants to drop a giant monster-shark on our heads so he can conquer Earth."

"So, how do we stop him?" I say. "*Can* we stop him?"

Wentwhistle slams on the brakes and skids to a halt outside Bay Crossroads. "Let's work on saving your little girlfriend first. That is, unless he hasn't turned her already."

33

My stomach churns when I survey the parking lot of Bay Crossroads Ministry.

Stupid, stupid, stupid. You know this is a bad idea, right?

How is it a bad idea? We just got here.

You want so bad to be the hero, to save your little girlfriend. What if they've already served her up? What if she's one of them?

I...would know if that happened. I just would.

No, you wouldn't. Now, you're just going to get everybody killed.

Win's hand on my shoulder brings me back to reality. "Mickey?" he whispers. "Get it together, man."

But that's hard to do because I'm freaking out. What's not helping is Bay Crossroads. It has radically changed since Katie Sue's funeral.

The blackened ruins of the church remind me of a war zone. Most of the windows are gone, shattered glass piled beneath smoldering aluminum frames. The three crosses on the roof are twisted into a huge metallic triangle, and a snarling one-eyed shark with snaky limbs sits at the center.

Wentwhistle gets out of the van. "Love what they've done with the place."

Holding his spear, Win scrambles through the sliding

door. I bring up the rear, holding my own blaster and the bag of hair spray. Wentwhistle crouches behind a beat-up F-150. Staying low, I offer her can of Aqua-Net.

"No thanks, Mr. Finley," she says. "I'm already loaded for bear."

She's not kidding. In addition to her bomber jacket and sturdy work boots, Wentwhistle wears an Army surplus helmet with a red, white, and blue peace sign painted on. She has a blaster spear slung over her shoulder, and brandishes a hook in one hand, silver conch shell in the other.

"What the heck is that thing?" I say, touching the shell.

"You like it? This is my good luck charm. I bring it every time I go into battle."

Win joins us and inspects the shell. "Does it do anything?"

"Not that I know of." She fastens the conch to her belt. "But this might prove useful."

She retrieves the jeweled pendant from around her neck. Its emerald eye shimmers and a wave of sickness roils my gut. My pulse races and sweat beads on my forehead.

Wentwhistle narrows her eyes, giving me a long, studied look. "Mr. Finley, are you alright?"

I wipe the sweat from my brow. "Yeah, I'm solid," I lie.

"Are you sure?" She tucks the pendant in her jacket. "Does this little trinket upset you?"

"What?" I shake the cobwebs out of my head. "No, I don't care about that thing." But I do, and I can tell from the expression on her face that she doesn't believe me.

"Hey, check out the ride," Win whispers, nodding to a nearby car. "Who comes to church in something like that?"

It's a beauty all right, a muscle car with chrome runners and mag wheels. Double-headlights glare above a thin-lipped grill. A fresh coat of metallic-green paint gives the hot rod a factory-showroom sheen. But a sinking feeling hits my stomach.

This is Uncle John's Challenger.

My blood runs cold, and I struggle to breathe. "Y'all?" I say. "That's my uncle's car. He's here."

"Makes sense," Wins says, "He went bad, right?"

I shake my head, fighting back tears. "Yeah, but I didn't think I'd have to fight him."

Wentwhistle pats me on the shoulder. "Mr. Finley, you may not have a choice."

"You don't understand," I say. "I'm not afraid of Uncle John. Well, I am, actually. But the real problem is, push comes to shove, I don't know if I can bring myself to hurt him."

"Here's the thing." She points to the church. "It's not him, anymore. And I doubt anyone else in that place is human. Mickey?" She grasps my wrists. "If we don't stop Blight here and now, he'll bring that shark to Earth and people will die. Maybe thousands." She stares into my eyes and a chill runs down my spine. "Maybe millions."

"She's right, man," Win says.

All the pent-up rage and terror of the last week boils the blood in my veins. I'm lucky to be alive, and now they want me to help save the world? How can I do that when I can't even save myself?

"Egad, Finley." Wentwhistle grabs my shoulder. "Buck up, will you?"

I let out a sigh. "Okay." Shouldering the bag of Aqua-Net, I collect my spear. "Y'all are right. I'm ready." Except I'm not, but what choice do I have?

"Good." Wentwhistle turns to us. "Now, we need a plan to get in—"

"Man, let's just go," Win says.

She grabs his arm and whispers, "Not yet. We can't just barge in there like Thomas Magnum."

He smiles and gives me a thumbs up. "See, Mickey?

Everybody knows my show."

"So, what *do* we do?" I say.

"See over there?" Wentwhistle points to a door on the side of the building. "We cut through the parking lot and get inside."

"Then what happens?" Win says.

"We find the Carson girl."

My cheeks flush with anger toward Pastor Paul. "What about her dad?"

Wentwhistle shrugs. "If he's good, we take him with us. If he's not…" She taps the blade of her hook. "…we take him out."

Win grasps his blaster. "Now, you're talking." He peers over the truck's hood while Wentwhistle puts on her goggles. Then she grabs her hook and leads the way, followed by Win and me. We stay low and move fast. Broken glass crunches under our feet. Using the vehicles as cover, we get to a hedge ten yards from the door.

"Get ready to cover me." Wentwhistle gathers herself and touches the conch. From somewhere inside the building a guttural chant starts up.

"*Metokl. Tzihuatl. Azokuitli.*"

"What's that they're singing?" I whisper.

"Some kind of prayer, I think." With knuckles white on the hook, she turns to us. "You fellas ready?"

Win raises his blaster. "Ready as I'm gonna be." He shoots past us toward the door, trotting crazy-fast.

"Oh brother." Wentwhistle charges after him.

Aerosol cans clanking, I struggle to catch up.

We breach the door and find ourselves in a dark hallway reeking of bait and brine. Shark-squidlings quiver on the carpet, and the walls drip with green ooze. A broken picture frame hangs at an odd angle, its canvas slashed with three claw marks. We reach the end of the corridor. To the left lies another hallway leading to the break room where I met Becca Mae and Wade. I hear someone speak in a muffled voice, followed by a high-pitch giggle.

"Hold up," I say. "Let me go first."

Win tenses as though electrified. "Careful, Mickey."

I hesitate. Can I do this? Sure I can, I have to for Becca Mae.

Wentwhistle gives me a thumbs up. "Go on ahead. We're with you."

Treading cautiously, I make my way down the hall, keeping to the shadows.

Twenty feet down, I find the break room. A dull greenish glare spills from the entryway. Two voices, a boy's and a girl's, echo down the hallway. Then my shoe squeaks on the linoleum. The chatter stops, and the hallway goes silent for a moment.

Finally, the girl says, "So, what's going to happen afterwards?"

Oh, crap. I recognize that voice.

It's Becca Mae.

"They're going to set you up on a throne, with a crown and everything," a boy says. "It's going to be so beautiful, baby."

"I'm so glad." She's slurring her words, like maybe she's on something.

"Sure, you are," the boy says. I recognize his voice, too.

Wade.

I motion for the others to join me. Win taps the trigger on his blaster spear. "Come on, Mickey. Let's go in."

I raise a finger to my lips "No. Give it a second."

Wade struts out of the room, dressed in a dark green robe and a wreath of blackened briars around his head.

Freddie, scabby face puffy and red from the fireball at the boathouse, materializes from the shadows.

"Thought that dude was toast," Win whispers.

I elbow Win and give him a look.

The pair disappear into the chapel at the end of the hall.

"Let's go." I slink along the wall until I reach the break room.

Win accidentally pokes me with his blaster. "Man, you are clumsy."

"Me?" I whisper.

"Yes, you," he says

"Would you two keep it down?" Wentwhistle adjusts her goggles.

"Whatever," I say, bringing my blaster to bear. Part of me wants to run away, get as far from this church as I can, but then what happens to Becca Mae?

"Mickey." Win nudges me. "Get in that room."

I step inside.

Becca Mae lies on a seaweed-covered table. Her languid body is swathed in light green robes held together at the waist by a single brass chain decorated with a platinum starfish and seashells. Her eyelids shimmer with peacock blue liner, and her cornflake-colored mane spreads over the table's edge. Becca Mae's eyes flicker open when we enter, her dilated pupils floating huge in those liquid brown irises.

Sitting up slowly, she smiles. "Mickey? What are you doing here?" Her speech is definitely slurred, and she carries an odor of rancid peaches.

I prop my blaster against the wall and rush to her side. "We're going to get you out of here."

"Mickey, no, stop." She puts her hands on my chest and shoves me away. "You don't understand what's going to happen."

Up close, Becca Mae's breath smells of something sickly sweet like spoiled pears. Her eyes dart like gnats, never focusing on one spot. Is she high?

Wentwhistle steps between us and waves a hand in front of Becca Mae's eyes. "Ms. Carson," she says, "are you well enough to travel?"

Becca Mae giggles. "Hey Mickey? Where'd you dig up granny?"

Wentwhistle glances at me. "Your honey's been drugged, Mr. Finley." She snaps her fingers in front of Becca Mae's face. "Seeing trails, kid?"

Becca Mae tries to rise but slips on the seaweed, nearly falling from the table. "Oh, wow." Her laughter is faster than a chattering nail gun. "Get a load of clumsy girl here!"

"Come on, love." Wentwhistle gets an arm around her waist, helping her to her feet. "Let's get you out of here."

Becca Mae sways for a moment, then turns on Wentwhistle. "No. Wade said Daddy wants me to do my duty. There's a whole choir of angels waiting to crown me in glory." She jabs a finger in Wentwhistle's chest for emphasis. "In glory!"

I try to restrain her arms. "Hey, Becca Mae. Whatever Wade promised you—"

She presses her nose to mine, the stench of her breath unbearable. "Silly-Billy. Wade didn't promise me nothing. *Daddy* did."

"Hey, this is a bad spot," Win says, hands fidgeting on his weapon. "We got to get out of here."

The sound of footsteps clatter from down the hall, accompanied by a man's voice.

"Make sure everybody's had a taste." It's Wade. "Especially the ones who took the vaccine. We'll check on my cousin in a minute."

"Right," someone replies.

"Hah!" Becca Mae laughs. "You hear that? Wade's coming to kick your a—"

"That's enough out of you, friend." Wentwhistle reaches into her satchel and draws a small packet. Quick as a snake, she snaps the packet under Becca Mae's nose, and a smell like lavender fills the room.

"Hey," Becca Mae says, "what did you—" Her eyes roll into her head, and she sprawls to the floor.

I rush to her side. "Jeez, what was that stuff?"

"Shut up and help me carry her." Wentwhistle tosses the packet on the ground.

We each get under an arm and drag Becca Mae as far as the door. "Remember how we did this in the marsh?" I pull an Aqua-Net can from the satchel.

"Right on," he nods. "You toss it, I blast it."

Footsteps echo from down the hall. In the darkness, I spy two gray-skinned kzelocs approaching.

Wentwhistle frowns. "Are you sure this is the best way to—"

"Watch me." I dash into the hall and toss the can like a softball. One of the monsters picks it up and Win zaps him. The Aqua-Net ignites, and a fireball envelops the kzelocs. Their screams flood the corridor like a braking freight train. Two other goons materialize and leap over their liquified friends. Pounding down the hall, their double-fanged jaws open wide to reveal spiny tongues.

"That didn't work like I thought it would," Win says. He fires again and cuts one off at the knees. The other flies backward, leveled by a blast from Wentwhistle's hook. Fire spreads to the walls, filling the corridor with smoke.

I shield Becca Mae while reaching for more Aqua-Net. She wakes and throws her arms around me.

"You shouldn't have come," she coos. "All y'all in deep trouble, now."

Wentwhistle turns to me. "Can you carry her?"

"I think so." I drop the can and hoist Becca Mae over my shoulders.

Shouting echoes through the inferno. "Somebody get a hose. The rest of y'all, fan out. Don't let them get away."

Win and Wentwhistle lay down cover fire while I bundle Becca Mae down the hall. At the exit, I lower my shoulder and glass explodes from the aluminum frame.

Suddenly, we're outside. A streaking meteorite illuminates the dark clouds above before slamming into the ground.

A crowd of gray-skinned monsters ring the exit. One licks its lips with a barbed tongue. Another sniffs the air like a dog, then spits a slimy, tentacled thing from its mouth. Together, they rush forward.

Dropping Becca Mae, I raise my blaster, but something slams into my shoulder, knocking the weapon from my hand. I turn, taking a punch in the mouth for my troubles. Pain explodes in my head, and I slump to the ground.

Win battles a couple of monsters. "Hey, let me go, man!" He decks one but the second throws him to the sidewalk.

There's a loud whistle, and the crowd parts to make room for Wade, who arrives smiling. Freddie is at his side, tentacles squirming from where his jaw used to be.

"My, my, my, Pop-Tart," Wade snarls as he steps toward me. "You came all this way for nothing." He snaps his fingers and two kzelocs drag Becca Mae away. "Didn't get the girl, neither."

The crowd parts for another man, small, with a mustache dangling under his nose. He's dressed like the priests on T'kahuatl—black robes held together by a green sash.

"Mickey," Pastor Paul says, "what were you doing with my daughter?"

I smile. "Actually, don't know if you know about this, but me and Becca Mae? We're going steady and she wanted me to—"

"Shut up, Pop-Tart." Wade decks me, and I fall to the asphalt.

"Going steady?" Becca Mae's laugh is a rapid-fire barrage. "Mickey, you ain't even asked me out on a date."

Wentwhistle darts out of the church, hook in hand. She nails one of the kzelocs holding Becca Mae. The second creature lashes out, but Wentwhistle sends it reeling with a point-blank blast.

Then she slides the hook under Becca Mae's throat. "Pastor? Back off or I'll kill the girl."

"Now, now." Pastor Paul throws up a hand, freezing Wade and the others. "There's no need for any more violence." He approaches Wentwhistle. "We can work something out. You're a collector, right?" He produces a gold necklace from his robes. "These are pretty, aren't they? I've got plenty more."

"Back off," Wentwhistle says. "I mean it." She flexes her wrist, and a red cut opens where the hot blade meets Becca Mae's flesh.

Becca Mae cries, "Mickey? Tell her to stop."

Freddie's face-tentacles flicker like snakes. Glowering at Wentwhistle, he utters a series of growls and chirps.

"Hey, granny?" Wade says. "Freddie says you're a stupid old cow who's going to die."

The mob howls like jackals.

Win closes ranks with us. "Oh yeah? Make the first move, and we'll see what happens."

Pastor Paul raises his hands as if he's bestowing a blessing on the assembled congregation. "Like I said, we don't want anyone to get hurt. Why can't we talk this out?"

Wentwhistle scowls. "We're done talking. You need a human sacrifice to bring your god back to life, right? Why am I not surprised it's your own daughter?"

Becca Mae screams, "Daddy, what's she talking about? You

said I was going to be Queen."

"That's right, my sweet girl. So very right." The minister smiles like he's about to give a benediction. "And I promise you'll be crowned with glory in heaven for bringing Azokuitli to this world."

"*Metokl Tzihuatl Azokuitli!*" The mob chants in unison. "Blessed be the Rising!"

"This is crazy," I say, trying to stand.

Freddie plants a foot on my back, pinning me.

Wade turns to Wentwhistle. "Granny, don't be a fool. Let her go or we'll mess you up good."

She sneers. "No can do. Now step aside, or we'll—"

Freddie coughs and a black dart sails through the air.

Wentwhistle grabs her own neck and falls to the ground.

Win goes for Wade, but someone bludgeons him from behind. Uncle John stands over him, bad eye oozing green pus, lips bent in a slack-jawed frown.

Pastor Paul kneels next to me and runs his fingers through my hair. "You poor, deluded boy. So brave, so willing to fight. I can see why Becca likes you so much."

He snaps his fingers. A couple of kzelocs drag Becca Mae back into the church.

She squirms in their grip. "Daddy, I changed my mind. I don't want to be no queen. Don't make me."

"Take her away." He turns his back on her screaming and motions toward a matronly crone standing in the crowd. "Drug Becca again, would you? Double the dosage. Last thing I want is for it to hurt."

The old woman nods and disappears into the church.

I glare at Wade. "Dude? I'm going to get out of this." He steps toward me, but I can't shut up. "And when I do, you're going to regret the day you met me because I'm going to—"

He grinds my face into the asphalt with his shoe. "No,

Craig E. Higgins

you won't. But guess what? This afternoon, you're going to witness something nobody on this planet's seen in thousands of years. And then, Pop-Tart..." He reaches down, grabs my chin, and shakes it from side to side. "...you're going to die."

From somewhere above, I hear a loud ringing, sounding for all the world like a great, cracked bell tolling the end of the world.

34

We're tied to the railing around a swimming pool behind Bay Crossroads, Win to my left, Wentwhistle to my right. She's still unconscious thanks to Freddie's tongue-dart. The pool is drained of water. Dank, green moss covers its walls, and a stench like fish guts wafts from an open drain.

Kzelocs with gray complexions and expressionless faces stand in a line stretching around the pool. Their clothes are filthy and shredded. All are disfigured—some more than others. Had they turned into monsters the last few weeks, or long before?

A quartet of beekeepers guard three aluminum fold-out tables set up near the diving board. Other kzelocs serve smoking kibble from deep metal pans. Flies buzz around the fried concoctions, but nobody seems to notice. And no one objects to the way their food squiggles like maggots in the pans. An aroma hangs in the air that stinks like a mixture of burned vegetable oil, sulfur, and spillage from a septic tank.

"Man, what is that? Fried mirliton?" Jeez, I think I'm going to puke.

Win takes in a whiff. "Whew! It's rank, whatever it is."

Members of the football team stumble along, vacant

eyes black as coal. A few feet behind them stands a girl from Alice's cheerleader mafia, followed by the kid I talked to at the vaccination line at school. He mumbles to himself, fingers toying with the headphone cord looped around his neck. I recognize others. Mr. Kraftner, my English teacher. Doctor Carmelo, who took care of me at the hospital. And one of Uncle John's VFW buddies who used to come by the house to play cards. All are soulless scarecrows, numbering maybe in the hundreds. Not all are from town. How far away did they come?

Mr. Kraftner staggers to the head of the line. Flesh slips like diseased slugs from his mottled face, and there are huge bald patches on his head. With one clawed hand, he reaches into a pan and slops a double ration of kibble into his bowl. As he eats, a clot of hair and scalp sloughs from his head. Something slithers out of a pan, sheds its crispy batter, and devours the fleshy hairball. With a smile, Kraftner picks up the fleeing beast, pops it between his lips, and swallows.

"Gross, man." Win coughs.

But Kraftner's not done. Dropping his bowl, the English teacher digs into the pan, greedily stuffing more of the rancid concoction into his mouth. A beekeeper grabs him from behind, and a big kzeloc strides over.

"Uncle John," I whisper.

The thing that used to be my uncle yanks the monster off his feet by the collar. "That's too much. Others have to eat."

Kraftner bats his fists against the big man's chest. "No, I haven't had my share, you understand? I'm still hungry. Still hungry."

"Still hungry, eh?" Uncle John smiles and drags the English teacher behind some bushes. "Let's fix that."

The thick hedges jostle, clumps of leaves flying into the air. I hear a rupturing sound like somebody popping a hot water bottle, followed by the snapping of something dry and brittle.

Kraftner screeches like a parakeet. "No, give that back! I... need that."

"Not for long," Uncle John says.

"No!" The English teacher screams. "Stop it, stop it, stop it!"

The bushes bend and weave in time to a rhythmic wrenching noise. Kraftner's screams turn to moans. Finally, silence prevails.

Uncle John emerges, wiping his hands on his filthy overalls. "Show's over," he says.

The ruined things return to their feast.

I shake my head. "I can't believe he just did that."

"Oh yeah?" Win nods to the far side of the pool. "Then you ain't going to believe this."

A procession arrives, consisting of Pastor Paul, Wade, and Freddie, leading six kzelocs carrying Becca Mae on a wooden litter covered in shells, seaweed, and translucent nettles. They're surrounded by beekeepers and bug-faced T'Kalul wearing full battle dress and carrying blaster spears. Behind them a band of bug-heads toots loudly on bone horns, one of them sawing away on what looks like a two-stringed, fat-bodied guitar.

I shout at Win over the noise. "That's them—the aliens."

Pastor Paul turns abruptly and silences the proceedings with a wave of his hand. Then, six T'Kalul set Becca Mae's litter on end so she stands facing us. Lying back against the platform, she rolls her head from side to side, a blissful smile on her face. Oblivious to the crowd, she fiddles with brass chains binding her to the litter. Wade rubs his knuckles and whispers something to Freddie. Uncle John joins them, scouring the crowd with his one good eye.

Out of the shadows, a fourth figure emerges onto the

pool deck. Like Pastor Paul, he wears dark robes, only his are accented by golden lightning bolts. Jet-black bangs fall across his forehead, his broken nose tilted like a bent shark fin.

"And that's Midian Blight," I say.

Wentwhistle begins to come around. The skin around the wound from Freddie's dart is an angry purple color. Coughing, she shakes her head. "Sorry…so tired," she says. "What did I miss?"

Win says, "Lady, how are you even alive? Last dude I saw took one of those darts, pretty much died on the spot."

"Oh, I've been darted before. A body develops a tolerance after a while." She turns to me. "Mr. Finley, is that who I think it is?"

"Yep," I say. "Blight's here."

"Oh, my. The big cheese himself." It's like she's glad the two of them finally crossed paths. A greenish worm emerges from her wound, inches up her cheek, and disappears into her disheveled hair.

"Um, are you okay?" I ask.

She shivers. "No," she says, gaze riveted on the cleric. "No, I certainly am not, Mr. Finley. But Blight's presence seals the deal. They're almost ready."

"What do we do?" Win strains against his ropes, rattling the railing.

"Nothing, for now," Wentwhistle says.

Blight raises his arms.

Wade claps three times.

A hush descends over the proceedings.

The cleric gestures toward the blackened sky. "Soon, our dread god of destruction will rise in glory. Behold his servant, Midian Blight."

"Oh, poop," Wentwhistle sighs. "Get over yourself, would you?"

Blight steps to the edge of the empty pool. "Lift your voices, my children. Say his name."

In unison, the crowd chants, *"Metokl Tzihuatl Azokuitli. Metokl Tzihuatl Azokuitli."*

He waves a hand, and they go silent. "Azokuitli be praised. Today he returns to destroy this world, so that we, his children, might inherit it." With another gesture, the asteroid above begins moving over the sun.

"Behold, T'kahuatl ascends into convergence!" Blight shouts.

A tear runs down Wentwhistle's cheek. "This is very, very, very bad."

Win tries to work a hand free. "What happens next?"

"Blight brings his asteroid into position," Wentwhistle says, "setting up the correct trajectory for the shark to enter our world." She nods at Becca Mae. "All they need now is transport for the girl."

"Transport?" Win says. "You mean, up to the asteroid?"

"That's right."

"But if Becca's the sacrifice, why not just kill her here?" Win says.

"Yeah. Or can't he just zap her to the asteroid?" I say.

"Blight can't teleport her off-world, like you did, Mr. Finley." Wentwhistle coughs, a dark line of spittle trailing down her chin. "Mixing her atoms in transit might ruin her purity as a vessel. Azokuitli would not be pleased."

I glare at her. "You didn't just call Becca Mae a vessel, did you?"

Win struggles against the ropes, tendons in his neck straining. "There must be some way to stop this."

Wentwhistle glances at him and shakes her head. "Sorry, Win. I think our luck's just about run out."

Something glows through the fabric of her shirt.

"Say, Doc?" That thing's acting up."

She drops her gaze. "So, it is. For all the good that does us."

A column of T'Kalul warriors pushes through the crowd, followed by six beekeepers. Two of the soldiers place a squat, open brass cylinder the size of a car tire in front of the platform. I can just make out a nest of green wires inside, arcing with blazing lightning. Awash in the golden light, Becca Mae's eyes roll back in her head, and her chin drops to her chest.

Blight lifts his hands to the crowd. "Speak his name."

The chant goes up again. "*Metokl Tzihuatl Azokuitli. Metokl Tzihuatl Azokuitli.*"

Dropping his robes, he stands resplendent in a tunic of emerald scales accented by a harness encrusted with brass talons, shark's teeth, and beetle shells. On his belt hangs a dark, glassy knife. The beekeepers remove their helmets. Just as I suspected, they're T'Kalul. The whole crew fall to their knees, hissing in a semi-circle at Blight's feet.

Two kzeloc women in shapeless dresses approach bearing a brass headband decorated with bones and fish scales, a shark nose protruding like a hood ornament. Slowly, the handmaidens lower the crown on the cleric's head, then drift into the crowd.

Blight draws his dagger and stands atop the brass drum. Becca Mae opens her eyes. With two deft motions, the cleric cuts her bonds. Shaking like a leaf, she falls to the deck but pushes up to her knees. At a low rumble in the distance, I look up in time to see the asteroid complete its transit of the sun. Darkness shrouds the swimming pool deck and the air chills almost to freezing.

There's a stench of burning ozone beneath Wentwhistle's shirt, the pendant is glowing bright as a neon sign. "Well, that's weird," she says. A triangle-shaped outline burns through the coarse fabric, revealing the medallion beneath.

I turn to her. "What's that thing doing?"

"Darnation, it hurts!" Wentwhistle thrashes like a rat in a cage. "Get this thing off me!"

Shaking her head from side to side, she wriggles the pendant from her neck. It lands at my feet, glowing red-hot. The emerald jewel flares brightly, but the amethyst is dark as a lump of coal.

"Wentwhistle, what does this mean?" I say.

"Wait." Pastor Paul puts out a hand, glaring at Blight. "This is my daughter, my offering." The minister gets to his knees. "Where's my tribute?"

The cleric sneers. "Do you want something for your sacrificial lamb?"

"I've been faithful to you, loyal for years." Pastor Paul grabs Blight's arm. "Done everything you've asked—"

"You haven't answered me." The cleric brushes the minister's hand aside. "What do you *want*?"

"Well, I want to be one of you, and not like them." He gestures toward the mob. "Make me like you."

"It cannot be." Blight shakes his head. "You are not one of us. I can make you a kzeloc, but that is little better than the mud worm state you are now."

"You don't understand." Pastor Paul makes a fist and thumps his chest. "Make me like *you!*" He points to the asteroid blocking out the sun. "I want to live up there and be a god!"

Raising their blaster spears, the T'Kalul huddle closer, mandibles clicking.

"A god?" Blight backhands Pastor Paul across the face and he falls to the deck. "What a joke." The cleric laughs. "This work is thousands of years in the making. My people traveled across two galaxies to come here." He raises his arms like a TV preacher. "That we might make this place our home."

Blight kicks the whimpering minister. "A god? You're a worm cast, Paul. A bottom feeder. Unworthy even to be a witness to things you will never understand!"

The minister rises to his feet and grabs Becca Mae's wrist. "Make me like you or I'll take her away. You know I have the power to do that. It's in our bargain, remember? Blood begets blood? Blood protects blood?"

Weird. Wade said that to me once.

"Wentwhistle?" I say, "You know what they're talking about?"

"Haven't a clue," she says.

Becca Mae groggily raises her head. "Daddy? What are you doing?" She tries to rise but slips to the deck.

"Those were my words, Paul," Blight says, stepping toward them. "Alright, I lied." He claps his hands. "I can give you power, after a fashion, but you know not what you ask. The risks—"

"Don't try to trick me, wizard." Pastor Paul is screaming now. "I want what's mine!"

The cleric's eyes flash like twin emerald fires. "Very well."

Blight nods to Wade. He pulls Becca Mae aside while the beekeepers surround the minister. Raising their arms, the aliens join hands, forming a circle. One clicks its mandibles, and then the rest join in. Smoke rises from the deck, enveloping the minister.

Pastor Paul laughs. "Yes, I was born for this! I was—"

Green fires burst to life around him, engulfing his body. The minister screams and drops to his knees. Long spines burst from his back and stomach.

"Whoa," Win says. "What're they doing to him?"

Wentwhistle shakes her head. "He's getting his reward, the idiot."

The flames rise in intensity, giving off a stench like

gunpowder mixed with fish guts. Pastor Paul curls into a fetal position. Smoke enshrouds him completely.

Blight claps his hands. "Enough."

The beekeepers step aside, and the fumes dissipate. What's left of the minister curls inside a burning circle. His skin is gray and covered with sores. Three knobby, spider-like legs stick out of his belly, and his back is a mess of squirming tentacles.

But the worst of it is Pastor Paul's face. His cheekbones jut through the skin like crude knives, and beetle-like mandibles sprout from what's left of his lower jaw. His eyes are gone, replaced by bobbling, glassy orbs. Dark fluid runs from under the new organs, staining his gray cheeks.

The wretched thing crawls toward Blight, but some beekeepers drag him away.

Becca Mae gets to her feet and smiles. "Metokl Tzihuatl Azokuitli," she says.

Win is beside himself. "Man, that was her dad! Doesn't she care?"

Wentwhistle shakes her head. "She's out of it, Win. Lost in his power."

"That's messed up, man."

The handmaids approach Becca Mae and let down her hair. Her cornflake-colored mane unravels, framing her round face. Becca Mae steps onto the brass disc, beaming like she just won a beauty pageant.

Blight runs the flat of his dagger across her cheek. "The pain will be brief, but yours is the glory to bring about the Rising."

Becca Mae bows her head. "May Azokuitli let this be."

With both hands, the cleric raises the knife to the heavens.

The cylinder spins, light swirling into a blinding coil.

The only other illumination is the baleful glow of the

pendant at my feet.

Something big flashes in the sky then descends, exploding just over the horizon. A tremor passes beneath us, buckling the deck. Fissures open and everyone scrambles for footing.

"Whoa. They have earthquakes in Mississippi?" Win says.

Kzelocs wail and stumble around like puppets with clipped strings. The T'Kalul close ranks around Blight and Becca Mae, leveling their blasters at the mindless crowd. Smoke rises at my feet, and I glance down. The pendant begins to quake, green jewel's glare overwhelming in the near darkness. Then the blazing emerald shatters and the amethyst ignites, bathing us in warm light. A blast of heat spreads outward from the pool, the empty basin filling with a purple glow that grows brighter with each passing second.

Blight barks orders to the warriors protecting him. Three remain to guard Becca Mae while the rest take up firing positions around the deck. Wade, Freddie, and Uncle John join him near the spinning brass disk.

A purple fireball erupts out of the pool. The railing we're roped to shatters, and we're free.

Rubbing her wrists, Wentwhistle shouts, "Go get Becca Mae."

"Right." Shaking free of the ropes, I get to my feet.

She turns to Win. "Help him."

He offers her a hand. "What about you?"

Wentwhistle coughs. "Give me a minute, alright? I'll catch up to you." She doesn't look good.

The pendant lies at my feet, its amethyst sparkling. Don't know why, but its presence no longer makes me feel sick. I hang it around my neck.

Win pats my shoulder. "You ready?"

I nod. "Yeah."

We take off for the other side of the deck. Things get

crazy on the way there. Milky feelers, thick as a man's leg, slither over the pool's edge. One grabs the ankle of a kzeloc and drags it away.

"That's nuts," Win says, avoiding the snaking limbs.

Suddenly, a luminescent bulb floats upwards from the bottom of the pool, supported by a long, snaky trunk. Round white petals and waxy oval leaves sprout from rapidly branching limbs. The jellyfish tree rises high into the air, illuminated by a great magenta corona.

"Wow," I say, gazing up at the monstrous plant. "She came."

The kzelocs panic and scatter. We push through the fleeing mob and reach Blight's crew. A T'Kalul soldier lowers his staff but Win bowls him over and grabs the weapon. Another bug-head fires, singeing the ground at our feet. Win blasts the alien, sending it rolling off the deck. I move past him, reaching for a T'Kalul's spear lying on the ground.

A sailing dart pings off the deck. I glance up and there's Freddie, jaw-tentacles swirling. He lurches toward me, neck bulging like a bullfrog.

Does he have another stinger in him? It won't matter if I take him out.

Freddie closes on me before I can get off a shot. Pursing his lips, he spits a projectile that pierces my shirt but misses my skin. Wielding the blaster like a club, I take a swing at his head. He ducks and lands a punch. Pain explodes in my gut, and I drop the spear. Win arrives and throws a right at Freddie's head. His fist gets stuck in the monster's face-tentacles.

"Aw, man." Yanking his arm free, Win kicks the monster in the groin. Freddie just laughs, tentacles flaring.

Behind him, a tendril squirms along the deck.

"Hey, Freddie." I get to my feet. "Watch your step."

The limb coils around his foot and drags him hissing into the burning pool.

Craig E. Higgins

Win tosses me his spear. "We can still make it." He retrieves another weapon off the ground, and we dash toward Becca Mae.

Two beekeepers bar our way, but Win blasts the concrete in front of them, sending them reeling.

Up ahead, the cylinder spins wildly, like something's gone wrong with it. Becca Mae falls to the deck screaming. Tumbling onto its side, the disk rolls toward us. Me and Win jump out of the way, and it crashes into a couple T'Kalul, sending them sprawling.

Becca Mae stands, arms outstretched, her head tilted to the asteroid above our heads. I reach for her, but I'm flattened by a blow from behind. Glancing up, I gaze at the face of my attacker. Uncle John looms over me.

"Mick, you've disappointed me for the last time."

35

A meteorite smashes into the pool deck, heaving chunks of concrete in all directions. Uncle John is catapulted into the air and comes down hard.

Win dashes toward us, firing his weapon. "Mickey, watch out."

Uncle John sidesteps the blast and rushes him, flinging Win aside like a discarded newspaper. Win rolls with the fall and comes up swinging, but Uncle John catches his fist in one meaty palm. Snarling, he backhands Win, smacking him to the deck.

Now, it's just me and him.

Uncle John turns to me. "Mick, it's time you came home." A worm squirms out of the corner of his bad eye. "Your aunt's worried sick about you."

"No, she's not." My legs shake and sweat pours from my brow despite the chill. Even when he was human, there was no way I could take Uncle John. What do I do now?

He holds out his hand. "Mick, there's no need to fight." Spittle drips from his lips. "We're family."

Wrong on both accounts, buddy.

Uncle John roars and sprints toward me, reaching with

those big hands. His fingertips burst open, revealing sharp talons. Dark fluid gurgles from his lips.

I can either kill him or he'll eat me. And that's no choice at all.

I level the weapon to fire. But before he gets to me, a milky-white feeler coils lashes his ankle and upends him. Dragged toward the pool, Uncle John's screams and claws at the concrete. Helpless like he is, one shot will take him out. My gut churns, and the voices return.

You can't hurt him. Can't, can't, can't.

But he tried to kill me.

Don't do it. Don't, don't, don't.

"Alright, I won't." I blast the tendril, releasing a hot geyser of milky liquid.

The jellyfish erupts in bright pink light, illuminating everything like a thousand suns. Fleeing kzelocs burst into magenta flames. All around us, the monsters drop like flies, immolated in the unforgiving glow. Smoke floods the air and there's a stench like rotted bait on the wind. Jeez, what an awful stink!

Rising from the concrete, Uncle John lopes away, trying to run from the glare. He passes me without a glance, flames bursting from his back. Pushing through the mob, he reaches the double gate and exits into the darkness beyond.

The jellyfish shudders, its outer skin peeling like an orange. A slender figure emerges, features obscured by the pink glare. But I make out the swirling tresses framing her head and shoulders. I know who it is.

"Win." I point to the sky. "It's Katie Sue."

She lowers slowly to the deck on a gigantic frond and approaches on bare feet. Her t-shirt and slacks have been replaced by a sleeveless gown stitched from dark, oval leaves. Her limbs are entwined with vines, and she's wearing a crown of thorny branches. Katie Sue's Spanish moss hair waves like silk in the chill air. An amethyst glow radiates beneath the pale skin just below her collarbones.

There's something unsettling about her face. Blazing magenta irises swim in twin coal black seas where the whites of her eyes used to be. Katie Sue wears a cruel expression, high cheekbones stretching the flesh around her upper lip now curled into a sneer.

Win steps forward slowly. "Katie, is that you?"

She smiles and the cruel facade melts away. "Yes. How y'all been?"

I approach, even though I'm still not sure what to expect. "Katie Sue, you came for us."

"I did." Her voice rings like an echo from the bottom of the sea. "She sent me." Katie Sue gestures to the jellyfish tree. "We are here to stop the Rising."

"Well, you must be the famous dead girl." It's Wentwhistle. "That *Temizkuan* there in the swimming pool?"

Katie Sue nods. "It is."

"Who?" Win says.

Wentwhistle turns to us. "Temizkuan is the T'Kalul life goddess. She's Azokuitli's opposite, sort of."

A burst of energy sears the ground at our feet. Bug-faced warriors rush toward us. Katie Sue turns to face them, arms outstretched. Thick, spear-tipped roots burst through the concrete, impaling many of them. Katie Sue makes a fist and vines rip through the concrete, wrapping themselves around the remaining creatures. Win raises his weapon and cuts a swath through the entangled warriors.

I survey the deck. Midian Blight and Wade stand near the diving board with Becca Mae.

Blight steps forward, cracking his knuckles. "Ah, the one who carries the heart of Temizkuan in her breast," he says to

Katie Sue. "I wanted to kill you, and now you are here."

"You can try." She makes a fist, steam rising from her hands. "But this Rising won't happen." She points to Becca Mae. "Give me my sister and return to T'kahuatl."

"I don't think so." Blight snaps his fingers. A pair of beekeepers drag Becca Mae away.

"Y'all can't stop this," she says as they push her through the gate.

"Don't let them take her." Wentwhistle points to the fleeing trio.

I turn to Win but he is busy trading fire with the T'Kalul. Katie Sue remains focused on Blight. There's nobody to rescue Becca Mae but me, even if she doesn't want to be rescued.

I run, catching up to them in the parking lot. A beekeeper turns and lobs something green and slimy that hits me in the chest. I grab the monster and try to pull it off, but it lashes a tentacle around my wrist, holding on for dear life. I twist free, but the beast snaps its jaws, nearly taking out a chunk of my arm. Grabbing the back of its head, I rip the creature off my chest and smash it to the ground.

"Wait right there, chummy," I say.

Picking up the spear, I raise the weapon above my head and stab the monster's squishy torso. Green muck splatters across my face and chest. Bile rises in my throat. I can't believe I just did that.

A truck backfires. I turn and catch sight of Becca Mae being shoved into a green BDM van. The vehicle speeds out of the lot, gravel flying under its wheels.

"Crap!" I kick an overturned car and howl in pain.

No chance of catching them now.

I trot through the gate and onto the deck. Katie Sue stands, twirling her arms like a majorette. Blackened roots sprout from the concrete, snaking their way toward Blight. Green eyes flashing, the cleric claps his hands together. Emerald flame ignites along the knotty limbs, reducing them to ash.

Enraged, Katie Sue turns to the great tree and thrusts her arms skyward. "Temizkuan, help me," she cries.

Glowing white-hot, the bulbous head shoots a searing bolt of light directly at Blight. Smirking, the cleric raises his fist, and a dome of green light descends, shrouding him and Wade. The beam hits the dome and fragments into a shower of sparks.

Blight roars with glee. "You'll have to do better than that."

What remains of the deck suddenly buckles and caves in on itself. A jet of lava erupts from a nearby fissure, spewing onto the concrete. Blight nods to Wade and the pair dart toward the fiery trench, the rest of the T'Kalul in tow.

"Where y'all going?" Katie Sue flicks a wrist, and a knotty root bursts through the deck. She snaps it off at its base, fashioning a spear. "I'm not done with you, Blight."

He pauses at the lip of the fissure, illuminated by the fire. "You can't stop me." Cruel shadows dance across his mangled features. "No-one can."

Katie Sue flings the projectile. It spirals through the darkness, making a beeline for Blight's heart.

With a smirk, the cleric snaps his fingers. The weapon lurches to a stop in mid-air. "Oh, no, no, no," he says, waving his hand. "Go back the way you came."

The spear turns abruptly, and flies back toward Katie Sue.

Just then, a shambling figure emerges onto the deck. The spear hits him in the chest, passes through him, and embeds in a brick wall.

"No!" I blast the ground at Blight's feet, but he's already gone, joining Wade and the remaining T'Kalul in the fiery lava.

A meteorite hits nearby and a tremor rocks the deck,

throwing everyone except Katie Sue to the ground. The fissure closes over, scattering dust and ash in all directions. Silence descends on the battle-torn deck.

Temizkuan's jellyfish-head buzzes softly, but otherwise deathly quiet settles over the grounds. A cold wind knifes through my clothes, chilling me to the bone. Crap, but I hope I'm not in shock. My head hurts like somebody drove sharp nails through my skull. To top it off there's soot, ash, and concrete dust everywhere, making it hard to breathe.

Getting to my feet, I catch sight of Wentwhistle tending to Win. There's an ugly burn on his arm. I'm guessing it came from a T'Kalul blaster.

"He'll be alright. He's taken a beating, though," Wentwhistle says.

I kneel beside them. "That's good. I—"

My legs go rubbery, but Katie Sue appears and grabs my arm. "Sit still, Mickey," she says. "I'm going to get everyone fixed up. It's going to be okay."

"No, it's not," I say when I clear my head. "Katie Sue, I'm so sorry." I raise my head to look at her. "I tried to get to Becca Mae. I really, really tried." My eyes grow moist, and I start to cry. "But I screwed it up." I punch the concrete again and again, bloodying my knuckles. "Screwed up, screwed up, screwed—"

"Hey, stop that." Katie Sue grabs my wrists. "We *all* failed Becca." She casts a glance at the open gate. "I'm the one with the power, and I should've done something sooner."

"And why didn't you?" Wentwhistle steps toward her, nose inches from Katie Sue's. "I mean, here you show up after the apocalypse starts with an alien deity in your pocket. But we could've used your help a couple of days ago. You know that, right?"

That's totally not fair. "Hey, cool it." I put a hand on

Wentwhistle's arm. "You don't know what she's been through—"

"Actually, your friend's got a point." Katie Sue steps toward the body of the thing impaled on the spear. "Reason why I couldn't help before was..." She shakes her head. "I was communing with Temizkuan, learning all I could about the Rising. When everything went crazy, I had to fight Blight's army off to protect my sanctuary."

Wentwhistle frowns. "And we're supposed to believe that?"

"Believe what you want." Katie Sue knelt next to the monstrosity. "But Mickey, when we talked in the woods, I could've come to help y'all." She gently runs her hand across the thing's bumpy forehead. "Maybe then, this one wouldn't be dead."

Stepping toward her, I get a closer look at the monster's face. Despite the thick mandibles and glassy eyes, I recognize the creature. "Aw, man... Katie Sue?"

She looks at me with magenta irises flashing in the darkness. "What is it?"

"This is your dad. This is Pastor Paul."

Win steps behind me, holding his wounded arm. "He's not lying, Katie. We all saw him change."

A plum-colored tear runs down her cheek. "I know."

Oh, crap. She just killed her own father. How can she possibly live with herself, even if she's dead?

"He should've stayed out of it." Katie Sue sits and cradles his head in her lap. "And I should've..." A shudder runs across her pale shoulders. "You know, I guess it doesn't matter now."

Cursing, Win kicks a T'Kalul's helmet across the deck. "No, they can't just get away with this."

"Oh, yes they can," Wentwhistle says. "They've got the asteroid in place, the girl for the sacrifice, everything." She turns to us and a worm crawls out of her hair, slinking down her forehead. "We've been played for suckers, friends." She snags the slimy thing off her face and flings it on the ground. "Blight's been one step ahead of us the whole…" Wentwhistle's left eye rolls up in her head, and dark fluid drips from her nostrils. She staggers and falls forward.

I rush to her side. "Aw, man, don't die on us."

Win helps me lay Wentwhistle on the concrete. Her breathing is labored, skin clammy to the touch.

Katie Sue kneels by the fading Wentwhistle and inspects the wound on her neck. "We need to get her to the barn."

"But the barn's across town," I say.

She points to the tree. "We're closer than you think."

Me and Win carry Wentwhistle to the pool. A large frond lowers from the canopy, and we roll her into the safety of its embrace. Instantly, she is whisked away. More fronds descend for the three of us. There's a rush of air as we're swept up into the tree. Lights blind my eyes, and a deafening buzzing overwhelms me. Then, everything is darkness, and my mind is filled with nothing. But, maybe that's okay because right now, nothingness feels better than the hollowness of worrying about how much more we can lose.

36

When I open my eyes, lavender fills the skies above. I'm face up on a purple grass palette, blades soft against my back. Sweet pine mixed with lilac perfumes the air. I figure the scent originates with the blossom-studded shrubs dotting the verdant landscape stretching past the horizon's gentle curve.

I shake my head, but nothing changes. "Wait, this isn't the barn."

Win stands over me and offers a hand. "No, we someplace else."

I try to stand, but a wave of nausea sends me staggering.

"You've been out for a couple of hours." He steadies me. "Yeah, you'll feel sick at first. But once you get your bearings, you get used to it."

Another wave washes over me. I cover my mouth, but my stomach settles, and my vision clears. "Where the heck are we?"

Win points to a tall, conical hut maybe fifty yards away. It's made of animal pelts stretched over ebony lodge poles. "That's…hard to explain. Let's go talk to Katie."

I follow him to the hut. He pushes the flap aside. Acrid smoke floods my nostrils, nearly choking me. On a cot made of hide, Wentwhistle lays moaning, gray hair splayed round her head. Katie Sue kneels beside her. She's dressed in a buckskin tunic and thick leggings underneath a coat of white petals. Her hair is held in a ponytail, the silky-white tresses descending to the small of her back. In one hand, she holds a pot brimming with a noxious broth. In the other, a magnolia blossom.

The memory of Katie Sue holding her dead father burns in my memory. I want to ask how she's feeling, but this totally feels like the wrong time. With forehead creased and eyes a little glassy, she stares at Wentwhistle as if into a crystal ball. Not wanting to be a distraction, I keep my mouth shut.

"Hold her up so I can give her the medicine." Katie Sue nods to Win.

He drops to his knees and gently lifts Wentwhistle's head.

Katie Sue spoons the broth into her mouth. The older woman coughs as the vile liquid slips down her throat.

Katie Sue's magenta eyes flash in the dark, cramped interior. "Mickey? Can you grab me that mortar and pestle?"

"What?" I say.

Win points to a bowl sitting on a small table. "Dude, she means those."

She crumbles the blossom into the vessel and begins to grind it into a paste. "Your friend is hurt bad. I can't just put my hands on her."

"And that's why we're here?" I say.

"Yes." Humming, Katie Sue dips a finger in. A "pop" sounds, and a sliver of smoke erupts from the bowl.

The smell is overpowering, but I hope it works. "Man, that's potent."

"It has to be." Katie Sue smears lightning bolts of paste on Wentwhistle's face. "She'll have to lay here for a spell while the medicine does its work." She closes her eyes and places a hand on top of the older woman's. "Let's talk outside." Katie Sue gets to her feet and vanishes through the flap.

We leave the hut and walk down a pebbled path. Outside, a warm breeze sends dandelion seeds airborne. I kick a rock, sending it spinning off into the high grass. "So, where are we, exactly? Is this supposed to be T'kahuatl? Because I've been there, and this isn't it."

Katie Sue shakes her head. "No. Temizkuan remembers the T'Kalul before they began their long journey among the stars." She gestures toward the purple and lavender fields. "T'kahuatl is a perversion of where they came from."

"So, you mean where we're at is like their home-world?" Win says.

"Sort of..." She frowns. "More like a memory of that place, but real. Or at least, real enough."

"And they all dressed like you?" I point to the tunic she's wearing.

Katie Sue grins. "Well, I took some liberties. This is how I would've dressed if, you know, I was living there."

Win shrugs. "That works, I guess."

Something roars in the distance.

She points to a creature with a bulbous head and compound insect eyes lumbering nearby. "These creatures could roam hundreds of miles in a week. Nobody ever messed with them. They just did what they wanted, had enough food, and never hurt nobody."

I keep a wary eye on the lumbering beast. "That thing isn't going to eat *us*, is he?"

"No." She laughs. "Try to understand. What we're seeing is a *memory*, an illusion."

"What killed it?" Win says. "The aliens' planet, I mean."

"Temizkuan won't tell me." Katie Sue casts her gaze towards the sky. "She reveals what she wants to. I can show you this." She raises her hands over her head and conjures a shimmering black oval, flapping like a tapestry in the memory of a long-ago breeze.

In the center, a big red sphere appears. Smaller spheres of different colors appear, falling into concentric orbits around the first. Flecks of sparkling light wink in the background.

I figure them for stars and take a guess at what's happening. "Wait a minute. Is that our solar system?"

Win scratches his head. "No." He turns to Katie Sue. "It's theirs, right?"

"Yes." Katie Sue points toward a pad of purple grass beneath our feet. "Y'all have a seat."

Hypnotized by the display, I can't resist sitting cross-legged on the grass. Win joins me.

Katie Sue points to a coral-colored sphere, fourth in sequence. "Thousands of years ago, this big space rock breached the T'Kalul solar system." Suddenly, a small orange projectile blazes into view, aimed at the coral planet. "Word got out that it looked like they were going to get hit, and everybody was afraid they were going to die. And they probably would've, except their high priests figured out how to save the people."

"I get it," I say. "Blight was one of those holy men, right?"

"Correct." Katie Sue smiles like a proud teacher whose student just got the right answer. "Midian Blight—well, they called him something else back then he was just a bug. Him and some scientists built all this stuff that turns an asteroid into a living world."

She waves her hand. The sun and planets are replaced by scenes of bug-headed aliens in some underground complex, testing rockets and constructing giant machines. The oval shimmers again, and the picture changes to a landscape of blocky pyramids rising from lush jungle, an orange sky overhead.

"That's what T'kahuatl looks like." I punch Win in the arm. "Not a fun place to visit."

Win glares at me before pointing to the images. "So, they turned their moon into, like, a mini planet? How'd they get it to move?"

"Excellent question," Wentwhistle says, approaching us on the pebble path. "And I'm dying to hear the answer." She takes a seat next to me and whispers into my ear, "Mr. Finley, don't trust this one too much. She's one of *them*, after all."

I shake my head. "Lady, you wouldn't be alive if it wasn't for her."

Win turns to Wentwhistle. "Hey, shouldn't you be resting?"

"You kidding?" She waves him off. "I'm fit as a fiddle."

But he's right. Dark circles sit under Wentwhistle's eyes, and her complexion is pale, almost ashen.

I try changing the subject. "What happened next?"

With a wave of Katie Sue's hand, the images inside the burning oval fade, replaced by the coral planet and the hurtling projectile in space. "Well, once they created the technology, Blight and his followers set in motion their plan to capture the asteroid." She twirls her finger, and the space rock settles into orbit around the T'Kalul home-world. "And once the orbit stabilized, they copied into it every aspect of their planet's biosphere and magmatic structure, magnetic fields, and what have you."

Inside the oval, glittering particles form, swirling on one side of the space rock. Then the orange sphere moves, slowly at first, gaining steam as it speeds to the edge of the display.

Win's jaw hangs open. I'm blown away, too. How could the bugs have accomplished all this?

"So, they called this traveling world T'kahuatl, or Wandering Sanctuary," Katie Sue says. "And for millennia, the T'Kalul traveled the space-ways until they found a planet capable of supporting life."

Wentwhistle snaps her fingers. "Earth."

Katie Sue nods. "That's right. Once in our solar system, they set T'kahuatl in orbit behind the moon, on the dark side."

"Wait, wait. I get it," Win says. "We can't see anything on the dark side. It's like a blind spot."

"That's right."

"So, everybody got out?" Wentwhistle says.

"What do you mean by *everybody*?" Katie Sue says.

"Exactly what I said." Wentwhistle points to the fleeing projectile. "Did all the T'Kalul escape from the home-world or was it just a few?"

Katie Sue shrugs. "Temizkuan isn't sure."

"Won't answer a direct question, huh?" Wentwhistle chuckles. "Well, at least some things are starting to make sense. I've long suspected the T'Kalul were more refugees than conquerors. Digs I've been on, we always found hand weapons and pottery, a few star maps, stuff like that. But it's not like the bug-heads were this mighty army or something."

Katie Sue waves her hand, and the oval's display devolves into a kaleidoscope of sparks and flashes. "The journey in space took its toll on the people, and many died. Even the leaders were affected." A picture of Midian Blight gels in the center. "The hero became a tyrant, and he turned the people away from Temizkuan to follow a darker god."

"Azokuitli," I say.

"Azokuitli." Katie Sue nods.

"And so, the shark's their equalizer, yeah?" Wentwhistle stands. "The spearhead of the Rising."

"That's right."

"Well, I'd say we're caught up here." Wentwhistle's knees wobble and she staggers but rights herself.

Win turns to her. "You sure you're okay?"

Her laugh is a hollow chuckle. "Oh, yeah. Never been better."

So, that's it. We stop an intergalactic shark-monster before it destroys Earth. No pressure, right? I get to my feet. "Then we need to get going. How long do you figure we have before the Rising?"

"Not long," Katie Sue says, fingertips touching the oval. "Time passes slowly in this place, but when we return we won't have but a day to stop them, if that."

"But that's going to be easy, right?" Win says. "I mean, we find Becca, and Blight's screwed because he can't do his ceremony."

"Yeah," I say. "If he can't teleport her to T'kahuatl—"

"Teleportation is not his only option. A tremor runs across Katie Sue's shoulders. "Blight may have another way to..." She trails off and a plum-colored tear rolls down her cheek. "Get Becca off...the planet."

"Katie Sue?" Win says.

From out of nowhere, dark clouds crawl across the lavender sky. Smoky embers rain onto the ground.

"What's happening? Katie Sue, you've got to fix it." I brush a cinder from my hair. "You've got to."

"I've got to?" She glares at me, teardrops staining her face. "What do you think I am, the Bionic Woman?"

"Yes."

Katie Sue shifts her gaze to the smoldering clouds, eyes moist and frowning. Then she turns, sits on a nearby rock, folds her knees against her chest, and cries.

I reach out a hand but Win stops me. "Man, she just, you know, she lost her dad. Give her some space, okay?"

"Okay, I'm sorry. You're right."

The knife turns in my gut.

Stupid, stupid, stupid. You're only worried about yourself.

Oh, man. That's not true. And of all the times for you to—

"She said this place was some kind of illusion," Wentwhistle says. "Whole thing'll probably fall apart soon."

Katie Sue shivers in the smoldering rain, dust and purple grasses swirling around her feet. I don't know what to do for her. Days ago, she told me that, more than anything, she needed a friend. What kind of friend am I if I don't try to help her now?

Brushing past Win, I knelt beside her. "Hey, look. I suck, okay? Sometimes I think nobody's ever been hurt but me."

"I'm not upset with you." She brushes a strand of moss-hair from her cheek. It's just...I died and came back. And I thought God left me, you know? But Temizkuan brought me peace. I'm content with the path she set out for me. But this?" She points to the gyre of burning soot descending from the sky, "I don't rightly know what I can do about this. It's too big, you know? Just too big." She turns to me, magenta eyes flooding with purple tears. "Not only that, but we lost Becca. And Daddy's gone—"

"I'm sorry about your dad. And I know I'll never understand, you know, where you're at right now. But, Katie Sue, we still need you. Becca Mae needs you."

"I know that." She nods. "But I mean, how could this happen to Daddy, you know? How could I—"

"Don't do this to yourself." I take hold of her icy hand. "It's Blight's fault, what happened. And how could you know your dad would get in the way?"

"I just...with all the things I can do now, I should've been able to *see* him. *Know* it was him. *Save* him." Katie Sue gazes into the sky and shakes her head." The purple bulge on her chest pulsates.

"Katie Sue, there's something you've got to know." My gut churns, because once again I'm about to be the bearer of terrible news. "Your dad, right? He was working with Blight."

Katie Sue blinks. "What?"

"Him and Blight had some kind of deal, and Becca Mae was part of it."

Crying, she shakes her head. "Daddy wouldn't do that. He just...wouldn't."

"Hey, kid." Wentwhistle knelt in front of her. "I know it's hard, betrayal. I had someone I love very much betray me. He left me to die." She runs a finger across her own throat. "I would've been pushing up daisies if it was up to him."

"Who was this?" I say.

"Third ex-husband," she says. "So, we've all been screwed over. And believe me, it sucks the big one, no matter how many times it happens."

Katie Sue presses her fist to her temples. "You think you understand, but you don't. You have no idea what it is to be me."

"That's right," Wentwhistle says, brushing moss-hair from the girl's face. "I can't understand, just like you can't understand the things I've been through, or Mr. Finley here, or Win."

"Stop trying to patronize me." Katie Sue buries her head in her hands. "I let Daddy die. Nobody's worse than me."

"Katie Sue?" I say. "You know who deliberately hurts people? Midian Blight. What *you* did wasn't intentional."

She runs her fingertips over her pulsating bruise. "This thing in my chest? It's keeping me alive. Lets me speak for a goddess. But you know what? Sometimes it's almost like sleeping with the enemy."

Wentwhistle shakes her head. "I doubt that. Temizkuan is the Life-Giver, the guide. Whatever else she is, she can't be as bad at that monster getting ready to wipe out the Gulf."

"Yeah," Win says. "We know you're hurting, man, but you

got to help us before it's too late."

"Guess I don't have much choice, considering the circumstances." Katie Sue stands, closes her eyes, and takes a deep breath. Steam rises round her body, warming the air.

"Okay," she says, "we're going to go back, now."

The pinkish sky above dissolves, descending in a downpour of sparkling dust and embers. Darkness pervades, and through the deluge I make out the wooden rafter of a gabled roof. A cold wind blows against my skin, and a sulfur stench permeates my nostrils.

We're back in the barn.

Katie Sue raises her arms. Blackened embers from the other world float from the ground and stitch themselves together in mid-air to form a fluffy coat. She draws the cape tight around her shoulders. "Alright. We need to come up with a plan if we're going to defeat Blight. He's got one thing left to do to raise Azokuitli."

"Sacrifice Becca on the asteroid," Win says.

"That's not happening," I say, fists balled. "How do we stop him?"

37

We spend the next hour debating Blight's whereabouts. Win suggests the cleric must be holed up somewhere near Bay Crossroads. Wentwhistle argues for a search of the cemetery.

Katie Sue silences us with one hand. "For Midian Blight to get Becca where he wants her, he'll need a rocket ship."

"That's right!" the older woman says with a snap of her fingers. "The sacrifice-ee can't be teleported off-world." She turns to Katie Sue. "You mentioned something about that, didn't you?"

"Yes." I sit underneath Katie Sue's tree and try to piece it all together, watching the jellyfish-head cast colored shards of light on the ceiling. "So, he needs a ship of some kind? If the T'Kalul have a freaking traveling planet, wouldn't Blight have access to, I don't know, a UFO or something?"

Wentwhistle shakes her head. "No. The T'Kalul are actually pretty primitive in some ways. Their magic is advanced, but for them space travel that doesn't involve hitching a ride on asteroids boils down to rockets, mostly. Not much more advanced than NASA." She grabs a stick and sketches something in the dirt.

"So, could this projectile be hiding in plain sight, maybe?"

337

I say. "Something so conspicuous that people just got used to it being there, and didn't think about what it was?"

Win turns to me. "There any tall buildings in town? Or, like a grain silo?"

"No to both," I say. "Tallest thing in Bay St. Louis is the water tower, and you can't exactly hide a rocket in that."

Wentwhistle finishes her drawing with a flourish. "Ahem! I think the answer's obvious. Take a look."

We crowd around her handiwork. It's a crude sketch of the twin towers of St. Adolphus, with those onion domes pointing at a rock lying in the dirt.

"See, those are our birdies right there." Wentwhistle grins like the cat who caught the canary.

"So, they're keeping Becca Mae at St. Adolphus." Why didn't I think of that in the first place? "But if Blight's holed up there, he's bound to have some serious backup."

"That's true," Win says. "And they'll be watching for anything coming in."

"Coming in, maybe," Katie Sue says, eyes blazing like fireworks. "But what about from underneath?"

An hour later we are huddled inside the belly of a gigantic wooden boring drill Katie Sue grew from Temizkuan's trunk. Its front end consists of a conical bit made from thick thorny roots woven so tight they're hard as steel. The back end of the log lies open. As we travel, I catch sight of mud flowing along the bottom rim. The cramped interior is incredibly hot and uncomfortable. Even though we've only traveled a few minutes, the oxygen is running low, so it's getting hard to breathe.

The drill comes to a sudden stop, its nose facing upward. After a moment, Katie Sue climbs to the top and punches the bit aside. Outside there's a crash of something heavy smashing against stone, making the log rattle. A dim green light floods the interior.

Win turns to me. "Man, you ready for this?"

I shake my head. "No, but what choice do we have?"

Katie Sue climbs over the rim and vanishes into the darkness above. After a moment, she yells, "Coast is clear. Y'all come up, now."

Me and the others follow, lugging our weapons and gear. The drop is about three feet, and I land hard on the cobblestone.

Win steps over and helps me to my feet. "You alright, Mickey?"

"Yeah." I brush dust and wood chipping off my knees, trying to clear my head.

Wentwhistle slips to the floor, making a perfect dismount. "Finley, you need to learn how to take a fall."

I crack a smile, still smarting from the stinging in my knees. "Thanks for the encouraging words."

Win scowls, his eyes darting in every direction. "Where are we again?"

"St. Adolphus." Katie Sue approaches, bare feet almost gliding across the floor. "The basement, from the look of it."

"And how far we got to go?" he says.

She points to the ceiling. "I would guess three stories, assuming they've already loaded Becca onto a rocket."

I take stock of our surroundings. We're in a square room maybe thirty feet across with a ten-foot-high ceiling. Marble tentacle reliefs bracket the walls of a cavernous foyer just beyond the door. The walls are decorated with oil paintings rendered on black velvet. One features green-robed T'Kalul priests cracking whips over the heads of humans dragging a cyclopean slab up the steps of a pyramid.

Another features a girl lying on a stone altar, black sky above her head veined in spidery gold. She wears a headdress of charcoal-black feathers and gold-metallic bikini, a big turquoise disc dangling from her nose. A dark-haired man dressed in black robes holds a crude stone knife over her chest.

"Egad, but these are the hormonal fantasies of a twelve-year-old boy." Wentwhistle shakes her head. "Not only is Blight a megalomaniac, he's developmentally challenged."

I catch sight of the floor. In the center there's a mosaic of a one-eyed shark bursting from the top of pyramid. "Oh, I don't know. This stuff would be kind of cool if it wasn't so evil."

"Finley, you disappoint me." She inspects the painting of the girl with the priest. "Lots of dust on these things, and the oils are faded. Bet they've been up here a long time."

"Alright, y'all," Katie Sue says, stepping toward us. "Everybody ready to go?"

"Ready as I'll ever be." Win lugs a blaster spear over his shoulder.

I'm packing a blaster and three cans of Aqua-Net, with the pendant dangling around my neck. Wentwhistle wears two hooks on her belt like some kind of demented gunslinger.

Katie Sue's outfit is both bizarre and lethal looking. She's ditched the leafy gown for a full-body carapace of thick magnolia branches lashed together by strips of jellyfish hide.

Win eyes her unusual get-up. "Man, that's pretty rad. Why couldn't you make me a suit?"

"Sorry." She shrugs. "Temizkuan doesn't carry anything in your size."

A dull warmth permeates my chest. I reach into my t-shirt and pull out the pendant. The amethyst shines brightly, the comforting warmth of its glow spreading across my chest like an electric blanket. I don't know why, but ever since the emerald blew itself out this thing makes me feel better.

Wentwhistle grabs my wrist. "Would you put that away?"

She points to the shiny object. "You'll get us shot at twenty paces."

"Sorry." I hide the pendant under my shirt.

Katie Sue speaks with an edge in her voice. "Mickey, Temizkuan instructs me. We will need that when we get inside the rocket silo."

I frown. "Why? What does it do?"

Her tone is all business now. "That device is a *kazetotl*, a gatekeeping device. A key."

"That's wild," Win says.

Something skitters across the floor in the darkness ahead.

Me and Win level our blasters, and Wentwhistle raises the hook above her head. A rat twitches his whiskers at us, then scampers through an open archway.

We lower our weapons.

"I should've guessed," Wentwhistle says, frowning. "Rumor is Blight's been on the Gulf Coast for years. He's been running this little cult with nobody in town the wiser."

"That doesn't matter right now," Katie Sue says, setting off toward the archway. "Let's keep moving."

Cautiously, we pass under the arch and make our way down a corridor with polished wooden walls inlaid with sculptures of strange insects, sharks, and centipedes. Wentwhistle stops to inspect a display case containing a replica of blocky pyramids rising above a jungle.

She turns to me. "Do these look like the structures you saw on T'kahuatl?"

"Sure do." I run my fingers across the glass. "But the plants and stuff don't. You figure these were modeled on something built on Earth?"

"Precisely, Boy Wonder," Wentwhistle bends down for a closer look. "Judging from the architecture, I'd say this is Mesoamerican, pre-Olmec. Or..." She steps away from the case. "...something somebody wanted the locals back then to *think* was pre-Olmec."

We check out some other cases. One is stocked with feathered headdresses, beaded shawls, and leather skirts. Another holds a collection of knives with blades made from shiny black glass.

"Obsidian." Wentwhistle points to the weapons. "Aztec from the looks of them. These could be worth a fortune."

Suddenly, the floor beneath our feet trembles. From somewhere deep within the building, a low rumble accelerates to a roar, shaking the foundation.

My heart leaps in my chest. Jeez, but this is getting scary. If I didn't know better, I would say the entire coast was sliding into the Gulf. "What was that?" I say.

"They're warming up the engines." Katie Sue raises an armored fist. "We're running out of time."

With one clean motion, she shatters the glass, and reaches inside.

"Here." She tosses a feathered crown to me. "We might need this."

I hold the cumbersome artifact up to the light. "What for?"

"Not sure." She shrugs. "Temizkuan instructs me."

I'm not about to argue with a dead girl wearing tree armor. "Sure." I stuff the headdress in my bag and follow the others down the next passageway. It curves to the right and opens into a vaulted antechamber whose earthen floor is dotted with small, polished stones of different colors, connected by inlaid black glass.

Wentwhistle runs her hands over the surface. "I think this is a star map, like the ones I have in the van."

"Cool." Stepping into the room, I slip on one of the stones and drop my spear. It clatters to the floor, kicking off an echo which reverberates through the adjoining doorway.

"Oh crap," Win whispers. "Hope nobody heard that."

Down the corridor, distant voices grumble amid the crunch of rough footfalls.

"We've been found out," Katie Sue extends her hands in the air, fingertips pulsating with purple light. "They're coming."

The clamor grows to a rumble like a buffalo stampede. How many guys does Blight have guarding this place?

A T'Kalul emerges from the darkness, brass helmet gleaming like a new penny. Two others dog its heels. Katie Sue turns and thrusts her hands upward. Vines rip through the floor and entangle the first creature. Win blasts another off its feet and back into the corridor. But the remaining warrior evades a shot from Wentwhistle's hook.

Instantly, the T'Kalul is on me, hands clutching my neck. I throw an elbow, then plant my heel on its knee. The warrior staggers backward. Retrieving my spear, I blast the T'Kalul in the gut. It staggers for a moment on wobbly legs, then crashes to the floor. Glass shrapnel scatters in its wake.

The bug-head tries to rise but Katie Sue descends, punching it in the back. With a flash of magenta light, the T'Kalul lies still. Katie Sue clenches her fists, and more vines pop through the ground, encasing the remaining soldiers.

"Y'all okay?" she asks.

Win brushes a chunk of green pulp off his shirt. "Think so."

Footfalls and furious clicking echo down the hallway. Wentwhistle clears her throat. "Hate to spoil the moment, but we can't stay here."

Katie Sue clenches both fists. Spiky roots and thorny vines pierce the floor, creating an impenetrable bramble. For a moment, screeching fills the hallway, then dwindles into complete silence.

Win steps toward the doorway and peers down the hall.

"Katie? I think you got them."

With a flick of her wrist, the spiky foliage collapses into ash. She steps into the corridor. "Come on. Becca's down here."

Her purple glowing fingertips illuminate the root-choked hallway. Following her lead, we step over the bodies of fallen T'Kalul.

"Man, oh man, Katie Sue," I say. "What do you even need us for?"

"I don't." She turns and smiles, magenta eyes flashing in the near darkness. "But Becca will when I…" Her voice trails off.

Win steps toward her. "Katie?"

Katie Sue snaps out of it at the sound of his voice. "Sorry," she says. "Temizkuan fears we won't be in time. We need to hurry."

The corridor ends in an intersection. Wentwhistle peers to the right, then the left. She turns to Katie Sue. "Which way?"

"Give me a moment." Katie Sue presses both fists against her forehead, mumbles something inaudible, and then says, "Temizkuan isn't sure. We'll have to split up."

Furious clicking reverberates from the other end of the hallway.

Wentwhistle draws something from her satchel. "Never know when a good road flare's going to come in handy." She strikes the charge, and a blinding light sizzles in the darkness.

The sound of trampling footsteps echoes around us. I turn to Wentwhistle. "Well, if we're splitting up, who's going with who?"

"Win?" Katie Sue says. "You and Colleen go left. Mickey comes with me."

Wentwhistle tilts her head and squints. "Are you sure this is a good idea, splitting the team?"

"You have a better one?"

"No."

They're almost on us. "We need something to slow them down," I say.

"Allow me." Wentwhistle trains her hook on a support arch down the hallway. She fires and a high-pitched shriek floods the corridor. Rock and masonry rain down and block the passageway.

She must be reading my mind. "That was quick thinking," I say.

"Mr. Finley, you ain't seen nothin' yet." Wentwhistle turns to Win. "Come on, kid."

"Wait," he says. "How we gettin' back out?"

Katie Sue points to the sky. "There're rockets upstairs. We'll just airlift ourselves out, if need be. One other thing." She opens her hand and a magnolia blossoms in her palm. "If y'all run into trouble, toss this at whatever's chasing you and call Temizkuan's name three times. That'll level the playing field."

Wentwhistle pockets the bloom. "Sounds spiffy. You ready, Win?"

He nods. "Yeah. Let's go."

"Mr. Finley? It's vital—absolutely vital—you survive this. Dig?"

Man, this lady's weird in an utterly cool way. "Right on, Wentwhistle."

Win stops, sets down his pike, and says, "Be cool, man."

"You, too."

He draws me in for a hug, then retrieves his weapon and joins Wentwhistle. They disappear into the blackness, the flare's cherry glow lighting their way.

"Okay." Katie Sue extends a hand, and I take it. "You ready?"

"As I'll ever be, I guess."

"Then let's go."

38

Me and Katie Sue walk down a corridor that ends in another circular room. The walls are covered with blackened bones arranged in geometric patterns—triangles, hexagons, and octagons.

Marble tentacles climb the corners and connect at the base of a chandelier made from emeralds set in fish skulls, dried out fins, and mummified insect wings. Light from the chandelier flickers green, bathing the room in a sickly, underwater light. This place is all kinds of creepy.

"What's all this?" I say.

"Not sure." Katie Sue eyes the fishy overhead light fixture. "If you haven't figured it out by now, the children of Azokuitli are a weird bunch, but maybe we can use one of the jewels up there to light our way."

"Can't you just use your magic powers?"

She chuckles. "I have to conserve something in case we run into trouble."

And we haven't run into trouble already? "Oh, okay." We stand in front of a circular stone depression about three feet across. "Say, Katie Sue?"

"Yes?" she says, frowning. Tendrils snake from her hand,

wend upward, and snag an emerald.

"What do you think this is?" I point to the floor. "Some kind of pool?"

"Not sure." She rubs the jewel, making it glow brighter. "Maybe they used it for rendering."

"Rendering?"

"Yeah, you know, like turning animals into food?"

The thought makes my stomach turn. "You mean like pigs or chickens?"

"That's right." She raises her eyebrows. "You never been to a hog slaughtering?"

"No. That's gross."

A case housing the embalmed remains of a T'Kalul priest catches my eye. "Do you think there's any hope for my folks?" I say, inspecting the cadaver through the glass.

"If they've fallen under Blight's influence, I'd doubt it at this point."

"I know, I know. But do you think maybe they could change back? You know, like if we stop Blight?"

The emerald radiates a warm green glow that makes Katie Sue look coldly beautiful and kind of cruel. It's like some alien part of her surfaced in this dungeon of horrors.

"Doubtful," she says, stepping away. Then she turns to me with pursed lips. "You have to accept the fact they aren't human anymore."

"Just like you aren't human?"

The gem in her fist begins to smoke. "What's that supposed to mean?"

"I don't mean nothing by that. It's just…I'm confused, you know? How come you're independent of Blight? Why can't he control you like he does my uncle and everyone else?"

"Mickey, you've got to understand." She touches the spot on her chest. "Temizkuan lives inside me. And Blight has absolutely no influence over her."

"So, you work for her?"

"What?"

"Do you work for her?" Nervous, I scrape the floor with the toe of my shoe. "Is Temizkuan like, I don't know, your boss or something?"

Her gaze turns wary. "Where is this coming from? Why do you doubt—"

"You know, it's getting to where you don't even *sound* like Katie Sue anymore." I probably should shut up, but the words keep coming. "You know stuff she wouldn't know, and you have all these superpowers. I mean, you just wiped out a bunch of dudes without even thinking about it."

"You mean those bug-heads? They were trying to kill us."

"The Katie Sue I knew wouldn't do something like that." My heart pounds faster than pistons in a high-performance engine. "So, who are you, really?"

She goes silent. Her eyes flash magenta fire and bony spines burst from her forehead.

I'm surely about to die. "Whoa."

"Oh gosh." Gingerly, she touches a spike and shakes her head. "This is new."

Whew. Guess she's not going to kill me. "What do you think those things are for?"

Katie Sue furrows her brow. "I'm not sure. But everything sounds louder. Like, really loud." She inches to the center of the chamber, stops, and cocks her head. Then, she points to the floor. "Becca's down there."

"Down where?"

The jewel emits a burst of light, casting eerie shadows around the chamber. A grinding sound reaches my ears. I watch the circular depression slide open in the floor. We're standing on the edge of a deep, dark hole.

I turn to Katie Sue. "How did you know to do that?"

"Come," she says.

I really don't want to go down in the hole, but I guess I have no choice. Taking a deep breath, I follow. "Katie Sue, we're right by the bay, so you can't build anything below sea level out here. How come there's all these subterranean levels to this place?"

Her eyes flash like fireflies. "Who said we're by the bay?" She turns and descends a long spiral staircase, the green gem illuminating her way.

The staircase ends in a big room, maybe fifty feet across. The walls are made of gigantic, misshapen stone blocks, glistening with slime. Tall, glass tubes, filled with an amber liquid, stand at odd intervals around the room. Four of them are occupied. I count two embalmed T'Kalul in priest's robes, and another in full battle dress. The last tube contains the remains of a short, squat humanoid, wearing nothing but a tattered loincloth and brass harness crisscrossing its sunken chest. The left side of its face is distorted, one eye nothing more than a bulging, milky pearl, a spiny mandible for a chin.

A brass plate at the base says. *Kh'lomo, aged twenty-five. Husking failed, 1137 A.D.*

I turn to Katie Sue. "What do you think this guy's deal was?"

"Not sure." She inspects the case. "This might've been one of Midian's early human bodies."

"That's sick." Distracted by a shiver going up my spine, I nearly trip over a cable running from a tube. "What's this?"

"Don't know." Me and Katie Sue track the cable to a bank of television monitors. Amber colored cursors blink on the black screens, and each is wired to a keyboard.

"Huh." I sit down in front of a screen. Then it hits me.

"Wait, these are computers." I tap the spacebar and a prompt appears on the screen.

Query?

Katie Sue sits next to me. "What are you up to over here?"

"This is just like Atari." With two fingers, I type, *Hi, how are you?* then press the Enter key.

Something hums underneath the table. The computer's response flashes on the cursor line.

Cannot process your request. Query?

"This is not like Atari," Katie Sue says, shifting her gaze to a black plastic box next to the keyboard. "What do we have here?"

The box looks featureless save for a small triangle-shape sunk into the surface.

Katie Sue furrows her brow. "You know, I wonder..." She turns to me. "Mickey, where's the kazetotl?"

"The what?" Oh, wait, I know what she's talking about. "Oh yeah, the key." I draw the pendant from my shirt, and hand it to her. Katie Sue hesitates for a moment, then fits it into the slot. The amethyst glows and the pendant locks into place, a perfect fit.

The cursor hops across the screen, displaying a repetitive heap of cheery news.

Four hours...twenty-three minutes...
ten-point-two seconds until arrival.
The RISING is here...
Four hours...twenty-three minutes...
ten seconds until arrival.
The RISING is here...

"Four hours." Katie Sue frowns and hands the pendant back to me. "Not a lot of time to stop Blight."

Dim lights spring to life on the ceiling, and the grinding of machinery running at full tilt fills the air. In the center of the room, an oval-shaped section of the floor slides away. A curious machine, like a pipe organ, rises to the surface. Huge brass canisters are attached to what looks like a giant beetle sitting on a television screen.

"You play?" Katie Sue points to the contraption.

That thing looks like it would eat me if I put my hands on it. "No."

Out of the corner of my eye, I catch something floating in one of the glass tubes. The liquid inside is murky, as though its contents had disintegrated a long time ago. Then something bumps against the glass and bobs up and down like a leaf in a whirlpool. I nearly gag when I realize what it is. The figure in the soup was human once. But now it's little more than jaundiced skin stretched tight across a skeleton. The carcass is dressed in what appears to be a police officer's uniform. A tentacled, shark-nosed creature sticks out of its bloated belly.

Katie Sue places a hand on the cylinder. "Looks like they're still conducting experiments on people."

Stomach acid rises in my throat. I don't want to look, but it's hard to take my eyes off the dancing remains. "How long you think this guy's been here?"

She inspects the brass plate at the cylinder's base. "Apparently since nineteen-seventy-five."

"Five years? Oh, crap."

"It actually makes sense." In the glass, Katie Sue's reflection is superimposed over the skeleton's fleshless grin. "Blight wanted to test his parasites before using them on big groups." She taps the glass next to the thing sticking out of the cadaver's abdomen. "Probably wanted to get the mixture right, so he could turn the whole town into Azokuitli worshippers."

"Does that matter?"

"It matters more than you think," she says. "A god needs followers, or else he's not much of a god, is he?"

"I reckon." I point to the pipe organ with its weird insect decoration. "What about that thing over there?"

"Your guess is as good as mine." Katie Sue approaches the contraption. Sitting at the keys, she taps one bass note then takes a step back.

The beetle's eyes light up, and the carapace splits open. Wings vibrate in its back, the buzzing filling the room with atonal static.

I cover my ears, but it does little good. "Man, can you turn that thing off?"

Katie Sue taps the same key, and the beetle's wings cease humming.

"Whew…" I approach the organ.

The organ's TV flickers to sudden life. An image of a brass metal triangle, set with three jewels, floats into view.

Katie Sue licks her lips. "That's a kazetotl. Like yours, but fully intact."

The image fades, replaced by a close-up of a tentacled, one-eyed shark.

"Azokuitli," I say.

A second symbol appears on screen, a magnolia topped by a bulging jellyfish canopy.

"Blessed Temizkuan," Katie Sue says.

The tree fades, and a moth with crystal-blue human eyes blinking on its wings flutters on screen.

I turn to her. "You know this one?"

Katie Sue presses her fingertips against her temples.

"Temizkuan doesn't say."

Of course, she doesn't. How convenient. "I guess that's a mystery for another time."

Katie Sue makes a sudden snap to attention. "Sure. We've got to find Becca." She stands and jostles the organ. A high-pitched whine erupts from its speakers, and a door falls open revealing a hidden compartment. Something heavy slips out of the chamber and crashes to the floor.

"Huh?" I reach down to retrieve the object, almost cutting off a finger in the process. "Wow, this thing's deadly."

"What is it?" Katie Sue says.

The dagger is made from smooth black glass, with crude, serrated edges. "Don't they have some of these upstairs?"

"Sort of," Katie Sue takes the knife and balances it on one finger, testing the weight. "But why hide it in an organ?"

I shrug. "I don't know."

"And this one *isn't* like the ones upstairs." She slashes the blade in the air, twirling it in a circle. "It's bigger. Probably had some special purpose."

"Maybe it's for bigger sacrifices?"

Katie Sue frowns. "That's not funny."

The air turns bone-chilling cold, and something scrapes along the floor, making a scratching sound.

I level my spear in the direction of the disturbance. "Who's there?"

A sound like oil splashing in a fifty-gallon drum fills the room.

Katie Sue's eyes blaze like magenta flares. "Show yourself."

The shadowy figure slinks into view, its head a nest of snaky tentacles.

"Don't play with us. Show yourself." I've got my thumb on the blaster's trigger.

"Aw, Pop-Tart," a girl's voice says. "That ain't no way to

treat an old friend."

"It can't be." I nearly choke on my own tongue.

A glass cylinder shatters. The organ lights up, and the beetle revs to a fever pitch. What's left of Alice Walsh slithers into view.

"Y'all miss me?"

39

Alice slinks along on muddy tentacles, her torso shimmering and luminescent. Humanoid arms end in fin-shaped hands that are tipped with barbed talons. Oily mucous seeps from the girl-monster's pitted face, and her rough cheeks are stained plum. Fangs glitter behind her scaly lips, and a mass of tentacles writhe like snakes on her head.

"No, no, no." I drop the blaster and the sound of it hitting the ground seems far away.

"Yeah, yeah, yeah, Pop-Tart." A single eye in the center of her face sparkles with feline menace. "You let this happen to me when you done ran off."

"You told me to let you go. That's what you said."

"It's *your* fault I'm this way." She jabs a claw to her chest. "All your fault, and you're going to pay for it!"

She lunges, toppling one of the computer monitors. The device crashes to the floor, the screen shattering into a thousand pieces.

"We don't have time for this." Katie Sue steps in front of me and levels the knife at the creature. "Where's my sister?"

"You ain't ever going to find out." Alice sneers, a green pus bubbling on her lips. "Little Blondie's being loaded on a pod right now."

Smoke billows from Katie Sue's fists. "You're Wade's little friend, right?"

"Me and Wade ain't together no more." The girl-monster cackles, closing the distance. "But I serve the Master 'til I die."

Katie Sue scowls, her horned brows twitching like antennae. "Famous last words."

Sharp roots burst through the floor, skewering Alice. She shrieks in pain but manages to free herself.

The pair lock into a blur of white hair, flashing eyes, and lashing tentacles. Katie Sue ducks one flailing limb but a second wrenches away the knife, shattering her arm guard in the process. Wood splinters in all directions, and I duck behind the organ to avoid impalement. Breaking Alice's grip, she leapfrogs a third tentacle, and snatches the blade off the floor.

"That won't do you no good, hon." The girl-monster coils a limb around Katie Sue's waist.

"Getting familiar there?" Katie Sue slashes down, severing a tentacle.

Alice screams, her limb flopping on the floor like a fish, spewing green fluid.

"You're going to pay for that." She coils her remaining limbs under herself, muscles tensing for a strike. "Y'all ain't getting out of here."

If we don't get past Alice, everything goes to crap. I rise from behind the organ, leveling my spear at the diseased girl.

Knives turn in my stomach.

Stupid, stupid, stupid. You can't stop that freaky witch.

Just shut up, okay?

You can't do anything at a—

Something heavy and wet snaps against my head.

Dropping my spear, I crash to the floor and come eye to eye with a snaking limb. Twisting my hip, I roll free, avoiding the deadly appendage.

Time slows to a crawl.

Alice sends a tentacle looping around Katie Sue's neck, strangling her. The black knife falls from her hands and skitters along the floor. Then a second limb rises, the business end barbed like a spear.

Oh crap, she's going to gut Katie Sue. Scrambling to my feet, I search for my spear. Something falls from my bag and rolls along the floor.

A can of Aqua-Net.

Screaming like a cat, Alice thrusts the tentacle into Katie Sue's chest, shattering her wooden breastplate. Dropping to her knees, Katie Sue clenches her fist and thorny vines explode through the ceiling, ensnaring the girl-monster.

They're locked into it to the death. But that gets us no closer to Becca Mae. I've got to do something.

Rising to one knee, I lift the can and shout, "Hey, Alice!"

"Not now, Pop-Tart." Alice twists her head, pus oozing from her lips. "I'm going to kill you later."

"Nah, you won't." I shake the can and roll the Aqua-Net across the floor. It comes to rest against her body. Then I pick up my blaster.

She laughs. "Now, you're just being stupid."

"Oh really?" I fire and the can detonates, sending flaming hairspray cascading all over Alice.

Her screams flood the air. "What did you do?" Flames gallop along her back, igniting her tentacled hair. "What did you do?"

Katie Sue twists free. Smoke fills the room, a mix of aerosol, burning oil, and spoiled fish guts. I almost wretch, the stink worse than a dead refrigerator full of spoiled meat.

The roar of the bonfire grows to deafening proportions. Alice writhes, mouth hanging open, her wails drowned amid the crackling flames.

Amid the chaos, I notice what's left of Katie Sue's wooden armor dangles from her body.

"Hey, shouldn't you, I don't know, cover up a little?" I say.

She folds her arms over her chest. "Can you not look?"

Leafy vines slither through cracks in the stone floor and peel away the remains of the armor, exposing her pale skin.

I avert my gaze. "Sorry." There's a rush of air mingled with a sound like crickets chirping.

"Okay, you can turn around," she says.

Katie Sue's dressed in a sleeveless tunic made of oval leaves stitched with glowing lavender-colored tree roots.

"Wow. Looks good."

"I guess," she says. "Thinking about starting my own fashion line when this is over." She turns to face the girl-monster writhing in the flames. "Alice Walsh, right? Sorry about the mess, honey."

"Shut up. Just shut up!" Alice squats on her mangled tentacles, her flesh charred and blackened, green fluid oozing from her mouth. "I'll get out of this, I swear I will. Y'all ain't heard the last from—"

A huge chunk of masonry falls from the ceiling, flattening Alice.

Katie Sue regards the smoking remains. "The rest of the room's going to cave in soon. Any ideas on getting us out of here?"

"Not really." Truth is, I can barely stand. "Can't you just use your magic?"

"Use my magic?" She shrugs. "That's no way to talk to the avatar of a goddess."

"Well, what else would *you* call it?"

"Just be respectful." Katie Sue grins, and I know she's kidding. "I'm not some TV hot-chick genie in a belly-dancer costume, thank you *very* much."

"Oh brother." I shake my head. "Dude, just fix it."

"I will." She waves her hand in the air and white light blossoms on the opposite wall.

"What's that?" I say.

"Our ticket out of here."

I cast a wary eye at the mountain of smoking debris on the floor. "What about Alice?"

She shrugs. "I don't think she can hurt us anymore."

A tentacle bursts through the pile.

"Oh crap." I level my spear.

Purple flames ignite around Katie Sue's clenched fists.

The limb gropes blindly for a moment, then lies still.

"Whew." I rub sweat from my brow.

"Here." Katie Sue brushes something from my cheek. "You got some soot on you."

"Thanks." I stand and a glint from something near the organ catches my eye. "Hey, it's your knife."

She points to the weapon. "You take it."

Katie Sue turns toward the light on the wall, and I follow. Behind us, the rest of the ceiling is coming down, raining rock and masonry. Glass cylinders shatter, spilling their contents. A chunk of debris smashes the organ into a thousand pieces.

Eyes blazing magenta fire, Katie Sue makes a fist and the wall implodes, creating a vacuum that almost knocks me off my feet. The hole glows red-hot and the temperature spikes.

"This way." Katie Sue points to the cavity, then disappears through the hole.

I run after her, leaping over the cavity's burning rim. We stand in a chamber hung with smoking roots stretching

Craig E. Higgins

upward into darkness.

"Come." She grabs a vine and plants a foot against the wall.

We pick our way through the shadows, the room below choked with rock and dust.

40

Me and Katie Sue climb along the roots against the wall. The blaster spear slung over my shoulder smacks against my back each time I reach for a higher handgrip. After a while, the muscles in my arms and legs burn, and I start coughing for lack of oxygen. I'm a little scared but can't think about how high we've climbed or I'll freak out and slip and fall into oblivion.

After what seems like forever, the chamber narrows into a vertical shaft. Katie Sue cranes her neck to face me.

"Think we're pretty close." She points to the dimly lit outline of a hole above our heads. "Be ready for anything when we get up there."

She scurries like a rabbit through the hole. Reaching the top, I place one hand on the rim and Katie Sue grabs my wrist, pulling me upward. The floor beneath me is concrete, and there's a heavy stench like gasoline which floods my nostrils, making me gag.

"Phew. What is this place?" I ask. "A chemical refinery?"

"No." Katie Sue's magenta eyes flash like fireflies in the near darkness. "Think we found our rockets."

"Guess so." I survey our surroundings. We're in a huge

chamber, maybe a football field across in length and two stories high. Across the room stand two parallel metal cylinders, each about thirty feet wide. Both sit on what look like inverted metal bowls spewing smoke and simmering flames between their rims and the floor.

"See what I mean?" she says. "These must be the base of the rockets."

"That makes sense." Gripping my blaster, I tread carefully, hair standing at attention on the back of my neck. I want very much to not be here right now, but lately my life's been beyond psycho. I have no illusions about getting everything I want out of this scenario.

Dim red and orange lights climb the walls. Next to one rocket stand two metal tanks attached by rubber hoses to a spigot. A huge hose like you'd see on an airport runway connects the spigot to the base of one of the rockets.

Katie Sue runs a hand along the thick tube. "They're almost done fueling." She places her fingertips to her temples and frowns. "Temizkuan instructs me that Becca's right above us."

She points toward a crown of light blazing above. The ceiling is laced with bleached, interlocking bones arranged to create images of what I guess are the T'Kalul on Earth. Femurs form the outlines of a pyramid looming over a jungle, hip bones, skulls, and rib cages represent aliens battling humans.

But the weird decor doesn't interest me as much as what's happening over our heads. The light above the ceiling filters through a layer of metal mesh surrounding the upper stages of the rockets. Guttural clicks and shrieks echo from the chamber above. An unsettling thought occurs to me. I turn to Katie Sue.

"You know what I don't get is, why do they have to sacrifice Becca in the first place? Or anybody, really? Is it like a superstitious thing?"

"Azokuitli is a god, and has to be appeased," she says.

"That's it?" I furrow my brow. "That's all you got?"

"Yeah, well I don't know the answer to your question." Katie Sue shrugs. "We need to focus on saving Becca."

Something like metal grinding against metal screams above our heads. A section of mesh slides away from the curvature of the rocket. Beyond the cylinder rests the bulbous base of one of the spires, its glassy sides shiny like obsidian.

Beyond that, I see the pitch-black sky. From out of the darkness, a gold-veined flash slashes across the clouds.

Katie Sue's face is suddenly illuminated in a wash of bright light, exposing a second set of features hidden under her translucent skin. Sharp, brass cheekbones bracket narrow breathing slits. Mandibles set in her lower jaw click like keys on a typewriter. Worst of all, her eyes are honeycombed like those of a wasp.

"Oh Jeez," I say, nearly tripping on my spear. "You're a bug-head."

Katie Sue turns. "What are you talking about?"

The lightning flashes again, and I get another terrible glimpse. "You're one of them, a T'Kalul."

"Mickey?"

A wave of nausea floods my gut.

Stupid, stupid, stupid. How did you miss this before?

Just shut up.

She's a monster like the rest of them.

"You're wrong," I say out loud. My knees buckle, and I'm sweating like I've just run a mile. I cover my eyes with my hands, too afraid to see more.

"Mickey? You've got to stop this, now."

"No, no, no." I shake my head furiously from side to side. "You're one of them, and you're going to kill me."

"I will do no such thing." Ice cold hands grasp my wrists. "Mickey, Blight's a sorcerer, remember? He's probably playing with your head. Look at me."

She pulls my hands from my face. I gaze at her and she's the same old Katie Sue—well, at least the chalk-white, purple-eyed version. "See? I'm no evil bug-head lady."

Wow, I must be really tired.

"I…I'm sorry. The lightning lit everything up and I swore I saw something…" I say, shaking my head. "I mean. I guess I didn't, right?"

Katie Sue smiles. "No, you didn't. And that's okay."

I'm so embarrassed, but I guess she's willing to let it slide.

A familiar voice echoes from the blackness above. "Mickey? That you?"

It's Win. I cup my hands and call out, "Yeah?"

The end of a long rope drops down, its end dangling a few feet above the floor.

"Grab on, and we'll pull you up," Win's voice says.

I turn to Katie Sue. "Looks like we got us a rescue party."

She nods. "You go first."

I wrap the rope underneath my arms, tie a secure knot, and give it a tug. "I'm ready."

The cord tightens around my chest, and I'm lifted upward, toes bumping against the rocket's side. Finally, I reach the top and fall onto a circular platform surrounding the base of the onion-dome. The room is small and shrouded in darkness save for red and orange lights flickering on a nearby bank of computer consoles.

Katie Sue calls from below. "Mickey, what's going on up there?"

I catch a whiff of something brine. "Win?" I say, "you here?"

Three figures emerge from the darkness but remain in

shadow. The taller one, dressed in what appears to be T'Kalul battle armor, makes a series of clicking noises with its mouth. Another laughs, his chuckle depressingly familiar.

It's Wade.

"Pop-Tart," he says, stepping toward me, "you are a certified *champeen* idiot."

"No!" I run to the edge. "Katie Sue, Wade's up here. Don't let him—"

Something hard comes down on my head, and the world goes dark.

"Get up."

A boot connects with my shoulder hard, waking me from delirium.

Pain erupts down my arm. "Wow, what was that about?"

"Get up."

The metal floor rumbles like a herd of wild horses, and the walls shake and buckle.

An overpowering diesel odor permeates my sinuses. Dark splotches stain my clothes and skin. "What's this?"

"Rocket fuel." Wade stands over me, dressed in burgundy robes. "Fella that works at the Stennis testing site outside of town requisitioned it for us. Master Blight don't turn all his servants into kzelocs." He runs his fingers through his blond locks. "Like me."

I take stock of my situation. Wade and his buddies have stripped me of all weapons, Aqua-Net, and the pendant. I'm sitting on the floor of a rounded, cone-shaped room that's maybe six feet at its highest point. Five curved metal brackets support walls covered in dials, levers, and brass cylinders. A single inverted teardrop-shaped window made of thick red glass casts ruby-colored shadows over the interior. In the center of the room stands a console brimming with illuminated bulbs and dancing lights. The control panel emits a humming noise which reverberates along the walls.

I glare at Wade. "This a rocket cockpit?" I ask.

"You're a big brain, aren't you, Pop-Tart? Can't put anything past you." He turns from me and steps toward the window, the darkness outside forming a perfect mirror for his cruel features. "Yep, you've got a seat on the train. Consider yourself lucky."

"Where are my friends?"

"The black kid and the granny? They're on another rocket. Granny seems to know some stuff. The other one might be alright for target practice."

If looks could punch somebody in the face, my eyes would deck Wade across the room. "What about Katie Sue?"

"Ah, crazy Katie." He snickers. "We already had Becca loaded up for transport, and when we showed Katie what would happen to Becca if she didn't back down, she gave up and let us put her on dry ice." Wade adjusts something on the console. "Becca's always been her weak spot." He cracks a grin. "Sisterly love. Isn't that the craziest thing?"

I'm not sure I believe him. "Why am I still alive?" I try to stand but a three-fingered claw grasps my shoulder, pushing me down. Turning, I stare up into the face of a T'Kalul warrior. The creature's compound eyes glitter in the infrared glow of the cramped compartment. He's telling me something, but all I hear is maddening chirping.

"Hey, Wade?" I say. "Tell this freak to get out of my face."

"Or what? You'll hairspray him to death?" Wade chuckles and then turns, a frown on his face. "As to your question, I'm not going to answer it. Except to say, if it weren't for me, you'd already be dead."

"Sorry if I don't feel grateful right now."

He pulls something from his robe. "Recognize this?"

It's the pendant. "Give me that back."

"Hah, that's funny." Wade drops the object back into the folds of his cloak. "Wouldn't do you that much good at this point, anyway." He snaps his fingers. The T'Kalul hauls me to my feet, then rips something shiny off its belt.

"Put those on," Wade says, gesturing to the shackles dangling in the warrior's other claw.

"No way."

"Suit yourself."

The T'Kalul punches me in the solar plexus. Pain explodes in my abdomen. I drop to my knees, all the wind knocked out of me. Unable to breathe, I try to stand but the alien cuffs me across the head, sending me to the floor.

Wade nods to the warrior, who yanks me to my feet. Grabbing my wrists, the T'Kalul pulls them behind my back and cuffs me.

"Boy, oh boy." Wade shakes his head. "Pop-Tart, you've been out of your league from the day we met. I take it you two took Alice out of the picture?"

I smile. "Yeah, we...did." I say between gasps of air. "And you? You're...going to...be next."

His laughter could peel paint off walls. "Actually, you did me the hugest favor! The Master was furious at me over that one. Alice could've screwed up *everything*! But now that trailer trash is gone, well..."

A black insect squiggles out of an open sore on Wade's forearm.

"Mmm. Looks pretty tasty." He swats the creature and pops it into his mouth. "A lot of things will make more sense when we get to the asteroid." A grin crosses Wade's face, and he grabs my chin. "Now, shut up, Pop-Tart. We're going to T'kahuatl."

I peer through the shadowed glass. Outside, gold veins

of lightning illuminate sulfurous black clouds. Down on the street, smoke drifts upward from wrecked vehicles. A few remaining humans scatter, chased by swarms of kzelocs. Beekeepers hop from a green van and pursue the stragglers, blasting them into dust.

My heart sinks in my chest. "What is all this?"

"BDM advance cleansing unit." Wade stands near an opening in the floor. "They're here to mop up any remaining resistance." He yawns. "It's good the area is pacified before the Rising."

"Oh yeah? And what'll they do when the National Guard gets here?" An image of Tommy in his midshipman's uniform flashes in my brain. "Or the Navy?"

Wade laughs. "Dream on, Pop-Tart. The Master created a ten-mile dead zone around the Gulf. They can't get in." He wrenches my shoulder so hard I think he's going to break it. "When the Rising happens, all the armies and navies and air forces will be swept aside by Azokuitli. Nukes will only feed the god's fury."

"So, that's it then," I say. "You win, and we lose."

Wade pats me on the head. "Blessed be the Rising," he says, stepping toward the window. The glass slides open, and Wade exits.

The remaining T'Kalul throws me against a wall.

I'm getting real sick of this dude tossing me around. "Yeah, you're stupid and ugly."

The T'Kalul opens its mouth, threatening me with a barbed dart on its tongue.

I push myself upright. "Am I supposed to be impressed?"

There's a rumble outside, and the whole compartment shakes. With my hands tied behind my back, it's impossible to keep my balance. I stumble to the floor. "A little help here?"

Clicking its mandibles, the warrior gestures toward a

nearby chair.

We must be taking off soon, so there's no point in arguing now. "You want me over there? Okay." I hop to my feet and stumble toward the seat.

The floor shakes again, and this time the cabin pressurizes, making my ears pop. I glance out the window and catch sight of smoke rising from the side of the rocket. Noises erupt from the console, its instrument lights flickering like exploding firecrackers. An overhead vent roars to life, blowing cold air into the compartment.

Sweat-soaked, I shiver in my t-shirt. "Hey," I say to the alien, "could you turn that thing down?"

A porthole opens in the center of the floor, exposing the top rung of a ladder in a vertical shaft. Another T'Kalul enters our compartment. This one wears a fancier uniform, with twin conch shells adorning its chest plate. The two creatures interlock their claws, then slap each other's shoulders.

"Is that like a secret handshake?" I say.

It ignores me, chattering with its mandibles at the other monster. The first bug-soldier nods, then unshackles me. But before I can make a move, it connects the metal bracelets on my wrists to magnets on the seat's armrests.

"Aw man, what if I need to use the bathroom?"

Satisfied I can't escape, they pop down the exit.

The pod's frame shakes, and the roar outside is louder than a bomb going off. Trails form along the edges of my vision, the room blurring into nonsense. A roar fills my ears, and gravity takes hold, pushing me into the seat.

Oh crap. I'm going into space!

My heartbeat slows, and a low guttural moan bellows in the pit of my stomach. Beads of sweat float in the air like glass trinkets. A sudden increase in pressure flattens my cheeks. Dark spots dance like gnats in front of my eyes. With great effort, I manage not to vomit.

The asteroid still blocks the sun, but now the black shape inverts colors like a photo negative. When you leave Earth, does light really do stuff like this?

A loud crack fills the air, and it occurs to me we've broken the sound barrier. My thoughts scatter into a million fragments, and a whisper explodes inside my head, growing to an unending hum. Before I black out, my vision dissolves into a swirling jumble of rainbow shards.

41

I wake to humid jungle air, the stench of which fills my nose with a mix of rotten bananas and rancid meat. My wrists are shackled to a pillar. Nearby, Win and Wentwhistle slump unconscious, manacled same as me.

I gaze at an amber sky. Amid charcoal gray clouds, a blue-green Earth glows like a jewel, casting spears of light through the clouds.

Yep, we're on T'kahuatl, alright, and that's not good.

A few yards away, a handful of T'Kalul priests confer, mandibles chattering. Wade and his preppy friends loiter nearby. Two wear green like the priests, but the blond bully struts around in burgundy, like he's bug-traitor royalty. Beside them stands a towering figure, long green-colored robes hanging from wide shoulders.

Uncle John.

Check that. It's not him anymore, just a monster that wears his flesh. Uncle John's face is a map of black stitches. Pus seeps from the sac over his ruined eye, and flies zigzag around his swollen head.

My pulse pounds in my temples, my mind clouded with confusion. I could've let John die during the fight at Bay

Crossroads, but I didn't. And now that big jewel up there in the sky is about to be eaten by a giant shark. Did I screw up by not killing him? Would taking Uncle John out have made a difference in the outcome?

A knife twists in my gut.

Stupid, stupid, stupid. It's all your fault what's happening here.

What? How is that even possible?

Everything's always your fault.

"I'm really getting sick of you," I mumble. "Just shut up and let me think."

Let you think? Let you think? That's where all the trouble starts!

I shake my head and take a deep breath, trying to get my head together. I got to focus, because maybe the world depends on it.

The voices persist.

You want proof? Take a look around.

I do, and a heart-wrenching sight makes my blood turn cold. Like the rest of us, Becca Mae is bound to a pillar. Her dress is in tatters, her head crowned with a garland of green flowers. In front of her stands an altar made of black glass shot through with amber streaks. Green smoke drifts from a nearby brazier. Irregular scratches crisscross the altar's sides as if someone or something had been frantic to escape before being ripped to shreds.

A clutch of bug-priests hover near Becca Mae. Beside them a figure paces in black robes.

Midian Blight.

Other T'Kalul and kzelocs cluster around, pushing and shoving, scrambling for a good view. But no Katie Sue. Wade said she gave up. So, shouldn't she be here?

Did they kill her instead?

Speaking of the devil, Wade saunters over.

"Well, well, Pop-Tart." A slimy worm oozes from his ear.

"Back to the land of the living—at least for now." He pops the writhing morsel in his mouth and swallows it with a grin.

I wish I had the biggest can of Aqua-Net in the world, just so I could melt that stupid smile off his face. "You think this is funny?"

"Actually, yeah." His smirk widens, the gaps between his teeth wider than sewer grates. "Little people like yourself never get it. I *want* this to happen. I've been marked." He raises his arm, revealing something slithering beneath the skin. "And everybody that's ever crossed me? Made me look stupid? They're all going to get it now."

"What are you talking about? You're a rich boy. Everything's been handed to you your whole life."

Wade slaps me, the blow lightning fast, leaving my cheek stinging. "You don't know anything about me. Or my life. But now—" He thumps his chest. "—the Master will raise the god, and we'll all be kings. All those who serve."

Heavy footsteps echo on the slate behind him. Wade jumps, almost bumping into Uncle John.

"The Master wants you at the altar," the giant says.

Wade scowls, but the two depart.

Win opens his eyes. "Man, where are we?"

"On top of a pyramid."

"A pyramid?"

"Yep. On the asteroid."

"Seriously? We really here?"

"I wish I was lying, but I'm not."

"Man, that's so messed up."

I try bashing my shackles against the pillar. My only reward is a pair of scraped palms.

Win winces on my behalf. "Any idea what they're going to do to us?"

"No. But I think we're screwed."

"Ain't that the truth."

Midian Blight nods to his priests, and they move to either side of the altar. Drifting to the center of the platform, the cleric stops and claps his hands.

The crowd falls silent.

Blight begins humming in a low guttural growl, waving his arms in disjointed circles. The priests join in, adding a clicking rhythm to the cleric's atonal drone. Green smoke belches into the sky, accompanied by a biting odor like burning tires.

Smiling, Blight spreads his arms wide and three robed T'Kalul push through the crowd, playing instruments like the ones the band used at Bay Crossroads. Banging a drum, the leader of the trio chirps a slow cadence that sets my teeth on edge.

Two gray-skinned kzeloc women appear, yoked to a cart bearing a rectangular, black-lacquered box. The lid is decorated with a pink jellyfish ensnared in a tree. I could be wrong, but it sure looks like a coffin.

Blight lowers his hands and the racket ceases. With a clap, he summons a young kzeloc from the crowd. Dressed in a loincloth, the little monster kneels before Blight and hands him a triangle-shaped object.

Crap, he's got a kazetotl. "He's got a pendant like mine," I say to Win.

"Looks that way," Win says.

The cleric stands, arms outstretched, kazetotl in one hand and a big ceremonial dagger in the other. "This day fulfills the dreams of the space-faring people, once lost over the seas of eternity. Our race has suffered as no other. But behold, our hour of redemption is at hand. I bring you…our deliverer!"

The monstrous crowd howls its approval.

Wentwhistle opens her eyes and strains against her shackles. "Somebody get the number of the bus that hit me?"

Blight nods and four priests step forward. Plumes of emerald fire belch into the orange sky. The crowd cheers again, the humid air reverberating with their fervent screaming and clicking.

"Now, Azokuitli blesses us," Blight says, turning to the coffin, "with two who bear our sacred mark."

Bear our sacred mark? "Wentwhistle, what's he talking about?"

"Not sure." She squints into the green haze. "But it can't be good."

"So," Blight says, "let us weigh the worthiness of the sacrifices we offer the god." He gestures toward Becca Mae. "This one holds the legacy of our people in her veins."

Becca Mae's part T'Kalul? That makes no sense.

"But in here…" Blight waves the dagger over the coffin. "…lies another with the same gift, yet possesses something even more precious. Observe."

He nods and the women throw back the lid.

Inside, Katie Sue is dressed in black robes like the cleric. Her eyelids flutter open, and Blight helps her out of the coffin. He nods to two T'Kalul soldiers. "Tie the other one down."

They approach Becca Mae, cut her bonds, and strap her to the altar. Wade steps forward, kisses her forehead, and bows to Blight. Becca Mae tosses her head from side to side, mumbling something inaudible.

"The girl's still zonked out," Wentwhistle says.

Blight turns to Katie Sue. "You, woman, are the avatar of Temizkuan, almost a goddess yourself." He chuckles and the crowd joins in.

Win frowns. "These dudes are weird."

The cleric raises his hand, and the laughter stops. "Now, I offer you a choice."

Katie Sue staggers, her eyes half-open. Is she drugged, too?

"A choice?" she says.

"Yes." Blight points the dagger at her. "In truth, your tether to Temizkuan is not so strong here. But *my* powers are at their greatest."

She raises her head. "What do you want?"

"What lives *within* you." With one deft flick of the wrist, Blight slits the top of her robe, and it falls open. The pulsating blemish on her chest glows purple through the skin. "I want the heart of Temizkuan."

"Never." Katie Sue slaps the blade away. "With her power added to yours, you'll burn out this solar system. Kill everyone and everything—including yourself."

Blight laughs. "Temizkuan lies to you. But if you won't relent, it doesn't matter." He waves the knife at Becca Mae. "You care about this one, yes? In life, you were her sister." He lifts the blade above the girl's chest.

"No!" Katie Sue raises her hands.

Blight nods, and a smiling Wade runs a rough hand over Becca Mae's sweaty cheek.

"Here is your choice," Blight says. "Give up the heart, or…" The cleric snaps his fingers. "…I'll sacrifice the girl to Azokuitli and give what's left of her to my servant."

Wade rubs his hands together. "Ohhh, yes."

A plum-colored teardrop seeps from Katie Sue's eye. "You cannot do this. You dare not."

"I do anything for the survival of my people." Blight runs the blade along Becca Mae's cheek. "Anything for my god."

"Not this." Katie Sue snarls at the cleric. "You bring that shark to life, and it'll destroy everything."

"Of course." Blight snaps his fingers. "Let's get on with it."

Uncle John and a T'Kalul grab Katie Sue and wrestle her into the coffin. The cleric gazes at Becca Mae.

She opens her eyes and turns to him, a smile on her face.

"Am I a queen yet?"

"Not yet, little one," he says, raising the knife above his head. "But soon, you shall be majestic, a queen above a thousand, thousand queens."

"Stop!" Katie Sue emerges from the coffin and stands to face Blight. "I'll do it. Just don't hurt Becca!"

Blight smiles, lowering the weapon.

A roar erupts from somewhere in the jungle. Monsters blast out of the treetops and fly across the barren sky.

42

Wade and Uncle John drag Becca Mae from the altar and throw her to the ground.

She shakes her head and tries to stand. "Wait, what's going on?" Getting to her feet, she tries to reclaim her place on the slab. "No, I'm going to be a queen. I was promised—"

Wade backhands her, sending her sprawling on the cracked slate. Becca Mae hugs her knees to her chest and cries, her hair a tousled mess.

Katie Sue steps out of the coffin, her face an expressionless mask. Silently, she approaches the altar.

My nerves are shot, and I'm beyond exhausted, but the craziness unfolding in front of me punches a hole in my gut. Did we come all this way just to lose?

I turn to Win. "What now?"

He bucks against his restraints. "Man, I don't know. Wentwhistle?"

The older woman frowns. "Boys, I'm afraid we're out of our depth here."

A golden lightning bolt slashes the orange sky, sending a flock of bird-like creatures wheeling off toward the horizon.

Blight rounds on Katie Sue. "Come, it is time."

She lies on the slab. The cleric rubs his hands together. Emerald smoke rises from the stone, snaking along her body.

Uttering an incantation in an inhuman tongue, Blight clenches his fist. Stiff as a board, Katie Sue's body rises off the slab and floats in midair.

Blight steps forward and lays his hands on her body. "Oh, heart of Temizkuan, come out." He smiles, showing incisors sharp as switchblades. "Bring your life to your brother-god."

A sudden tremor rocks the ground, shaking the pyramid. The platform rumbles beneath my feet, and a dull roar echoes in my ears. A sharp breeze snaps like a cold towel against my body and my gut twists into a knot. I have to resist a burning urge to pee.

"Come out, Temizkuan." Green sweat beads on the magician's cheeks. "My power is greater here. You must obey!"

Around the edge of the platform, the crowd chants in a monotone cadence.

"*Metokl. Tzihuatl. Azokuitli. Metokl. Tzihuatl. Azokuitli.*"

A crack splits the center of the platform, followed by a second that bisects the first. My pillar rumbles and seems to loosen at the base. Maybe I can topple the stone and free myself? I try shaking the column from side to side, but the hard stone holds in place.

Crap.

Still, I've got one advantage. The crowd of chanting priests and the rest of the monsters are lost in some religious ecstasy, locked into whatever Blight's doing to Katie Sue.

But even if I bust loose without anybody noticing, what *then* do I do?

In the distance, something screams like a cat with its tail caught in a door. Blight sweeps his arms wildly. Eyes closed, Katie Sue shakes her head, biting her lip so hard, purple blood trickles down her chin. The air above her body starts to shimmer, and a sphere of emerald light blossoms and hovers over her chest.

Staring up to the heavens, the cleric chants, *"Metokl. Tzihuatl. Azokuitli."*

The crowd joins him. *"Metokl. Tzihuatl. Azokuitli."*

Another fissure opens in the platform. My pillar totters.

Okay, that's got to be it. Taking a deep breath, I crouch as far as my bonds will let me and leap, slamming my back against the hard stone of the pillar. The force makes the pillar tumble, taking me with it. My bonds snap and I roll to a stop next to Win.

He turns to me. "Alright, Mickey. You did it!"

"Yeah." I smile. "I did."

"Get me loose, now."

I cut his cords with a sharp rock.

"There we are," Wentwhistle says, now free of her own restraints and rubbing her wrists.

Win frowns at her. "Hey, how'd you do that?"

"Marrakech rope trick. But that's not important now. What matters is we stop this thing." She steps behind me and breaks what's left of my shackles. "On my signal, you two go after Blight while I get Katie Sue."

"No, no, no." I shake my head. "That's a crazy idea."

"You got a better one? Getting her off that altar, wrecks Blight's ritual." She points toward Earth, hovering in the orange sky. "And that might ruin his timetable. Maybe make it impossible for him to raise the god."

"Works for me." Win cracks his knuckles. "Whenever you're ready."

My stomach quivers like a tuna flopping in a net.

Stupid, stupid, stupid. Going to get everybody killed this time.

No, I'm not. You're the one who's stupid this time.

You get close to Blight and he's going to gut you!

"Shut up," I say, shaking my head. "I'm going to beat him, and beat him, and beat him—"

Win slaps my face, hard. "Hey, Mickey? Seriously man, you got to come back to us, okay? Your imaginary friend ain't here."

Wentwhistle puts her hands on her hips and stares into my eyes. "Mr. Finley, we need you to hold it together."

"Look, I'm sorry," I say, ashamed for being afraid. "But seriously? I'm useless here." I want to cry, and puke, and run away, all at the same time, but I can't decide which should come first, and that makes it worse.

"What?" Win grabs my shoulder. "C'mon, man. We need you."

"No, you don't." I'm shaking all over like a fever's got hold of me. "All everybody ever does is die on me. And you know why?" I punch myself repeatedly in the leg, stinging my thigh. "Because I'm stupid, and weak, and I can't do anything right because they won't let me!"

I bury my face in my hands. Somebody grabs my wrists. It's Wentwhistle.

"Who won't let you?"

"I don't know. The voices."

"Tell the voices to take a hike," she says. "We're kind of busy here."

The cat-screech blares again as Blight thrusts his hands into the light above Katie Sue. Her chest heaves and her eyes snap open like window blinds.

The stones beneath our feet rumble and shift. "What's up with the earthquake?" I say.

Wentwhistle frowns. "Big shark daddy's coming, I'm guessing from underground."

Emerald flame geysers out of the fractured platform. Rock dust belches into the sky, scattering Blight's warriors. Wade loses his footing and tumbles to the ground. The rest of the monsters retreat to the edges of the platform.

Time seems to slow in tempo with the blood in my temples. Heat radiating from the cracks in the platform hits me like a blast furnace. I take a deep breath and wipe the sweat from my brow. Deep inside my head the voices chatter on, but distant now like the half-forgotten parts of a bad dream. And I make peace with myself, with what's happening. That I might die. So, it's now or never. Either we do this, or we don't.

"Okay," I turn to Win. "You ready?"

He smiles. "Now, there's the stone-cold Mickey Finley, right there."

Blight balls his hands into fists and raises them to the heavens. "Now rise, Dread One. Rise, Rise, Rise, Rise, Rise!"

Something purple and slimy bursts from Katie Sue's chest and squiggles into the green light.

"Omigosh," I yell, pointing at the squirming thing. "That's the artichoke!"

There's a screech, and the creature's bulbous head ignites, burning down to dust. Sparks fly and the glowing sphere balloons into an expanding cloud that envelops Katie Sue and Blight.

A piercing scream fills the air. We clamp our hands to our ears to block the sound. Win slips to his knees like he's praying. Wentwhistle braces herself against the remains of a pillar, shouting something at me but I can't make out what she's saying.

Katie Sue's body pivots and turns in mid-air until she hovers upright in front of us, a purple flame blooming on her chest. Her mouth hangs open and her magenta eyes flare like supernovas. Smoke rises from her hair, and patches of skin from her bare arms flit upward like charred kindling.

Blight raises both arms, then thrusts them downward. "Oh

Temizkuan, let this vessel begone!"

Purple flame explodes through the green corona surrounding the two of them, blinding me. I scream until I'm hoarse. Another blast rips across the platform, knocking me to the ground. Groping through smoke, and noise, my heart pounds like a tidal wave against a freighter's hull.

Here we go. I'm going to be dead soon.

Win drags me to my feet. "Hey," he says, voice cutting through the whine in my ears, "get up, man."

The smoke clears and I see a green sphere. Inside, what's left of Katie Sue burns to a blackened skeleton that disintegrates into flickering sparks. Only Blight remains, his broken face bathed acid green. "Azokuitli comes now. Blessed be the Rising!"

I stand there, arms limp at my sides. No, no, no. This can't be happening. My gut churns but the voices don't come, and I don't care because nothing they can say would make me feel worse than I do anyway.

Wentwhistle stumbles toward me and throws her arms around my shoulders. "Mickey," she says in my ear, "I'm so sorry."

Another burst of flame belches from underground. Wade gets to his feet and runs toward Becca Mae. Grabbing her by the hair, he drags her from the altar. They get about five feet before a tremor shakes the platform, making him lose his balance.

I turn to Win. "We gotta stop him." He nods and we launch ourselves at the pair.

"Hey, Wade," I yell, grabbing a big stone and planting my feet. "Where you going?"

"Pop-Tart." He sneers, fist twisting into a bony crab-claw. "You're a freaking idiot."

"Nah." I weigh the distance, about the heft of the stone.

"C'mon, Wade. Just you and me."

Win steps in front of me. "Mickey, don't."

Wentwhistle bolts past and launches herself. She throws a kick that catches Wade on the knee. Howling, he snaps his claw-hand at her, but she sidesteps the blow. Crouching, she balls her fist and plants one on his jaw, knocking him backward.

Eyes wide, Win turns to me. "You just see that?"

"She's full of surprises," I say, running toward the pair.

Wiping his cut lip, Wade grins. "You'll die for that."

Wentwhistle throws another kick, but the bully blocks it with his claw. "End of the line, sister." Clamping her ankle with his pincers, he tosses her onto the smoking altar.

Blood rushes to my cheeks, and cold rage boils in my chest. I'm going to kill this guy.

"That's it, man." I charge Wade.

Laughing, he sidesteps my rush and clips my back with his claw. Crap, but that hurt! I drop to my knees, the rock slipping from my hands. A coppery taste of blood fills my mouth.

Win slams into Wade and nearly takes him down. The blond bully laughs and slashes his shoulder with a bony claw. Win tries to rise but Wade plants a boot on his back, pinning him to the hard stone.

Grabbing the shard, I take off running. Wade turns toward me a split-second too late. Lunging, I bury the sharp stone in his neck. He screams and stumbles backward, ripping the rock out of his skin. Dark fluid spills from the wound.

"Nice one," he gasps. "Want to try that again?"

"Wade?" It's a girl's voice.

I turn and there stands Becca Mae, fists balled at her side. "You drugged me?"

Wade shrugs. "You know, it wasn't really like that."

"You did, didn't you?" Her eyes narrow to slits. "What were you gonna do? Treat me like you did Alice?"

"Becca, we can work this—"

Snarling, she punches Wade in the hole under his chin. Blood arcs above his head.

"You don't...do that." Slamming her to the ground, he gives her a kick. She curls into a fetal position. "You don't do that to me."

"That's it, man!" I rush him, staying low like I would in wrestling. He lashes at me, but I duck and drive a knee into his groin. Wade tumbles, crashing head-first to the ground.

Becca Mae lies crumpled in a heap.

"Are you alright?" I say.

Her eyes go wide, and she screams, "Mickey, watch out!"

There's a rush of air and something slams into me. I stumble and hit the ground.

Wade pounces, landing on top of me. "Goodbye, Pop-Tart."

Win lunges, jabbing a spear into the wound on Wade's neck. "You done?" he tells the bully.

Wade smiles. "Don't point that thing at me." He gestures toward an emerald light. "See, I got backup."

Engulfed in the green light, Blight raises his arms.

Win turns and fires. The energy bolt passes harmlessly through Blight. Seizing his opportunity, Wade bolts, joining a mob on the edge of the platform. Blight waves a hand and vanishes in a ball of light that dissipates into blackness.

"Mickey!" Becca Mae screams. The ground beneath us erupts in a hundred places. The sound is deafening, like standing in front of a jet turbine about to explode. A wide fissure opens between us, noxious smoke boiling up from underground. Gritting my teeth, I step back a few feet and rush forward, leapping the spreading gap in a single bound. I clear the lip, but the edge crumbles. I teeter on the edge of a smoking abyss.

Crap, I can't die like this.

Shifting my weight, I throw myself forward into the arms of Becca Mae, and we fall to the ground.

"You okay?" she says.

"Yeah."

She kisses my cheek. "Wade drugged me—"

"It's okay." I crush her against me, drinking in her perfume. "We're going to make it."

"Are we?"

With the look she gives me, I just can't help myself. I kiss her, the moment passing slowly like a teardrop gliding along the edge of a glass slipper. The taste of her lips is sweeter than a thousand marshmallows soaked in Coca-Cola.

Becca Mae draws back and frowns. "This isn't the right time—"

"No, it's not." I squeeze her arm. "But maybe later."

She shakes her head. "No promises, okay?"

An aftershock and a blast of volcanic heat shakes us from our embrace. Win and Wentwhistle emerge from the smoke on the opposite side of the fissure.

"Hang on a second," Wentwhistle shouts. "We'll get over to you."

Another massive tremor rolls through, and the ground opens in a huge gash swallowing slabs of rock and fallen bodies. All that remains is a lanky figure gyrating near the edge of the hole.

It's Uncle John, tentacles wiggling from his mouth and ruined eye. He idiot-dances in a circle, knees buckling and shoulders bobbing like a chicken with its head cut off. Did the others leave him behind? Why do I care? He's a monster now.

Behind Uncle John, a pale green fin, big as a jetliner's wing, bursts through the fissure, followed by its floppy twin. A stench like ammonia floods the air and Becca Mae starts gagging. A mob of screaming T'Kalul and kzelocs leap from the platform, scrambling for safety. Slowly a gargantuan body the size of a battleship emerges, its bulbous head sporting a pointed snout as big as the prow of an aircraft carrier. Glittering fangs as large as telephone poles drip in double-rows from its awful mouth. A slit-pupiled eye as wide as the moon stares from its fleshy flank.

Shrouded in shadow, Uncle John stops dancing and turns, facing the towering beast.

With a great snarl, the monster descends and clamps Uncle John's upper torso in its massive jaws.

"No!" I scream, running toward the widening rift. Becca Mae grabs my arm and pulls me to safety.

"What're you doing?" She gestures toward the creature. "What is that thing?"

"That's Azokuitli." I shake my head and swallow a lump in my throat. "We've failed."

The creature slurps Uncle John's remains into its mouth and lets out a roar. The shark hoists itself up onto the platform. Its bellowing screech a disorienting sound, like the cutting of a thousand violin strings.

Win drops his weapon, his complexion ashen.

Wentwhistle sinks to her knees. "We're too late. It's here." Blotting out the Earth above, the creature rears high on its haunches. "This *is* the Rising."

43

The huge temple starts collapsing with the shark's emergence. Screaming, the beast points its shrapnel-fanged nose at Earth, high above the horizon. Green muck sloughs from its flanks like tree sap. A stench of brine mixed with burning ozone nearly flattens me, and I'm positively, absolutely sure we are about to die.

"Aw man." Win points to the sky. "That thing's coming to kill the Earth."

"Egad! Blight's gone and done it, hasn't he?" Wentwhistle turns to me and Becca Mae. "Mr. Finley, can you make another of those jumping-jack leaps?"

I glance down. The gap is almost five feet across. "I doubt it."

She steps over the body of a fallen T'Kalul. "Wait, I've got an idea." Reaching down, she detaches a hook from the warrior's belt. "Let's try this."

I frown. "What's that going to do?"

Wentwhistle grins. "Time to improvise." Crouching, she jams the borrowed sickle beneath a massive block lying near the edge.

"What are you doing?" Win shouts.

She turns to him. "Step back."

He does and she fires the hook, its backlash knocking her and Win to the ground. The block falls hard but its size manages to keep it straddled across the fissure.

Wentwhistle stands and shouts at us. "Make tracks, you two."

I grab Becca Mae's hand and we dash over the improvised bridge. Win shouts.

"We need to get off this thing."

"First," Becca Mae says, pushing between us, "we gotta stop that shark."

"You're funny." Wentwhistle chuckles. "Right now, all we can do is run."

We reach the edge of the platform. Holding Becca Mae's hand, I vault down the steps, rock crumbling beneath my feet. Flames from fissures in the broken slats belch smoke into the blackening sky. Becca Mae trips over a fallen warrior but I drag her to her feet.

Five steps from the ground, something whips past my ear. I turn and see a kzeloc a few steps above, its yellow eyes blazing and a tongue-dart lolling in its mouth. A blast from Win makes the creature tumble backward. An explosion near my feet sends me and Becca Mae to the jungle floor. Seconds later, the others catch up to us.

Wentwhistle points to the shark, straddling the top of the pyramid. "Is it getting bigger? I can't tell."

"Stupid thing's already huge," Win says.

Towering over the collapsing structure, the shark shakes like a dog flinging water off its fur. Hot steam like rocket exhaust bursts from the beast's haunches, and a noxious gas cloud wafts along the temple's sides filling the air with a stench like fish guts.

"Jeez," I say, "is that thing going to crap its way to Earth?"

A flash of purple light erupts from the jungle canopy. The trees near the origin of the blast crumple and burn.

Win turns and says, "You see that?"

"What is it?" I say.

"Sheesh." Wentwhistle replaces the hook on her belt. "This can't be good, can it?"

The violet glow extends underneath the foliage, shafts of light shooting through the trees.

"You know what?" Becca Mae leans in for a look. "I think we're going to be okay."

"What?" I frown. "How can you be so sure?"

The shimmering light snakes along until it reaches the tree line. Then a moving wave of earth, the size of a Greyhound bus plows toward us, spreading white flower petals in its wake.

"Is that like an animal, or something?" Win points to the moving pile.

The mound stops about a hundred yards from the pyramid's base. Purple vines, thick as Grecian columns, burst upward. Sailing high into the air, the creepers converge to form an intertwining structure the size of a small car. Plum-colored artichoke leaves emerge and envelop the structure, overlapping each other like fish scales.

"Oh my," Wentwhistle says. "I might be wrong, but is that some kind of…cocoon?"

"Yeah," Becca Mae says. "That's *exactly* what it is."

Lavender light shoots through thousands of tiny pinprick openings in the hardening shell.

"This is crazy," Win shouts to me.

It sheds its heavy leaves, revealing a pulpy mass at the center that looks like a teardrop. Roots shoot through the growth's surface and descend to the ground. Then, a black stalk thicker than a redwood bursts from the mound below. The stalk climbs until its tip pierces the bottom of the glowing teardrop. The mass above the ground dissolves, revealing a slender figure standing atop a leafy pallet.

Becca Mae grips my arm. "Omigosh, it's Katie!"

Holy crap. I can't believe it but somehow, she's come back to save us.

Squirming black vines cover Katie Sue and her white hair is blazing like a corona. She raises her arms and the stalk beneath her thickens to twice its girth. Branches explode from the trunk, teeming with oval-shaped leaves and thick white petals.

After a flash, Katie Sue vanishes into a purple light that swirls and hardens, gaining mass and form. In seconds, what remains atop the pallet is a shimmering bulb sprouting milky tendrils.

"My word," Wentwhistle says, her eyes wide as half-dollars, "she brought Temizkuan to the party."

The feelers slither downward, embedding themselves in the trunk's thickening bark. A leafy canopy rises and envelops the jellyfish-head.

"So…what?" Win says. "She going to fight the shark?"

I turn to him. "Yeah, she is. We're going to beat this thing—"

A fist drives into my jaw, knocking me down. Glancing up, I meet my attacker's gaze. It's Wade, backed by two gray-skinned kzelocs and a T'Kalul.

"You're going to beat nobody," he says, leveling his crab-claw at me. "Not now, not ever."

Win slashes Wade across the head with his spear. The bully reels, falling backward. The T'Kalul tries to level his blaster at me, but Wentwhistle draws her hook first. A high-pitched scream erupts from the vibrating blade, and the warrior sails into the dirt.

"We need to get out of here," she says, the ground beneath

us trembling.

Becca Mae grabs my hand. "C'mon, let's go."

A couple T'Kalul emerge from the smoking ruins. One opens its thin lips, revealing a dart on the end of its tongue. Wentwhistle raises her knee and snap-kicks the warrior in the mandibles. The projectile slips from its mouth, sizzling in the dust. Win aims a blast at the other one, but the T'Kalul lunges for him, knocking the spear from his hands.

Becca Mae points to Wade, getting to his feet. "Mickey, he's not done."

"Yes, he is." I get to my feet. Don't know what it takes to put this guy down, but I'm going to find out.

The bully stops a few feet away, smiling. "You can't do it yourself, Pop-Tart." He snaps his crab-claw at me. "Need some little girl to protect you, huh?"

"Shut up, Wade." I rush him and throw a punch.

Wade ducks and swings, his slash cutting my shirt and nearly gutting me. I plant my heel hard into his foot. Cursing, he takes a swipe at my head, nearly cutting my scalp. Grabbing Wade under his arms, I hoist him over my hip, and he falls face-first into the dirt.

Becca Mae approaches to kick Wade in the stomach. He grabs her ankle and throws her. She hits solid rock, making a sickening crunch sound. Crumpling in a heap, she lies still. Too still.

"Becca Mae?" I rush toward her, too close to where Wade lies. He clips my leg with his claw, sending me sprawling. I roll on the ground, clutching my knee.

Getting to his feet, Wade approaches slowly. "End of the line, Pop-Tart." He extends his crab-claw, the bony appendage forms into a gnarled spike. "Gonna gut you."

My hand touches something cold. I turn my head and glimpse Win's blaster spear. It's come to this. Wade's not going to stop unless I put him down for good.

He jumps with his spike-hand cocked above his head, poised to strike. I raise the spear and fire. The energy burst catches Wade mid-air, searing his gut. Screaming, he sails backward and lands in the mud.

I rise and approach him, holding the weapon in both hands. He struggles up on one elbow, his human hand held out in surrender. "Hey, man. Cool it, okay?" Green pulp oozes from his chest. His face is ashen, blood trickling from his lip. "We're done."

He's got to be kidding. "No, we're not." Raising the spear, I slash his face and blood sprays across his shirt.

"C'mon, man!" he says, tears running down his cheek.

I thrust the blaster down hard on his nose, and it splatters into a green ruin. "We're done, huh?" I strike again, this time pulping his ear. "We're done?" A third blow snaps his collarbone. "You think *this* is done?"

I raise the spear again, but somebody grabs my wrists from behind.

"No, Mickey," Becca Mae says. "Leave him be."

Wade smiles, his teeth spattered in gore. "Nice one, Becca." Holding his gut, he staggers to his feet. "I knew I could count on you."

"Don't thank me," she says.

This is a really bad idea. "We can't just let him go."

Becca Mae shakes her head. "Yes, we can." She turns to the bully. "I'm saving your life, Wade, because Katie would want me to. But I don't ever want to see you again."

He chuckles and blood streams down his chin. "Whatever you say, cuz." Turning, he stumbles past a mound of smoking rubble and vanishes into the darkness.

Win and Wentwhistle approach.

"Hey man, you okay?" Win says.

"I'll be alright." I shrug. "What's happening with—"

A deafening screech pierces the smoky haze. I catch sight of one of Azokuitli's tentacles lashing the side of the pyramid, showering rock and dust in all directions.

Wentwhistle points to a clump of overturned trees. "Over there."

We run and take cover. Becca Mae crouches next to me.

"Mickey, I'm scared. What do we do?"

"I don't know." I stare at the orange sky above. Smoke rises from the collapsed ruins, and there are bodies everywhere. There were still a lot of T'Kalul and kzelocs left standing before the shark rose, but I'm guessing the survivors ran for safety in the jungle.

Above us, two gods tower, trying to kill each other.

Shrieking, Azokuitli slithers down the pyramid, its unblinking eye blazing with green fire. Temizkuan stands nearly as tall as the beast. Her roots, ripped from the pockmarked ground, have transformed into makeshift, taloned feet.

Is Katie Sue still inside? Did she give up her life to bring it here? I can't be sure either way.

Azokuitli wraps its tentacles around the trunk of the great tree, but Temizkuan does not yield. With a shrug, the goddess thrusts spiny branches into the shark. Brown liquid gushes from its belly, igniting fires where the gunk hits the ground. The shark screams and spits a torrent of dark sludge into Temizkuan's canopy, igniting it. A pungent stench like rotten oranges floods the air. The jellyfish writhes and struggles to shake free of the ensuing flames.

"She's not going to make it," Win says.

Wentwhistle shakes her head. "We don't know that."

Temizkuan's head balloons and then exhales a burst of blazing sparks at Azokuitli. Tiny sparks flare to life on the shark's skin and it tumbles, tentacles lashing blindly. Roaring in frustration, the shark closes its jaws on the tree's canopy, its spiny teeth piercing the jellyfish beneath.

Milky liquid spews into the air but as we look on, a purple light mushrooms inside the gelatinous mass, illuminating the sky.

Shielding my eyes with my hand, I turn to Wentwhistle. "What's it doing?" I shout.

"Something lethal, I hope," she says.

Azokuitli screeches and swats Temizkuan with its snout. The light goes out, but the goddess rears up, her taloned toes digging into the ground. Lunging, the shark clamps its jaws around her thick trunk. Purple sap flows like a river, and the great tree seems to waver.

Relaxing its bite, Azokuitli turns, fins flapping like wings. generating a hot wind that blasts the ground beneath its tentacles.

I wrap Becca Mae in my arms. "Hang on."

Suddenly, Azokuitli goes airborne. In seconds, the shark god is only a black dot against the sky.

The Earth hangs like a blue marble. How long will it take for the shark to reach Bay St. Louis? Will it kill everyone in the city? What about the Gulf Coast? The world? My eyes grow moist and my gut churns, but the voices don't come, and it doesn't matter because we failed and now everybody's going to die.

Becca Mae puts her hand on my cheek. "Hey, don't cry."

Was I crying? "I just…we came so close, you know? So close."

Wentwhistle grabs my arm. "Wait a minute." She points to Temizkuan. "It's not over."

Light blossoms from inside Temizkuan's canopy. Rising to its full height, the goddess points her head at the fleeing shark. The glow inside the jellyfish blazes to an inferno, its heat searing the air. There's a sudden odor of burning ozone, like thousands of spotlights all burning out at once. Then a beam of purple light erupts from the tree.

Drilling skyward, the beam pierces Azokuitli. The shark god explodes in a fireball. Chunks of meat, guts, and cartilage rain down in a sickening torrent. The jungle ignites in patches, and my nostrils fill with the stench of fish guts mixed with rotted bait. Other bits of Azokuitli land amid the ruins. Tiny chunks of noxious-smelling flesh flop and wiggle as though still alive. Becca Mae buries her head in my chest and shrieks.

One plops on Win's lap. He tosses it away. "Man, so disgusting!"

After a while, the downpour stops, and we emerge from our makeshift shelter. Temizkuan teeters above us, her canopy gone and great clots of milky fluid dripping down its bark.

With a shudder, the jellyfish-head disentangles from the tree. Gravity takes hold, and the opaque bulb tumbles to rest between the root-taloned feet.

Becca Mae approaches the gelatinous mass. Carefully, she reaches forward to inspect the organism. The jellyfish splits open and white gunk spills forth. A girl's pale arm slips through the gash.

Becca Mae gasps and leaps backward. Me and Win rush forward, me with the blaster in my hands.

Katie Sue crawls out of the jellyfish and sinks to the ground. She's covered in some oily gel with only a few vines covering her skinny frame. Her labored breathing sounds shallow, and an ugly purple wound sits in the middle of her chest where Blight tore out the artichoke.

"Hey." She gasps.

I nod to Win. He helps me carry Katie Sue to a stone outcropping to prop her against. Wentwhistle drapes her jacket over the girl's shoulders.

"Funny," Katie Sue says. "It's so hot here but I'm starting to…" She struggles to breathe. "…feel cold."

Wentwhistle makes a face I've come to know all too well. "Don't worry, love. You won't be feeling that way much longer."

"Oh, good. That's good." Katie Sue turns her head and looks at me. Her pupils are milky like she's got cataracts, unseeing. Perhaps it's better this way. "Mickey, where's Becca?"

Becca Mae stands over us, her complexion almost as pale as her sister's. "Right here, Katie."

"Oh, good." Katie Sue coughs and dark purple fluid trickles down her chin. "I was afraid you didn't make it."

"I made it." Becca Mae kneels at her sister's side, and tousles the girl's mossy white hair. "Everybody's okay, thanks to you."

"Me?" Katie Sue laughs hoarsely. "Don't know how much…I did." She shivers and plum-colored fluid drips from her nose. "Most of it was Temizkuan and…" She turns to me. "…y'all did a lot."

Win paces in a circle, then kicks a rock. "Katie, you going to be okay, man," he says, tears staining his cheek. "We'll get you on one of those rocket ships and we'll, I don't know, we'll save you."

Wentwhistle shakes her head. "No time for that, I'm afraid."

I brush my fingers across Katie Sue's forearm. "This is just so…I mean, is there anything you want right now? Anything you need us to do, or—"

"I'm fine, really." She grasps my hand, her grip stronger than I would think possible for a twice-dead woman. "I've had…a great life, Mickey. And then I had another life…because of you."

She can't mean that. I ruined everything for her. Killed her, even. "Katie Sue, please don't say that."

"No, I'm serious." She puts my hand in Becca Mae's. "I want you two to...to take care of each other. Y'all are bonded because...of everything that's happened."

Becca Mae is crying now, eyes red, snot coming out of her nose. "Katie, I love you so much. What am I going to do without you?"

"Take care of each other," Katie Sue says. "Both of you do that...for me, okay?"

She stiffens then seems to melt, a look of peace on her still pretty face. Then her head lolls to the side and she stops moving.

Wentwhistle leans down and closes her eyes. "Godspeed, little May Queen."

Becca Mae looks up at me, eyes full of tears. I kneel and hold her in my arms, rocking her like I would a baby.

"Oh, Lord, Lord, Lord." Win holds his head in his hands.

Wentwhistle puts her arm around his shoulder. "Win, there's nothing I can say right now—nothing to make it better."

"I know." He lifts his head and tries to smile. "Katie was real good people, you know? I didn't know her that long, but I guess that doesn't really matter, does it?"

"It doesn't." Wentwhistle steps toward me and Becca Mae. "Becca? I think we can find a rocket to take us home. Do you want to bring your sister?"

Sniffling, Becca Mae shakes her head. "She wouldn't want anybody to see her like this. And there ain't nobody to help me bury her that isn't already here."

"Here, then." Wentwhistle turns to me. "Mr. Finley, is there another temple nearby? I'm thinking it might house a rocket pad."

"Maybe, but I don't know." I stand and help Becca Mae to

her feet. "I've only been here one other time."

"Alright. We need to tend to our fallen comrade." She picks up a T'Kalul spear.

"Wait." Becca Mae tugs my arm. "Look."

I turn and see Katie Sue's body, enveloped in a lavender haze. Sparkles fleck from her skin, alighting into the air, accompanied by a whiff of fresh magnolias. Then a purple flame envelops her body and Katie Sue ascends as golden dust, a memory of spirit and magic, echoing in the shadows of the sky, out into the cosmos.

Epilogue

Wasn't too hard finding a rocket back to Earth. We ran into a lost patrol of T'Kalul on our way to a launch pad and got into a fight. Nobody actually got hurt on either side. Win blasted a tree near one warrior, and they all ran like scared rabbits. Guess they'd had enough by that point. We never ran into Wade, either. To this day, I still don't understand why Becca Mae wanted to show him mercy.

Blight died with the shark, I guess. Though I'm convinced someday they'll return, and there'll be more trouble. But you can't live your life worrying about a thing like that.

Back on Earth, Tommy came home right after the National Guard cleared the roads and let the outside world access Bay St. Louis.

Together, me and him surveyed the remains of the house, and decided we could fix it up. With a little help from some survivors of Bay Crossroads, we went on a construction binge. The work was hard, but Tommy insisted it would toughen me up. I got some mean roofing skills that winter. Learned about drywall, got up to my armpits in paint, hammers, and nails. Maybe I'll do construction for a living someday.

Win helped us for a few weeks. Turns out, his folks got out

of town before the stuff really hit the fan. But the experience made them want to go back to Cincinnati, so off they went.

Me and Tommy searched for Aunt Margene, but never found her. The little bundle of murderous joy she kept in the potato-chip can vanished with her. For all I know, they are out on the highway somewhere, thumbing a ride for parts unknown.

Becca Mae moved in with her grandparents up in Jackson. Me and her hung out on the front porch swing of her old house the night before she left. Freshly scrubbed, her hair smelled of butterscotch and her body cleaved to mine, warm and soft. I told her I was really into her. It was scary to say that, but after what we'd been through, I just had to let her know.

She said she'd known for a while how I felt. She even smiled and said she felt the same.

We kissed a little, and then a lot. But we didn't talk about what Katie Sue said before she died the second time, that we were bonded to each other. After everything that happened, it was too weird and too heavy a thing to think about.

She set some boundaries. "You're awesome, Mickey, but I'm just not ready for a relationship right now."

And I got that. I mean, we both had a lot of people to bury, and she was leaving town. The timing was all wrong.

Becca Mae did say this, though. "Maybe someday, I don't know, we could be something, like…" She smiled. "…*really* something." She signed that promissory note with her lips.

I left her porch that night, my heart pounding like I'd just been on the best roller coaster at the greatest carnival the world has ever seen.

Becca Mae left me her address, and I'm hoping to visit this summer.

Wentwhistle offered me a job. It doesn't pay much, and the

hours are weird, but she told me she needs somebody to drive the van while she, "goes to find some stuff", as she put it. We didn't discuss the details, but I'm guessing we're searching for more alien artifacts, weapons, things like that, which means we'll probably get into more trouble eventually. But that's cool. I'm excited and scared and totally ready for that. Or, at least, I think I am. We'll just have to see what happens.

I get to thinking sometimes about everything that happened last winter. Some days, even though I know she's not really there, I go to the cemetery to talk to Katie Sue. She never answers, at least in the way you and I might think of it. But it comforts me to bring flowers I picked myself and sit by her grave.

I know this sounds weird, but I'm sure I'll see her again.

Count on that.

And you know something else? The voices aren't as bad as they used to be. I mean, they're still there, but they don't sound as loud, or something. It's as if there's been this permanent change over the last six months, and they can't hurt or control me anymore.

If the voices ever get bad again? I'll stuff them in a bottle and ship them out with the afternoon surf when it pulls out to the Gulf.

Some things in my life will never be the same.

But I'm all the stronger for it.

To Be Continued…

Recovering Catholic school boy Craig E. Higgins is a fan of sword-and-sorcery and Southern lit. His tales combine teen angst with deep-fried cosmic weirdness.

Active in several writers' groups, Higgins presents here his first novel, *Artichoke Stars and Chicken-Fried Sharks*. The writer and his wife live in the Nevada desert between glitzy Las Vegas and mysterious Area 51.

Made in the USA
Middletown, DE
28 October 2024